HEAVY WEATHER

"Brilliant . . . Fascinating . . . Exciting
. . . A full complement of thrills."
—*The New York Times Book Review*

"A remarkable and individual sharpness of
vision . . . Sterling hacks the future, and
an elegant hack it is."—*Locus*

"So believable are the speculations that
. . . one becomes convinced that the world
must and will develop into what Sterling
has predicted."—*Science Fiction Age*

"Sharp . . . Intriguing . . . A near-future
thriller."—*Publishers Weekly*

THE DIFFERENCE ENGINE
(with William Gibson)

"Bursting with the kind of demented speculation and obsessive detailing that has made both Gibson's and Sterling's work stand out."—*San Francisco Chronicle*

"Highly imaginative . . . [A] splendid effort."—*Chicago Tribune*

"Smartly plotted, wonderfully crafted, and written with sly literary wit . . . spins marvelously and runs like a dream."
—*Entertainment Weekly*

A GOOD OLD-FASHIONED FUTURE

STORIES BY
BRUCE STERLING

BANTAM BOOKS
NEW YORK   TORONTO   LONDON   SYDNEY   AUCKLAND

A GOOD OLD-FASHIONED FUTURE

A Bantam Spectra Book / June 1999

SPECTRA and the portrayal of a boxed "s" are trademarks of Bantam
Books, a division of Random House, Inc.

These stories were previously published in other formats:
"Maneki Neko" was published in *The Magazine of Fantasy
and Science Fiction*, May 1998, copyright © Mercury Press, Inc.
First published in *Hayakawa's Science Fiction Magazine*.
"Big Jelly" was published in *Asimov's*, November 1994,
copyright © Dell Magazines.
"The Littlest Jackal" was published in *The Magazine of Fantasy
and Science Fiction*, March 1996, copyright © Mercury Press, Inc.
"Sacred Cow" was published in *Omni*, January 1993,
copyright © Omni Publications International Limited.
"Deep Eddy" was published in *Asimov's*, August 1993,
copyright © Dell Magazines.
"Bicycle Repairman" was published in *InteractionsL: The Sycamore Hill
Anthology*, edited by John Kessel, Mark L. Van Name, and Richard
Butner, Tor Books, 1996.
"Taklamakan" was published in *Asimov's*, October/November 1998,
copyright © Dell Magazines.

ISBN 0-553-57642-9

Published simultaneously in the United States and Canada

Bantam Books are published by Bantam Books, a division of Random
House, Inc. Its trademark, consisting of the words "Bantam Books" and the
portrayal of a rooster, is Registered in U.S. Patent and Trademark Office
and in other countries. Marca Registrada. Bantam Books, 1540 Broadway,
New York, New York 10036.

PRINTED IN THE UNITED STATES OF AMERICA

OPM   10   9   8   7   6   5   4   3   2   1

CONTENTS

MANEKI NEKO

"I can't go on," his brother said.

Tsuyoshi Shimizu looked thoughtfully into the screen of his pasokon. His older brother's face was shiny with sweat from a late-night drinking bout. "It's only a career," said Tsuyoshi, sitting up on his futon and adjusting his pajamas. "You worry too much."

"All that overtime!" his brother whined. He was making the call from a bar somewhere in Shibuya. In the background, a middle-aged office lady was singing karaoke, badly. "And the examination hells. The manager training programs. The proficiency tests. I never have time to live!"

Tsuyoshi grunted sympathetically. He didn't like these late-night videophone calls, but he felt obliged to listen. His big brother had always been a decent sort, before he had gone through the elite courses at Waseda University, joined a big corporation, and gotten professionally ambitious.

"My back hurts," his brother groused. "I have an ulcer. My hair is going gray. And I know they'll fire me. No matter how loyal you are to the big companies, they have no loyalty to their employees anymore. It's no wonder that I drink."

"You should get married," Tsuyoshi offered.

"I can't find the right girl. Women never understand me." He shuddered. "Tsuyoshi, I'm truly desperate. The market pressures are crushing me. I can't breathe. My life has got to change. I'm thinking of taking the vows. I'm serious! I want to renounce this whole modern world."

Tsuyoshi was alarmed. "You're very drunk, right?"

His brother leaned closer to the screen. "Life in a monastery sounds truly good to me. It's so quiet there. You recite the sutras. You consider your existence. There are rules to follow, and rewards that make sense. It's just the way that Japanese business used to be, back in the good old days."

Tsuyoshi grunted skeptically.

"Last week I went out to a special place in the mountains . . . Mount Aso," his brother confided. "The monks there, they know about people in trouble, people who are burned out by modern life. The monks protect you from the world. No computers, no phones, no faxes, no e-mail, no overtime, no commuting, nothing at all. It's beautiful, and it's peaceful, and nothing ever happens there. Really, it's like paradise."

"Listen, older brother," Tsuyoshi said, "you're not a religious man by nature. You're a section chief for a big import-export company."

"Well . . . maybe religion won't work for me. I did think of running away to America. Nothing much ever happens there, either."

Tsuyoshi smiled. "That sounds much better! America is a good vacation spot. A long vacation is just what you need! Besides, the Americans are real friendly since they gave up their handguns."

"But I can't go through with it," his brother wailed. "I just don't dare. I can't just wander away from everything that I know, and trust to the kindness of strangers."

"That always works for me," Tsuyoshi said. "Maybe you should try it."

Tsuyoshi's wife stirred uneasily on the futon. Tsuyoshi

lowered his voice. "Sorry, but I have to hang up now. Call me before you do anything rash."

"Don't tell Dad," Tsuyoshi's brother said. "He worries so."

"I won't tell Dad." Tsuyoshi cut the connection and the screen went dark.

Tsuyoshi's wife rolled over, heavily. She was seven months pregnant. She stared at the ceiling, puffing for breath. "Was that another call from your brother?" she said.

"Yeah. The company just gave him another promotion. More responsibilities. He's celebrating."

"That sounds nice," his wife said tactfully.

Next morning, Tsuyoshi slept late. He was self-employed, so he kept his own hours. Tsuyoshi was a video format upgrader by trade. He transferred old videos from obsolete formats into the new high-grade storage media. Doing this properly took a craftsman's eye. Word of Tsuyoshi's skills had gotten out on the network, so he had as much work as he could handle.

At ten A.M., the mailman arrived. Tsuyoshi abandoned his breakfast of raw egg and miso soup, and signed for a shipment of flaking, twentieth-century analog television tapes. The mail also brought a fresh overnight shipment of strawberries, and a jar of homemade pickles.

"Pickles!" his wife enthused. "People are so nice to you when you're pregnant."

"Any idea who sent us that?"

"Just someone on the network."

"Great."

Tsuyoshi booted his mediator, cleaned his superconducting heads, and examined the old tapes. Home videos from the 1980s. Someone's grandmother as a child, presumably. There had been a lot of flaking and loss of polarity in the old recording medium.

Tsuyoshi got to work with his desktop fractal detail

generator, the image stabilizer, and the interlace algorithms. When he was done, Tsuyoshi's new digital copies
would look much sharper, cleaner, and better composed
than the original primitive videotape.

Tsuyoshi enjoyed his work. Quite often he came
across bits and pieces of videotape that were of archival
interest. He would pass the images on to the net. The
really big network databases, with their armies of search
engines, indexers, and catalogs, had some very arcane
interests. The net machines would never pay for data,
because the global information networks were non-
commercial. But the net machines were very polite, and
had excellent net etiquette. They returned a favor for a
favor, and since they were machines with excellent, enormous memories, they never forgot a good deed.

Tsuyoshi and his wife had a lunch of ramen with
naruto, and she left to go shopping. A shipment arrived by
overseas package service. Cute baby clothes from Darwin,
Australia. They were in his wife's favorite color, sunshine
yellow.

Tsuyoshi finished transferring the first tape to a new
crystal disk. Time for a break. He left his apartment, took
the elevator, and went out to the corner coffee shop. He
ordered a double iced mocha cappuccino and paid with a
chargecard.

His pokkecon rang. Tsuyoshi took it from his belt and
answered it. "Get one to go," the machine told him.

"Okay," said Tsuyoshi, and hung up. He bought a
second coffee, put a lid on it, and left the shop.

A man in a business suit was sitting on a park bench
near the entrance of Tsuyoshi's building. The man's suit
was good, but it looked as if he'd slept in it. He was holding his head in his hands and rocking gently back and
forth. He was unshaven and his eyes were red-rimmed.

The pokkecon rang again. "The coffee's for him?"
Tsuyoshi said.

"Yes," said the pokkecon. "He needs it."

Tsuyoshi walked up to the lost businessman. The man

looked up, flinching warily, as if he were about to be kicked. "What is it?" he said.

"Here," Tsuyoshi said, handing him the cup. "Double iced mocha cappuccino."

The man opened the cup, and smelled it. He looked up in disbelief. "This is my favorite kind of coffee. . . . Who are you?"

Tsuyoshi lifted his arm and offered a hand signal, his fingers clenched like a cat's paw. The man showed no recognition of the gesture. Tsuyoshi shrugged, and smiled. "It doesn't matter. Sometimes a man really needs a coffee. Now you have a coffee. That's all."

"Well. . . ." The man cautiously sipped his cup, and suddenly smiled. "It's really great. Thanks!"

"You're welcome." Tsuyoshi went home.

His wife arrived from shopping. She had bought new shoes. The pregnancy was making her feet swell. She sat carefully on the couch and sighed.

"Orthopedic shoes are expensive," she said, looking at the yellow pumps. "I hope you don't think they look ugly."

"On you, they look really cute," Tsuyoshi said wisely. He had first met his wife at a video store. She had just used her credit card to buy a disk of primitive black-and-white American anime of the 1950s. The pokkecon had urged him to go up and speak to her on the subject of Felix the Cat. Felix was an early television cartoon star and one of Tsuyoshi's personal favorites.

Tsuyoshi would have been too shy to approach an attractive woman on his own, but no one was a stranger to the net. This fact gave him the confidence to speak to her. Tsuyoshi had soon discovered that the girl was delighted to discuss her deep fondness for cute, antique, animated cats. They'd had lunch together. They'd had a date the next week. They had spent Christmas Eve together in a love hotel. They had a lot in common.

She had come into his life through a little act of grace, a little gift from Felix the Cat's magic bag of tricks.

Tsuyoshi had never gotten over feeling grateful for this. Now that he was married and becoming a father, Tsuyoshi Shimizu could feel himself becoming solidly fixed in life. He had a man's role to play now. He knew who he was, and he knew where he stood. Life was good to him.

"You need a haircut, dear," his wife told him.

"Sure."

His wife pulled a gift box out of her shopping bag. "Can you go to the Hotel Daruma, and get your hair cut, and deliver this box for me?"

"What is it?" Tsuyoshi said.

Tsuyoshi's wife opened the little wooden gift box. A maneki neko was nestled inside white foam padding. The smiling ceramic cat held one paw upraised, beckoning for good fortune.

"Don't you have enough of those yet?" he said. "You even have maneki neko underwear."

"It's not for my collection. It's a gift for someone at the Hotel Daruma."

"Oh."

"Some foreign woman gave me this box at the shoe-store. She looked American. She couldn't speak Japanese. She had really nice shoes, though. . . ."

"If the network gave you that little cat, then you're the one who should take care of that obligation, dear."

"But dear," she sighed, "my feet hurt so much, and you could do with a haircut anyway, and I have to cook supper, and besides, it's not really a nice maneki neko, it's just cheap tourist souvenir junk. Can't you do it?"

"Oh, all right," Tsuyoshi told her. "Just forward your pokkecon prompts onto my machine, and I'll see what I can do for us."

She smiled. "I knew you would do it. You're really so good to me."

Tsuyoshi left with the little box. He wasn't unhappy to do the errand, as it wasn't always easy to manage his pregnant wife's volatile moods in their small six-tatami apartment. The local neighborhood was good, but he was hoping to find bigger accommodations before the child was born. Maybe a place with a little studio, where he could expand the scope of his work. It was very hard to find decent housing in Tokyo, but word was out on the net. Friends he didn't even know were working every day to help him. If he kept up with the net's obligations, he had every confidence that someday something nice would turn up.

Tsuyoshi went into the local pachinko parlor, where he won half a liter of beer and a train chargecard. He drank the beer, took the new train card, and wedged himself into the train. He got out at the Ebisu station, and turned on his pokkecon Tokyo street map to guide his steps. He walked past places called Chocolate Soup, and Freshness Physique, and The Aladdin Mai-Tai Panico Trattoria.

He entered the Hotel Daruma and went to the hotel barbershop, which was called the Daruma Planet Look. "May I help you?" said the receptionist.

"I'm thinking, a shave and a trim," Tsuyoshi said.

"Do you have an appointment with us?"

"Sorry, no." Tsuyoshi offered a hand gesture.

The woman gestured back, a jerky series of cryptic finger movements. Tsuyoshi didn't recognize any of the gestures. She wasn't from his part of the network.

"Oh well, never mind," the receptionist said kindly. "I'll get Nahoko to look after you."

Nahoko was carefully shaving the fine hair from Tsuyoshi's forehead when the pokkecon rang. Tsuyoshi answered it.

"Go to the ladies' room on the fourth floor," the pokkecon told him.

"Sorry, I can't do that. This is Tsuyoshi Shimizu, not Ai Shimizu. Besides, I'm having my hair cut right now."

"Oh, I see," said the machine. "Recalibrating." It hung up.

Nahoko finished his hair. She had done a good job. He looked much better. A man who worked at home had

to take special trouble to keep up appearances. The pokkecon rang again.

"Yes?" said Tsuyoshi.

"Buy bay rum aftershave. Take it outside."

"Right." He hung up. "Nahoko, do you have bay
rum?"

"Odd you should ask that," said Nahoko. "Hardly
anyone asks for bay rum anymore, but our shop happens
to keep it in stock."

Tsuyoshi bought the aftershave, then stepped outside
the barbershop. Nothing happened, so he bought a manga
comic and waited. Finally a hairy, blond stranger in
shorts, a tropical shirt, and sandals approached him. The
foreigner was carrying a camera bag and an old-fashioned
pokkecon. He looked about sixty years old, and he was
very tall.

The man spoke to his pokkecon in English. "Excuse
me," said the pokkecon, translating the man's speech into
Japanese. "Do you have a bottle of bay rum aftershave?"

"Yes I do." Tsuyoshi handed the bottle over. "Here."

"Thank goodness!" said the man, his words relayed
through his machine. "I've asked everyone else in the
lobby. Sorry I was late."

"No problem," said Tsuyoshi. "That's a nice pokkecon you have there."

"Well," the man said, "I know it's old and out of
style. But I plan to buy a new pokkecon here in Tokyo. I'm
told that they sell pokkecons by the basketful in
Akihabara electronics market."

"That's right. What kind of translator program are
you running? Your translator talks like someone from
Osaka."

"Does it sound funny?" the tourist asked anxiously.

"Well, I don't want to complain, but. . . ." Tsuyoshi
smiled. "Here, let's trade meishi. I can give you a copy of a
brand-new freeware translator."

"That would be wonderful." They pressed buttons

and squirted copies of their business cards across the network link.

Tsuyoshi examined his copy of the man's electronic card and saw that his name was Zimmerman. Mr. Zimmerman was from New Zealand. Tsuyoshi activated a transfer program. His modern pokkecon began transferring a new translator onto Zimmerman's machine.

A large American man in a padded suit entered the lobby of the Daruma. The man wore sunglasses, and was sweating visibly in the summer heat. The American looked huge, as if he lifted a lot of weights. Then a Japanese woman followed him. The woman was sharply dressed, with a dark blue dress suit, hat, sunglasses, and an attaché case. She had a haunted look.

Her escort turned and carefully watched the bellhops, who were bringing in a series of bags. The woman walked crisply to the reception desk and began making anxious demands of the clerk.

"I'm a great believer in machine translation," Tsuyoshi said to the tall man from New Zealand. "I really believe that computers help human beings to relate in a much more human way."

"I couldn't agree with you more," said Mr. Zimmerman, through his machine. "I can remember the first time I came to your country, many years ago. I had no portable translator. In fact, I had nothing but a printed phrasebook. I happened to go into a bar, and . . ."

Zimmerman stopped and gazed alertly at his pokkecon. "Oh dear, I'm getting a screen prompt. I have to go up to my room right away."

"Then I'll come along with you till this software transfer is done," Tsuyoshi said.

"That's very kind of you." They got into the elevator together. Zimmerman punched for the fourth floor. "Anyway, as I was saying, I went into this bar in Roppongi late at night, because I was jetlagged and hoping for something to eat . . ."

"Yes?"

"And this woman . . . well, let's just say this woman was hanging out in a foreigner's bar in Roppongi late at night, and she wasn't wearing a whole lot of clothes, and she didn't look like she was any better than she ought to be. . . ."

"Yes, I think I understand you."

"Anyway, this menu they gave me was full of kanji, or katakana, or romanji, or whatever they call those, so I had my phrasebook out, and I was trying very hard to puzzle out these pesky ideograms . . ." The elevator opened and they stepped into the carpeted hall of the hotel's fourth floor. "So I opened the menu and I pointed to an entree, and I told this girl. . . ." Zimmerman stopped suddenly, and stared at his screen. "Oh dear, something's happening. Just a moment."

Zimmerman carefully studied the instructions on his pokkecon. Then he pulled the bottle of bay rum from the baggy pocket of his shorts, and unscrewed the cap. He stood on tiptoe, stretching to his full height, and carefully poured the contents of the bottle through the iron louvers of a ventilation grate set high in the top of the wall.

Zimmerman screwed the cap back on neatly, and slipped the empty bottle back in his pocket. Then he examined his pokkecon again. He frowned, and shook it. The screen had frozen. Apparently Tsuyoshi's new translation program had overloaded Zimmerman's old-fashioned operating system. His pokkecon had crashed.

Zimmerman spoke a few defeated sentences in English. Then he smiled, and spread his hands apologetically. He bowed, and went into his room, and shut the door.

The Japanese woman and her burly American escort entered the hall. The man gave Tsuyoshi a hard stare. The woman opened the door with a passcard. Her hands were shaking.

Tsuyoshi's pokkecon rang. "Leave the hall," it told him. "Go downstairs. Get into the elevator with the bellboy."

Tsuyoshi followed instructions.

The bellboy was just entering the elevator with a cart full of the woman's baggage. Tsuyoshi got into the elevator, stepping carefully behind the wheeled metal cart. "What floor, sir?" said the bellboy.

"Eight," Tsuyoshi said, ad-libbing. The bellboy turned and pushed the buttons. He faced forward attentively, his gloved hands folded.

The pokkecon flashed a silent line of text to the screen. "Put the gift box inside her flight bag," it read.

Tsuyoshi located the zippered blue bag at the back of the cart. It was a matter of instants to zip it open, put in the box with the maneki neko, and zip the bag shut again. The bellboy noticed nothing. He left, tugging his cart.

Tsuyoshi got out on the eighth floor, feeling slightly foolish. He wandered down the hall, found a quiet nook by an ice machine, and called his wife. "What's going on?" he said.

"Oh, nothing." She smiled. "Your haircut looks nice! Show me the back of your head."

Tsuyoshi held the pokkecon screen behind the nape of his neck.

"They do good work," his wife said with satisfaction. "I hope it didn't cost too much. Are you coming home now?"

"Things are getting a little odd here at the hotel," Tsuyoshi told her. "I may be some time."

His wife frowned. "Well, don't miss supper. We're having bonito."

Tsuyoshi took the elevator back down. It stopped at the fourth floor. The woman's American companion stepped onto the elevator. His nose was running and his eyes were streaming with tears.

"Are you all right?" Tsuyoshi said.

"I don't understand Japanese," the man growled. The elevator doors shut.

The man's cellular phone crackled into life. It emitted a scream of anguish and a burst of agitated female English. The man swore and slammed his hairy fist against the elevator's emergency button. The elevator stopped with a lurch. An alarm bell began ringing.

The man pried the doors open with his large hairy fingers and clambered out into the fourth floor. He then ran headlong down the hall.

The elevator began buzzing in protest, its doors shuddering as if broken. Tsuyoshi climbed hastily from the damaged elevator, and stood there in the hallway. He hesitated a moment. Then he produced his pokkecon and loaded his Japanese-to-English translator. He walked cautiously after the American man.

The door to their suite was open. Tsuyoshi spoke aloud into his pokkecon. "Hello?" he said experimentally. "May I be of help?"

The woman was sitting on the bed. She had just discovered the maneki neko box in her flight bag. She was staring at the little cat in horror.

"Who are you?" she said, in bad Japanese.

Tsuyoshi realized suddenly that she was a Japanese American. Tsuyoshi had met a few Japanese Americans before. They always troubled him. They looked fairly normal from the outside, but their behavior was always bizarre. "I'm just a passing friend," he said. "Something I can do?"

"Grab him, Mitch!" said the woman in English. The American man rushed into the hall and grabbed Tsuyoshi by the arm. His hands were like steel bands.

Tsuyoshi pressed the distress button on his pokkecon.

"Take that computer away from him," the woman ordered in English. Mitch quickly took Tsuyoshi's pokkecon away, and threw it on the bed. He deftly patted Tsuyoshi's clothing, searching for weapons. Then he shoved Tsuyoshi into a chair.

The woman switched back to Japanese. "Sit right there, you. Don't you dare move." She began examining the contents of Tsuyoshi's wallet.

"I beg your pardon?" Tsuyoshi said. His pokkecon was lying on the bed. Lines of red text scrolled up its little screen as it silently issued a series of emergency net alerts.

The woman spoke to her companion in English. Tsuyoshi's pokkecon was still translating faithfully. "Mitch, go call the local police."

Mitch sneezed uncontrollably. Tsuyoshi noticed that the room smelled strongly of bay rum. "I can't talk to the local cops. I can't speak Japanese." Mitch sneezed again.

"Okay, then I'll call the cops. You handcuff this guy. Then go down to the infirmary and get yourself some anti-histamines, for Christ's sake."

Mitch pulled a length of plastic whipcord cuff from his coat pocket, and attached Tsuyoshi's right wrist to the head of the bed. He mopped his streaming eyes with a tissue. "I'd better stay with you. If there's a cat in your luggage, then the criminal network already knows we're in Japan. You're in danger."

"Mitch, you may be my bodyguard, but you're breaking out in hives."

"This just isn't supposed to happen," Mitch complained, scratching his neck. "My allergies never interfered with my job before."

"Just leave me here and lock the door," the woman told him. "I'll put a chair against the knob. I'll be all right. You need to look after yourself."

Mitch left the room.

The woman barricaded the door with a chair. Then she called the front desk on the hotel's bedside pasokon. "This is Louise Hashimoto in room 434. I have a gangster in my room. He's an information criminal. Would you call the Tokyo police, please? Tell them to send the organized crime unit. Yes, that's right. Do it. And you should put your hotel security people on full alert. There may be big trouble here. You'd better hurry." She hung up.

Tsuyoshi stared at her in astonishment. "Why are you doing this? What's all this about?"

"So you call yourself Tsuyoshi Shimizu," said the woman, examining his credit cards. She sat on the foot of the bed and stared at him. "You're yakuza of some kind, right?"

"I think you've made a big mistake," Tsuyoshi said.

Louise scowled. "Look, Mr. Shimizu, you're not dealing with some Yankee tourist here. My name is Louise Hashimoto and I'm an assistant federal prosecutor from Providence, Rhode Island, USA." She showed him a magnetic ID card with a gold official seal.

"It's nice to meet someone from the American government," said Tsuyoshi, bowing a bit in his chair. "I'd shake your hand, but it's tied to the bed."

"You can stop with the innocent act right now. I spotted you out in the hall earlier, and in the lobby, too, casing the hotel. How did you know my bodyguard is violently allergic to bay rum? You must have read his medical records."

"Who, me? Never!"

"Ever since I discovered you network people, it's been one big pattern," said Louise. "It's the biggest criminal conspiracy I ever saw. I busted this software pirate in Providence. He had a massive network server and a whole bunch of AI freeware search engines. We took him in custody, we bagged all his search engines, and catalogs, and indexers. . . . Later that very same day, these *cats* start showing up."

"Cats?"

Louise lifted the maneki neko, handling it as if it were a live eel. "These little Japanese voodoo cats. Maneki neko, right? They started showing up everywhere I went. There's a china cat in my handbag. There's three china cats at the office. Suddenly they're on display in the windows of every antique store in Providence. My car radio starts making meowing noises at me."

"You *broke* part of the network?" Tsuyoshi said, scandalized. "You took someone's machines away? That's terrible! How could you do such an inhuman thing?"

"You've got a real nerve complaining about that. What about *my* machinery?" Louise held up her fat, eerie-looking American pokkecon. "As soon as I stepped off the airplane at Narita, my PDA was attacked. Thousands and thousands of e-mail messages. All of them pictures of cats. A denial-of-service attack! I can't even communicate with the home office! My PDA's useless!"

"What's a PDA?"

"It's a PDA, my Personal Digital Assistant! Manufactured in Silicon Valley!"

"Well, with a goofy name like that, no wonder our pokkecons won't talk to it."

Louise frowned grimly. "That's right, wise guy. Make jokes about it. You're involved in a malicious software attack on a legal officer of the United States Government. You'll see." She paused, looking him over. "You know, Shimizu, you don't look much like the Italian mafia gangsters I have to deal with, back in Providence."

"I'm not a gangster at all. I never do anyone any harm."

"Oh no?" Louise glowered at him. "Listen, pal, I know a lot more about your set-up, and your kind of people, than you think I do. I've been studying your outfit for a long time now. We computer cops have names for your kind of people. Digital panarchies. Segmented, polycephalous, integrated influence networks. What about all these *free goods and services* you're getting all this time?"

She pointed a finger at him. "Ha! Do you ever pay *taxes* on those? Do you ever *declare* that income and those benefits? All the free shipments from other countries! The little homemade cookies, and the free pens and pencils and bumper stickers, and the used bicycles, and the helpful news about fire sales. . . . You're a tax evader! You're living through kickbacks! And bribes! And influence peddling! And all kinds of corrupt off-the-books transactions!"

Tsuyoshi blinked. "Look, I don't know anything about all that. I'm just living my life."

"Well, your network gift economy is undermining the lawful, government-approved, regulated economy!"

"Well," Tsuyoshi said gently, "maybe my economy is better than your economy."

"Says who?" she scoffed. "Why would anyone think that?"

"It's better because we're *happier* than you are. What's wrong with acts of kindness? Everyone likes gifts. Midsummer gifts. New Year's Day gifts. Year-end presents. Wedding presents. Everybody likes those."

"Not the way you Japanese like them. You're totally crazy for gifts."

"What kind of society has no gifts? It's barbaric to have no regard for common human feelings."

Louise bristled. "You're saying I'm barbaric?"

"I don't mean to complain," Tsuyoshi said politely, "but you do have me tied up to your bed."

Louise crossed her arms. "You might as well stop complaining. You'll be in much worse trouble when the local police arrive."

"Then we'll probably be waiting here for quite a while," Tsuyoshi said. "The police move rather slowly, here in Japan. I'm sorry, but we don't have as much crime as you Americans, so our police are not very alert."

The pasokon rang at the side of the bed. Louise answered it. It was Tsuyoshi's wife.

"Could I speak to Tsuyoshi Shimizu please?"

"I'm over here, dear," Tsuyoshi called quickly. "She's kidnapped me! She tied me to the bed!"

"Tied to her *bed*?" His wife's eyes grew wide. "That does it! I'm calling the police!"

Louise quickly hung up the pasokon. "I haven't kidnapped you! I'm only detaining you here until the local authorities can come and arrest you."

"Arrest me for what, exactly?"

Louise thought quickly. "Well, for poisoning my bodyguard by pouring bay rum into the ventilator."

"But I never did that. Anyway, that's not illegal, is it?"

The pasokon rang again. A shining white cat appeared on the screen. It had large, staring, unearthly eyes.

"Let him go," the cat commanded in English.

Louise shrieked and yanked the pasokon's plug from the wall.

Suddenly the lights went out. "Infrastructure attack!" Louise squawled. She rolled quickly under the bed.

The room went gloomy and quiet. The air conditioner had shut off. "I think you can come out," Tsuyoshi said at last, his voice loud in the still room. "It's just a power failure."

"No it isn't," Louise said. She crawled slowly from beneath the bed, and sat on the mattress. Somehow, the darkness had made them more intimate. "I know very well what this is. I'm under attack. I haven't had a moment's peace since I broke that network. Stuff just happens to me now. Bad stuff. Swarms of it. It's never anything you can touch, though. Nothing you can prove in a court of law."

She sighed. "I sit in chairs, and somebody's left a piece of gum there. I get free pizzas, but they're not the kind of pizzas I like. Little kids spit on my sidewalk. Old women in walkers get in front of me whenever I need to hurry."

The shower came on, all by itself. Louise shuddered, but said nothing. Slowly, the darkened, stuffy room began to fill with hot steam.

"My toilets don't flush," Louise said. "My letters get lost in the mail. When I walk by cars, their theft alarms go off. And strangers stare at me. It's always little things. Lots of little tiny things, but they never, ever stop. I'm up against something that is very very big, and very very patient. And it knows all about me. And it's got a million arms and legs. And all those arms and legs are people."

There was the noise of scuffling in the hall. Distant voices, confused shouting.

Suddenly the chair broke under the doorknob. The door burst open violently. Mitch tumbled through, the sunglasses flying from his head. Two hotel security guards were trying to grab him. Shouting incoherently in English, Mitch fell headlong to the floor, kicking and thrashing. The guards lost their hats in the struggle. One tackled

Mitch's legs with both his arms, and the other whacked and jabbed him with a baton.

Puffing and grunting with effort, they hauled Mitch out of the room. The darkened room was so full of steam that the harried guards hadn't even noticed Tsuyoshi and Louise.

Louise stared at the broken door. "Why did they do that to him?"

Tsuyoshi scratched his head in embarrassment. "Probably a failure of communication."

"Poor Mitch! They took his gun away at the airport. He had all kinds of technical problems with his passport. . . . Poor guy, he's never had any luck since he met me."

There was a loud tapping at the window. Louise shrank back in fear. Finally she gathered her courage, and opened the curtains. Daylight flooded the room.

A window-washing rig had been lowered from the roof of the hotel, on cables and pulleys. There were two window-washers in crisp gray uniforms. They waved cheerfully, making little catpaw gestures.

There was a third man with them. It was Tsuyoshi's brother.

One of the washers opened the window with a utility key. Tsuyoshi's brother squirmed into the room. He stood up and carefully adjusted his coat and tie.

"This is my brother," Tsuyoshi explained.

"What are you doing here?" Louise said.

"They always bring in the relatives when there's a hostage situation," Tsuyoshi's brother said. "The police just flew me in by helicopter and landed me on the roof." He looked Louise up and down. "Miss Hashimoto, you just have time to escape."

"What?" she said.

"Look down at the streets," he told her. "See that? You hear them? Crowds are pouring in from all over the city. All kinds of people, everyone with wheels. Street noodle salesmen. Bicycle messengers. Skateboard kids. Take-out delivery guys."

Louise gazed out the window into the streets, and shrieked aloud. "Oh no! A giant swarming mob! They're surrounding me! I'm doomed!"

"You are not doomed," Tsuyoshi's brother told her intently. "Come out the window. Get onto the platform with us. You've got one chance, Louise. It's a place I know, a sacred place in the mountains. No computers there, no phones, nothing." He paused. "It's a sanctuary for people like us. And I know the way."

She gripped his suited arm. "Can I trust you?"

"Look in my eyes," he told her. "Don't you see? Yes, of course you can trust me. We have everything in common."

Louise stepped out the window. She clutched his arm, the wind whipping at her hair. The platform creaked rapidly up and out of sight.

Tsuyoshi stood up from the chair. When he stretched out, tugging at his handcuffed wrist, he was just able to reach his pokkecon with his fingertips. He drew it in, and clutched it to his chest. Then he sat down again, and waited patiently for someone to come and give him freedom.

BIG JELLY

By Rudy Rucker and Bruce Sterling

The screaming metal jellyfish dragged long, invisible tentacles across the dry concrete acres of the San Jose airport. Or so it seemed to Tug—Tug Mesoglea, math-drunk programmer and fanatic aquarist. Tug was working on artificial jellyfish, and nearly everything looked like a jellyfish to him, even airplanes. Tug was here in front of the baggage claim to pick up Texas billionaire Revel Pullen.

It had taken a deluge of phone-calls, faxes, and e-mail to lure the reclusive Texan venture-capitalist from his decrepit, polluted East Texas oil-fields, but Tug had now coaxed Revel Pullen to a second face-to-face meeting in California. At last, it seemed that Tug's unconventional high-tech startup scheme would charge into full-scale production. The prospect of success was sweet.

Tug had first met Revel in Monterey two months earlier, at the spring symposium of the ACM SIGUSC, that is, the Association for Computing Machinery's Special Interest Group for Underground and Submarine Computation.

At the symposium, Tug had given a badly botched presentation on artificial jellyfish. He'd arrived with five hundred copies of a glossy desktop-published brochure: "Artificial Jellyfish: Your Route to Postindustrial Global

Competitiveness!" But when it came time for Tug's talk, his 15-terabyte virtual jellyfish–demo had crashed so hideously that he couldn't even reboot his machine—a cheap Indonesian Sun–clone laptop that Tug now used as a bookend. Tug had brought some slides as a backup, but of course the slide-tray had jammed. And, worst of all, the single working prototype of Tug's plastic artificial jellyfish had burst in transit to Monterey. After the talk, Tug, in a red haze of shame, had flushed the sodden rags of decomposing gel down the conference center's john.

Tug had next headed for the cocktail lounge, and there the garrulous young Pullen had sought him out, had a few drinks with him, and had even picked up the tab—Tug's wallet had been stolen the night before by a cute older busboy.

Since Tug's topic was jellyfish, the raucous Pullen had thought it funny to buy rounds of tequila jelly-shots. The slimy jolts of potent boozy Jell-O had combined with Revel's bellowed jokes, brags, and wild promises to ease the pain of Tug's failed speech.

The next day, Tug and Revel had brunched together, and Revel had written Tug a handsome check as earnest money for pre-development expenses. Tug was to develop an artificial jellyfish capable of undersea oil prospecting.

As software applications went, oil-drilling was a little roughnecked and analog for Tug's taste, but the money certainly looked real enough. The only troubling aspect about dealing with Revel was the man's obsession with some new and troublesome organic slime which his family's oldest oil-well had recently tapped. Again and again, the garish Texan had steered the conversation away from jellyfish and onto the subject of ancient subterranean slime.

Perched now on the fire-engine red hood of his expensive Animata sports car, Tug waited for Revel to arrive. Tug had curly dark hair and a pink-cheeked complexion. He wore shorts, a sport shirt, and Birkenstock sandals with argyle socks. He looked like a depraved British schoolboy. He'd bought the Animata with his house-money nest-egg when he'd learned that he would never, ever be rich enough to buy a house in California. Leaning back against the windshield of his car, Tug stared at the descending airplanes and thought about jellyfish trawling through sky-blue seawater.

Tug had whole tankfuls of jellies at home: one tank with flattish moon jellies each with its four whitish circles of sex organs, another tank with small clear bell jellies from the eel grass of Monterey bay, a large tank with sea nettles that had long frilly oral arms and whiplike purple tentacles covered with stinging cells, a smaller tank of toadstool-like spotted jellies from Jellyfish Lake in Palau, a special tank of spinning comb-jellies with trailing ciliated arms, a Japanese tank with umbrella jellies—and more.

Next to the arsenal of tanks was the huge color screen of Tug's workstation. Tug was no biologist; he'd blundered under the spell of jellies while using mathematical algorithms to generate cellular models of vortex sheets. To Tug's mathematician's eye, a jellyfish was a highly perfected relationship between curvature and torsion, just like a vortex sheet, only a jellyfish was working off dynamic tension and osmotic stress. Real jellyfish were gnarlier than Tug's simulations. Tug had become a dedicated amateur of coelenteratology.

Imitating nature to the core, Tug found a way to evolve and improve his vortex sheet models via genetic programming. Tug's artificial jellyfish algorithms competed, mutated, reproduced, and died inside the virtual reality of his workstation's sea-green screen. As Tug's algorithms improved, his big computer monitor became a tank of virtual jellyfish, of graphic representations of Tug's equations, pushing at the chip's computational limits, slowly pulsing about in dimly glowing simulation-space.

The living jellies in the tanks of true seawater provided an objective standard toward which Tug's programs could try to evolve. At every hour of the day and night, video cameras peered into the spot-lit water tanks, ceaselessly analyzing the jellyfish motions and feeding data into the workstation.

The recent, crowning step of Tug's investigations was his manufacturing breakthrough. His theoretical equations had become actual piezoplastic constructions—soft, watery, gelatinous robot jellies of real plastic in the real world. These models were produced by using an intersecting pair of laser beams to sinter—that is, to join together by heating without melting—the desired shape within a matrix of piezoplastic microbeads. The sintered microbeads behaved like a mass of cells: each of them could compress or elongate in response to delicate vibratory signals, and each microbead could in turn pass information to its neighbors.

A completed artificial jellyfish model was a floppy little umbrella that beat in steady cellular waves of excitation and relaxation. Tug's best plastic jellyfish could stay active for up to three weeks.

Tug's next requirement for his creations was "a killer application," as the software tycoons called it. And it seemed he might have that killer app in hand, given his recent experiments in making the jellyfish sensitive to chemical scents and signals. Tug had convinced Revel—and half-believed himself—that the artificial jellies could be equipped with radiosignaling chips and set loose on the sea floor. They could sniff out oil-seeps in the ocean bottom and work their way deep into the vents. If this were so, then artificial jellyfish would revolutionize undersea oil prospecting.

The only drawback, in Tug's view, was that offshore drilling was a contemptible crime against the wonderful environment that had bred the real jellies in the first place. Yet the plan seemed likely to free up Texas venture capital, enough capital to continue his research for at least another year. And maybe in another year, thought Tug, he would have a more ecologically sound killer app, and he would be able to disentangle himself from the crazy Texan.

Right on cue, Revel Pullen came strolling down the

exit ramp, clad in the garb of a white-trash oil-field worker: a flannel shirt and a pair of Can't-Bust-'Em overalls. Revel had a blond crewcut and smooth dark skin. The shirt was from Neiman-Marcus and the overalls were ironed, but they seemed to be genuinely stained with dirt-fresh Texas crude.

Tug hopped off the hood of his car and stood on tiptoe to wave, deliberately camping it up to jangle the Texan's nerves. He drew up a heel behind him like Marilyn Monroe waving in *The Misfits*.

Nothing daunted, Revel Pullen headed Tug's way with an exaggerated bowlegged sprawl and a scuff of his python-skin boots. Revel was the scapegrace nephew of Amarillo's billionaire Pullen Brothers. The Pullen clan were malignant market speculators and greenmail raiders who had once tried to corner the world market in molybdenum.

Revel himself, the least predictable of his clan, was in charge of the Pullen Brothers' weakest investments: the failing oil wells that had initially brought the Pullen family to prominence—beginning with the famous Ditheree Gusher, drilled near Spindletop, Texas, in 1892.

Revel's quirk was his ambition to become a high-tech tycoon. This was why Revel attended computer-science meetings like SIGUSC, despite his stellar ignorance of everything having to do with the movement of bytes and pixels.

Revel stood ready to sink big money into a technically sexy Silicon Valley start-up. Especially if the start-up could somehow do something for his family's collapsing oil industry and—though this part still puzzled Tug—find a use for some odd clear fluid that Revel's engineers had recently been pumping from the Ditheree hole.

"Shit howdy, Tug," drawled Revel, hoisting his polyester/denim duffel bag from one slim shoulder to another. "Mighty nice of y'all to come meet me."

Beaming, Tug freed his fingers from Revel's insistent grip and gestured toward the Animata. "So, Revel! Ready to start a business? I've decided we should call it Cteno-

phore, Inc. A *ctenophore* is a kind of hermaphroditic jellyfish which uses a comblike feeding organ to filter nutrients
from the ocean; they're also called comb-jellies. Don't you
think Ctenophore is a perfect name for our company?
Raking in the dollars from the economy's mighty sea!"

"Not so loud!" Revel protested, glancing up and
down the airport pavement in a parody of wary street-
smarts. "As far as any industrial spy knows, I'm here in
California on a personal vacation." He heaved his duffel
into the back of Tug's car. Then he straightened, and
reached deep into the baggy trouser-pocket of his Can't-
Bust-'Ems.

The Texan dragged out a slender pill-bottle filled with
clear viscous jelly and pressed the crotch-warmed vial into
Tug's unwilling palm, with a dope-dealer's covert insis-
tence. "I want you to keep this, Tug. Just in case anything
should . . . you know . . . happen to me."

Revel swiveled his narrow head to scan the passers-by
with paranoid alertness, briefly reminding Tug of the last
time he'd been here at the San Jose airport: to meet his
ailing father, who'd been fingerpaint-the-wall-with-shit senile and had been summarily dumped on the plane by
Tug's uncle. Tug had gotten his father into a local nursing
home, and last summer Tug's father had died.

Life was sad, and Tug was letting it slip through his
fingers—he was an unloved gay man who'd never see
thirty again, and now here he was humoring a nutso het
from Texas. Humoring people was not something Tug excelled at.

"Do you really have enemies?" said Tug. "Or do you
just think so? Am I supposed to think you have enemies?
Am I supposed to care?"

"There's money in these plans of ours—real foldin'
money," Revel bragged darkly, climbing into the Animata's passenger seat. He waited silently until Tug took
the wheel and shut the driver's-side door. "All we really
gotta worry about," Revel continued at last, "is control-

ling the publicity. The environmental impact crap. You didn't tell anybody about what I e-mailed you, did you?"

"No," snapped Tug. "That cheap public-key encryption you're using has garbled half your messages. What are you so worried about, anyway? Nobody's gonna care about some slime from a played-out oil well—even if you do call it *Urschleim*. That's German, right?"

"Shhhhh!" hissed Revel.

Tug started the engine and gunned it with a bluish gust of muscular combustion. They swung out into the endless California traffic.

Revel checked several times to make sure that they weren't being trailed. "Yes, I call it *Urschleim*," he said at last, portentously. "In fact, I've put in a trademark for that name. Them old-time German professors were on to something. *Ur* means *primeval*. All life came from the Urschleim, the original slime! Primeval slime from the inner depths of the planet! You ever bitten into a green almond, Tug? From the tree? There's some green fuzz, a thin little shell, and a center of clear, thick slime. That's exactly how our planet is, too. Most of the original Urschleim is still flowing, and oozing, and lyin' there 'way down deep. It's just waitin' for some bright boy to pump it out and exploit its commercial potential. Urschleim is life itself."

"That's pretty grandiose," said Tug evenly.

"Grandiose, hell!" Revel snapped. "It's the only salvation for the Texas oil business, compadre! God damn it, if we Texans don't drill for a living, we'll be reduced to peddling chips and software like a bunch of goddamn Pacific Rim computer weenies! You got me wrong if you think I'll give up the oil business without a fight!"

"Sure, sure, I'm hip," Tug said soothingly. "My jellyfish are going to help you find more oil, remember?" It was easy to tell when Revel had gone nonlinear—his Texan drawl thickened drastically and he began to refer to his beloved oil business as the "aisle bidness." But what was the story with this *Urschleim*?

Tug held up the pill-bottle of clear slime and glanced

at it while steering with one hand. The stuff was thixotropic—meaning a gel that becomes liquid when shaken. You'd tilt the vial and all the Urschleim would be stuck in one end, but then, if you shook the bottle a bit, the slime's state would change and it would run down to the other end like ketchup suddenly gushing from a bottle. Smooth, clear ketchup. Snot.

"The Ditheree hole's oozin' with Urschleim right now!" said Revel, settling a pair of Italian sunglasses onto his freckled nose. He looked no older than twenty-five. "I brought three gallons of it in a tank in my duffel. One of my engineers says it's a new type of deep-lying oil, and another one says it's just water infected with bacteria. But I'm with old Herr Doktor Professor von Stoffman. We've struck the cell fluid of Mother Earth herself: undifferentiated tissue, Tug, primordial ooze. Gaia goo. Urschleim!"

"What did you do to make it start oozing?" asked Tug, suppressing a giggle.

Revel threw back his head and crowed. "Man, if OPEC got wind about our new high-tech extraction techniques. . . . You don't think I got enemies, son? Them sheikhs play for keeps." Revel tapped his knuckles cagily against the car's closed window. "Hell, even Uncle Sam'd be down on us if he knew that we've been twisting genes and seeding those old worn-out oil beds with designer bacteria! They eat through tar and paraffin, change the oil's viscosity, unblock the pores in the stone, and get it all fizzy with methane. . . . You wouldn't think the ol' Ditheree had it in 'er to blow valves and gush again, but we plumbed her out with a new extra-virulent strain. And what did she gush? Urschleim!"

Revel peered at Tug over the tops of his designer sunglasses, assuming what he seemed to think was a trustworthy expression. "But that ain't the half of it, Tug. Wait till I tell you what we did with the stuff once we had it."

Tug was impatient. Gusher or not, Revel's bizarre maunderings were not going to sell any jellyfish. "What did you think of that artificial jellyfish I sent you?"

Revel frowned. "Well, it looked okay when it showed up. About the size of a deflated football. I dropped it in my swimmin' pool. It was floatin' there, kinda rippling and pulsing, for about two days. Didn't you say that sucker would run for weeks? Forty-eight hours and it was gone! Disintegrated I guess. Chlorine melted the plastic or something."

"No way," protested Tug, intensely. "It must have slipped out a crack in the side of your pool. I built that model to last three weeks for sure! It was my best prototype. It was a chemotactic artificial jellyfish designed to slither into undersea vents and find its way to underground oil beds."

"My swimming pool's not in the best condition," allowed Revel. "So I guess it's possible that your jellyfish did squeeze out through a crack. But if this oil-prospecting application of yours is any good, the thing should have come back with some usable geology data. And it never did come back that I noticed. Face it, Tug, the thing melted."

Tug wouldn't give in. "My jellyfish didn't send back information because I didn't put a tracer chip in it. If you're going to be so rude about it, I might as well tell you that I don't think oil prospecting is a very honorable application. I'd really rather see the California Water Authority using my jellies to trace leaks in irrigation and sewage lines."

Revel yawned, sinking deeper into the passenger seat. "That's real public-spirited of you, Dr. Mesoglea. But California water ain't worth a dime to me."

Tug pressed onward. "Also, I'd like to see my jellyfish used to examine contaminated wells here in Silicon Valley. If you put an artificial jellyfish down a well, and leave it to pulsate down there for a week or two, it could filter up all kinds of trace pollutants! It'd be a great public-relations gambit to push the jelly's antipollution aspects. Considering your family history, it couldn't hurt to get the Pullen family in the good graces of the Environmental Protection

people. If we angle it right, we could probably even swing
a federal development grant!"

"I dunno, hombre," Revel grumbled. "Somehow it
just don't seem sportin' to take money from the
Feds. . . ." He gazed mournfully at the lushly exotic
landscape of monkey-puzzle trees, fat pampered yuccas,
and orange trees. "Man, everything sure looks *green* out
here."

"Yes," Tug said absently, "thank God there's been a
break in the drought. California has plenty of use for a
jellyfish that can monitor water-leaks."

"It's not the water that counts," said Revel, "it's the
carbon dioxide. Two hundred million years' worth of
crude oil, all burned to carbon dioxide and spewed right
into the air in just a few decades. Plant life's goin' crazy.
Why, all the plant life along this highway has built itself
out of car exhausts! You ever think o' that?"

It was clear from the look of glee on Revel's shallow
features that this thought pleased him mightily. "I mean, if
you traced the history of the carbon in that weirdass-
lookin' tree over there . . . hunnert years ago it was
miles down in the primeval bowels of the earth! And since
we eat plants to live, it's the same for people! Our flesh,
brain, and blood is built outa burnt crude-oil! We're creatures of the Urschleim, Tug. All life comes from the primeval goo."

"No way," said Tug heatedly. He took a highway exit
to Los Perros, his own local enclave in the massive sprawl
that was Silicon Valley. "One carbon atom's just like the
next one. And once you're talking artificial life, it doesn't
even have to be an 'atom' at all. It can be a byte of information, or a microbead of piezoplastic. It doesn't matter
where the material came from—life is just a pattern of
behavior."

"That's where you and me part company, boy." They
were tooling down the main drag of Los Perros now, and
Revel was gaping at some chicly dressed women. "Dig it,
Tug, thanks to oil, a lot of carbon in your yuppie neigh-

bors comes from Texas. Like or not, most modern life is
fundamentally Texan."

"That's pretty appalling news, Revel," smiled Tug. He
took the last remaining hilly corners with a squeal of his
Michelins, then pulled into his driveway. He parked the
Animata under the rotting, fungus-specked redwood deck
of the absurdly overpriced suburban home that he rented.
The rent was killing him. Ever since his lover had moved
out last Christmas, Tug had been meaning to move into a
smaller place, but somewhere deep down he nursed a hope
that if he kept the house, some nice strong man would
come and move in with him.

Next door, Tug's neighbors were flinging water-
balloons and roaring with laughter as they sizzled up a
huge aromatic rack of barbecued tofu. They were rich
Samoans. They had a big green parrot named Toatoa. On
fine days, such as today, Toatoa sat squawking on the ga-
ble of the house. Toatoa had a large yellow beak and a
taste for cuttlebone and pumpkin-seeds.

"This is great," Revel opined, examining the
earthquake-split walls and peeling ceiling Sheetrock. "I
was afraid we'd have some trouble findin' the necessary
space for experiments. No problem, though, with you ren-
tin' this sorry dump for a workshop."

"I live here," said Tug with dignity. "By California
standards this is a very good house."

"No wonder you want to start a company!" Revel
climbed the redwood stairs to Tug's outdoor deck, and
dragged a yard-long plastic pressure cylinder from within
his duffel bag, flinging aside some balled-up boot socks
and a set of watered-silk boxer shorts. "You got a garden
hose? And a funnel?" He pulled a roll of silvered duct tape
from the bottom of his bag.

Tug supplied a length of hose, prudently choosing one
that had been severely scorched during the last hillside
brushfire. Revel whipped a French designer pocketknife
from within his Can't-Bust-'Ems and slashed off a three-

foot length. He then deftly duct-taped the tin funnel to the
end of the hose, and blew a few kazoo-like blasts.

Next Revel flung the crude horn aside and took up the
pressure cylinder. "You don't happen to have a washtub,
do you?"

"No problem," Tug said. He went into the house and
fetched a large plastic picnic cooler.

Revel opened the petcock of the pressure cylinder and
began decanting its contents into the cooler. The black
nozzle slowly ejaculated a thick clear gel, rather like silicone putty. Pint after pint of it settled languorously into
the white pebbly interior of the hinge-topped cooler. The
stuff had a sulfurous, burning-rubber reek that Tug associ-
ated with Hawaii—a necessarily brief stay he'd had on the
oozing, flaming slopes of Kilauea.

Tug prudently sidled across the deck and stood up-
wind of the cooler. "How far down did you obtain this
sample?"

Revel laughed. "Down? Doc, this stuff broke the
safety-valves on old Ditheree and blew drillin' mud over
five counties. We had an old-time blue-ball gusher of it. It
just kept comin', pourin' out over the ground. Kinda, you
know, *spasmodic*. . . . Finally ended up with a lake of
clear hot pudding higher than the tops of pickups."

"Jesus, what happened then?" Tug asked.

"Some evaporated. Some soaked right into the sub-
soil. Disappeared. The first sample I scored was out of the
back of some good ol' boy's Toyota. Lucky thing he had
the tailgate up, or it woulda all run out."

Revel pulled out a handkerchief, wiped sweat from his
forehead, and continued talking. "Of course, once we got
the rig repaired, we did some serious pump-work. We Pullens happen to own a tank farm near Nacogdoches, a couple of football fields' worth of big steel reservoirs. Hasn't
seen use since the OPEC embargo of the '70s. The tanks
were pretty much abandoned on site. But every one of
them babies is brim-full with Revel Pullen's trademark
Urschleim right now." He glanced up at the sun, looking a

bit wild-eyed, and wiped his forehead again. "You got any beer in this dump?"

"Sure, Revel." Tug went into the kitchen for two bottles of Etna Ale, and brought them out to the deck.

Revel drank thirstily, then gestured with his makeshift horn. "If this don't work, well, you're gonna think I'm crazy." He pushed his Italian shades up onto the top of his narrow crewcut skull, and grinned. He was enjoying himself. "But if it *does* work, ol' son—you're gonna think *you're* crazy."

Revel dipped the end of the funnel into the quiescent but aromatic mass. He swirled it around, then held it up carefully and puffed.

A fat lozenge-shaped gelatinous bubble appeared at the end of the horn.

"Holy cow, it blows up just like a balloon," Tug said, impressed. "That's some kind of viscosity!"

Revel grinned wider, holding the thing at arm's length. "It gets better."

Tug Mesoglea watched in astonishment as the clear bubble of Urschleim slowly rippled and dimpled. A long double crease sank into the taut outer membrane of the gelatinous sphere, encircling it like the seam on an oversized baseball.

Now, with a swampy-sounding plop, the bubble came loose from the horn's tin muzzle and began to float in midair. A set of cilia emerged along the seam and the airborne jelly began to bob and beat its way upward.

"Urschleim!" whooped Revel.

"Jesus Christ," Tug said, staring in shocked fascination. The air jelly was still changing before his eyes, evolving a set of interior membranes, warping, pulsing, and rippling itself into an ever more precise shape, for all the world like a computer graphics program ray-tracing its image into an elegant counterfeit of reality. . . .

Then a draft of air caught it. It hit the eaves of the house sturdily, bounced, and drifted up over the roof and into the sky.

"I can hardly believe it," said Tug, staring upward. "Spontaneous symmetry breaking! A self-actuating reaction/diffusion system. This slime of yours is an excitable medium with emergent behavior, Revel! And that spontaneous fractalization of the structures . . . can you do it again?"

"As many times as you want," said Revel. "With as much Urschleim as you got. Of course, the smell kinda gets to you if you do it indoors."

"But it's so odd," breathed Tug. "That the slime out of your oil well is forming itself into jellyfish shapes just as I'm starting to build jellyfish out of plastic."

"I figure it for some kind of a morphic resonance thing," nodded Revel. "This primeval slime's been trapped inside the Earth so long it's truly achin' to turn into something live and organic. Kind of like that super-weird worm and bacteria and clam shit that grows out of deep undersea vents."

"You mean *around* the undersea vents, Revel."

"No, Tug, right *out* of 'em. That's the part most people don't get."

"Whatever. Let me try blowing an Urschleim air jelly."

Tug dabbled the horn's tin rim in the picnic cooler, then huffed away at his own balloon of Urschleim. The sphere began to ripple internally, just as before, with just the same dimples and just the same luscious double crease. Tug had a sudden déjà vu. He'd seen this shape on his computer screen.

It started to float away, but frugal Revel darted forward and repeatedly slashed at it with his Swiss knife, finally causing the air jelly to break into a flying burst of clear snot that splashed all over Tug's feet and legs. The magic goo felt tingly on Tug's skin. He wondered nervously if any of the slime might be passing into his bloodstream. Revel scooped most of the slime off the deck and put it back in the cooler.

"What do you think?" asked Revel.

"I'm overwhelmed," said Tug, shaking his head. "Your Urschleim jellyfish look so much like the ones I've been building in my lab. Let's go in. I'll show you my jellyfish while we think this through." Tug led Revel into the house.

Revel insisted on bringing the Urschleim-containing cooler and the empty pressure canister into the house. He even got Tug to throw an Indian blanket over them, "in case we get company."

Tug's jellyfish tanks filled up an entire room with great green bubbling glory. The aquarium room had been a domestic video game parlor during the early 1980s, when the home's original builder, a designer of shoot-'em-up computer twitch-games, had shored up the floor to accommodate two dozen massive arcade-consoles. This was a good thing, too, for Tug's seawater tanks were a serious structural burden, and far outweighed all of Tug's other possessions put together, except maybe the teak waterbed that his ex-lover had left. Tug had bought the tanks themselves at a knockdown auction from the federal-seizure sale of an eccentric Oakland cocaine dealer, who had once used them to store schools of piranha.

Revel mulled silently over the tanks of jellyfish. Backlit by greenish glow from the spotlights of a defunct speed-metal crew, Tug's jellies were at their best. The backlighting brought out their most secret, most hidden interior curvatures, with an unblinking brilliance that was well-nigh pornographic.

Their seawater trace elements and Purina Jellyfish Lab Chow cost more than Tug's own weekly grocery bill, but his jelly menagerie had come to mean more to Tug than his own nourishment, health, money, or even his love-life. He spent long secret hours entranced before the gently spinning, ciliated marvels, watching them reel up their brine shrimp prey in mindless, reflexive elegance, absorbing the food in a silent ecstasy of poisonous goo. Live, digestive goo, that transmuted through secret alchemical biology into pulsating, glassy flesh.

Tug's ex-lover had been pretty sporting about Tug's goo-mania, especially compared to his other complaints about Tug's numerous perceived character flaws, but Tug figured his lover had finally been driven away by some deep rivalry with the barely organic. Tug had gone to some pains to Windex his noseprints from the aquarium glass before Revel arrived.

"Can you tell which ones are real and which ones I made from scratch?" Tug demanded triumphantly.

"You got me whipped," Revel admitted. "It's a real nice show, Tug. If you can really teach these suckers some tricks, we'll have ourselves a business."

Revel's denim chest emitted a ringing sound. He reached within his overalls, whipped out a cellular phone the size of a cigarette-pack, and answered it. "Pullen here! What? Yeah. Yeah, sure. Okay, see you." He flipped the phone shut and stowed it.

"Got you a visitor coming," he announced. "Business consultant I hired."

Tug frowned.

"My uncle's idea, actually," Revel shrugged. "Just kind of standard Pullen procedure before we sink any real money in a venture. We got ourselves one of the best computer-industry consultants in the business."

"Yeah? Who?"

"Edna Sydney. She's a futurist, she writes a high-finance technology newsletter that's real hot with the boys in suits."

"Some strange woman is going to show up here and decide if my Ctenophore, Inc. is worth funding?" Tug's voice was high and shaky with stress. "I don't like it, Revel."

"Just try 'n' act like you know what you're doing, Tug, and then she'll take my uncle Donny Ray a clean bill of health for us. Just a detail really." Revel laughed falsely. "My uncle's a little over-cautious. Belt-and-suspenders kinda guy. Lot of private investigators on his payroll and stuff. The old boy's just tryin' to keep me outa trouble, basically. Don't worry about it none, Tug."

Revel's phone rang again, this time from the pocket on his left buttock. "Pullen here! What? Yeah, I know his house don't look like much, but this is the place, all right. Yeah, okay, we'll let you in." Revel stowed the phone again, and turned to Tug. "Go get the door, man, and I'll double check that our cooler of Urschleim is out of sight."

Seconds later, Tug's front doorbell rang loudly. Tug opened it to find a woman in blue jeans, jogging shoes, and a shapeless gray wool jersey, slipping her own cellular phone into her black nylon satchel.

"Hello," she said. "Are you Dr. Mesoglea?"

"Yes, I am. Tug Mesoglea."

"Edna Sydney, Edna Sydney Associates."

Tug shook Edna Sydney's dainty blue-knuckled hand. She had a pointed chin, an impressively large forehead, and a look of extraordinary, almost supernatural intelligence in her dark brown shoebutton eyes. She had a neat cap of gray-streaked brown hair. She looked like a digital pixie leapt full-blown from the brain of Thomas Edison.

While she greeted Revel, Tug dug a business card from his wallet and forced it on her. Edna Sydney riposted with a card from the satchel that gave office addresses in Washington, Prague, and Chicago.

"Would you care for a latte?" Tug babbled. "Tab? Pineapple-mango soda?"

Edna Sydney settled for a Jolt Cola, then gently maneuvered the two men into the jellyfish lab. She listened attentively as Tug launched into an extensive, arm-waving spiel.

Tug was inspired. Words gushed from him like Revel's Urschleim. He'd never before met anyone who could fully understand him when he talked techie jargon absolutely as fast as he could. Edna Sydney, however, not only comprehended Tug's jabber but actually tapped her foot occasionally and once politely stifled a yawn.

"I've seen artificial life devices before," Edna allowed,

as Tug began to run out of verbal ectoplasm. "I knew all those Santa Fe guys before they destroyed the futures exchanges and got sent off to Leavenworth. I wouldn't advise trying to break into the software market with some new genetic algorithm. You don't want to end up like Bill Gates."

Revel snorted. "Gates? Geez, I wouldn't wish that on my worst enemy." He chortled aloud. "To think they used to compare that nerd to Rockefeller! Hell, Rockefeller was an oil business man, a family man! If Gates had been in Rockefeller's class, there'd be kids named Gates running half the states in the Union by now."

"I'm not planning to market the algorithms," Tug told the consultant. "They'll be a trade secret, and I'll market the jelly simulacra themselves. Ctenophore, Inc. is basically a manufacturing enterprise."

"What about the threat of reverse engineering?"

"We've got an eighteen-month lead," Revel bragged. "Round these parts, that's like eighteen years anywhere else! Besides, we got a set of ingredients that's gonna be mighty hard to duplicate."

"There hasn't been a lot of, uh, sustained industry development in the artificial jellyfish field before," Tug told her. "We've got a big R&D advantage."

Edna pursed her lips. "Well, that brings us to marketing, then. How are you going to get your products advertised and distributed?"

"Oh, for publicity, we'll do COMDEX, A-Life Developers, BioScience Fair, *MONDO 3000,* the works," Revel assured her. "And get this—we can ship jellies by the Pullen oil pipelines anywhere in North America for free! Try and match that for ease of distribution and clever use of an installed base! Hell, it'll be almost as easy as downloadin' software from the Internet!"

"That certainly sounds innovative," Edna nodded. "So—let's get to the crux of matters, then. What's the killer app for a robot jellyfish?"

Tug and Revel traded glances. "Our exact application is highly confidential," Tug said tentatively.

"Maybe *you* could suggest a few apps, Edna," Revel told her, folding his arms cagily over the denim chest of his Can't-Bust-'Ems. "Come on and *earn* your twenty thousand bucks an hour."

"Hmmm," the consultant said. Her brow clouded, and she sat in the armchair at Tug's workstation, her eyes gone distant. "Jellyfish. Industrial jellyfish . . ."

Greenish rippling aquarium light played across Edna Sydney's face as she sat in deep thought. The jellyfish kept up their silent, eternal pulsations; kept on bouncing their waves of contraction out and back between the centers and the rims of their bells.

"Housewares application," said Edna presently. "Fill them with lye and flush them through sinks and commodes. They agitate their way through sink traps and hairballs and grease."

"Check," said Tug alertly. He snatched a mechanical pencil from the desktop and began scribbling notes on the back of an unpaid bill.

"Assist fermentation in septic tanks by loading jellies with decomposition bacteria, then setting them to churn the tank sludge. Sell them in packs of thousands for city-sized sewage-installations."

"Outrageous," said Tug.

"Microsurgical applications inside plugged arteries. Pulsates plaque away gently, but disintegrates in the ventricular valves to avoid heart attacks."

"That would need FDA approval," Revel hedged. "Maybe a few years down the road."

"You can get a livestock application done in eighteen months," said Edna. "It's happened in recombinant DNA."

"Copacetic," said Revel. "Lord knows the Pullens got a piece o' the cattle business!"

"If you could manufacture Portuguese men-of-war or other threatening toxic jellies," Edna said, "then you could set a few thousand right offshore in perhaps Hilton Head or Puerto Vallarta. After the tourist trade crashed, you could buy up shoreline property cheap and make a real killing." She paused. "Of course, that would be illegal."

"Right," Tug nodded, pencil scratching away. "Although my plastic jellyfish don't sting. I suppose we could implant pouches of toxins in them. . . ."

"It would also be unethical. And wrong."

"Yeah, yeah, we get it," Revel assured her. "Anything else?"

"Do the jellyfish reproduce?" asked Edna.

"No, they don't," Tug said. "I mean, not by themselves. They don't reproduce and they don't eat. I can manufacture as many as you want to any spec, though."

"So they're not truly alive, then? They don't evolve? They're not Type III a-life?"

"I evolved the algorithm for their behavior in my simulations, but the devices themselves are basically sterile robots with my best algorithms hard-coded in," Tug geeked fluently. "They're jellyfish androids that run my code. Not androids, coelenteroids."

"It's probably just as well if they don't reproduce," said Edna primly. "How big can you make them?"

"Well, not much bigger than a basketball at present. The lasers I'm currently using to sinter them are of limited capacity." Tug neglected to mention that he had the lasers out on unauthorized loan from San Jose State University, thanks to a good friend in lab support at the School of Engineering. "In principle, a jellyfish could be quite large."

"So they're currently too small to live inside," said Edna thoughtfully.

Revel smiled. " 'Live inside,' huh? You're really something special, Edna."

"That's what they pay me for," she said crisply. She glanced at the screen of Tug's workstation, with its rich background color drifting from sky-blue to sea-green, and with a vigorous pack of sea nettles pumping their way forward. "What genetic operators are you using to evolve your algorithms?"

"Standard Holland stuff. Proportional reproduction, crossover, mutation, and inversion."

"The Chicago a-life group came up with a new schemata-sensitive operator last week," said Edna. "Preliminary tests are showing a 40 percent speed-up for searching intractable sample spaces."

"Terrific! That would really be useful for me," said Tug. "I need that genetic operator."

Edna scribbled a file location and the electronic address of a downloading site on Tug's business card and gave it back to him. Then she glanced at a dainty wristwatch inside her left wrist. "Revel's uncle paid for a full hour plus travel. You two want to spring for a retainer, or do I go?"

"Uh, thanks a lot, but I don't think we can swing a retainer," Revel said modestly.

Edna nodded slowly, then touched one finger to her pointed chin. "I just thought of an angle for using your jellyfish in hotel swimming-pools. If your jellyfish don't sting, you could play with them like beach balls, they'd filtrate the water, and they could shed off little polyps to look for cracks. I just hate the hotel pools in California. They're surrounded by anorexic bleached blondes drinking margaritas made of chemicals with forty letters in their names. Should we talk some more?"

"If you don't like your pool, maybe you could take a nice dip in one of Tug's tanks," Revel said, with a glance at his own watch.

"Bad idea, Revel," Tug said hastily. "You get a good jolt from those natural sea nettles and it'll stop your heart."

"Do you have a license for those venomous creatures?" Edna asked coolly.

Tug tugged his forelock in mock contrition. "Well, Ms. Sydney, amateur coelenteratology's kind of a poorly policed field."

Edna stood up briskly, and hefted her nylon bag. "We're out of time, so here's the bottom line," she said. "This is one of the looniest schemes I've ever seen. But I'm going to phone Revel's uncle with the go-ahead as soon as I get back into Illinois airspace. Risk-taking weirdos like you two are what makes this industry great, and the Pullen family can well afford to back you. I'm rooting for you boys. And if you ever need any cut-rate Kazakh programmers, send me e-mail."

"Thanks, Edna," Revel said.

"Yes," said Tug. "Thank you for all the good ideas." He saw her to the door.

"She didn't really sound very encouraging," Tug said after she left. "And her ideas were ugly, compared to ours. Fill my jellyfish with lye? Put them in septic tanks and in cow arteries? Fill them with poison to sting families on vacation?" He flung back his head and began camping back and forth across the room imitating Edna in a shrieking falsetto. "They're not Type III a-life? Oh dear! How I hate those anorexic blondes! Oh my!"

"Look, Tug, if Edna was a little underwhelmed it's just 'cause I didn't tell her everything!" said Revel. "A trade secret is a trade secret, boy, and three's a crowd. That gal's got a brain with the strength o' ten, but even Edna Sydney can't help droppin' certain hints in those pricey little newsletters of hers. . . ."

Revel whistled briefly, pleased with his own brilliance.

Tug's eyes widened in sudden, cataclysmic comprehension. "I've got it, Revel! I think I've got it! When you first saw an Urschleim air jelly—was it before or after you put my plastic jellyfish in your swimming pool?"

"After, compadre. I only first thought of blowing Urschleim bubbles last week—I was drunk, and I did it to make a woman laugh. But you sent me that sorry-ass melting jellyfish a full six weeks ago."

"That 'sorry-ass melting jellyfish' found its way out a crack in your swimming pool and down through the shale beds into the Ditheree hole!" cried Tug exultantly. "Yes!

That's it, Revel! My equations migrated right out into your goo!"

"Your software got into my primeval slime?" said Revel slowly. "How exactly is that s'posed to happen?"

"Mathematics represents optimal form, Revel," said Tug. "That's why it slips in everywhere. But sometimes you need a seed equation. Like if water gets cold, it likes to freeze; it freezes into a mathematical lattice. But if you have really cold water in a smooth tank, the water might not know how to freeze—until maybe a snowflake drifts into it. To make a long story short, the mathematical formations of my sintered jellyfish represent a low-energy phase space configuration that is stably attractive to the dynamics of the Urschleim."

"That story's too long for me," said Revel. "Let's just test if you're right. Why don't we throw one of your artificial jellies into my cooler full of slime?"

"Good idea," Tug said, pleased to see Revel plunging headlong into the scientific method. They returned to the aquaria.

Tug mounted a stepladder festooned with bright-red anti-litigation safety warnings, and used a long-handled aquarium net to fetch up his best artificial jelly, a purple-striped piezoplastic sea nettle that he'd sintered up just that morning, a homemade, stingless *Chrysaora quinquecirrha*.

Revel and Tug strode out to the living room with the plastic sea nettle pulsating gamely against the fine-woven mesh of the net.

"Stand back," Tug warned and flipped the jelly into the four inches of Urschleim still in the plastic picnic cooler.

The slime heaved upward violently at the touch of the little artificial jellyfish. Once again Revel blew some Texan hot air into the goo, only this time it all lifted up at once, all five liters of it, forming a floating sea nettle the size of a large dog.

Revel shouted. The Urschleim jelly drifted around the

room, its white oral arms swaying like the train of a wedding dress.

"Yee haw! Shit howdy!" shouted Revel. "This one's different from all the Urschleim ones I've seen before. People'd buy this one just for fun! Edna's right. It'd be a hell of a pool toy, or, heck, a plain old land toy, as long as it don't fly away."

"A toy?" said Tug. "You think we should go with the recreational application? I like it, Revel! Recreation has positive energy. And there's a lot of money in gaming."

"Just like tag!" Revel hooted, capering. "Blind man's bluff!"

"Watch out, Revel!" One swaying fringe of the dog-sized ur-jelly made a sudden whipping snatch at Revel's leg. Revel yelped in alarm and tumbled backward over the living-room hassock.

"Christ! Get it off me!" Revel cried as the enormous jelly reeled at his ankle, its vast gelatinous bulk hovered menacingly over his upturned face. Tug, with a burst of inspiration, slid open the glass doors to the deck.

Caught in a draft of air, the jelly released Revel, floated out through the doors, and sailed off over Tug's redwood deck. Tug watched the dog-sized jelly ascending serenely over the neighbors' yard. Engrossed in beer and tofu, the neighbors failed to notice it.

Toatoa the parrot swooped off the roof of the Samoans' house and rose to circle the great flying sea nettle. The iridescent green parrot hung in a moment of timeless beauty near the translucent jelly, and then was caught by one of the lashing oral arms. There was a frenzy of green motion inside the Urschleim sea nettle's bell, and then the parrot had clawed and beaked its way free. The nettle lost a little altitude, but then sealed up its punctures and began again to rise. Soon it was a distant, glinting dot in the blue California sky. The moist Toatoa cawed angrily from her roof-top perch, flapping her wings to dry.

"Wow!" said Tug. "I'd like to see that again—on digital video!" He smacked his forehead with the flat of his

hand. "But now we've got none left for testing! Except—
wait!—that little bit in the vial." He yanked the vial from
his pocket and looked at it speculatively. "I could put a
tiny Monterey bell jelly in here, and then put in some na-
nophones to pick up the phonon jitter. Yeah. If I could get
even a rough map of the Urschleim's basins of chaotic
attraction—"

Revel yawned loudly and stretched his arms. "Sounds
fascinatin', Doc. Take me on down to my motel, would
you? I'll call Ditheree and get some more Urschleim delivered to your house by, oh, 6 A.M. tomorrow. And by day
after tomorrow I can get you a lot more. A whole lot
more."

Tug had rented Revel a room in the Los Perros Inn, a
run-down stucco motel where, Tug told Revel as he
dropped him off, Joe DiMaggio and Marilyn Monroe had
once spent a honeymoon night.

Fearing that Tug harbored a budding romantic notion
of a honeymoon night for himself, Revel frowned and
muttered, "Now I know why they call this the Granola
State: nuts, flakes, and fruits."

"Relax," said Tug. "I know you're not gay. And
you're not my type anyway. You're way too young. What I
want is a manly older guy who'll cherish me and take care
of me. I want to snuggle against his shoulder and feel his
strong arms around me in the still of the night." Perhaps
the Etna Ale had gone to Tug's head. Or maybe the
Urschleim had affected him. In any case, he didn't seem at
all embarrassed to be making these revelations.

"See you tomorrow, old son," said Revel, closing his
door.

Revel got on the phone and called the home of Hoss
Jenkins, the old forehand of the Ditheree field.

"Hoss, this is Revel Pullen. Can you messenger me out
another pressure tank of that goo?"

"That goo, Revel, that goo! There's been big-ass balloons of it floatin' out of the well. You never should of
thrown those gene-splice bacteria down there."

"I told you before, Hoss, it ain't bacteria we're dealing with, it's primeval slime!"

"Ain't many of us here that agree, Revel. What if it's some kind of plague on the oil wells? What if it spreads?"

"Let's stick to the point, Hoss. Has anybody noticed the balloons?"

"Not yet."

"Well, just keep folks off our property. And tell the boys not to be shy of firing warning shots—we're on unincorporated land."

"I don't know how long this can stay secret."

"Hoss, we need time to try and find a way to make a buck off this. If I can get the right spin on the Urschleim, folks'll be *glad* to see it coming out of Ditheree. Just between you and me, I'm out here with the likeliest old boy to figure out what to do. Not that he's much of a *regular fella,* but that's neither here nor there. Name of Tug Mesoglea. I think we're on to something big. Send that tank of goo out to Mesoglea's address, pronto. Here it is. Yeah, and here's his number, and while we're at it, here's my number at the motel. And, Hoss, let's make that *three* tanks, the same size as the one you filled up for me yesterday. Yeah. Try and get 'em out here by six A.M. tomorrow. And start rounding out a Pullen pipeline connection between our Nacogdoches tank farm and Monterey."

"Monterey, California, or Monterrey, Mexico?"

"California. Monterey's handy and it's out of the way. We'll need someplace real quiet for the next stage I'm planning. There's way too many professional snoops watching everybody's business here in Silicon Valley, drivin' around scanning cellular phones and stuff—you're receiving this call as encrypted, aren't you, Hoss?"

"Sure thing, boss. Got my Clipper Chip set to maximum scramble."

"Good, good, just making sure. I'm trying to be cautious, Hoss, just like Uncle Donny Ray."

Hoss gave a snort of laughter on the other end of the line, and Revel continued. "Anyhoo, we need someplace

kind of out of the way, but still convenient. Someplace
with some spare capacity, but a little run-down, so's we
can rent lots of square footage on the cheap and the city
fathers don't ask too many prying questions. . . . Ask
Lucy to sniff around and find me a place like that in Monterey."

"There's already hundreds of towns like that in
Texas!"

"Yeah, but I want to do this out here. This deal is a
software kind o' thing, so it's gotta be California."

Revel woke around seven A.M., stirred by the roar of the
morning rush-hour traffic. He got his breakfast at a California coffee shop that called itself "Southern Kitchen,"
yet served orange-rind muffins and sliced kiwi-fruits with
the eggs. Over breakfast he called Texas, and learned that
his assistant, Lucy, had found an abandoned tank farm
near a defunct polluted military base just north of Monterey. The tank-farm belonged to Felix Quinonez, who had
been the base's fuel supplier. The property, on Quinonez's
private land, included a large garage. The set-up sounded
about perfect.

"Lease it, Lucy," said Revel, slurping his coffee. "And
fax Quinonez two copies of the contract so's me and him
can sign off down at his property today. I'll get this Tug
Mesoglea fella to drive me down there. Let's say two
o'clock this afternoon? Lock it in. Now has Hoss found a
pipeline connection? He has? Straight to Quinonez's
tanks? Bless you, honey. Oh, and one more thing? Draw
up incorporation papers for a company called Ctenophore, Inc., register the company, and get the name trade-
marked. C-T-E-N-O-P-H-O-R-E. What it means? It's a
kind of morphodite jellyfish. Swear to God. I learned it
from Tug Mesoglea. If you should put Mesoglea's name
on my incorporation papers? Are you teasin' me, Lucy?
Are you tryin' to make ol' Revel mad? Now book me and
Mesoglea a suite in a Monterey hotel, and fax the incorpo-

ration papers to me there. Thanks, darlin'. Talk to ya
later."

The rapid-fire wheeling and dealing filled Revel with
joy. Expansively swinging his arms, he strolled up the hill
to Tug's house, which was only a few blocks off. The air
was clear and cool, and the sun was a low bright disk in
the immaculate blue sky. Birds fluttered this way and
that—sparrows, grackles, robins, humming-birds, and the
startlingly large California bluejays. A dog barked in the
distance as the exotic leaves and flowers swayed in
the gentle morning breeze.

As he drew closer to Tug's house, Revel could hear the
steady screeching of the Samoans' parrot. And when he
turned the corner of Tug's block, Revel saw something
very odd. It was like there was a ripple in the space over
Tug's house, an undulating bluish glinting of curved air.

Wheeling about in the midst of the glinting was the
furious Toatoa. A school of small airborne bell jellies were
circling around and around over Tug's house, now fleeing
from and now pursuing the parrot, who was endeavoring,
with no success, to puncture them. Revel yelled at the
cloud of jellyfish, but what good would that do? You
could as soon yell at a volcano or at a spreadsheet.

To Revel's relief, the parrot retreated to her house
with a broken tailfeather, and the jellies did not follow
her. But now—were the air bells catching the scent plume
of the air off Revel's body? They flocked and spiraled el-
dritchly. Revel hurried up Tug's steps and into his house,
right past the three empty cylinders of Urschleim lying outside Tug's front door.

Inside Tug's house reeked of subterranean sulfur. Air
jellies of all kinds pressed this way and that. Sea nettles,
comb-jellies, bell jellies, spotted jellies, and even a few giant siphonophores—all the jellies of different sizes, with
the smaller ones beating frantically faster than the bigger
ones. It was like a children's birthday party with lighter-
than-air balloons. Tug had gone utterly bat-shit with the
Urschleim.

"Hey, Tug!" Revel called, slapping a sea nettle away from his face. "What's goin' on, buddy? Is it safe in here?"

Tug appeared from around a corner. He was wearing a long blonde wig. His cheeks were high pink with excitement, and his blue eyes were sparkling. He wore bright lipstick, and a tight red silk dress. "It's a jelly party, Revel!"

A huge siphonophore shaped like a mustachioed rope of mucus came bumping along the ceiling toward Revel, its mane of oral arms soundlessly a-jangle.

"Help!"

"Oh, don't worry so," said Tug. "And don't beat up a lot of wind. Air currents are what excites them. Here, if you're scared, come down to my room while I slip into something less confrontational."

Revel sat on a chair in the corner of Tug's bedroom while Tug got back into his shorts and sandals.

"I was so excited when all that slime came this morning that I put on my dress-up clothes," Tug confessed. "I've been dancing with my equations for the last couple of hours. There doesn't seem to be any limit to the size of the jellyfish I can blow. We can make Urschleim jellyfish as big as anything!"

Revel rubbed his cheek uncertainly. "Did you figure anything more out about them, Tug? I didn't tell you before, but back at Ditheree we're getting spontaneous air jelly releases. I mean—I sure don't understand how the hell they can fly. Did you get that part yet?"

"Well, as I'm sure you know, the scientific word for jellyfish is 'coelenterate,'" said Tug, leaning toward the mirror to take off his lipstick. "'Coelenterate' is from 'hollow gut' in Latin. Your average jellyfish has an organ called a *coelenteron*, which is a saclike cavity within its body. The reason these Urschleim fellows can fly is that somehow the Urschleim fill their coelenterons with, of all things, helium! Nature's noblest gas! Traditionally found seeping out of the shafts of oil wells!" Tug whooped, waggled his ass, and slipped off his wig.

Revel clambered angrily to his feet. "I'm glad you're having fun, Doc, but fun ain't business. We're in retail now, and like they say in retail, you can't do business from an empty truck. We need jellies. All stocks, all sizes. You ready to set up shop seriously?"

"What do you mean?"

"I mean build product, son! I done called my man Hoss Jenkins at Ditheree, and we're gonna be ready to start pumping Urschleim cross-country by pipeline around noon our time tomorrow. That is, if you're man enough to handle the other end of the assembly line here in California."

"Isn't that awfully sudden?" Tug hedged, wiping off his mascara. "I mean, I do have some spreadsheets and business plans for a factory, but . . ."

Revel scoffed, and swatted at the jelly-stained leg of his Can't-Bust-'Ems. "Where have you been, Tug? This is the twenty-first century. Ain't you ever heard of just-in-time manufacturing? Hell, in Singapore or Taiwan they'd have already set up six virtual corporations and had this stuff shipped to global markets yesterday!"

"But I can't run a major manufacturing enterprise out of my house," Tug said, gazing around him. "Even my laser-sintering equipment is on a kind of, uhm, loan, from the University. We'll need lasers for making the plastic jellies to seed the big ones."

"I'll buy you lasers, Tug. Just give me the part numbers."

"But, but, we'll need workers. People to answer the phone, men to carry things . . ." Tug paused. "Though, come to think of it, we could use a simple Turing imitation program to answer the phones. And I know where we can pick up a few industrial robots to do the heavy lifting."

"Now you're talking sense!" Revel nodded. "Let's go on upstairs!"

"But what about the factory building?" Tug called after Revel. "We can't fit the business into my poor house. We'll need a lot of floor space, and a tank to store the

Urschleim, with a pipeline depot nearby. We'll need a power hookup, an Internet node, and—"

"And it has to be some outta-the-way locale," said Revel, turning to grin down from the head of the stairs. "Which I already leased for us this morning!"

"My stars!" said Tug. "Where is it?"

"Monterey. You're drivin'." Revel glanced around the living-room, taking in the odd menagerie of disparate jellyfish floating about. "Before we go," he cautioned, "you better close the door to your wood-stove. There's a passel of little air jellies who've already slipped out through your chimney. They were hassling your neighbor's parrot."

"Oh!" said Tug, and closed the wood-stove's door. The big siphonophore slimed its arms across Tug. Instead of trying to fight away, Tug dangled his arms limply and began hunching his back rhythmically—like a jellyfish. The siphonophore soon lost interest in him and drifted away. "That's how you do it," said Tug. "Just act like a jellyfish!"

"That's easier for you than it is for me," said Revel, picking up a twitching plastic moon jelly from the floor. "Let's take some of these suckers down to Monterey with us. We can use them for seeds. We can have like a tank of these moon jellies, some comb-jellies, a tank of sea nettles, a tank of those big street-loogie things over there—" He pointed at a siphonphore.

"Sure," said Tug. "We'll bring all my little plastic ones, and figure out which ones make the best Urschleim toys."

They set a sheet of plastic into the Animata's trunk, loaded it up with plastic jellyfish doused in seawater, and set off for Monterey.

All during the trip down the highway, Revel jabbered into his cellular phone, jolting various movers and shakers into action: Pullen family clients, suppliers, and gophers, in Dallas, Houston, San Antonio—even a few discreet calls to Djakarta and Macao.

Quinonez's tank farm was just north of Monterey, squeezed up against the boundaries of what had once been Fort Ord. During their occupancy of these rolling dunes, the army had so thoroughly polluted the soil that the land was now legally unusable. The base, which had been closed since the 1990s, was a nature preserve cum hazardous waste site. Those wishing to stroll the self-guiding nature trails were required to wear respirators and disposable plastic shoe-covers.

Tug guided the Animata along a loop road that led to the back of the Ord Natural Waste Site. Inland from the dunes were vast fields of brussels sprouts and artichokes. In one of the fields six huge silvery tanks rested like visiting UFOs.

"There it is, Tug," said Revel, putting away his phone. "The home of Ctenophore, Inc."

As they drew closer, they could see that the great storage tanks were marred with graffiti and pocked with rust. Some of the graffiti was richly psychedelic, but most was Aztec gang-code glyphs about red and blue, South and North, the numbers 13 and 14, and so on. The gangs' points of dispute grew ever more abstract.

Between the tanks and the road there was a vast gravel parking lot with yellowed thistles pushing up through it. At one side of the lot was a truly enormous steel and concrete garage, practically the size of an airplane hangar. Painted on the wall in fading electric pink, yellow, and blue was *Quinonez Motorotive—Max Nix We Fix!*

"Park here, Tug," said Revel. "Mr. Quinonez is supposed to show up and give us the keys."

"How did you get the lease lined up already?"

"What do you think I've been doing on the phone, Doc? Ordering pizza?"

They got out of the Animata, and stood there in the sudden, startling silence beneath the immense, clear California sky. In the distance a sputtering motor made itself heard, then pushed closer. Revel wandered back toward the nearest oil-tank and peered at it. Now the motor arrived in the form of a battered multicolored pickup truck driven by a rugged older man with iron gray hair and a heavy mustache.

"Hello!" sang Tug, instantly in love.

"Good afternoon," said the man, getting out of his pickup. "I'm Felix Quinonez." He stuck out his hand and Tug eagerly grasped it.

"I'm Tug Mesoglea," said Tug. "I handle the science, and my partner Revel Pullen over there handles the business. I think we're leasing this property from you?"

"I think so, too," said Quinonez, baring his strong teeth in a flashing smile. He let go of Tug's hand, giving Tug a thoughtful look. An ambiguous look. Did Tug dare hope?

Now Revel came striding over. "Quinonez? I'm Revel Pullen. Did you bring the contract Lucy faxed you? Muy bueno, my man. Let's sign the papers on the hood of your pickup, Texas style!"

The ceremony completed, Quinonez handed over the keys. "This is the key to the garage, this is for the padlock on the pipeline valve, and these here are for the locks on the stairways up onto the tanks. We've been having some trouble keeping kids out of here."

"I can see that from the free paint-jobs you been getting," said Revel, staring over at the graffiti-bedecked tanks. "But the rust I'm seeing is what worries me. The corrosion."

"These tanks have been empty and out of use for quite a few years," granted Quinonez. "But you weren't planning on filling them, were you? As I explained to your assistant, the hazardous materials license for this site was revoked the day Fort Ord was closed."

"I certainly *am* planning on filling these tanks," said Revel, "or why the hell else would I be renting them? But the materials ain't gonna be hazardous."

"You're dealing in beet-sugar?" inquired Quinonez.

"Never you mind what's going in the tanks, Felix. Just show me around and get me up to speed on your valves and pipelines." He handed the garage key to Tug. "Here, Doc, scope out the building while Felix here shows me his system."

"Thanks, Revel. But Felix, before you go off with him, just show me how the garage lock works," said Tug. "I don't want to set off an alarm or something."

Revel watched disapprovingly while Tug walked over to the garage with Felix, chattering all the way.

"You must be very successful, Felix," gushed Tug as the leathery-faced Quinonez coaxed the garage's rusty lock open. Grasping for more topics to keep the conversation going, Tug glanced up at the garage's weathered sign. "*Motorotive*, that's a good word."

"A cholo who worked for me made it up," allowed Quinonez. "Do you know what *Max Nix We Fix* means?"

"Not really."

"My Dad was in the army in the sixties. He was stationed in Germany, he had an easy deal. He was in the motor vehicle division, of course, and that was their slogan. *Max Nix* is German for 'it doesn't matter.' "

"How would you say *Max Nix* in Spanish?" inquired Tug. "I love Spanish."

"*No problema,*" grinned Felix. Tug felt that there was definitely a good vibration between them. Now the lock on the garage door squeaked open, and Felix held it open so that Tug could pass inside.

"The lights are over here," said Felix, hitting a bank of switches. The cavernous garage was like a vast barn for elephants—there were thirty vehicle-repair bays on either side like stalls; each bay was big enough to have once held a huge green army truck.

"Hey, Quinonez," came Revel's holler. "I ain't got all day!"

"Thanks so much, Felix," said Tug, reaching out to the handsome older man for another handshake. "I'd love to see more of you."

"Well, maybe you will," said Felix softly. "I am not a married man."

"That's lovely," breathed Tug. The two made full eye contact. No problema.

Later that afternoon, Tug and Revel settled into a top-floor suite of a Monterey seaside hotel. Tug poured a few buckets of hotel ice onto the artificial jellyfish in his trunk. Revel got back into the compulsive wheeler-dealer mode with his portable phone again, his demands becoming more unseemly and grandiose as he and Tug worked their way, inch by amber inch, through a fifth of Gentleman Jack.

At three in the morning, Tug crashed headlong into bed, his last conscious memory the clink and scrape of Revel razoring white powder on the suite's glass-topped coffee-table. He'd hoped to dream that he was in the arms of Felix Quinonez, but instead he dreamed once again about debugging a jellyfish program. He woke with a terrible hangover.

Whatever substance Revel had snorted—it seemed unlikely to be anything so mundane and antiquated as mere cocaine—it didn't seem to be bothering him next morning. Revel lustily ordered a big breakfast from room-service.

As Revel tipped the busboy lavishly and splashed California champagne into their beaker of orange juice, Tug staggered outside the suite to the balcony. The Monterey air was rank with kelp. Large immaculate seagulls slid and twisted along the sea-breeze updrafts at the hotel's walls. In the distance to the north, a line of California seals sprawled on a rocky wharf like brown slugs on broken concrete. Dead tin-roofed canneries lined the shore to the south, some of them retrofitted into tourist gyp-joints and discos, others empty and at near-collapse.

Tug huffed at the sea air until the vise-grip loosened at his temples. The world was bright and chaotic and beautiful. He stumbled into the room, bolted down a champagne mimosa and three forkfuls of scrambled eggs.

"Well, Revel," he said finally, "I've got to hand it to you. Quinonez Motorotive is ideal in every respect."

"Oh, I've had Monterey in mind since the first time we met here at SIGUSC," Revel admitted, propping one boot-socked foot on the tabletop. "I took to this place right away. This is my kind of town." With his lean strangler's mitts folded over his shallow chest, the young oilman looked surprisingly at peace, almost philosophical. "You ever read any John Steinbeck, Tug?"

"Steinbeck?"

"Yeah, the Nobel Prize–winning twentieth-century novelist."

"I never figured you for a reading man, Revel."

"I got into Steinbeck's stuff when I first came to Monterey," Revel said. "Now I'm a big fan of his. Great writer. He wrote a book set right here in Cannery Row . . . you ever read it? Well, it's about all these drunks and whores living on the hillsides around here, some pretty interesting folks, and the hero's this guy who's kind of their mentor. He's an ichthyologist who does abortions on the side. Not for the money though, just because it's the 1940s and he likes to have lots of sex, and abortion happens to be this thing he can hack 'cause of his science background. . . . Y'see, Tug, in Steinbeck's day, Cannery Row actually canned a hell of a lot of fish! Sardines. But all the sardines vanished by 1950. Some kind of eco-disaster thing; the sardines never came back at all, not to this day." He laughed. "So you know what they sell in this town today? Steinbeck."

"Yeah, I know," said Tug. "It's kind of a postmodern culture-industry museum-economy tourist thing."

"Yeah. Cannery Row cans Steinbeck now. There's Steinbeck novels, and tapes of the crappy movie adaptations, and Steinbeck beer-mugs, and Steinbeck key chains, Steinbeck bumper-stickers, Steinbeck iron-on patches, Steinbeck fridge-magnets . . . and below the counter, there's Steinbeck blow-up plastic love-dolls so that the air-filled author of Grapes of Wrath can be subjected to any number of unspeakable posthumous indignities."

"You're kidding about the love-dolls, right?"

"Heck no, dude! I think what we ought to do is buy one of 'em, blow it up, and throw it into a cooler full of Urschleim. What we'd get is this big Jell-O Steinbeck, see? Maybe it'd even *talk*! Like deliver a Nobel Prize oration or something. Except when you go to shake his hand, the hand just snaps off at the wrist like a jelly polyp, a kind of dough-lump of dead author flesh, and floats through the air till it hits some paper and starts writing sequels. . . ."

"What the hell was that stuff you snorted last night, Revel?"

"Bunch of letters and numbers, old son. Seems like they change 'em every time I score."

Tug groaned as if in physical pain. "In other words you're so fried, you can't remember."

Revel, jolted from his reverie, frowned. "Now, don't go Neanderthal on me, Tug. That stuff is pure competitive edge. You wouldn't act so shocked about it, if you'd spent some time in the boardrooms of the Fortune 500 lately. Smart drugs!" Revel coughed rackingly and laughed again. "The coolest thing about smart drugs is, that if they even barely work, you just *gotta* take 'em, no matter how square you are! Otherwise, the Japanese CEOs kick your ass!"

"I think it's time to get some fresh air, Revel."

"How right you are, hombre. We gotta settle in at Quinonez's tank farm this morning. We've got a Niagara of Urschleim headed our way." Revel glanced at his watch. "Fact is, the stuff oughta be rollin' in a couple of hours from now. Let's go on down and get ready to watch the tanks fill up."

"What if one of the tanks splits open?"

"Then I expect we won't use that particular tank no more."

When Tug and Revel got to Quinonez Motorotive, they found several crates of newly delivered equipment waiting for them. Tug was as excited as Christmas morning.

"Look, Revel, these two boxes are the industrial robots, that box is the supercomputer, and this one here is the laser-sintering device."

"Yep," said Revel. "And over here's a drum of those piezoplastic beads and here's a pallet of titaniplast sheets for your jellyfish tanks. You start gettin' it all set up, Doc, while I check out the pipeline valves one more time."

Tug unlimbered the robots first. They were built like short squat humanoids, and each came with a telerobotic interface that had the form of a virtual reality helmet. The idea was that you put on the helmet and watched through the robot's eyes, meanwhile talking the robot through some repetitive task that you were going to want it to do. The task in this case was to build jellyfish tanks by lining some of the garage's big truck bays with titaniplast—and to fill up the tanks with water.

The robot controls were of course trickier than Tug had anticipated, but after an hour or so he had one of them slaving away like the Sorcerer's Apprentice. He powered up the second robot and used it to bring in and set up the new computer and the laser-sintering assemblage. Then he crossloaded the first robot's program onto the second robot, and it, too, got to work turning truck bays into aquaria.

Tug configured the new computer and did a remote login to his workstation back in Los Perros. In ten minutes he'd siphoned off copies of all the software he needed, and ghostly jellyfish were shimmering across the computer's new screen. Tug went out and looked at the robots; they'd finished five aquaria now, and water was gushing into them from connections the busy robots had made to the Quinonez Motorotive watermain.

Tug opened the trunk of his car and began bringing in artificial jellyfish and throwing them into the new tanks. Meanwhile Revel was moving about on the big storage tanks, crawling all over them like an excited fly on fresh

meat. Spotting Tug, Revel whooped and waved from the
top of a tank. "The slime's comin' soon," hollered Revel.
Tug waved back and returned to his computer.

Checking his e-mail, Tug saw that he'd finally gotten a
coelenteratological monograph concerning one of the
ctenophores he'd been most eager to model: the Venus's-
girdle, or *Cestus veneris,* a comb-jelly native to the Mediterranean, shaped like a wide, tapering belt covered with
cilia. The Venus's-girdle was a true ctenophore, and its
water-combing cilia were said to diffract sunlight into gorgeous rainbows. It might be fun to wrap one of them
around your waist for dress-up. Ctenophore, Inc. could
make fashion accessories as well as toys! Smiling as he
worked, Tug began transferring the report's data to his
design program.

The roar of the Urschleim coming through the pipeline
was like a subway underground. Initially taking it for an
earthquake, Tug ran outside and collided with the jubilant
Revel.

"Here she comes, pardner!"

The nearest of the giant tanks boomed and shuddered
as the slime began coursing into it. "So far, so good!" said
Revel.

Tanks two and three filled up uneventfully, but a long
vertical seam midway up on tank four began to gape open
as the tank was filling. Scampering about like a meth-biker
roughneck, Revel yanked at the pipeline valves and di-
verted the Urschleim flow from tank four into tanks five
and six, which tidily absorbed the rest of the shipment.

As the roaring and booming of the pipeline delivery
died down, the metal of tank four gave a dying shriek and
ripped open from top to bottom. Floundering in vast chaotic motion, the sides of the great tank unrolled to fall
outward like a snipped ribbon, tearing loose from the huge
disk top, which glided forward some twenty yards like a
giant Frisbee.

An acre or more of slime gushed out of the burst tank
to flood the tank farm's dry weedy soil. The thousands of

gallons of glistening Urschleim mounded up on the ground like a clear tapioca pudding.

Tug started running toward the spill, fearful for Revel's safety. But, no, there was Revel, standing safe off to one side like a triumphant cockroach. "Come on, Tug!" he called. "Come look at this!" Tug kept running and Revel met him at the edge of the Urschleim spill.

"This is just like the spill at Ditheree!" exclaimed Revel. "But you'll see, spillin' Urschleim on the ground don't mean a thing. You ready to start fillin' orders, Tug?" His voice sounded tinny and high, like the voice of an indestructible cartoon character.

"The stuff is warm," said Tug, leaning forward to feel the great knee-high pancake of Urschleim. His voice, too, had a high, quacking quality. Here and there fat bubbles of gas formed beneath the Urschleim and burst plopping holes in it. The huge Urschleim flapjack was giving off gas like a dough full of yeast. But the gas was helium, which is why their voices were high and—

"I just realized how the Urschleim makes helium," squawked Tug. "Cold fusion! Let's run back in the garage, Revel, and find out whether or not we've got radiation sickness. Come on. I mean it. Run!"

Back in the garage they caught their breath for a while. "Why would we have radiation sickness?" puffed Revel finally.

"I think your Urschleim is fusing hydrogen atoms together to make helium," said Tug. "Depending on the details of the process, that could mean anything from warming the stuff up, to killing everyone in the county."

"Well, it ain't killed anyone down in Ditheree so far," Revel scoffed. "And come to think of it, one of my techs did check the first batch over with a Geiger counter. It ain't radioactive, Tug. How could it be? We're gonna use it to make toys!"

"Toys? You've already got orders?"

"I got a fella owns a chain of variety stores down in Orange County, wants ten thousand jellies to sell for swimming-pool toys. All shapes and sizes. I told him I'd send 'em out down the pipeline to his warehouse early tomorrow morning. He's takin' out ads in tomorrow's papers."

"Heavens to Betsy!" exclaimed Tug. "How are we going to pull that off?"

"I figure all you need to do is tap off Urschleim a bucketful at a time, and just dip one of your artificial jellyfish into each bucketful. The ur-snot will glom right on to the math and start acting like a jellyfish. You sell the slime jellyfish, and keep the plastic jellyfish to use as a seed again and again."

"We're going to do that ten thousand times by tomorrow morning?"

"Teach the damn robots to do it!"

Just about then, Felix Quinonez showed up in his truck to try and find out what they'd just spilled out of tank four. Revel blustered at him until he went away, but not before Tug managed to set a dinner date for that evening.

"Jesus, Tug," snapped Revel. "What in hell you want to have supper with that old man for? I hope to God it ain't because of—"

"Hark," sang Tug. "The love that dare not speak its name! Maybe I can get myself a Venus's-girdle sintered up in time. I think it would be a stunning thing to wear. The Venus's-girdle is a ctenophore native to the Mediterranean. If I can make mine come out anywhere near as gorgeous as the real thing, then we'll sell *twenty* thousand of them to your man in Orange."

Revel nodded grimly. "Let's git on in the garage and start workin', son."

They tried to get the robots to help with making the ten thousand jellies, but the machines were slow and awkward at this task. Tug and Revel set to work making the jellies themselves—tapping off Urschleim, vivifying it with the magic touch of a plastic jellyfish, and throwing the Urschleim jellyfish into one of the aquaria for storage.

They put nets over the storage aquaria to keep the creatures from floating off. Soon the nets bulged upward with a dizzying array of Urschleim coelenteroids.

When dinnertime rolled around, Tug, to Revel's displeasure, excused himself for his date with Felix Quinonez.

"I'll just work on through," yelled Revel. "I *care* about business, Tug!"

"I'll check back with you around midnight."

"Fine!" Revel drew out his packet of white powder and inhaled deeply. "I can go all night, you lazy heifer!"

"Don't overwork yourself, Revel. If we don't finish all the jellyfish tonight we can finish them early tomorrow morning. How many do we have done anyway?"

"I'm counting about three thousand," said Revel. "Damn but those robots are slow."

"Well, I'll be back later to drive you back to the hotel. Don't do anything crazy while I'm gone."

"You're the one who's crazy, Tug!"

Tug's dinner with Felix Quinonez went very well, even though Tug hadn't had time to sinter himself that Venus's-girdle. After the meal they went back to Felix's house and got to know each other better. The satiated Tug dropped off to sleep, and by the time he got back to the tank farm to pick up Revel, it was nearly dawn.

A stiff breeze was blowing from the south, and a dying moon hung low in the west over the sea. Patches of fog swept northward across the moon's low disk. The great tanks of Urschleim were creaking and shivering. Tug opened the garage door to find the whole interior space filled with Urschleim jellies. Crouched cackling at one side of the garage was the wasted Revel. Streaming out of five jury-rigged pipes next to Revel were unbreakable fresh Urschleim jellyfish, blowing out of the pipes like bubbles from a magic bubble wand. Every now and then an air-bubble would start to swell too large before plopping free, and one of the two robots would step forward and snip it off.

"Reckon we got enough yet, Tug?" asked Revel. "I done lost count."

Tug did a quick estimation of the volume of the garage divided by the volume of an air jelly and came up with two hundred thousand.

"Yes, Revel, I'm sure that's way more than enough. Stop it now. How did you get around having to dip the plastic jellyfish into the slime?"

"The smart nose knows," said Revel, horning up a thumbnail of white powder. "How was your big date?"

"My date was fine," said Tug, pushing past Revel to turn off the valves on the five pipes. "It could even be the beginning of a steady thing. Thank God this garage isn't wood, or these air jellies would lift off the roof. How are you going to feed them all into the pipeline to Orange County, Revel?"

"Got the robots to rig a collector up top there," said Revel, gesturing toward the distant ceiling. "You think it's time to ship 'em out? Can do!" Revel slapped a large toggle switch that one of the robots had jury-rigged into the wall. The deep throb of a powerful electric pump began.

"That's good, Revel, let's get the jellies out of here. But you still didn't tell me how you got the jellies to come out of the pipe all ready-made." Tug paused and stared at Revel. "I mean how could they come out ready-made without your having to dip a plastic jellyfish in them. What did you do?"

"Hell, I can tell by your face you already know the answer," snapped Revel defensively. "You want to hear it? Okay, I went and put one of your goddamn precious plastic jellies in each of the big tanks. Same idea as back at Ditheree. Once the whole tank's got your weird math in it, the pieces that bubble out form jellies naturally. We got sea nettles in tank number one, moon jellies in number two, those spotted jellies in tank three, bell jellies in tank five, and ctenophores in tank six. Comb-jellies. Tank four's busted, you recall."

"Busted," said Tug softly. Outside the screeching of

metal rose above the sighing of the wind and the chug of the pipeline pump that was sucking the garage's jellies off the ceiling and pipelining them off to Orange County. "Busted."

A huge crash sounded from the tank field.

Tug helped the disoriented Revel out into the driveway in front of the garage. Tank number six was gone, and a spindle-shaped comb-jelly the size of a blimp was bouncing across the sloping field of artichoke plants that lay north of the tank farm. The great moving form was live and shiny in the slanting moonlight. Its transparent flesh glowed faintly from the effects of cold fusion.

"The other tanks are going to break up, too, Revel," Tug murmured. "One by one. It's the helium."

"Them giant air jellies are gonna look plumb beautiful when the sun comes up," said Revel, squinting at his watch. "It'll be great publicity for Ctenophore, Inc. Did I tell you I got the papers for it drawn up?"

"No," said Tug. "Shouldn't I sign them?"

"No need for you to sign, old son," said Revel. "The Urschleim's mine, and so's the company. I'm putting you on salary! You're our chief scientist!"

"God damn it, Revel, don't play me for a sucker. I wanted stock. You knew that."

A dark figure shuffled up behind them and tapped Revel's shoulder with its metal claw. It was one of the industrial robots, carrying Revel's portable phone.

"There's a call on your phone, Mr. Pullen. From Orange County. You set the phone down earlier while you were ingesting narcotics."

"Busy, busy!" exclaimed Revel. "They must be wantin' to transfer payment for our shipment. We're in business, Tug, my man. And just to make sure there's no hard feelings, I'll pay your first year's salary in advance! Tomorrow, that is."

As Revel drew out his portable phone, another of the great metal tanks gave way, releasing a giant, toadstool-like spotted jelly. Outlined against the faint eastern sky, it was an awesome sight. The wind urged the huge quivering thing northward, and its great stubby tentacles dragged stubbornly across the ground. Tug wished briefly that Revel were screaming in the jelly's grip instead of screaming into his telephone.

"*Lost* 'em?" Revel said, screeching. "What the hell you mean? We shipped 'em to you, and you owe us the money for 'em. Your warehouse roof blew off? That's not my fault, is it? Well, yes, we did ship some extras. Yes, we shipped you twenty to one. We figured you'd have a high demand. So that makes it our fault? Kiss my grits!" He snapped the phone shut and scowled.

"So all the jellies in Orange County got away?" said Tug softly. "It's looking kind of bad for Ctenophore, Inc., isn't it, Revel? It's going to be tough to run that operation *alone*." With a roar, a third storage tank gave way like a hatching egg, releasing a moon jelly the size of an ice-skating rink. The first rays of the rising sun shimmered on its great surface. In the distance there were sirens.

In rapid succession the two remaining tanks burst open, unleashing a bell jelly and a mammoth sea nettle. A vagary of the dawn breeze swept the sea nettle toward Tug and Revel. Instead of fleeing it, Revel ran crazily toward it, bellowing in mindless anger.

Tug watched Revel for a moment too long, for now the huge sea nettle lashed out two of its dangling oral arms and snagged the both of them. Swelling its hollow gut a bit larger, the vast sea nettle rose a few hundred feet into the air, and began drifting north along Route One toward San Francisco.

By swinging themselves around and climbing frenziedly, Tug and Revel were able to find a perch together in the tangled tissues on the underside of the enormous sea nettle. The effort and the clear morning air seemed finally to have cleared Revel's head.

"We're lucky these things don't sting, eh, Doc? I gotta hand it to you. Say, ain't this a hell of a ride?"

The light of the morning sun refracted wonderfully

through the giant lens-like tissues of the helium-filled sea nettle.

"I wonder if we can steer it?" said Tug, feeling around in the welter of dangling jelly frills all around them. "It'd be pretty cool to set down at Crissy Field right near the Golden Gate Bridge."

"If anyone can steer it, Tug, you're the man."

Using his knowledge of the jelly's basins of chaotic attraction, Tug was indeed able to adjust the giant sea nettle's pulsings so as to bring them to hover over Crissy Field's great grassy sward, right at the mouth of the San Francisco Bay, first making a low pass over the hilly streets of San Francisco. Below were thousands of people, massed to greet them.

They descended lower and lower, surrounded by a buzzing pack of TV-station helicopters. Anticipating a deluge of orders for Ctenophore products, Revel phoned up Hoss Jenkins to check his Urschleim supply.

"We've got more goo than oil, Revel," shouted Hoss. "It's showin' up in all our wells and in everybody else's wells all across Texas. Turns out there wasn't nothing primeval about your slime at all. It was just a mess of those gene-splice bacteria like I told you all along. Them germs have floated down from the air jellies and are eatin' up all the oil they can find!"

"Well, keep pumping that goo! We got us a global market here! We got cold fusion happening, Hoss! Not to mention airships, my man, and self-heating housing! And that probably ain't but the half of it."

"I sure hope so, Revel! Because it looks like all the oil business left in Texas is about to turn into the flyin' jelly business. Uncle Donny Ray's asking lots of questions, Revel! I hope you're prepared for this!"

"Hell yes, I'm prepared!" Revel snapped. "I spent all my life waitin' for a chance like this! Me 'n' ol' Tug are the pioneers of a paradigm-shatterin' postindustrial revolution, and anybody who don't like it, can get in the breadlines like those no-neck numbskulls from IBM." Revel snapped the phone shut.

"What's the news, Revel?" asked Tug.

"All the oil in Texas is turning into Urschleim," said Revel. "And we're the only ones who know what to do about it. Let's land this thing and start makin' us some deals."

The giant sea nettle hovered uneasily, rippling a bit in the prop-wash of the anxious helicopters. Tug made no move to bring them lower. "There's no *we* and no *us* as long as you're talking that salary bullshit," said Tug angrily. "If you want me to bust ass and take risks in your startup, it has to be fifty-fifty down the line. I want to be fully vested! I want to be on the board! I want to call my share of the shots!"

"I'll think about it," Revel hedged.

"You better think fast, Revel." Tug looked down between his legs at the jostling crowd below. "Look at them all. You don't really know how the hell we got here or what we're doing, Revel. Are you ready to face them alone? It's nice up here in this balloon, but we can't ride a balloon forever. Sooner or later, we're gonna have to walk on our own two feet again, and look people right in the eye." He reached up into the tissues of the giant sea nettle, manipulating it.

Now the sun-baked quake-prone ground began rising up steadily again. Tattooed local hipsters billowed away from beneath them in San Francisco's trademark melange of ecstasy and dread.

"What are you going to say to them when I land us?" demanded Tug harshly.

"Me?" Revel said, surprised. "You're the scientist! You're the one who's s'posed to explain. Just feed 'em some mathematics. Chaos equations and all that bullshit. It don't matter if they can't understand it. 'There's no such thing as bad publicity,' Tug. P.T. Barnum said that."

"P.T. Barnum wasn't in the artificial life business, Revel."

"Sure he was," said Revel, as the great jellyfish touched down. "And, okay, what the hey, if you'll stick with me and do the talkin', I'll go ahead and cut you in for 50 percent."

Tug and Revel stepped from the jellyfish and shook hands, grinning gamely, in a barrage of exploding flash-bulbs.

THE LITTLEST JACKAL

"I hate Sibelius," said the Russian mafioso.

"It's that Finnish nationalist thing," said Leggy Starlitz.

"That's *why* I hate Sibelius." The Russian's name was Pulat R. Khoklov. He'd once been a KGB liaison officer to the air force of the Afghan government. Like many Afghan War veterans, Khoklov had gone into organized crime since the Soviet crackup.

Starlitz examined the Sibelius CD's print-job and plastic hinges with a dealer's professional eye. "Europeans sure pretend to like this classic stuff," he said. "Almost like pop, but it can't move real product." He placed the CD back in the rack. The outdoor market table was nicely set with cunningly targeted tourist-bait. Starlitz glanced over the glass earrings and the wooden jewelry, then closely examined a set of lewd postcards.

"This isn't 'Europe,'" Khoklov sniffed. "This is a Czarist Grand Duchy with bourgeois pretensions."

Starlitz fingered a poly-cotton souvenir jersey with comical red-nosed reindeer. It bore an elaborate legend in the Finno-Ugric tongue, a language infested with umlauts. "This is Finland, ace. It's European Union."

Khoklov was kitted-out to the nines in a three-piece linen suit and a snappy straw boater. Life in the New Russia had been very good to Khoklov. "At least Finland's not NATO."

"Look, fuckin' Poland is NATO now. Get over it."

They moved on to another table, manned by a comely Finn in a flowered summer frock and jelly shoes. Starlitz tried on a pair of shades from a revolving stand. He gazed experimentally about the marketplace. Potatoes. Dill. Carrots and onions. Buckets of strawberries. Flowers and flags. Orange fabric canopies over wooden market tables run by Turks and Gypsies. People were selling salmon straight from the decks of funky little fishing boats.

Khoklov sighed. "Lekhi, you have no historical perspective." He plucked a Dunhill from a square red pack.

One of Khoklov's two bodyguards appeared at once, alertly flicking a Zippo. "No proper sense of *culture,*" insisted Khoklov, breathing smoke and coughing richly. The guard tucked the lighter into his Chicago Bulls jacket and padded off silently on his spotless Adidas.

Starlitz, who was trying to quit, bummed a smoke from Khoklov, which he was forced to light for himself. Then he paid for the shades, peeling a salmon-colored fifty from a dense wad of Finnish marks.

Khoklov paused nostalgically by the Czarina's Obelisk, a bellicose monument festooned with Romanov aristo-fetish gear in cast bronze. Khoklov, whose politics shaded toward Pamyat rightism with a mystical pan-Slavic spin, patted the granite base of the Obelisk with open pleasure.

Then he gazed across the Esplanade. "Helsinki city hall?"

Starlitz adjusted his shades. When arranging his end of the deal from a cellar in Tokyo, he hadn't quite gathered that Finland would be so relentlessly bright. "That's the city hall all right."

Khoklov turned to examine the sun-spattered Baltic. "Think you could hit that building from a passing boat?"

"You mean me personally? Forget it."

"I mean someone in a hired speedboat with a shoulder-launched surplus Red Army panzerfaust. Generically speaking."

"Anything's possible nowadays."

"At night," urged Khoklov. "A pre-dawn urban commando raid! Cleverly planned. Precisely executed. Ruthless operational accuracy!"

"This is summer in Finland," said Starlitz. "The sun's not gonna set here for a couple of months."

Khoklov, tripped up in the midst of his reverie, frowned. "No matter. You weren't the agent I had in mind in any case."

They wandered on. A Finn at a nearby table was selling big swollen muskrat-fur hats. No sane local would buy these items, for they were the exact sort of pseudo-authentic cultural relics that appeared only in tourist economies. The Finn, however, was flourishing. He was deftly slotting and whipping the Mastercards and Visas of sunburnt Danes and Germans through a handheld cellular credit checker.

"Our man arrives tomorrow morning on the Copenhagen ferry," Khoklov announced.

"You ever met this character before?" Starlitz said. "Ever done any real business with him?"

Khoklov sidled along, flicking the smoldering butt of his Dunhill onto the gray stone cobbles. "I've never met him myself. My boss knew him in the seventies. My boss used to run him from the KGB HQ in East Berlin. They called him Raf, back then. Raf the Jackal."

Starlitz scratched his close-cropped, pumpkin-like head. "I've heard of *Carlos* the Jackal."

"No, no," Khoklov said, pained. "Carlos retired, he's in Khartoum. This is Raf. A different man entirely."

"Where's he from?"

"Argentina. Or Italy. He once ran arms between the Tupamaros and the Red Brigades. We think he was an Italian Argentine originally."

"KGB recruited him and you didn't even know his nationality?"

Khoklov frowned. "We never recruited him! KGB never had to recruit any of those seventies people! Baader-Meinhof, Palestinians. . . . They always came straight to us!" He sighed wistfully. "American Weather Underground—how I wanted to meet a groovy hippie revolutionary from Weather Underground! But even when they were blowing up the Bank of America the Yankees would never talk to real communists."

"The old boy must be getting on in years."

"No no. He's very much alive, and very charming. The truly dangerous are always very charming. It's how they survive."

"I like surviving," Starlitz said thoughtfully.

"Then you can learn a few much-needed lessons in charm, Lekhi. Since you're our liaison."

Raf the Jackal arrived from across the Baltic in a sealed Fiat. It was a yellow two-door with Danish plates. His driver was a Finnish girl, maybe twenty. Her dyed-black hair was braided with long green extensions of tattered yarn. She wore a red blouse, cut-off jeans, and striped cotton stockings.

Starlitz climbed into the passenger seat, slammed the door, and smiled. The girl was sweating with heat, fear, and nervous tension. She had a battery of ear-piercings. A tattooed wolf's-head was stenciled up her clavicle and nosing at the base of her neck.

Starlitz twisted and looked behind him. The urban guerrilla was scrunched into the Fiat's back seat, asleep, doped, or dead. Raf wore a denim jacket, relaxed-fit Levi's, and Ray·Bans. He'd taken his sneakers off and was sleeping in his rumpled mustard-yellow socks.

"How's the old man?" Starlitz said, adjusting his seat belt.

"Ferries make him seasick." The girl headed up the

Esplanade. "We'll wake him at the safehouse." She shot him a quick sideways glance of kohl-lined eyes. "You found a good safehouse?"

"Sure, the place should do," said Starlitz. He was pleased that her English was so good. After four years tending bar in Roppongi, the prospect of switching Japanese for Finnish was dreadful. "What do they call you?"

"What did they tell you to call me?"

"Got no instructions on that."

The girl's pale knuckles whitened on the Fiat's steering-wheel. "They didn't inform you of my role in this operation?"

"Why would they wanna do that?"

"Raf is our agent now," the girl said. "He's not your agent. Our operations coincide—but only because our interests coincide. Raf belongs to my movement. He doesn't belong to any kind of Russians."

Starlitz twisted in his seat to stare at the slumbering terrorist. He envied the guy's deep sense of peace. It was hard to tell through the Ray·Bans, but the smear of sweat on his balding forehead gave Raf a look of unfeigned ease. Starlitz pondered the girl's latest remark. He had no idea why a college-age female Finn would claim to be commanding a 51-year-old veteran urban guerrilla.

"Why do you say that?" he said at last. This was usually a safe and useful question.

The girl glanced in the rear-view. They were passing a sunstruck green park, with bronze statues of swaggering Finnish poets and mood-stricken Finnish dramatists. She took a corner with a squeak of tires. "Since you need a name, call me Aino."

"Okay. I'm Leggy. . . . or Lekhi. . . . or Reggae." He'd been getting a lot of "Reggae" lately. "The safehouse is in Ypsallina. You know that neighborhood?" Starlitz plucked a laminated tourist map from his shirt pocket. "Take Mannerheimintie up past the railway station."

"You're not Russian," Aino concluded.

"Nyet."

"Are you Organizatsiya?"

"I forget what you have to do to officially join the Russian mafia, but basically, no."

"Why are you involved in the Ålands operation? You don't look political."

Leggy found the lever beneath the passenger seat and leaned back a little, careful not to jostle the slumbering terrorist. "You're sure you want to hear about that?"

"Of course I want to hear. Since we are working together."

"Okay. Have it your way. It's like this," Starlitz said. "I've been in Tokyo working for an all-girl Japanese metal band. These girls made it pretty big and they bought this disco downtown in Roppongi. I was managing the place. . . . Besides the headbanging, these metal-chicks ran another racket on the side. Memorabilia. A target-market teenage-kid thing. Fan mags, key chains, T-shirts, CD-ROMs. . . . Lotta money there!"

Aino stopped at a traffic light. The cobbled crosswalk filled with a pedestrian mass of sweating, sun-dazed Finns.

"Anyway, after I developed that teen market, I found this other thing. These cute little animals. 'Froofies.' Major hit in Japan. Froofy Velcro shoes, Froofy candy, sodas, backpacks, badges, lunchkits . . . Froofies are what they call 'kawai.' "

Aino drove on. They passed a bronze Finnish general on horseback. He had been a defeated general, but he looked like defeating him again would be far more trouble than it was worth. "What's kawai?"

Starlitz rubbed his stubbled chin. " 'Cute' doesn't get it across. Maybe 'adorable.' Big-money-making adorable. The kicker is that Froofies come from Finland."

"I'm a Finn. I don't know anything called Froofies."

"They're kids' books. This little old Finnish lady wrote them. On her kitchen table. Illustrated kid-stories from the forties and fifties. Of course lately they've been made into manga and anime and Nintendo cassettes and a whole bunch of other stuff. . . ."

Aino's brows rose. "Do you mean Flüüvins? Little blue animals with heads like big fat pillows?"

"Oh, you know them, then."

"My *mother* read me Flüüvins! Why would Japanese want Flüüvins?"

"Well, the scam was—this old lady, she lives on this secluded island. Middle of the Baltic. Complete ass-end of nowhere. Old girl never married. No manager. No agent. Obviously not getting a dime off all this major Japanese action. Probably senile. So the plan is—I fly over to Finland. To these islands. Hunt her down. Cut a deal with her. Get her signature. Then, we sue."

"I don't understand you."

"She lives in the Åland Islands. Those islands are crucial to your people, and the Organizatsiya, too. So you see the general convergence of interests here?"

Aino shook her green-braided head. "We have serious political and economic interests in the Ålands. Flüüvins are silly books for children."

"What's 'serious?' I'm talking plastic action figures! Cartoon drinking glasses. Kid-show theme songs. When a thing like this hits, it's major revenue. Factories churning round the clock in Shenzhen. Crates full of stuff into mall anchor-stores. Did you know that the 'California Raisins' are worth more than the entire California raisin crop? That's a true fact!"

Aino was growing gloomy. "I hate raisins. Californians use slave ethnic labor and pesticides. Raisins are nasty little dead grapes."

"I'm copacetic, but we're talking Japan here," Starlitz insisted. "Higher per-capita than Marin County! The ruble's in the toilet now, but the yen is sky-high. We get a big shakedown settlement in yen, we launder it in rubles, and we clear major revenue completely off the books. That's serious as cancer."

Aino lowered her voice. "I don't believe you. Why are

you telling me such terrible lies? That's a very stupid cover story for an international spy!"

"You had to ask." Starlitz shrugged.

They found the safehouse in Ypsallina. It was a duplex. The other half of the duplex was occupied by a gullible Finnish yuppie couple with workaholic schedules. Starlitz produced the keys. Aino went in, checked every room and every window with paranoid care, then went back to the Fiat and woke Raf.

Raf wobbled into the apartment, found the bathroom. He vomited with gusto, then turned on the shower. Aino brought in a pair of bulging blue nylon sports bags. There was no phone service, but Khoklov's people had thoughtfully left a clone-chipped cellular on the bedroom dresser.

Starlitz, who had been in the safehouse before, retrieved his laptop from the kitchen closet. It was a Japanese portable with a keyboard the length of a cricket bat, a complex mess of ASCII, kanji, katakana, hiragana, and arcane function keys. It had a cellular modem.

Starlitz logged in to a Helsinki Internet service provider and checked the metal-band's website in Tokyo. Nothing much happening there. Sachiho was doing TV tabloid shows. Hukie had gone into production. Ako was in the studio for a solo album. Sayoko was pregnant. Again.

Starlitz tried his hotlist and found a new satellite JPEG file of developments on the ground in Bosnia. Starlitz was becoming very interested in Bosnia. He hadn't been there yet, but he could feel the lure increasing steadily. The Japanese scene was basically over. Once the real-estate bubble had busted, the glitz had run out of the Tokyo street-party and now the high yen was chasing the gaijin off. But Bosnia was clearly a very coming scene for the mid-90s. Not Bosnia per se (unless you were a merc, or crazy) but the surrounding safe-areas where the arms and narco people were setting up: Slovenia, Bulgaria, Macedonia, Albania.

Practically every entity that Starlitz found of interest was involved in the Bosnian scene. UN. USA. NATO. European Union. Russian intelligence, Russia mafia (interlocking directorates there). Germans. Turks. Greeks. Ndrangheta. Camorra. Israelis. Saudis. Iranians. Moslem Brotherhood. An enormous gaggle of mercs. There was even a happening Serbian folk-metal scene where Serb chicks went gigging for hooting audiences of war criminals. It was cool the way the Yugoslav scene kept recomplicating. It was his kind of scene.

Raf emerged from the bathroom. He'd shaved and had caught his thinning wet hair in a ponytail clip. He wore his jeans; his waistline sagged but there was muscle in his hairy shoulders.

Raf unzipped one of the sports bags. He tunneled into a baggy black T-shirt.

Starlitz logged off.

Raf yawned. "Dramamine never works. Sorry."

"No problem, Raf."

Raf gazed around the apartment. The pupils of his dark eyes were two shrunken pinpoints. "Where's the girl?"

Starlitz shrugged. "Maybe she went out to cop some Chinese."

Raf found his shades and a packet of Gauloises. Raf might have been Italian. The accent made this seem plausible. "The boot of the car," he said. "Could you help?"

They hauled a big wrapped tarpaulin from the trunk of the Fiat and into the safehouse. Raf deftly untied the tarp and spread its contents across the chill linoleum of the kitchenette.

Rifles. Pistols. Ammo. Grenades. Plastique. Fuse wire. Detonator. Starlitz examined the arsenal skeptically. The hardware looked rather dated.

Raf deftly reassembled a stripped and greased AK-47. The rifle looked like it had been buried for several years, but buried by someone who knew how to bury weapons properly. Raf slotted the curved magazine and patted the tarnished wooden butt.

"Ever seen a Pancor Jackhammer?" asked Starlitz. "Modern gas-powered combat shotgun, all-plastic, bullpup design? Does four twelve-gauge rounds a second. The ammo drums double as landmines."

Raf nodded. "Yes, I do the trade shows. But you know—as a practical matter—you have to *let people know* that you can kill them."

"Yeah? Why is that?"

"Everyone knows the classic AK silhouette. You show civilians the AK"—Raf brandished the rifle expertly—"they throw themselves on the floor. You bring in your modern plastic auto-shotgun, they think it's a vacuum cleaner."

"I take your point."

Raf lifted a bomb-clustered khaki webbing belt. "See these pineapples? Grenades like these, they have an inferior killing radius, but they truly *look like grenades*. What was your name again, my friend?"

"Starlitz."

"Starlet, you carry these pineapples on your belt into a bank or a hotel lobby, you will never have to use them. Because people *know* pineapples. Of course, when you *use* grenades, you don't want to use these silly things. You want these rifle-mounted BG-15s, with the rocket propellant."

Starlitz examined the scraped and greasy rifle-grenades. The cylindrical explosive tubes looked very much like welding equipment, except for the stenciled military Cyrillic. "Those been kicking around a while?"

"The Basques swear by them. They work a charm against armored limos."

"Basque. I hear that language is even weirder than Finnish."

"You carry a gun, Starlet?"

"Not at the mo'."

"Take one little gun," said Raf generously. "Take that

Makarov nine-millimeter. Nice combat handgun. Vintage
Czech ammo. Very powerful."

"Maybe later," Starlitz said. "I might appropriate a
key or so of that plastique. If you don't mind."

Raf smiled. "Why?"

"It's really hard finding good Semtex since Havel shut
down the factories," Starlitz said moodily. "I might feel
the need 'cause . . . I got this certain personal problem
with video installations."

"Have a cigarette," said Raf sympathetically, shaking
his pack. "I can see that you need one."

"Thanks." Starlitz lit a Gauloise. "Video's all over the
place nowadays. Banks got videos . . . hotels got videos
. . . groceries . . . cash machines . . . cop cars. . . .
Man, I *hate* video. I always hated video. Nowadays, video
is really getting on my nerves."

"It's panoptic surveillance," said Raf. "It's the Specta-
cle."

Starlitz blew smoke and grunted.

"We should discuss this matter further," Raf said intently. "Work in the Struggle requires a solid theoretical
grounding. Then you can focus this instinctive proletarian
resentment into a coherent revolutionary response." He
began sawing through a wrapped brick of Semtex with a
butterknife from the kitchen drawer.

Starlitz ripped the plastique to chunks and stuffed
them into his baggy pockets.

The door opened. Aino had returned. She had a companion: a very tall and spectrally pale young Finn with an
enormous cotton-candy wad of steely purple hair. He
wore a pearl-buttoned cowboy shirt and leather jeans. A
large gold ring pierced his nasal septum and hung over his
upper lip.

"Who is this?" smiled Raf, swiftly tucking the
Makarov into the back of his belt.

"This is Eero," said Aino. "He programs. For the
movement."

Eero gazed at the floor with a diffident shrug. "Many

people are better hackers than myself." His eyes widened suddenly. "Oh. Nice guns!"

"This is our safehouse," said Raf.

Eero nodded. The tip of his tongue stole out and played nervously with the dangling gold ring.

"Eero came quickly so we could get started at once," Aino said. She looked at the greasy arsenal with mild disdain, the way one might look at a large set of unattractive wedding china. "Now where is the money?"

Starlitz and Raf exchanged glances.

"I think what Raf is trying to say," said Starlitz gently, "is that traditionally you don't bring a contact to the safehouse. Safehouses are for storing weapons and sleeping. You meet contacts in open-air situations or public locales. It's just a standard way of doing business."

Aino was wounded. "Eero's okay! We can trust him. Eero's in my sociology class."

"I'm sure Eero is fine," said Raf serenely.

"He brought a cellphone," Starlitz said, glancing at the holster on Eero's chrome-studded leather belt. "Cops and spooks can track people's movements through mobile cellphones."

"It's all right," Raf said gallantly. "Eero is your friend, my dear, so we trust him. Next time we are a bit more careful with our operational technique. Okay?" Raf spread his hands judiciously. "Comrade Eero, since you're here, take a little something. Have a grenade."

"Truly?" said Eero, with a self-effacing smile. "Thank you." He tried stuffing a pineapple, without success, into the tight leather pocket of his jeans.

"Where is the money?" Aino repeated.

Raf shook his head gently. "I'm sure Mister Starlet is not so foolish to bring so much cash to our first meeting."

"The cash is at a dead drop," Starlitz said. "That's a standard method of transferral. That way, if you're surveilled, the oppo can't make out your contacts."

"The tactical teachings of good old Patrice Lumumba

University," said Raf cheerfully. "You were an alumnus, Starlet?"

"Nope," said Starlitz. "Never was the Joe College type. But the Russian mob's chock-full of Lumumba grads."

"I understand this money transfer tactic," murmured Eero, swinging the grenade awkwardly at the end of one bony wrist. "It's like an anonymous remailer at an Internet site. Removing accountability."

"Is the money in U.S. dollars?" said Aino.

Raf pursed his lips. "We don't accept any so-called dollars that come from Russia, remember? Too much fresh ink."

"It's in yen," said Starlitz. "Three point two million U.S."

Raf brightened. "Point two?"

"It was three mill when we finalized the deal, but the yen had another uptick. Consider it a little gift from our Tokyo contacts. Don't launder it all in one place."

"That's good news," said Aino, with a tender smile.

Starlitz turned to Eero. "Is that enough bread to get you and your friends set up in the Ålands with the networked Suns?"

Eero blinked limpidly. "The workstations have all arrived safely. No more problems in America with computer export restrictions. We could ship American computers straight to Russia if we liked."

"That's swell. Any problem getting proper crypto?"

Eero picked at a purple wisp of hair with his free hand. "The Dutch have been most understanding."

"Any problem leasing the bank building in the Ålands, then?"

"We *bought* the building. With money to spare. It was a cannery, but the Baltic has been driftnetted, so. . . ." Eero shrugged his bony shoulders. "It has a little Turkish restaurant next door. So the programmers have plenty of pilaf and shashlik. Finn programmers . . . we like our pilaf."

"Pilaf!" Raf enthused, all jolliness. "I haven't had a decent pilaf since Beirut."

Starlitz narrowed his eyes. "How about your personnel? Any problems there?"

Eero nodded. "We wish we had more people on the start-up, of course. Technical start-ups always want more people. Still, we have enough Finnish hackers to boot and run your banking system. We are mostly very young people, but if those Russian math professors can login from Leningrad—sorry, Petersburg—then we should have no big problems. The Russian math people, they were all unemployed, unfortunately for them. But they are very good programmers, very solid skills. The only problem with our many young hackers from Finland. . . ." Eero absently switched the grenade from hand to hand. "Well, we are so very excited about the first true Internet money-laundry. We tried very hard not to talk, not to tell anyone what we are doing, but . . . well, we're so proud of the work."

"Tell your mouse-jockeys to sit on the news a while longer," Starlitz said.

"Really, it's too late," Eero told him meekly.

Starlitz frowned. "Well, how many goddamn people have you Finn cowboys let in on this thing, for Christ's sake?"

"How many people read the alt newsgroups?" Eero said. "I don't have those figures, but there's alt.hack, alt.2600, alt.smash.the.state, alt.fan.blacknet. . . . Many."

Starlitz ran his hand over his head. "Right," he said. Like most Internet disasters, the situation was a fait accompli. "Okay, that development has torn it big-time. Aino, you did right to bring this guy here right away. The hell with proper operational protocol. We gotta get that bank up and running as soon as possible."

"There's nothing wrong with publicity," Raf said. "We need publicity to attract business."

"There'll be business all right," Starlitz said. "The Russian mob is already running the biggest money-laundry since the Second World War. The arms and narco crowd worldwide are banging down the doors. Black electronic cash is a vital component of the emergent global system. The point is—we got a very narrow window of opportunity here. If our little crowd is gonna get anything out of this set-up, we have gotta be there with a functional online money-laundry just when the system really needs one. And just before *everybody else* realizes that."

"Then publicity is vital," Raf insisted. "Publicity is our oxygen! With a major development like this one, you must seize and create your own headlines. It's like Leila Khaled always says: 'The world has to hear our voice.'"

Aino blinked. "Is Leila Khaled still alive?"

"Leila lives!" Raf said. "Wonderful woman, Leila Khaled. She does social work in Damascus with the orphans of the Intifada. Soon she will be in the new Palestinian government."

"Leila Khaled," said Aino thoughtfully. "I envy her historical experience so much. There's something so direct and healthy and physical about hijacking planes."

Eero couldn't seem to find a place inside his clothing for the grenade. Finally he placed it daintily on the kitchen counter and regarded it with morose respect.

"Any other questions?" Raf asked Starlitz.

"Yeah, plenty," Starlitz said. "The Organizatsiya's got their pet Russian math professors working the technical problems. I figure the Russians can hack the math—Russians do great at that. But black-market online money laundering is a *commercial customer service* operation. Customer service is definitely not a Russian specialty."

"So?"

"So we can't hang around waiting for clearance from Moscow mafia muckety-mucks. If this scheme is gonna work, we gotta slam it together and get it online pronto. We need quick results."

"Then you have the right man," said Raf briskly. "I always specialize in quick results." He shook Eero's hand. "You've been very helpful, Eero. It was pleasant to meet you. Enjoy your stay in the islands. We look forward to further constructive contacts. *Viva la revolución digitale!* Goodbye and good luck."

"You don't have the big money for us yet?" Eero said.

"Real soon now," Starlitz said.

"Could I have some cab fare please?"

Starlitz gave him a 100-mark Jean Sibelius banknote. "Hei hei," Eero said, with a melancholy smile. He tucked the note into his cowboy shirt pocket and left.

Starlitz saw the hacker to the door, and checked the street as the cadaverous Finn ambled off. He was unsurprised to see Khoklov's two bodyguards lurking clumsily in a white Hertz rental car, parked up the street. Presumably they were relaying signals from the plethora of covert listening devices that the Russians had installed in Raf's safehouse.

Eero drifted past the Russian mobsters in a daze of hacker self-absorption. Starlitz found the kid an interesting specimen. In Japan there were plenty of major Goth kids, but the vampire people-in-black contingent had never really crossbred with Japan's hacker population. Here in Finland, though, there were somber and lugubrious hairsprayed Cure fans pretty much across the social spectrum: car repair guys, hotel staff, pizza delivery, government clerks, the works.

When Starlitz returned, Raf was hunting in the kitchen for coffee. "Aino, let's review the political situation."

Aino perched obediently on a birchwood kitchen stool. "The Åland Islands are a chain in the Gulf of Bothnia between Finland and Sweden. They include Åland, Föglö, Kökar, Sottunga, Kumlinge, and Brändö."

"Yeah, right, okay," Starlitz grunted.

"The largest city is Mariehamm, with ten thousand inhabitants." She paused. "That's where the autonomous digital bank will be established."

"We're doing great so far."

"There are twenty-five thousand Åland citizens, mostly farmers and fishery people, but thirty percent are

engaged in the tourist industry. They run small-scale casinos and duty-free shops. The Ålands are a popular day-
tripping destination from continental Europe."

Starlitz nodded. He'd seen the shortlist of potential
candidates for a Russian offshore banking set-up. The
Ålands offered the tastiest possibilities.

Aino sat up straighter. "The inhabitants are Swedish-
speaking ethnics. In 1920, against their will and against a
popular plebiscite, they were ceded to Finland as part of a
negotiated settlement by the now-extinct League of Nations. In truth these oppressed people are neither Swedes
nor Finns. They are Ålanders."

"The islands' national liberation will proceed along
two fronts," said Raf, deftly setting a coffeepot to boil.
"The first is the Åland Island Liberation Front, which is,
essentially, my operation. The second front is Aino's people from the university, the Suomi Anti-Imperialist Cells,
who make it their cause to end the shameful injustice of
Finnish imperialism. The outbreak of armed struggle and a
terror campaign will provoke domestic crisis in Finland.
The cheapest and easiest apparent solution will be to grant
full autonomy to the Ålands. Since the islands are an easy
day-trip from Petersburg, this will leave the Organizatsiya
with a free hand for their banking operations."

"You're a busy guy, Raf."

"I've been resting on my laurels long enough," said
Raf, carefully rinsing three spanking-new coffee mugs.
"It's a new Europe now. Many fantastic new opportuni-
ties."

"Level with me. Do any of these Åland Island hicks
really want independence? They seem to be doing okay
just as they are."

Raf, surprised at the question, smiled.

Aino frowned. "Much work remains to be done in the
way of raising revolutionary consciousness in the Ålands.
But we in the Suomi Anti-Imperialist Cells will have the
resources to do that political work. Victory will be ours,
because the Finnish liberal-fascist state does not have the

capacity to restrain a captive nation against its will. Or if they *do*—" She smiled bitterly. "That will demonstrate the tenuousness of the current Finnish regime and its basic failure as a European state."

"Who have we got on the ground in the Ålands who can speak their local weirdo version of Swedish? Just in case we need to, like, phone in a claim or something."

"We have three people," Raf said. "The new premier, the new foreign minister, and of course the new economics minister, who will be in charge of easing things for the Russian operations. They are the shadow cabinet of the Ålands Republic."

"*Three* people?"

"Three people are plenty! There are only twenty-five thousand of them total. If the projections are right, the offshore bank will be clearing twenty-five million dollars in the first six months! Those islands are little rocks. It's potatoes and fish and casinos for rich Germans. The locals aren't players. The mob and their friends can buy them all."

"They matter," Aino said. "They matter to the Movement."

"But of course."

"The Ålands *deserve* their nation. If they don't deserve their nation, then *we Finns* don't deserve our nation. There are only five million Finns."

"We always yield to political principle," said Raf indulgently. He passed her a brimming mug. "Drink your coffee. You need to go to work."

Aino glanced at her watch, surprised. "Oh. Yes."

"Shall I cut the hash into gram bags? Or will you take the brick?"

She blinked. "You don't have to cut it, Raffi. They can cut it at the bar."

Raf opened one of the sports bags and passed her a fat brick of dope neatly wrapped in a Copenhagen newspaper.

"You work in a bar? That's a good cover job," Starlitz said. "What kind of hash is that?"

"Something very new in Europe," Raf said. "It's Azerbaijani hash."

"Ex-Soviet hash isn't really very good," sniffed Aino. "They don't know how to do it right. . . . I don't like to sell hash. But if you sell people drugs, then they respect you. They won't talk about you when cops come. I hate cops. Cops are fascist torturers. They should all be shot. Do you need the car, Raf?"

"Take the car," Raf said.

Aino fetched her purse and left the safehouse.

"Interesting girl," commented Starlitz, in the sudden empty silence. "Never heard of any Finn terror groups before. Germans, French, Irish, Basques, Croats, Italians. Never Finns, though."

"They're a bit behind the times in this corner of Europe. She's one of the new breed. Very brave. Very determined. It's a hard life for terrorist women." Raf carefully sugared his coffee. "Women never get proper credit. Women kidnap ministers, women blow up trains—women do very well at the work. But no one calls them 'armed revolutionaries.' They're always—what does the press say?—'maladjusted female neurotics.' Or ugly hardened lesbians with a father-figure complex. Or cute little innocents, seduced and brain-washed by the wrong sort of man." He snorted.

"Why do you say that?" Starlitz said.

"I'm a man of my generation, you know." Raf sipped his coffee. "Once, I wasn't advanced in my feminist thinking. It was being close to Ulrike that raised my consciousness. Ulrike Meinhof. A wonderful girl. Gifted journalist. Smart. Eloquent. Very ruthless. Quite good-looking. But Baader and that other one—what was her name? They treated her so badly. Always yelling at her in the safehouse—calling her a gutless intellectual, spoilt child of the bourgeoisie and so forth. My God, aren't we all spoilt

children of the bourgeoisie? If the bourgeoisie hadn't made
a botch of us, we wouldn't need to kill them."

A car pulled up outside. The engine died and doors
slammed.

Starlitz walked to the front window, peeked through
the blind.

"It's the yuppies from next door," he said. "Looks
like they're home early."

"We should introduce ourselves," Raf said. He began
combing his hair.

"Uh-oh, scratch that," Starlitz said. "That's the guy
who lives next door all right, but that's not the woman.
He's got a different woman."

"A girlfriend?" Raf said with interest.

"Well, it's a much younger woman. In a wig, net hose,
and red high heels." The door in the next duplex opened
and slammed. A stereo came on. It was playing a hot Cu-
ban rhumba.

"This is a golden opportunity," said Raf, shoving his
coffee mug aside. "Let's introduce ourselves now as his
new neighbors. He'll be very embarrassed. He'll never
look at us again. He'll never question us. Also, he'll keep
his wife away from us."

"That's a good tactic," Starlitz said.

"All right. Let me do the talking." Raf went to the
door.

"You still got that Makarov in the back of your belt,
man."

"Oh yes. Sorry." Raf tossed the pistol onto the sleek
Finnish couch.

Raf opened the front door. Then he back-stepped
deftly back into the apartment and shut the door firmly.
"There's a white rental car on the street."

"Yeah?"

"Two men inside it."

"Yeah?"

"Someone just shot them."

Starlitz hurried to the window. There were half a

dozen people clustered across the street. Two of them had just murdered Khoklov's bodyguards, suddenly emptying silenced pistols through the closed glass of the windows. The street was not entirely deserted, but killing people with silenced pistols was a remarkably unobtrusive affair if done with brio and accuracy.

Four men began crossing the street. They wore jeans, jogging shoes, and, despite the heat, box-cut Giorgio Armani blazers. Two of them were carrying dainty little videocams. All of them were carrying guns.

"Zionists," Raf announced. Briskly, but without haste, he retreated to his arsenal on the kitchen floor. He slung an AK over his shoulder, propped a second assault rifle within easy reach, then knelt around the corner of the kitchen wall, giving himself a clear line of fire at the front door.

Starlitz quickly weighed various possibilities. He decided to keep watching the window.

With swift and deadly purpose, the hit-team marched to the adjoining duplex. The door broke off its hinges as they kicked their way in. There were brief yelps of indignant surprise, and a quiet multiple stuttering. A burst of Uzi slugs pierced the adjoining wall and embedded themselves in the floor.

Raf rose to his feet, his plump face the picture of glee. He touched one finger to his lips.

Footsteps clomped rapidly up and down the stairs in the next apartment. Doors banged, drawers opened. A bedside telephone jangled as it was knocked from its table. In three minutes the hit-team was out the door.

Raf scurried to the window and knelt. He'd grabbed a small pocket Nikon from his sports bag. He clicked off a roll of snapshots as the hit squad retreated. "I'm so tempted to shoot them," he said, hitching the sling of his assault rifle, "but this is better. This is very funny."

"That was Mossad, right?"

"Yes. They thought I was the neighbor."

"They must have had a description of you and the girl.

And they know you're here in Finland, man. That's not good news."

"Let's phone in a credit for their hit. The Helsinki police might catch them. That would be lovely. Where is that cellphone?"

"Look, we were extremely lucky just now. We'd better leave."

"I'm always lucky. We have plenty of time." Raf gazed at his arsenal and sighed. "I hate to abandon these guns, but we have no car to carry them. Let's carry the guns next door, before we go! That should win us some nice press."

Starlitz met with Khoklov at two A.M. The midnight sun had given up its doomed attempt to sink and was now rising again in refulgent splendor. The two of them were strolling the spectrally abandoned streets of Helsinki, not too far from Khoklov's posh suite at the Arctia.

As European capitals went, Helsinki was a very young town. Most of it had been built since 1900, and quite a lot of that had been leveled by Russian bombers in the 1940s. Nevertheless the waterfront streets looked like stage sets for the Pied Piper of Hamelin, all copper-gabled roofs and leaded glass and quaint window turrets.

"I miss my boys," Khoklov grumbled. "Why did they have to ice my boys? Stupid bastards."

"Lot of Russian Jews in Israel now. Israel's very hip to the Russian mafia scene. Maybe it was a message."

"No. They're just out of practice. They thought my boys were guarding Raf. They thought that poor fat Finn was Raf. Raf makes them nervous. He's been on their hit-list since the Munich Olympics."

"How'd they know Raf was here?"

"It's those hackers at the bank. They've been talking too much. Three of our depositors are big Israeli arms dealers." Khoklov was tired. He'd been up all night explaining developments by phone to an anxious cabal of millionaire ex-Chekists in Petersburg.

"Since the word is out, we've got to move this into high gear, ace."

"I know that only too well." Khoklov opened a gun-metal pillbox and dry-swallowed a pink tab. "The Higher Circles in Organizatsiya—they love the idea of black electronic cash, but they're old-fashioned and skeptical. They say they want quick results, and yet they give me trouble about financing."

"I never expected those nomenklatura cats to come through for us," Starlitz said. "They're all ex-KGB bureaucrats, as slow as hell. If the Japanese shakedown works, we'll have the capital all right. You say they want results? What kind of results exactly?"

"You've met our golden boy now," said Khoklov. "What did you think of him? Be frank."

Starlitz weighed his words. "I think we're better off without him. We don't need him for a gig like this. He's over-qualified."

"He's good though, isn't he? A real professional. And he's always lucky. Lucky is better than good."

"Look, Pulat Romanevich. We've known each other quite a while, so I'm going to level with you. This guy is not right for the job. This Ålands coup is a business thing, we're trying to hack the structure of multinational cash-flows. It's the Infobahn. It's the nineties. It's borderless and it's happening. It's a high-risk start-up, sure, but so what? All Infobahn stuff is like that. It's global business, it's okay. But this is not a global business guy you've got here. This guy is a fuckin' golem. You used to arm him and pay him way back when. I'm sure he looked like some Che Guevara hippie poet rebel against capitalist society. But this guy is not an asset."

"You think he's crazy? Psychopathic? Is that it?"

"Look, those are just words. He's not crazy. He's what he is. He's a jackal. He feeds on dead meat from bigger crooks and spooks, and sometimes he kills rabbits.

He thinks straight people are sheep. He's got it in for consumer society. Enough to blow up our potential customers and laugh about it. The guy is a nihilist."

Khoklov walked half a block in silence, shoulders hunched within his linen jacket. "You know something?" he said suddenly. "The world has gone completely crazy. I used to fly MiGs for the Soviet Union. I dropped a lot of bombs on Moslems, and I got medals. The pay was all right. I haven't flown a jet in combat in eight years. But I loved that life. It suited me, it really did. I miss it every day."

Starlitz said nothing.

"Now we call ourselves Russia. As if that could help us. We can't feed ourselves. We can't house ourselves. We can't even exterminate a lousy bunch of fucking Chechnians. It's just like with these fucking Finns! We owned them for eighty years. Then the Finns got smart with us. So we rolled in with tanks and the sons of bitches ran into their forests in the dark and the snow, and they kicked our ass! Even after we finally crushed them, and stole the best part of their country, they just came right back! Now it's fifty years later, and the Russian Federation owes Finland a billion dollars. There are only five million Finns! My country owes every single Finn two hundred dollars each!"

"It's that Marxist thing, ace." They walked on in silence.

"We're past the Marxist thing," said Khoklov, warming to his theme as the pill took hold. "Now it's different. This time Russia has a kind of craziness that is truly big enough and bad enough to take over the whole world. Massive, total, institutional corruption. Top to bottom. Nothing held back. A new kind of absolute corruption that will sell *anything*: the flesh of our women, the future of our children. Everything inside our museums and our churches. Anything goes for money: gold, oil, arms, dope, nukes. We'll sell the soil and the forests and the Russian sky. We'll sell our souls."

They passed the bizarre polychrome facade of a

Finnish-Mexican restaurant. "Listen, ace," Starlitz said. "If it's the soul thing that's got you down, this guy won't help you there. It was a serious mistake to break him out of mothballs. You should have left him nodding-out in some bar in Baghdad listening to Bee Gees on vinyl. I don't know what you'll do about him now. You might try to bribe him with some kind of major ransom money, and hope he gets too drunk to move. But I don't think he'll do that for you. Bribes just flatter him."

"Okay," Khoklov said. "I agree. He's too dangerous, and he has too much past. After the coup, we kill him. I owe that much to Ilya and Lev, anyway."

"I appreciate that sentiment, but it's kinda late now, ace. You should have iced him when we knew where he was staying."

There was a distant hollow thump.

The Russian cocked his head. "Was that mortar fire?"

"Car bomb, maybe?" In the blue and lucid distance, filthy smoke began to rise.

Raf claimed that the abortive Israeli hit had been the twelfth attempt on his life. This might have been stretching the truth. It was only the second time that a Mossad hit-team had shot the wrong man in a neutral Scandinavian country.

Russians hated to commit themselves fully to a project. Seventy years of totalitarianism had left them with a terrific appetite for back-tracking, doublespeak, and doublecross. Raf, however, delighted in providing quick results.

Granted, his Ålands liberation campaign had had a few tactical setbacks. He'd had to abandon most of his favorite guns with the loss of his first safehouse. The Mossad team had escaped apprehension by the dumbfounded Finnish police. The car-bombing at the FinnAir office had cost Raf his yellow Fiat.

The Suomi Anti-Imperialist Cells excelled at spraying

radical political graffiti, but their homemade petrol bombs at the Jyväskylä police station had done only minor damage. The outspoken Helsinki newspaper editor had survived his kneecapping and would probably walk again.

Nevertheless, Raf's ex-KGB sponsors back in Petersburg were impressed with the veteran's initiative and can-do spirit. They'd supplied another payoff.

With a brimming war-chest of mafia-supplied Euroyen, Raf was on a roll. Raf had successfully infiltrated six Yankee mercs from the little-known but extremely violent American anarcho-rightist underground. Thanks to relaxed cross-border inspections in Europe and the dazed preoccupations of America's ninja tobacco inspectors, these Yankee gun-runners had boldly brought Raf an up-to-date and very lethal arsenal of NATO's remaindered best.

Raf also had ten Russian thugs on call. These men were combat-hardened mercenaries from the large contingent of thirty thousand ex-military professionals who guarded Russia's bankers. Russian bankers who were not mafia-affiliated were shot down in droves by the black marketeers. Russian bankers who were mafia-affiliated were generally killed by one another. These bankers' bodyguards were enjoying a booming trade. Being bodyguards, they naturally excelled at assassination.

These dangerous cliques of armed alien agitators would have been near-useless in Finland without the protection of locals on the ground. Raf had the Suomi Anti-Imperialist Cells to cover that front. The Suomi Anti-Imperialist Cells consisted of five hard-core undergraduates, plus a loose group of young fellow-travelers who would probably offer aid and shelter if pressed. The Cells also had an ideological guru, a radical Finnish nationalist professor and poet who had no real idea what his teachings had wrought among his nation's postmodern youth.

So Raf had twenty or so people ready to use guns and bombs at his direction. To the uninitiated, this might not have seemed an impressive force. However, by the conventional standards of European terrorism, Raf was doing splendidly. National movements such as ETA, IRA, and PLO tended to be somewhat larger, due to their extensive labor-pool of the embittered and oppressed, but Raf the Jackal was a creature of a different breed: a true revolutionary internationalist, a freelance with a dozen passports. His Åland Island Liberation Front was big. It was bigger than Germany's Baader-Meinhof. It was bigger than France's Action Directe. It was about as big as the Japanese Red Army, and considerably better financed. A group of this sort could change history. A far more primitive conspiracy had murdered Abraham Lincoln.

Starlitz was listening to international Finland Radio on the shortwave. It was tough to find decent English-language coverage of the ongoing terror campaign. Despite their continued selfless service in the UN blue-helmet contingent, neutral Finland didn't have a lot of foreign friends. The internal troubles of a neutral country didn't compel much general interest.

This would likely change, however, now that Raf had brought in outside experts. Raf was giving his Yankee new-hires an extensive rundown on the theory and practice of detonating acetylene bottles.

Aino had rented the state-supported handicrafts center through the good offices of her student activist group. The walls of the terrorist hideaway were covered with weird woolly hangings, massive hand-saws, pine-tar soaps, and eldritch Finnish glassware.

Aino was fully up-to-speed on improvised demolitions, so she had been appointed a look-out. She sat near a second-floor window overlooking the driveway, with a monster Finnish elk-rifle at hand. The job was tedious. Aino was leafing through a stack of English-language Flüüvin books which Starlitz had picked up at a Helsinki bookstore. Helsinki boasted bookstores half the size of aircraft hangars. The book thing was something to do during those long dark winters.

"How many of these did she write?" Aino said.

"Twenty-five. The hottest sellers are *Froofies Go to Sea* and *Papa Froofy and the Mushroom Tigers.*"

"They seem even stranger in English. It's strange that she cares so much about her little blue creatures. She worries about them so much, and gets so emotionally touched about them, and they don't even really exist." Aino flipped through the pages. "Look, here the Flüüvins are walking through the fire-mists on big stilts. That's a good picture. And look! There's that cave creature that carries the harmonica and complains all the time."

"That would be Speffy the Nerkulen."

"Speffy the Nerkulen." Aino frowned. "That isn't a proper Finnish name. It isn't Swedish, either. Not even Åland Swedish."

Starlitz turned off the shortwave, which was detailing Finnish agricultural production. "She imagined Speffy, that's all. Speffy the Nerkulen just popped out of her little gray head. But Speffy the Nerkulen sure moves major product in Hokkaido."

Aino riffled the pages of the paperback. "I could make a book like this. She wrote this book fifty years ago. She was my age when she wrote and drew this book. I could do this myself."

"Why do you say that?"

She looked up. "Because I could, I know I could. I can draw. I can tell stories. I'm always telling stories to people at the bar. Once I did a band poster."

"That's swell. How'd you like to come along with me and brace up the little old lady? I need a Finnish translator, and a former Froofy fan would be great. Besides, she can give you helpful tips on kid-lit."

Aino looked at him, surprised. Slowly, she frowned. "What are you saying? I'm a revolutionary soldier. You should respect my political commitment. You wouldn't talk to me that way if I was a twenty-year-old boy."

"If you were a twenty-year-old boy, you'd fuckin' spit on Speffy the Nerkulen."

"No I wouldn't."

"Yes you would. Young soldier boys are cheaper than dirt. They're a fuckin' commodity. Who needs 'em? But a young female Froofy fan could be a very useful cut-out in some dicey negotiations."

"You're still lying to me. You should stop. I'm not fooled."

Starlitz sighed. "Look. It's the truth. Try and get it straight. You think the Åland Islands are important, right? Important enough to blow up trains for. Well, Speffy the Nerkulen is the most important thing that ever came out of the Åland Islands. Froofies are the only Ålands product that you can't obtain anywhere else. Twenty-five thousand hick fishermen in the Baltic are doing *great* to produce a major worldwide pop hit like Speffy the Nerkulen. If the Ålands were Jamaica, he'd be Bob Marley."

One of Raf's new recruits entered the room. He was bearded and muscular, maybe thirty. He wore a Confederate flag T-shirt and carried a Colt automatic in a belt holster. "Hey," he said. "Y'all speak English?"

"Yo," said Starlitz.

"Where's the can?"

Starlitz pointed.

"Hey, babe," said the American, pausing. "That's a lady's rifle. You say the word, I'll give you something serious to shoot with."

Aino said nothing. Her grip tightened on the rifle's polished walnut stock.

The American grinned at Starlitz. "She's got no English, huh? She's a Russian, right? I heard there'd be lots of Russian chicks in this operation. Man. What a dollar'll do these days." He rubbed his hands.

"Posse Comitatus?" Starlitz hazarded.

"Aw hell no. We're not militia. Those militia boys, they're all in a sweat over UN black helicopters and the New World Order. . . . That's bullshit! We *know* the

New World Order. We got contacts. We're gonna be *inside* the goddamn black helicopters. Shoulder to shoulder with Ivan, this time!"

Finland had the most expensive booze in the world. This was Finnish social democratic policy, part and parcel with the world's lowest infant mortality rate. Nevertheless, Finns were truly fabulous drunks. The little Kasarmikatu bar was jammed with Finns methodically transiting from modest self-effacement to chest-pounding no-brakes bravado. A television barked above the shining racks of vodka and koskenkorva, showing broadcast news from across the Baltic. Another parliamentary crisis in Moscow. A furious Russian delegate was pounding the podium in a blue vinyl jacket and a Megadeth T-shirt.

The Japanese financier set down his apple juice and adjusted his sunglasses. "His Holiness the Master does not approve of drunkenness. Alcohol clouds the vision and occludes the flow of ki."

"I can't believe we found a Japanese who won't drink after a business deal," Khoklov bitched in Russian. The Japanese money-man didn't speak or understand Russian. The three of them were clustered in the darkest corner of the Helsinki bar.

Starlitz spoke in Russian. "Our star depositor here has got a very severe case of that Pacific Rim New Age thing. These Supreme Truth guys are completely nuts. However, they're richer than God."

Starlitz silently toasted the money-man with a shot of Finnish cranberry vodka. He'd convinced their backer that this pulverizing liquor was cranberry juice. He switched to fluent gutter Japanese. "Khoklov-san tells me that he admires your electric skullcap very much. He wants to try one for himself. He is seeking health benefits and increased peace of mind."

"Saaaaa . . ." riposted Mr. Inoue, patting the plasticized top of his shaven head. "The electroneural stabilizers of His Holiness the Master. They will soon be in mass production at our Fuji fortress."

"You got like a kids' version of those, right?" said Starlitz.

"Of course. His Holiness the Master has many children."

"So have you ever considered, like, a pop commercial version of those gizmos? Like with maybe a fully licensed cartoon character?"

Mr. Inoue blinked. "I was led to understand that Mister Khoklov's associates could supply us with military helicopters."

"The son of a bitch is on about the helicopters again," Starlitz explained in Russian.

Khoklov grunted. "Tell him we have a special on T-72 main battle tanks. Twenty million yen apiece. Just for him, though. No resales."

Starlitz conferred at length with Mr. Inoue. "He's not interested in tanks. He wants at least six Mil-17 choppers with poison gas dispensers. Also some Spetsnaz Ranger vets to train the cult's judo commando unit on their sacred island of Ishigakijima."

"Spetsnaz veterans? Very well. We've got plenty. Tell him he'll have to find them visas and put up earnest money. Those black berets aren't your average goons."

Starlitz conferred again. "He wants to know if you know anything about laser ablation uranium-enrichment techniques."

"Nyet. And I'm getting pretty tired of that question."

"He wants to know if you're interested in learning how they do that sort of thing at Mitsubishi Heavy Industries."

Khoklov groaned. "Tell him I appreciate the lead on industrial atomic espionage, but that crap went out with Klaus Fuchs and the Rosenbergs."

Starlitz sighed. "Let's give Inoue-san a little face here, Pulat Romanevich. His Holiness the Master predicts the world will end in 1997. We play along with the cult's loony apocalypse myths, and we can lock in their deposits all the way through winter ninety-six."

"Why do we need this plastic-headed lunatic?" Khoklov said. "He's a crooked exploiter of the gullible masses. He's running dummy companies inside Russia and recruiting Russian suckers for his ridiculous yoga cult. He needs us more than we need him. He's a long way from home. Put the strong-arm on him."

"Listen, ace. We need the cult's deposit money, because we need that yen disparity to cover the flow of black capital. Besides, I'm the Tokyo liaison for this gig! It's true the mafia could break his knees inside Russia, but back in Japan, his pals are building big stainless-steel bunkers full of giant microwaves."

"There are limits to my credulity, you know," Khoklov said testily. "Botulism breweries? Nerve gas factories? Hundreds of brainwashed New Age robots building computer chips for a half-blind master criminal in white pajamas? It's completely absurd, it's like something out of James Bond. Please inform this clown that he's dealing with real-life professionals."

Starlitz raised his hand and signaled. "Check please."

"Here you are sir," said Aino. "I hope you and your foreign friends are enjoying your stay in hospitable Helsinki."

After the Helsinki disco bombing, Raf moved his center of operations to the Ålands proper. The hardworking youngsters of the S.A.I.C. had found him another bolthole—a sauna retreat in the dense woods of Kökar Island. This posh resort belonged to a Swedish arms corporation who had once used it to entertain members of various Third World defense departments. Handy day-trips into the Ålands had assured them privacy and avoided potential political embarrassments on Swedish soil. This Swedish company had fallen on hard times due to the massive Russian bargain-basement armaments sales. They were happy to sublet their resort to Khoklov's well-heeled shell company.

"We can't all be Leninist ascetics," Raf declared cheerily. "One can still be a revolutionary in decent shoes."

"Decent shoes count for plenty in Russia these days," Starlitz agreed.

Raf leaned back in his lacquered bentwood chair. The resort's central office, with its stained glass windows and maniacally sleek Alvar Aalto furniture, seemed to suit him very well. "We've reached a delicate stage of the revolutionary process," Raf said, lacing his fingers behind his head. "Integrating the dual strike-forces of the liberation front."

"You mean introducing your Yankee guys to your Russian guys?"

"Yes. And what better neutral ground for that encounter than the traditional Finnish sauna?" Raf smiled. "Lads together! Nothing to hide! No clothes. No guns! Just fresh clean steam. And plenty of booze. And since the boys have been training so hard, I've prepared them a nice surprise."

"Women."

Raf chuckled. "They *are* soldiers, you know." He leaned forward onto the desk. "Did you examine this resort? We have certain expectations to keep up!"

Starlitz had examined the resort and the grounds. There had been more hookers through the place than Bofors had heavy machine guns. The grounds were private and extensive. Coups had been launched successfully from less likely places.

Starlitz nodded. "I get the drill. You know that I have a business appointment with that little old lady today. You set this up this way on purpose, just so I'd miss all the fun."

Raf paused, and thought this over. "You're not angry with me, are you, Starlitz?"

"Why do you say that, Raf?"

"Why be angry with me? I'm loaning you Aino. Isn't

that enough? I didn't have to give you a translator for your business scam. I'm trusting you, all alone on a little boat, with my favorite lieutenant. You should be grateful."

Starlitz stared at him. "Man, you're too good to me."

"You should look after Aino. My little jackal has been under strain. I know you are fond of her. Since you took such pains to speak with her behind my back."

"No, I'll leave her here with you tonight," Starlitz offered. "Let's see what your twenty naked, drunken mercs will do with a heavily armed poetry major."

Raf sighed in mock defeat. "Starlitz, you don't bullshit as easily as most really greedy people."

"Good of you to notice, man."

"Of course, I do want you to take Aino away for a while. She's young, and she would misinterpret this. Let's be very frank. These men I bought for us—they are brutal men who kill and die for pay. They must be given rewards and punishments that they can understand. They're whores with guns."

"I'm always happiest when I know the worst, Raf. You haven't told me the worst yet."

"Why should I confide in you? You never confide in me." Raf pushed an ashtray across the desk. "Have a cigarette."

Starlitz took a Gauloise.

Raf lit it with a flourish, then lit his own. "You talk a lot, Starlitz," he said. "You bargain well. But you never talk about yourself. Everything I discovered about you, I have found out through other people." Raf coughed a bit. "For instance, I know that you have a daughter. A daughter that you've never seen."

"Yeah, sure."

"*I* have seen your daughter. I have photos. She's not like you. She's cute."

"You've got photos, man?" Starlitz sat up. "Video?"

"Yes, I have photos. I have more than that. I have contacts in America who know where your daughter is living. She lives with those strange West Coast women. . . ."

"Yeah, well, I admit they're plenty strange, but it's one of those postnuclear family things," Starlitz said at last. "Would you like to meet your daughter? I could snatch her and deliver her to you here in the Ålands. That would be easy."

"The arrangement's not so bad as it stands," Starlitz said. "They let me send her kids' books. . . ."

Raf put his sock-clad feet on the desk. "Maybe you need to settle down, Starlitz. When a man gets to a certain age, he has to live with his decisions. Take me, for instance. Basically, I'm a family man."

"Wow."

"That's right. I've been married for twenty years. My wife's in a French prison. They caught her in '78."

"That's a long stretch."

"I have two children. One by my wife, one by a girl in Beirut. People think a man like Raf the Jackal must have no private life. They don't give me credit for my dreams. Did you know I've written journalism? I've even written poetry. Poetry in Italian and Arabic."

"You don't say."

"Oh, but I do say. I will say more, since it's just the two of us. No Russians here at the resort yet, to set up their tiresome bugging networks. . . . I have a good feeling about you, Starlitz. You and I, we're both postmodern men of the world. We saw an empire break to pieces. That had nothing to do with silly old Karl Marx, you know."

"Could be, man."

"It was the 1990s at work. Breaking up is very infective. It's everywhere now. It's out of control, like AIDS. Did you ever meet a Lebanese warlord? Jumblatt, perhaps? Berri? Splendid fellows. Men like lions."

"Never met 'em."

"That's a very good life, you know—becoming a warlord. It's what happens to terrorists when they grow up."

Starlitz nodded. It was a very dangerous thing to have

Raf so worried about his good opinion, but he couldn't help but be pleased.

"You seize a port," Raf explained. "You grow dope. You buy guns. It's like a little nation, but you don't need any lawyers, or any bureaucrats, or any ad-men, or any stupid bastards in suits. You have the guns, and you have the power. You tell them what to do, and they run and do it. Maybe it can't last forever. But as long as it lasts, it's heaven."

"This is good, Raf. You're leveling with me now. I appreciate that, I really do."

"The press says that I like to kill people. Well, *of course* I like to kill people! It's thrilling. It gives your life a heroic dimension. If it wasn't thrilling to kill people, people wouldn't buy tickets to movies where people are killed. But if I wanted to kill, I'd go to Chechnya, Georgia, Abkhazia. That's not the trick. Any idiot can become a warlord inside a war zone. The trick is to become a warlord where people are *fat* and *soft* and *rich*! You want to become a warlord *just outside* a massive, disintegrating empire. This is the perfect spot! I know I've had my little setbacks in the past. But the nineties are the sixties upside down. This time, I'm going to win, and *keep* what I win! I'm going to seize these little islands. I'll declare martial law and rule by decree."

"What about your three-man provisional government?"

"I've decided those boys are not reliable. I didn't like the way they talked about me. So, I'll short-cut the process, and produce very quick and decisive results. I'll take twenty-five thousand people hostage."

"How do you manage that?"

"How? By claiming that I have a Russian low-yield nuke, which in fact I don't. But who would dare to try my bluff? I'm Raf the Jackal! I'm the famous Raf! They know I'm capable of that."

"Low-yield nuke, huh? I guess the old terrie scenarios are the good ones. . . ."

"Of course I don't have any such nuke. But I do have ten kilos of cheap radioactive cesium. When they fly Geiger counters over—or whatever silly scientific thing those SWAT squads use—that will look very convincing. The Finns won't dare risk another Chernobyl. They still glow in the dark from that last one. So I'm being very reasonable, don't you agree? I'm only asking for a few small islands and a few thousand people. I'll observe the proper niceties, if they allow me that. I'll make a nice flag and some coinage."

Starlitz rubbed his chin. "The coinage thing should be especially interesting given the electronic bank angle."

Raf opened a desk drawer and produced a shotglass and a duty-free bottle of Finnish cloudberry liqueur. The booze in the Ålands was vastly cheaper than Finland's. "Singapore is only a little island," Raf said, squinting as he poured himself a shot. "Nobody ever complains about Singapore's nuclear weapon."

"I hadn't heard that, man."

"Of course they have one! They've had it for fifteen years. They bought the uranium from the South Africans during apartheid, when the Boers were desperate for money. And they built the trigger themselves. Singaporeans will take that kind of trouble. They are very industrious."

"Makes sense to me." Starlitz paused. "I'm still getting a general handle on your proposal. Give me the long-term vision, Raf. Let's say that you get what you want, and they somehow let you keep it. What then? Give me ten years down the road."

"People always asked me that question," Raf said, sipping. "You want one of these cloudberries? Little golden berries off the Finnish tundra, it surprises me how sweet they are."

"No thanks, but don't let me stop you, man."

"In the old days, people would ask me—mostly these were hostage negotiators, all the talking would get old and we'd all get rather philosophical sometimes. . . ." Raf screwed the cap precisely onto the liqueur bottle. "They'd say to me, 'Raf, what about this Revolution of yours? What kind of world are you really trying to give us?' I've had a long time to consider that question."

"And?"

"Did you ever hear the Jimi Hendrix rendition of 'The Star-Spangled Banner?' "

Starlitz blinked. "Are you kidding? That cut still moves major product off the back catalog."

"Next time, *really listen* to that piece of music. Try to imagine a country where that music *truly was* the national anthem. Not weird, not far-out, not hip, not a parody, not a protest against some war, not for young Yankees stoned on some stupid farm in New York. Where music like that was *social reality*. That is how I want people to live. People are sheep, and they don't have the guts to live that way. But if I get a chance, I can *make* them do it."

Starlitz liked speed launches. Piloting them was almost as much fun as driving. Raf's contacts had stolen one from Copenhagen and motored it across the Baltic at high speed. Since it was a classic dope-smuggler's vehicle, the Danish cops would assume it had been hijacked by dope people. They wouldn't be far wrong.

Starlitz examined the nautical map.

"I shot a cop today," Aino said.

Starlitz looked up. "Why do you say that?"

"I shot a cop dead. It was the constable in Mariehamm. I went into his little office. I told him someone stole the spare tire from my car. I took him around the back of his little office to see my car. I opened the trunk, and when he looked inside for the tire, I shot him. Three times. No, four times. He fell right into the trunk. So I threw him in the trunk and shut it. Then I drove away with him."

Starlitz folded the nautical map very carefully. "Did you phone in a credit?"

"No. Raf says it's better if we disappear the cop. We'll say he that defected back to Finland with the secret police files. That will be a good propaganda coup."

"You really iced this guy? Where's the body?"

"It's in this boat," Aino said.

"Take the wheel," said Starlitz. He left the cockpit and looked into the launch's fiberglass hold. There was a very dead man in uniform in it.

Starlitz turned to her. "Raf sent you to ice him all by yourself?"

"No," said Aino proudly, "he sent Matti and Jorma with me, but I made them keep watch outside." She paused. "People lie when they say it's hard to kill. Killing is very simple. You move your finger three times. Or four times. You imagine doing it, and then you plan it, and then you do it. Then it's done."

"How do you plan to deal with the evidence here?"

"We wrap the body in chains that I bought in the hardware store. We drop him into the Baltic between here and the little old lady's island. Here, take the wheel."

Starlitz went back to piloting. Aino hauled the dead cop out of the hold. The corpse outweighed her considerably, but she was strong and determined, and only occasionally squeamish. She hauled the heavy steel chains around the corpse with a series of methodical rattles, stopping every few moments to click them tight with cheap padlocks.

Starlitz watched this procedure while managing the wheel. "Was it Raf's idea to send along a corpse with my negotiations?"

Aino looked up gravely. "This is the only boat we have. I had to use this boat. We don't seize the ferries until later."

"Raf likes to send a message."

"This is *my* message. I killed this cop. I put him in this boat. He's a uniformed agent from the occupying power. He's a legitimate hard target." Aino tossed back her braids, and sighed. "Take me seriously, Mister Starlitz. I'm a young woman, and I dress like a punk because I like to, and maybe I read too many books. But I mean what I say. I believe in my cause. I come from a small obscure country, and my group is a small obscure group. That doesn't matter, because we are committed. We truly are an armed revolutionary strike force. I'm going to overthrow the government here and take over this country. I killed an oppressor today. That is a duty of an armed revolutionary."

"So you take the islands by force. Then what?"

"Then we'll be rid of these Åland ethnics. They'll be on their own. After that, we Finns can truly be Finns. We'll become a truly Finnish nation, on truly authentic Finnish principles."

"Then what?"

"Then we move into the Finno-Ugric lands that the Russians stole from us! We can take back Karelia. And Komi. And Kanti-Mansiysk." She looked at him and scowled. "You've never even heard of those places. Have you? They're sacred to us. They're in the Kalevala. But you, you've never even heard of them. . . ."

"What happens after that?"

She shrugged. "Is that my problem? I'll never see that dream fulfilled. I think the cops will kill me before then. What do you think?"

"I think these are gonna be kind of touchy book-contract negotiations."

"Stop worrying," Aino said. "You worry too much about trivial things." She gave a last methodical wrap of the chain, and heaved the dead cop overboard. The corpse bobbed face-down in the wake of the boat, then slowly sank from sight.

Aino reached over the fiberglass gunwale and cleaned her hands in the racing seawater. "Just talk slowly to her," she said. "The old lady writes in Swedish, did you know that? I found out all about her. That's her first language, Swedish. But they say her Finnish is very good. For an Ålander."

• • •

Starlitz pulled up at the little wooden dock. The entire island, shored in weed-slimed dark granite, was about twenty acres. The little old lady lived here with her even older and frailer brother. They'd both been born on the island, and had originally lived with their parents, but the father had died in 1950 and the mother in 1968.

The only access to the island was by boat. There were no phones, no electricity, and no plumbing. The home was a two-story stone mansion with a steep slate roof, a stone well, and a wooden outhouse. The eaves were carved and painted in yellow and red. There were some chickens and a couple of squat little island sheep. A skinny wooden derrick had a homemade lighthouse, with an oil lantern. A lot of seagulls around.

Starlitz yelled a loud 'ahoy' from the dock, which seemed the most polite approach, but there was no answer from the house. So they trudged up across the rocks and turf, and found the mansion's door and knocked. No response.

Starlitz tried the salt-warped door. It was unlocked. The windows were open and a faint breeze was playing through the parlor. There were hundreds of shelved books in Finnish and Swedish, some fluttering papers, and quite a few cheerily demented oil paintings. Some quite handsome bronze statuary and some framed Finnish theater posters from the 1930s. A wind-up Victrola.

Starlitz opened the hall closet and looked at the rough weather gear—oilskins and boots. "You know something? This little old lady is as tall as a house. She's a goddamned Viking." He left the parlor for the composition room. He found a wooden secretary and a fine velvet chair. Dictionaries, a Swedish encyclopedia. Some well-thumbed travel books and Nordic photography collections. "There's nothing in here," he muttered.

"What are you looking for?" said Aino.

"I dunno exactly. Something to explain how this works."

"Here's a note!" Aino called.

Starlitz went back into the parlor. He took the note, which had been written in copperplate longhand on lined Speffy the Nerkulen novelty notepaper.

"Dear Mister Starlins," read the note, "please pardon my not here being. I go to Helsingfors to testify. I go to Suomi Parliament as long needing for civic duty call. I regret I must miss you and hoping to speak with you about my many readers in Tokio another much more happier time. Sorry you must row so far and not have meet. Please help your self(s) to tea and biscuits all ready in kitchen. Goodbye!"

"She's gone to Helsinki," Starlitz said.

"She never travels anymore. I'm very surprised." Aino frowned. "She could have saved us a lot of trouble if she had a cellphone."

"Why would they want her in Helsinki?"

"Oh, they made her go there, I suppose. The local Ålanders. The local collaborationist power structure."

"What good do they think she can do? She's not political."

"That's true, but they are very proud of her here. After all, the children's clinic—The Flüüvin's Children's Clinic in Föglö?—that was hers."

"Yeah?"

"Also the park in Sottunga. The Flüüvin Park in Brändö and the Grand Flüüvin Festival Playground. She built all of those. She never keeps the money. She gives the money away. Mostly to the Flüüvin Pediatric Disease Foundation."

Starlitz pulled off his shades and wiped his forehead. "You wouldn't know exactly which pediatric diseases in particular have caught her fancy, right?"

"I never understood such behavior," said Aino. "Really, it must be a mental illness. A childless spinster from the unjust social order. . . . Denied any healthy sex life or outlets. . . . Living as a hermit with all her silly books and paintings all these years. . . . No wonder she's gone mad."

"Okay, we're going back," Starlitz said. "I've had it."

Raf and Starlitz were outside in the woods, slapping at the big slow-moving Scandinavian mosquitoes. "I thought we had an understanding," Raf said, over a muffled chorus of bestial howls from the sauna. "I told you not to bring her back here."

"She's your lieutenant, Raf. You straighten her out."

"You could have been more tactful. Invent some little deception."

"I didn't wanna get dumped off the boat." Starlitz scratched his bitten neck. "I face a very serious kink in my negotiations, man. My target decamped big-time and I got a very limited market window. This is Japanese pop culture we're talking here. The Japanese run product cycles in hyperdrive. They can burn out a consumer vogue in four weeks flat. There's nobody saying that Froofies will move long-term product like Smurfs or Seuss."

"I understand your financial difficulties with your Tokyo backers. If you can just be patient. We can take steps. We'll innovate. If necessary the Republic of the Ålands will nationalize literary production."

"Man, the point of this thing is to sue the guys in Japan who are *already ripping her off*. We gotta have something on paper that looks strong enough to stand up and bark in the courts in The Hague. You gonna strong-arm people anywhere over vaporous crap like intellectual property, it's gotta look heavy-duty, or they don't back off."

"Now you're frightening me," Raf said. "You should take a little time in the sauna. Relax. They're running videos."

"Videos right in all that goddamn steam, Raf?"

Raf nodded. "These are some very special videos."

"I fuckin' hate videos, man."

"They're Bosnian videos."

"Really?"

"Not easy to obtain. They're from the camps."

"You're showing those mercs atrocity videos?"

Raf spread his arms. "Welcome to twenty-first-century Europe!" he shouted at the empty shoreline. "Brand-new European apartheid regimes! Where gangs of war criminals abduct and systematically rape women from other ethnic groups. While the studio lights blaze and the minicams roll!"

"I'd heard those rumors," Starlitz said slowly. "Pretty hard to believe them, though."

"You go inside that sauna, and you'll believe those videos. It's quite incredible, but it's all quite real. You might not enjoy them very much, but you need to see this video documentation. You must come to terms with these practices in order to understand modern political developments. It's video that is like raw meat."

"Must be faked, man."

Raf shook his head. "Europeans always say that. They always ignore the rumors. They always discover the atrocities when it is five years too late. Then they act very shocked and concerned. Those videos exist, my friend. I've got them. And I've got more than that. I've got some of the women."

"You're kidding."

"I *bought* the women. I bartered for them with a pair of Stinger missiles. Fifteen Bosnian abductees. I had them shipped up here in sealed cargo trucks. I went to a lot of trouble."

"White slavery, man?"

"I'm not particular about color. It wasn't me who enslaved them. I'm the man who saved their lives. There were many other girls who were more stubborn or, who knows, probably less pretty. They're all dead in a ditch with bullets in the backs of their heads. These women are survivors. I wish I had more than fifteen of them, but I'm only getting started." Raf smiled. "Fifteen human souls! I rescued fifteen people! Do you know that's more people than I've ever personally killed?"

"What are you going to do with these women?"

"They'll entertain my loyal troops, first of all. I needed them for that, which gave me the idea. I admit this: it's very hard work in the sex-labor industry. But under my care, at least they won't be shot afterward."

Raf strolled along the rocky shoreline to the edge of the resort's dock. It was a nice dock, well outfitted. The fiberglass speed launch was tied up to one rubber-padded edge of it, but the dock could have handled a minor cruise ship.

"Those women will be grateful. Here, we will admit they exist! They haven't even had *identities*. And this world is full of people like them. After ten years of civil war, they sell slaves openly now in the Sudan. Kurds are gassed like vermin by Iraqis and shot out of hand by Turks. The Sinhalese are killing Tamils. We can't forget East Timor. All over the planet, groups of little people are quietly vanishing. You can find them cowering, hiding, all around the world, without papers, without legal identities. . . . The world's truly stateless people. My kind of people. But these are rich little islands—where there is room for thousands of them."

"This is a serious new wrinkle to the scheme, man. Did you clear it with Petersburg?"

"This development does not require debate," Raf said loftily. "It is a moral decision. People should not be killed in pogroms, by brutes who hate them merely because they are different. As a revolutionary idealist, I refuse to stomach such atrocities. These oppressed people need a great leader. A visionary. A savior. Me."

"Kind of a personality-cult thing, then."

Raf shook his long-haired head in sorrow. "Oh, you'd prefer them all quietly dead, I suppose! Like everyone else in the modern world who never lifts a hand to help them!"

"What if the locals complain?"

"I'll make the aliens into citizens. I'll have them out-vote all the locals. A warlord, justly voted into power by the will of the majority—wouldn't that be lovely? I'll raise a postmodern Statue of Liberty for the world's huddled masses. Not like that pious faker in New York harbor. Refugees aren't vermin, even if the rich despise them. They're displaced human beings without a place to rally. Let them rally here with me! By the time I leave power—years from now, when I'm old and gray—they'll be accomplishing great works in these little islands."

The hookers arrived on a fishing trawler. They looked very much like normal hookers from the world's fastest-growing hooker economy, Russia. They might have been women from the Baltic States. They looked like Slavic women at any rate. When they climbed from the trawler they looked rather seasick, but they seemed resolved. Not panicked, not aghast, not crushed by terror. Just like a group of fifteen more-or-less-young women, in microskirts and spandex, about to go through the hard work of having sex with strangers.

Starlitz was unsurprised to find Khoklov shepherding the hookers. Khoklov was accompanied by two brand-new bodyguards. The number of people aware of Raf's location was necessarily kept small.

"I hate working as a pimp," Khoklov groaned. He had been drinking on the boat. "At times like these, I truly know I've become a criminal."

"Raf says these girls are Bosnian slave labor. What's the scoop?"

Khoklov started in surprise. "What do you mean? What do you take me for? These girls are Estonian hook-ers. I brought them over from Tallinn myself."

Lekhi watched carefully as the bodyguards shep-herded their charges toward the whooping brutes inside the sauna. "That sure sounds like Serbo-Croatian those girls are talking, ace."

"Nonsense. That's Estonian. Don't pretend you can understand Estonian. Nobody understands that Finno-Ugric jabber."

"Raf told me these women are Bosnians. Says he bought them and he's going to keep them. Why would he say that?"

"Raf was joking with you."

"What do you mean, 'joking'? He says they're victims from a rapists' gulag! There's nothing funny about that! There just isn't any way to make that funny."

Khoklov gazed at Starlitz in mournful astonishment. "Lekhi, why do you want gulags to be 'funny'? Gulags aren't funny. Pogroms aren't funny. War is not funny. Rape is never funny. Human life is very hard, you see. Men and women truly suffer in this world."

"I know that, man."

Khoklov looked him over, then slowly shook his head. "No, Lekhi, you *don't* know that. You just don't know it the way that a Russian knows it."

Starlitz considered this. It seemed inescapably true. "Did you *ask* those girls if they were from Bosnia?"

"Why would I ask them that? You know the official Kremlin line on the Yugoslav conflict. Yeltsin says that our fellow Orthodox Slavs are incapable of such crimes. Those rape-camp stories are alarmist libels spread by Catholic Croats and Bosnian Muslims. Relax, Lekhi. These women here today, they are all Estonian professionals. You can have my word on that."

"Raf just gave me his word in a form that was highly otherwise."

Khoklov looked him in the eye. "Lekhi, who do you believe: some hippie terrorist, or a seasoned KGB officer and member in good standing of the Russian mafia?"

Starlitz gazed down at the flower-strewn Åland turf. "Okay, Pulat Romanevich. . . . For a moment there, I was actually considering taking some kind of, you know, action. . . . Well, never mind. Lemme get to the point. Our bank deal is falling apart."

Khoklov was truly shocked. "What do you mean? You can't be serious. We're doing wonderfully. Petersburg loves us."

"I mean that the old lady can't be bought. She's just too far away to touch. The deal is dead meat, ace. I don't know just how the momentum died, but I can sure smell the decay. This situation is not sustainable, man. I think it's time you and me got the hell out of here."

"You couldn't get your merchandising deal? That's a pity, Lekhi. But never mind that. I'm sure we can find some other capitalization scheme that's just as quick and just as cheap. There's always dope and weapons."

"No, the whole set-up stinks. It was the video thing that tipped me off. Pulat, did I ever tell you about the fact that I, personally, never show up on video?"

"What's that, Lekhi?"

"At least, I didn't used to. Back in the eighties, if you pointed a video camera at me it would crack, or split, or the chip would blow. I just never registered on videotape."

Slowly, Khoklov removed a silver flask from within his suit jacket. He had a long contemplative glug, then shuddered violently. He focused his eyes on Starlitz with weary deliberation. "I beg your pardon. Would you repeat that, please?"

"It's that whole video thing, man. That's why I got into the online business in the first place. Originally, I was a very analog kind of guy. But the video surveillance was seriously getting me down. I couldn't even walk down to the corner store for a pack of cigs without setting off half a dozen goddamn videos. But then—I discovered online anonymity. Online encryption. Online pseudonymity. That really helped my personal situation. Now I had a way to stay underground, stay totally unknown, even when I was being observed and monitored twenty-four hours a day. I found a way that I could go on being myself."

"Lekhi, are you drunk?"

"Nyet. Pay attention, ace. I'm leveling with you here."

"Did Raf give you something to drink?"

"Sure. We had a coffee earlier."

"Lekhi, you're on drugs. Do you have a gun? Give it to me now."

"Raf gave all the guns to the Suomi kids. They're keeping the guns till the mercs sober up. Simple precaution."

"Maybe you're still jetlagged. It's hard to sleep properly when the sun never sets. You should go lie down."

"Look, ace, I'm not the kind of fucking wimp who doesn't know when he's on acid. Normal people's rules just don't apply to me, that's all. I'm not a normal guy. I'm Leggy Starlitz, I'm a very, very strange guy. That's why I tend to end up in situations like this." Starlitz ran his hand over his sweating scalp. "Lemme put it this way. You remember that mafia chick you were banging, back in Azerbaijan?"

Khoklov took a moment to access the memory. "You mean the charming and lovely Tamara Akhmedovna?"

"That's right. The wife of the Party Secretary. I leveled with Tamara in a situation like this. I told her straight-out that her little scene was coming apart. I couldn't tell her why, but I just knew it. At the time, she didn't believe me, either. Just like you're not believing me now. You know where Tamara Akhmedovna is, right now? She's selling used cars in Los Angeles."

Khoklov had gone pale. "All right," he said. He whipped the cellular from an inner pocket of his jacket. "Don't tell me any more. I can see you have a bad feeling. Let me make some phone calls."

"You want Tamara's phone number?"

"No. Don't go away. And don't do anything crazy. All I ask is—just let me make a few contacts." Khoklov began punching digits.

Starlitz walked by the sauna. Four slobbering, buck-naked drunks dashed out and staggered down the trail in front of him. Their pale sweating hides were covered with crumpled green birch leaves from Finnish sauna whisks.

They plunged into the chilly sea with ecstatic grunts of ambiguous pain.

Somewhere inside, the New World Order comrades were singing "Auld Lang Syne." The Russians were having a hard time finding the beat.

Raf was enjoying a snooze in the curvilinear Aalto BarcaLounger when Khoklov and Starlitz woke him.

"We've been betrayed," Khoklov announced.

"Oh?" said Raf. "Where? Who is the traitor?"

"Our superiors, unfortunately."

Raf considered this, rubbing his eyelids. "Why do you say that?"

"They liked our idea very much," Khoklov said. "So they stole it from us."

"Intellectual piracy, man," Starlitz said. "It's a bad scene."

"The Ålands deal is over," Khoklov said. "The Organizatsiya's Higher Circles have decided that we have too much initiative. They want much closer institutional control of such a wonderful idea. Our Finnish hacker kids have jumped ship and joined them. They re-routed all the Suns to Kaliningrad."

"What is Kaliningrad?" Raf said.

"It's this weird little leftover piece of Russia on the far side of all three independent Baltic nations," Starlitz said helpfully. "They say they're going to make Kaliningrad into a new Russian Hong Kong. The old Hong Kong is about to be metabolized by the Chinese, so the mafia figures it's time for Russia to sprout one. They'll make this little Kaliningrad outpost into a Baltic duty-free zone cum European micro-buffer state. And they're paying our Finn hacker kids three times what we pay, plus air fare."

"The World Bank is helping them with development loans," Khoklov said. "The World Bank loves their Kalinngrad idea."

"Plus the European Union, man. Euros love duty-free zones."

"And the Finns, too," Khoklov said. "That's the very worst of it. The Finns have bought us out. Russia used to owe every Finn two hundred dollars. Now, Russia owes every Finn one hundred and ninety dollars. In return for a rotten little fifty million dollar write-off, my bosses sold us all to the Finns. They told the Finns about our plans, and they sold us just as if we were some lousy division of left-over tanks. The Finnish Special Weapons and Tactics team is flying over here right now to annihilate us."

Raf's round and meaty face grew dark with fury. "So you've betrayed us, Khoklov?"

"It's my bosses who let us down," Khoklov said sturdily. "Essentially, I've been purged. They have cut me out of the Organizatsiya. They liked the idea much more than they like me. So I'm expendable. I'm dead meat."

Raf turned to Starlitz. "I'll have to shoot Pulat Romanevich for this. You realize that, I hope."

Starlitz raised his brows. "You got a gun, man?"

"Aino has the guns." Raf hopped up from his lounger and left.

Khoklov and Starlitz hastily followed him. "You're going to let him shoot me?" Khoklov said sidelong.

"Look man, the guy has kept up *his* end. He always delivered on time and within specs."

They found Aino alone in the basement. She had her elk rifle.

"Where's the arsenal?" Raf demanded.

"I had Matti and Jorma take all the weapons from this property. Your mercenaries are terrible beasts, Raf."

"Of course they're beasts," Raf said. "That's why they follow a Jackal. Lend me your rifle for a moment, my dear. I have to shoot this Russian."

Aino slammed a thumb-sized cartridge into the breech and stood up. "This is my favorite rifle. I don't give it to anyone."

"Shoot him yourself, then," Raf said, backing up half

a step with a deft little hop. "His mafia people have blown the Movement's program. They've betrayed us to the Finnish oppressors."

"Police are coming from the mainland," Starlitz told her. "It's over. Time to split, girl. Let's get out of here."

Aino ignored him. "I told you that Russians could never be trusted," she said to Raf. Her face was pale, but composed. "What did American mercenaries have to do with Finland? We could have done this easily, if you were not so ambitious."

"A man has to dream," Raf said. "Everybody needs a big dream."

Aino centered her rifle on Khoklov's chest. "Should I shoot you?" she asked him, in halting Russian.

"I'm not a cop," Khoklov offered hopefully.

Aino thought about it. The rifle did not waver. "What will you do, if I don't shoot you?"

"I have no idea what I'll do," Khoklov said, surprised. "What do you plan to do, Raf?"

"Me?" said Raf. "Why, I could kill you with these hands alone." He held out his plump, dimpled hands in karate position.

"Lot of good that'll do you against a chopper full of angry Finnish SWAT team," Starlitz said.

Raf squared his shoulders. "I'd love to take a final armed stand on this territory! Battle those Finnish oppressors to the death! However, unfortunately, I have no arsenal."

"Run away, Raf," Aino said.

"What's that, my dear?" said Raf.

"Run, Raffi. Run for your life. I'll stay here with your stupid hookers, and your drunken, naked, mercenary losers, and when the cops come, I'm going to shoot some of them."

"That's not a smart survival move," Starlitz told her.

"Why should I run like you? Should I let my revolution collapse at the first push from the authorities, without even a token resistance? This is my sacred cause!"

"Look, you're one little girl," Starlitz said.

"So what? They're going to catch all your stupid whores, the men and the women, in a drunken stupor. The cops will put them all in handcuffs, just like that. But not me. I'll be fighting. I'll be shooting. Maybe they'll kill me. They're supposed to be good, these SWAT cops. Maybe they'll capture me alive. Then, I'll just have to live inside a little stone house. All by myself. For a long, long time. But I'm not afraid of that! I have my cause. I was right! I'm not afraid."

"You know," said Khoklov brightly, "if we took that speed launch we could be on the Danish coast in three hours."

Spray whipped their faces as the Ålands faded in the distance.

"I hope there aren't too many passport checks in Denmark," Khoklov said anxiously.

"Passports aren't a problem," Raf said. "Not for me. Or for my friends."

"Where are you going?" Khoklov asked.

"Well," said Raf, "perhaps the Ålands offshore bank scheme was a little before its time. I'm a visionary, you know. I was always twenty years ahead of my time—but nowadays maybe I'm only twenty minutes." Raf sighed. "Such a wonderful girl, Aino! She reminded me so much of . . . well, there have been so many wonderful girls. . . . But I must sacrifice my habit of poetic dreaming! At this tragic juncture, we must regroup, we must be firmly realistic. Don't you agree, Khoklov? We should go to the one locale in Europe that guarantees a profit."

"The former Yugoslavia?" Khoklov said eagerly. "They say you can make a free phone call anywhere in the world from Belgrade. Using a currency that doesn't even exist anymore!"

"Obvious potential there," said Raf. "Of course, it

requires operators who can land on their feet. Men of action. Men on top of their profession."

"Bosnia-Herzegovina," Khoklov breathed, turning his reddened face to yet another tirelessly rising sun. "The new frontier! What do you think, Starlitz?"

"I think I'll just hang out a while," Starlitz said. He gripped his nose with thumb and forefinger. Suddenly, without another word, Starlitz tumbled backward from the boat into the dark Baltic water. In a few short moments he was lost from sight.

SACRED COW

He woke in darkness to the steady racket of the rails. Vast unknowable landscapes, huge as the dreams of childhood, rumbled behind his shocked reflection in the carriage pane.

Jackie smoothed his rumpled hair, stretched stiffly, wiped at his mustache, tucked the railway blanket around his silk-pajamaed legs. Across the aisle, two of his crew slept uneasily, sprawled across their seats: Kumar the soundman, Jimmie Suraj his cinematographer. Suraj had an unlit cigarette tucked behind one ear, the thin gold chains at his neck bunched in an awkward tangle.

The crew's leading lady, Lakshmi "Bubbles" Malini, came pale and swaying down the aisle, wrapped sari-like in a souvenir Scottish blanket. "Awake, Jackie?"

"Yaar, girl," he said, "I suppose so."

"So that woke you, okay?" she announced, gripping the seat. "That big bump just now. That bloody lurch, for Pete's sake. It almost threw us from the track."

"Sit down, Bubbles," he apologized.

" 'Dozens die,' okay?" she said, sitting. " 'Stars, director, crew perish in bloody English tragic rail accident.' I can see it all in print in bloody *Stardust* already."

Jackie patted her plump hand, found his kit bag, extracted a cigarette case, lit one. Bubbles stole a puff, handed it back. Bubbles was not a smoker. Bad for the voice, bad for a dancer's wind. But after two months in Britain she was kipping smokes from everybody.

"We're not dying in any bloody train," Jackie told her, smiling. "We're filmwallas, darling. We were born to be killed by taxmen."

Jackie watched a battered railway terminal rattle past in a spectral glare of fog. A pair of tall English, wrapped to the eyes, sat on their luggage with looks of sphinxlike inscrutability. Jackie liked the look of them. Native extras. Good atmosphere.

Bubbles was restless. "Was this all a good idea, Jackie, you think?"

He shrugged. "Horrid old rail lines here, darling, but they take life damn slow now, the English."

She shook her head. "This country, Jackie!"

"Well," he said, smoothing his hair. "It's bloody cheap here. Four films in the can for the price of one feature in Bombay."

"I liked London," Bubbles offered bravely. "Glasgow, too. Bloody cold but not so bad . . . but Bolton? Nobody films in bloody Bolton."

"Business, darling," he said. "Need to lower those production costs. The ratio of rupees to meter of filmstock exposed . . ."

"Jackie?"

He grunted.

"You're bullshitting me, darling."

He shook his head. "Yaar, girl, Jackie Amar never bounced a crew check yet. Get some sleep, darling. Got to look beautiful."

Jackie did not title his own movies. He had given that up after his first fifty films. The studio in Bombay kept a whole office of hack writers to do titles, with Hindi rhyming dictionaries at their elbows. Now Jackie kept track of his cinematic oeuvre by number and plot summary in a gold-edged fake-leather notebook with detachable pages.

Jackie Amar Production No. 127 had been his first in merrie old England. They'd shot No. 127 in a warehouse in Tooting Bec, with a few rented hours at the Tower of London. No. 127 was an adventure/crime/comedy about a pair of hapless expatriate twins (Raj Khanna, Ram Khanna) who cook up a scheme to steal back the Koh-i-noor Diamond from the Crown Jewels of England. The Khanna brothers had been drunk much of the time. Bubbles had done two dance numbers and complained bitterly about the brothers' Scotch-tainted breath in the clinch scenes. Jackie had sent the twins packing back to Bombay.

No. 128 had been the first to star Jackie's English ingenue discovery, Betty Chalmers. Betty had answered a classified ad asking for English girls 18 to 20, of mixed Indian descent, boasting certain specific bodily measurements. Betty played the exotic Brit-Asian mistress of a gallant Indian military-intelligence attaché (Bobby Denzongpa) who foils a plot by Japanese yakuza gangsters to blow up the Tower of London. (There had been a fair amount of leftover Tower footage from film No. 127.) Local actors, their English subtitled in Hindi, played the bumbling comics from Scotland Yard. Betty died beautifully in the last reel, struck by a poisoned ninja blowdart, just after the final dance number. Betty's lines in halting phonetic Hindi had been overdubbed in the Bombay studio.

Events then necessitated leaving London, events taking the shape of a dapper and humorless Indian embassy official who had alarmingly specific questions for a certain Javed "Jackie" Amar concerning income-tax arrears for Rupees 6,435,000.

A change of venue to Scotland had considerably complicated the legal case against Jackie, but No. 129 had been born in the midst of chaos. Veteran soundman Wasant "Winnie" Kumar had been misplaced as the crew scrambled from London, and the musical score of No. 129 had been done, at hours' notice, by a friend of Betty's from Manchester, a shabby, scarecrow-tall youngster named Smith. Smith, who owned a jury-rigged portable mixing station clamped together with duct tape, had produced a deathly pounding racket of synthesized tablas and digitally warped sitars.

Jackie, despairing, had left the score as Smith had recorded it, for the weird noise seemed to fit the story, and young Smith had worked on percentage—which would likely come to no real pay at all. Western historicals were hot in Bombay this year—or at least, they had been, back in '48—and Jackie had scripted one in an all-night frenzy of coffee and pills. A penniless Irish actor had starred as John Fitzgerald Kennedy, with Betty Chalmers as a White House chambermaid who falls for the virile young president and becomes the first woman to orbit the Moon. An old film contact in Kazakhstan had provided some stock Soviet space footage with enthusiastic twentieth-century crowd scenes. Bubbles had done a spacesuit dance.

Somewhat ashamed of this excess—he had shot the entire film with only five hours sleep in four days—Jackie gave his best to No. 130, a foreign dramatic romance. Bobby Denzongpa starred as an Indian engineer, disappointed in love, who flees overseas to escape his past and becomes the owner of a seedy Glasgow hotel. No. 130 had been shot, by necessity, in the crew's own hotel in Glasgow with the puzzled but enthusiastic Scottish staff as extras. Bubbles starred as an expatriate cabaret dancer and Bobby's love interest. Bubbles died in the last reel, having successfully thawed Bobby's cynical heart and sent him back to India. No. 130 was a classic weepie and, Jackie thought, the only one of the four to have any chance in hell of making money.

Jackie was still not sure about the plot of No. 131, his fifth British film. When the tax troubles had caught up to him in Scotland, he had picked the name of Bolton at random from a railway schedule.

•　•　•

Bolton turned out to be a chilly and silent hamlet of perhaps sixty thousand English, all of them busy dismantling the abandoned suburban sprawl around the city and putting fresh paint and flowers on Bolton's nineteenth-century core. Such was the tourist economy in modern England. All the real modern-day businesses in Bolton were in the hands of Japanese, Arabs, and Sikhs.

A word with the station master got their rail cars safely parked on an obscure siding and their equipment loaded into a small fleet of English pedalcabs. A generous offer to pay in rupees found them a fairly reasonable hotel. It began to rain.

Jackie sat stolidly in the lobby that afternoon, leafing through tourist brochures in search of possible shooting sites. The crew drank cheap English beer and bitched. Jimmie Suraj the cameraman complained of the few miserable hours of pale, wintry European light. The lighting boys feared suffocation under the mountainous wool blankets in their rooms. Kumar the soundman speculated loudly and uneasily over the contents of the hotel's "shepherd's pie" and, worse yet, "toad-in-the-hole." Bobby Denzongpa and Betty Chalmers vanished without permission in search of a disco.

Jackie nodded, sympathized, tut-tutted, patted heads, made empty promises. At ten o'clock he called the studio in Bombay. No. 127 had been judged a commercial no-hope and had been slotted direct to video. No. 128 had been redubbed in Tamil and was dying a slow kiss-off death on the southern village circuit. "Goldie" Vachchani, head of the studio, had been asking about him. In Jackie's circles it was not considered auspicious to have Goldie ask about a fellow.

Jackie left the hotel's phone number with the studio. At midnight, as he sat sipping bad champagne and studying plot synopses from ten years back in search of inspiration, there was a call for him. It was his son Salim, the eldest of his five children and his only child by his first wife.

"Where did you get this number?" Jackie said.

"A friend," Salim said. "Dad, listen. I need a favor."

Jackie listened to the ugly hiss and warble of long-distance submarine cables. "What is it this time?"

"You know Goldie Vachchani, don't you? The big Bombay filmwalla?"

"I know Goldie," Jackie admitted.

"His brother's just been named head of the state aeronautics bureau."

"I don't know Goldie very well, mind you."

"This is a major to-do, Dad. I have the news on best private background authority. The budget for aeronautics will triple next Congress. The nation is responding to the Japanese challenge in space."

"What challenge is that? A few weather satellites."

Salim sighed patiently. "This is the fifties now, Dad. History is marching. The nation is on the wing."

"Why?" Jackie asked.

"The Americans went to the Moon eighty years ago."

"I know they did. So?"

"They polluted it," Salim announced. "The Americans left a junkyard of crashed machines up on our Moon. Even a junked motor car is there. And a golf ball." Salim lowered his voice. "And urine and feces, Dad. There is American fecal matter on the Moon that will last there in cold and vacuum for ten million years. Unless, that is, the Moon is ritually purified."

"God almighty, you've been talking to those crazy fundamentalists again," Jackie said. "I warned you not to go into politics. It's nothing but crooks and fakirs."

The hissing phone line emitted an indulgent chuckle. "You're being culturally inauthentic, daddyji! You're Westoxicated! This is the modern age now! If the Japanese get to the Moon first they'll cover it with bloody shopping malls."

"Best of luck to the damn fool Japanese, then."

"They already own most of China," Salim said, with sinister emphasis. "Expanding all the time. Tireless, soulless, and efficient."

"Bosh," Jackie said. "What about us? The Indian Army's in Laos, Tibet, and Sri Lanka."

"If we want the world to respect our sacred cultural values, then we must visibly transcend the earthly realm. . . ."

Jackie shuddered, adjusted his silk dressing gown. "Son, listen to me. This is not real politics. This is a silly movie fantasy you are talking about. A bad dream. Look at the Russians and Americans if you want to know what aiming at the Moon will get you. They're eating chaff today and sleeping on straw."

"You don't know Goldie Vachchani, Dad?"

"I don't like him."

"I thought I'd ask," Salim said sulkily. He paused. "Dad?"

"What?"·

"Is there any reason why the Civil Investigation Division would want to inventory your house?"

Jackie went cold. "Some mistake, son. A mixup."

"Are you in trouble, daddyji? I could try to pull some strings, up top. . . ."

"No no," Jackie said swiftly. "There's bloody horrid noise on this phone, Salim—I'll be in touch." He hung up.

Half an anxious hour with the script and cigarettes got him nowhere. At last he belted his robe, put on warm slippers and a nightcap, and tapped at Bubbles's door.

"Jackie," she said, opening it, her wet hair turbanned in a towel. Furnace-heated air gushed into the chilly hall. "I'm on the phone, darling. Long distance."

"Who?" he said.

"My husband."

Jackie nodded. "How is Vijay?"

She made a face. "Divorced, for Pete's sake! Dalip is my husband now, Dalip Sabnis, remember? Honestly, Jackie, you're so absentminded sometimes."

"Sorry," Jackie said. "Give Dalip my best." He sat in a chair and leafed through one of Bubbles's Bombay fan mags while she cooed into the phone.

Bubbles hung up, sighed. "I miss him so bad," she said. "What is it, okay?"

"My oldest boy just told me that I am culturally inauthentic."

She tossed the towel from her head, put her fists on her hips. "These young people today! What do they want from us?"

"They want the real India," Jackie said. "But we all watched Hollywood films for a hundred bloody years. . . . We have no native soul left, don't you know." He sighed heavily. "We're all bits and pieces inside. We're a jigsaw people, we Indians. Quotes and remakes. Rags and tatters."

Bubbles tapped her chin with one lacquered forefinger. "You're having trouble with the script."

Mournfully, he ignored her. "Liberation came a hundred bloody years ago. But still we obsess with the damn British. Look at this country of theirs. It's a museum. But us—we're worse. We're a wounded civilization. Naipaul was right. Rushdie was right!"

"You work too hard," Bubbles said. "That historical we just did, about the Moon, yaar? That one was stupid crazy, darling. That music boy Smith, from Manchester? He don't even speak English, okay. I can't understand a word he bloody says."

"My dear, that's English. This is England. That is how they speak their native language."

"My foot," Bubbles said. "We have five hundred million to speak English. How many left have they?"

Jackie laughed. "They're getting better, yes. Learning to talk more properly, like us." He yawned hugely. "It's bloody hot in here, Bubbles. Feels good. Just like home."

"That young girl, Betty Chalmers, okay? When she tries to speak Hindi I bust from laughs." Bubbles paused.

"She's a smart little cookie, though. She could go places in business. Did you sleep with her?"

"Just once," Jackie said. "She was nice. But very English."

"She's American," Bubbles said triumphantly. "A Cherokee Indian from Tulsa, Oklahoma, USA. When your advert said Indian blood, she thought you meant American Indians."

"Damn!" Jackie said. "Really?"

"Cross my heart it's true, Jackie."

"Damn . . . and the camera loves her, too. Don't tell anybody."

Bubbles shrugged, a little too casually. "It's funny how much they want to be just like us."

"Sad for them," Jackie said. "An existential tragedy."

"No, darling, I mean it's really funny, for an audience at home. Laugh out loud, roll in the aisles, big knee-slapper! It could be a good movie, Jackie. About how funny the English are. Being so inauthentic like us."

"Bloody hell," Jackie marveled.

"A remake of *Param Dharam* or *Gammat Jammat,* but funny, because of all English players, okay."

"*Gammat Jammat* has some great dance scenes."

She smiled.

His head felt inflamed with sudden inspiration. "We can do that. Yes. We will! And it'll make a bloody fortune!" He clapped his hands together, bowed his head to her. "Miss Malini, you are a trouper."

She made a pleased salaam. "Satisfaction guaranteed, sahib."

He rose from the chair. "I'll get on it straightaway."

She slipped across the room to block his way. "No no no! Not tonight."

"Why not?"

"None of those little red pills of yours."

He frowned.

"You'll pop from those someday, Jackieji. You jump

like a jack-in-box every time they snap the clapperboard. You think I don't know?"

He flinched. "You don't know the troubles of this crew. We need a hit like hell, darling. Not today, yesterday."

"Money troubles. So what? Not tonight, boss, not to worry. You're the only director that knows my best angles. You think I want to be stuck with no director in this bloody dump?" Gently, she took his hand. "Calming down, okay. Changing your mind, having some fun. This is your old pal Bubbles here, yaar? Look, Jackieji. Bubbles." She struck a hand-on-hip pose and shot him her best sidelong come-on look.

Jackie was touched. He got into bed. She pinned him down, kissed him firmly, put both his hands on her breasts, and pulled the cover over her shoulders. "Nice and easy, okay? A little pampering. Let me do it."

She straddled his groin, settled down, undulated a bit in muscular dancer's fashion, then stopped, and began to pinch and scratch his chest with absentminded Vedic skill. "You're so funny sometimes, darling. 'Inauthentic.' I can tap dance, I can bump and grind, and you think I can't wiggle my neck like a natyam dancer? Watch me do it, for Pete's sake."

"Stop it," he begged. "Be funny before, be funny afterward, but don't be funny in the middle."

"Okay, nothing funny darling, short and sweet." She set to work on him and in two divine minutes she had wrung him out like a sponge.

"There," she said. "All done. Feel better?"

"God, yes."

"Inauthentic as hell and it feels just as good, yaar?"

"It's why the human race goes on."

"Well then," she said. "That, and a good night's sleep, baby."

• • •

Jackie was enjoying a solid if somewhat flavorless breakfast of kippers and eggs when Jimmie Suraj came in. "It's Smith, boss," Jimmie said. "We can't get him to shut up that bloody box of his."

Jackie sighed, finished his breakfast, dabbed bits of kipper from his lips, and walked into the lobby. Smith, Betty Chalmers, and Bobby Denzongpa sat around a low table in overstuffed chairs. There was a stranger with them. A young Japanese.

"Turn it off, Smithie, there's a good fellow," Jackie said. "It sounds like bloody cats being skinned."

"Just running a demo for Mr. Big Yen here," Smith muttered. With bad grace, he turned off his machine. This was an elaborate procedure, involving much flicking of switches, twisting of knobs, and whirring of disk drives.

The Japanese—a long-haired, elegant youngster in a sheepskin coat, corduroy beret, and jeans—rose from his chair, bowed crisply, and offered Jackie a business card. Jackie read it. The man was from a movie company— Kinema Junpo. His name was Baisho.

Jackie did a namaste. "A pleasure to meet you, Mr. Baisho." Baisho looked a bit wary.

"Our boss says he's glad to meet you," Smith repeated.

"*Hai,*" Baisho said alertly.

"We met Baisho-san at the disco last night," Betty Chalmers said. Baisho, sitting up straighter, emitted an enthusiastic string of alien syllables.

"Baisho says he's a big fan of English dance-hall music," Smith mumbled. "He was looking for a proper dance hall here. What he thinks is one. Vesta Tilly, ta-ra-ra-boom-de-ay, that sort of bloody thing."

"Ah," Jackie said. "You speak any English, Mr. Baisho?"

Baisho smiled politely and replied at length, with much waving of arms. "He's also hunting for first editions of Noel Coward and J. B. Priestley," Betty said. "They're his favorite English authors. And boss—Jackie—Mr.

Baisho *is* speaking English. I mean, if you listen, all the vowels and consonants are in there. Really."

"Rather better than *your* English, actually," Smith muttered.

"I have heard of Noel Coward," Jackie said. "Very witty playwright, that Coward fellow." Baisho waited politely until Jackie's lips had stopped moving and then plunged back into his narrative.

"He says that it's lucky he met us because he's here on location himself," Betty said. "Kinema Junpo—that's his boss—is shooting a remake of *Throne of Blood* in Scotland. He's been . . . uh . . . appointed to check out some special location here in Bolton."

"Yes?" Jackie said.

"Said the local English won't help him because they're kind of superstitious about the place," Betty said. She smiled. "How 'bout you, Smithie? You're not superstitious, are you?"

"Nah," Smith said. He lit a cigarette.

"He wants us to help him?" Jackie said.

Betty smiled. "They have truckloads of cash, the Japanese."

"If you don't want to do it, I can get some mates o' mine from Manchester," Smith said, picking at a blemish. "They're nae scared of bloody Bolton."

"What is it about Bolton?" Jackie said.

"You didn't know?" Betty said. "Well, not much. I mean, it's not much of a town, but it does have the biggest mass grave in England."

"Over a million," Smith muttered. "From Manchester, London—they used to ship 'em out here in trains, during the plague."

"Ah," Jackie said.

"Over a million in one bloody spot," Smith said, stirring in his chair. He blew a curl of smoke. "Me grandfather used to talk about it. Real proud about Bolton they was, real civil government emergency and all, kept good order, soldiers and such. . . . Every dead bloke got his own marker, even the women and kids. Other places, later, they just scraped a hole with bulldozers and shoved 'em in."

"Spirit," Baisho said loudly, enunciating as carefully as he could. "Good cinema spirit in city of Boruton."

Despite himself, Jackie felt a chill. He sat down. "Inauspicious. That's what we'd call it."

"It was fifty years ago," Smith said, bored. "Thirty years before I was born. Or Betty here, either, eh? 'Bovine Spongiform Encephalopathy.' Mad Cow Disease. So what? BSE will never come back. It was a fluke. A bloody twentieth-century industrial accident."

"You know, I'm not frightened," Betty said, with her brightest smile. "I've even eaten beef several times. There's no more virions in it. I mean, they wiped out scrapie years ago. Killed every sheep, every cow that might have any infection. It's perfectly safe to eat now, beef."

"We lost many people in Japan," Baisho offered slowly. "Tourists who eated . . . ate . . . Engrish beef, here in Europe. But trade friction protect most of us. Old trade barriers. The farmers of Japan." He smiled.

Smith ground out his cigarette. "Another fluke. Your old granddad was just lucky, Baisho-san."

"Lucky?" Bobby Denzongpa said suddenly. His dark gazelle-like eyes were red-rimmed with hangover. "Yaar, they fed sheeps to the cows here! God did not make cows for eating of sheeps! And the flesh of Mother Cow is not for us to eat. . . ."

"Bobby," Jackie warned.

Bobby shrugged irritably. "It's the truth, boss, yaar? They made foul sheep, slaughterhouse offal into protein for cattle feed, and they fed that bloody trash to their own English cows. For years they did this wicked thing, even when the cows were going mad and dying in front of them! They knew it was risky, but they went straightaway on doing it simply because it was cheaper! That was a crime against nature. It was properly punished."

"That is enough," Jackie said coldly. "We are guests

in this country. We of India also lost many fellow country-
men to that tragedy, don't you know."

"Moslems, good riddance," Bobby muttered under his
breath, and got up and staggered off.

Jackie glowered at him as he left, for the sake of the
others.

"It's okay," Smith said in the uneasy silence. "He's a
bloody Asian racist, your filmstar walla there, but we're
used to that here." He shrugged. "It's just—the plague,
you know, it's all they talk about in school, like England
was really high-class back then and we're nothing at all
now, just a shadow or something. . . . You get bloody
tired of hearing that. I mean, it was all fifty bloody years
ago." He sneered. "I'm not the shadow of the Beatles or
the fucking Sex Pistols. I'm a working, professional, modern British musician, and got my union papers to prove
it."

"No, you're really good, Smithie," Betty told him. She
had gone pale. "I mean, England's coming back strong
now. Really."

"Look, we're not 'coming back,' lass," Smith insisted.
"We're already here right now, earning our bloody living.
It's life, eh? Life goes fucking on." Smith stood up, picked
up his deck, scratched at his shaggy head. "I gotta work.
Jackie. Boss, eh? Can you spare five pounds, man? I gotta
make some phone calls."

Jackie searched in his wallet and handed over a bill in
the local currency.

Baisho had five Japanese in his crew. Even with the help of
Jackie's crew, it took them most of the evening to scythe
back the thick brown weeds in the old Bolton plagueyard.
Every half-meter or so they came across a marker for the
dead. Small square granite posts had been hammered into
the ground, fifty years ago, then sheared off clean with
some kind of metal saw. Fading names and dates and com-

puter ID numbers had been chiseled into the tops of the posts.

Jackie thought that the graveyard must stretch around for about a kilometer. The rolling English earth was studded with plump, thick-rooted oaks and ashes, with that strange naked look of European trees in winter.

There was nothing much to the place. It was utterly prosaic, like a badly kept city park in some third-class town. It defied the tragic imagination. Jackie had been a child when the scrapie plague had hit, but he could remember sitting in hot Bombay darkness, staring nonplussed at the anxious shouting newsreels, vague images, shot in color no doubt, but grainy black and white in the eye of his memory. Packed cots in European medical camps, uniformed shuffling white people gone all gaunt and trembling, spooning up charity gruel with numb, gnarled hands. The scrapie plague had a devilishly slow incubation in humans, but no human being had ever survived the full onset.

First came the slow grinding headaches and the unending sense of fatigue. Then the tripping and flopping and stumbling as the nerves of the victim's legs gave out. As the lesions spread, and tunneled deep within the brain, the muscles went slack and flabby, and a lethal psychotic apathy set in. In those old cinema newsreels, Western civilization gazed at the Indian lens in demented puzzlement as millions refused to realize that they were dying simply because they had eaten a cow.

What were they called? thought Jackie. Beefburgers? Hamburgers. Ninety percent of Britain, thirty percent of Western Europe, twenty percent of jet-setting America, horribly dead. Because of hamburgers.

Baisho's set-design crew was working hard to invest the dreary place with proper atmosphere. They were spraying long white webs of some kind of thready aerosol across the cropped grass and setting up gel-filtered lights. It was to be a night shoot. Macbeth and Macduff would arrive soon on the express train.

Betty sought him out. "Baisho-san wants to know what you think."

"My professional opinion of his set, as a veteran Indian filmmaker?" Jackie said.

"Right, boss."

Jackie did not much care for giving out his trade secrets but could not resist the urge to cap the Japanese. "A wind machine," he pronounced briskly. "This place needs a wind machine. Have him leave some of the taller weeds, and set up under a tree. We've fifty kilos of glitter dust back in Bolton. It's his, if he wants to pay. Sift that dust, hand by hand, through the back of the wind machine and you'll get a fine effect. It's more spooky than hell."

Betty offered this advice. Baisho nodded, thought the idea over, then reached for a small machine on his belt. He opened it and began to press tiny buttons.

Jackie walked closer. "What's that then? A telephone?"

"Yes," Betty said. "He needs to clear the plan with headquarters."

"No phone cables out here," Jackie said.

"High tech," Betty said. "They have a satellite link."

"Bloody hell," Jackie said. "And here I am offering technical aid. To the bloody Japanese, eh."

Betty looked at him for a long moment. "You've got Japan outnumbered eight to one. You shouldn't worry about Japan."

"Oh, I don't worry," Jackie said. "I'm a tolerant fellow, dear. A very secular fellow. But I'm thinking, what my studio will say, when they hear we break bread here with the nation's competition. It might not look so good in the Bombay gossip rags."

Betty stood quietly. The sun was setting behind a bank of clouds. "You're the kings of the world, you Asians," she said at last. "You're rich, you have all the power, you have all the money. We need you to help us, Jackie. We don't want you to fight each other."

"Politics," Jackie mumbled, surprised. "It's . . . it's just life." He paused. "Betty, listen to old Jackie. They don't like actresses with politics in Bombay. It's not like Tulsa, Oklahoma. You have to be discreet."

She watched him slowly, her eyes wide. "You never said you'd take me to Bombay, Jackie."

"It could happen," Jackie muttered.

"I'd like to go there," she said. "It's the center of the world." She gripped her arms and shivered. "It's getting cold. I need my sweater."

The actors had arrived, in a motor-driven tricycle cab. The Japanese began dressing them in stage armor. Macduff began practicing kendo moves.

Jackie walked to join Mr. Baisho. "May I call on your phone, please?"

"I'm sorry?" Baisho said.

Jackie mimed the action. "Bombay," he said. He wrote the number on a page in his notebook, handed it over.

"Ah," Baisho said, nodding. *"Wakarimashita."* He dialed a number, spoke briefly in Japanese, waited, handed Jackie the phone.

There was a rapid flurry of digital bleeping. Jackie, switching to Hindi, fought his way through a screen of secretaries. "Goldie," he said at last.

"Jackieji. I've been asking for you."

"Yes, I heard." Jackie paused. "Have you seen the films?"

Goldie Vachchani grunted, with a sharp digital echo. "The first two. Getting your footing over in Blighty, yaar? Nothing so special."

"Yes?" Jackie said.

"The third one. The one with the half-breed girl and the Moon and the soundtrack."

"Yes, Goldie."

Goldie's voice was slow and gloating. "That one, Jackie. That one is special, yaar. It's a smasheroo, Jackie.

An ultrahit! Bloody champagne and flower garlands here,
Jackie boy. It's big. Mega."

"You liked the Moon, eh," Jackie said, stunned.

"Love the Moon. Love all that nonsense."

"I did hear about your brother's government appointment. Congratulations."

Goldie chuckled. "Bloody hell, Jackie. You're the
fourth fellow today to make that silly mistake. That Vachchani fellow in aeronautics, he's not my brother. My
brother's a bloody contractor; he builds bloody houses,
Jackie. This other Vachchani, he's some scientist egghead
fellow. That Moon stuff is stupid crazy, it will never happen." He laughed, then dropped his voice. "The fourth
one is shit, Jackie. Women's weepies are a drug on the
bloody market this season, you rascal. Send me something
funny next time. A bloody dance comedy."

"Will do," Jackie said.

"This girl Betty," Goldie said. "She likes to work?"

"Yes."

"She's a party girl, too?"

"You might say so."

"I want to meet this Betty. You send her here on the
very next train. No, an aeroplane, hang the cost. And that
soundtrack man, too. My kids love that damned ugly music. If the kids love it, there's money in it."

"I need them both, Goldie. For my next feature. Got
them under contract, yaar."

Goldie paused. Jackie waited him out.

"You got a little tax trouble, Jackie? I'm going to see
to fixing that silly business, yaar. See to that straightaway.
Personally."

Jackie let out a breath. "They're as good as on the
way, Goldieji."

"You got it then. You're a funny fellow, Jackie."
There was a digital clatter as the phone went dead.

The studio lights of the Japanese crew flashed on,
framing Jackie in the graveyard in a phosphorescent glare.
"Bloody hell!" Jackie shouted, flinging the phone away

into the air and clapping his hands. "Party, my crew! Big party tonight for every bloody soul, and the bill is on Jackie Amar!" He whooped aloud. "If you're not drunk and dancing tonight, then you're no friend of mine! My God, everybody! My God, but life is good."

DEEP EDDY

The Continental gentleman in the next beanbag offered "Zigaretten?"

"What's in it?" Deep Eddy asked. The gray-haired gentleman murmured something: polysyllabic medical German. Eddy's translation program crashed at once.

Eddy gently declined. The gentleman shook a zigarette from the pack, twisted its tip, and huffed at it. A sharp perfume arose, like coffee struck by lightning.

The elderly European brightened swiftly. He flipped open a newspad, tapped through its menu, and began alertly scanning a German business zine.

Deep Eddy killed his translation program, switched spexware, and scanned the man. The gentleman was broadcasting a business bio. His name was Peter Liebling, he was from Bremen, he was ninety years old, he was an official with a European lumber firm. His hobbies were backgammon and collecting antique phone-cards. He looked pretty young for ninety. He probably had some unusual and interesting medical syndromes.

Herr Liebling glanced up, annoyed at Eddy's computer-assisted gaze. Eddy dropped his spex back onto their neck chain. A practiced gesture, one Deep Eddy used a lot—*hey, didn't mean to stare, pal.* A lot of people were suspicious of spex. Most people had no idea of the profound capacities of spexware. Most people still didn't use spex. Most people were, in a word, losers.

Eddy lurched up within his baby-blue beanbag and gazed out the aircraft window. Chattanooga, Tennessee. Bright white ceramic air-control towers, distant wine-colored office blocks, and a million dark green trees. Tarmac heated gently in the summer morning. Eddy lifted his spex again to check a silent take-off westward by a white-and-red Asian jet. Infrared turbulence gushed from its distant engines. Deep Eddy loved infrared. That deep silent magical whirl of invisible heat, the breath of industry.

People underestimated Chattanooga, Deep Eddy thought with a local boy's pride. Chattanooga had a very high per-capita investment in spexware. In fact Chattanooga ranked third-highest in NAFTA. Number One was San Jose, California (naturally), and Number Two was Madison, Wisconsin.

Eddy had already traveled to both those rival cities, in the service of his Chattanooga users group, to swap some spexware, market a little info, and make a careful study of the local scene. To collect some competitive intelligence. To spy around, not to put too fine a point on it.

Eddy's most recent business trip had been five drunken days at a blowout All-NAFTA spexware conference in Ciudad Juarez, Chihuahua. Eddy had not yet figured out why Ciudad Juarez, a once-dreary maquilladora factory town on the Rio Grande, had gone completely hog-wild for spexing. But even little kids there had spex, brightly speckly throwaway kid-stuff with just a couple dozen meg. There were tottering grannies with spex. Security cops with spex mounted right into their riot helmets. Billboards everywhere that couldn't be read without spex. And thousands of hustling industry zudes with air-conditioned jackets and forty or fifty terabytes mounted right at the bridge of the nose. Ciudad Juarez was in the grip of rampant spexmania. Maybe it was all the lithium in their water.

Today, duty called Deep Eddy to Düsseldorf in Europe. Duty did not have to call very hard to get Eddy's attention. The mere whisper of duty was enough to dislodge Deep Eddy, who still lived with his parents, Bob and Lisa.

He'd gotten some spexmail and a package from the president of the local chapter. *A network obligation; our group credibility depends on you, Eddy. A delivery job. Don't let us down; do whatever it takes. And keep your eyes covered—this one could be dangerous.* Well, danger and Deep Eddy were fast friends. Throwing up tequila and ephedrine through your nose in an alley in Mexico, while wearing a pair of computer-assisted glasses worth as much as a car—now *that* was dangerous. Most people would be scared to try something like that. Most people couldn't master their own insecurities. Most people were too scared to live.

This would be Deep Eddy's first adult trip to Europe. At the age of nine he'd accompanied Bob and Lisa to Madrid for a Sexual Deliberation conference, but all he remembered from that trip was a boring weekend of bad television and incomprehensible tomato-soaked food. Düsseldorf, however, sounded like real and genuine fun. The trip was probably even worth getting up at 07:15.

Eddy dabbed at his raw eyelids with a saline-soaked wipey. Eddy was getting a first-class case of eyeball-burn off his spex; or maybe it was just sleeplessness. He'd spent a very late and highly frustrating night with his current girlfriend, Djulia. He'd dated her hoping for a hero's farewell, hinting broadly that he might be beaten or killed by sinister European underground networking-mavens, but his presentation hadn't washed at all. Instead of some sustained and attentive frolic, he'd gotten only a somber four-hour lecture about the emotional center in Djulia's life: collecting Japanese glassware.

As his jet gently lifted from the Chattanooga tarmac,

Deep Eddy was struck with a sudden, instinctive, gut-level conviction of Djulia's essential counter-productivity. Djulia was just no good for him. Those clear eyes, the tilted nose, the sexy sprinkle of tattoo across her right cheekbone. Lovely flare of her body-heat in darkness. The lank strands of dark hair that turned crisp and wavy halfway down their length. A girl shouldn't have such great hair and so many tatts and still be so tightly wrapped. Djulia was no real friend of his at all.

The jet climbed steadily, crossing the shining waters of the Tennessee. Outside Eddy's window, the long ductile wings bent and rippled with dainty, tightly controlled antiturbulence. The cabin itself felt as steady as a Mississippi lumber barge, but the computer-assisted wings, under spexanalysis, resembled a vibrating sawblade. Nerve-racking. *Let this not be the day a whole bunch of Chattanoogans fall out of the sky,* Eddy thought silently, squirming a bit in the luscious embrace of his beanbag.

He gazed about the cabin at his fellow candidates for swift mass death. Three hundred people or so, the European and NAFTA jet-bourgeoisie; well-groomed, polite. Nobody looked frightened. Sprawling there in their pastel beanbags, chatting, hooking fiber-optics to palmtops and laptops, browsing through newspads, making videophone-calls. Just as if they were at home, or maybe in a very crowded cylindrical hotel lobby, all of them in blank and deliberate ignorance of the fact that they were zipping through midair supported by nothing but plasmajets and computation. Most people were so unaware. One software glitch somewhere, a missed decimal point, and those cleverly ductile wings would tear right the hell off. Sure, it didn't happen often. But it happened sometimes.

Deep Eddy wondered glumly if his own demise would even make the top of the newspad. It'd be in there all right, but probably hyperlinked five or six layers down.

The five-year-old in the beanbag behind Eddy entered a paroxysm of childish fear and glee. "My e-mail, Mom!" the kid chirped with desperate enthusiasm, bouncing up and down. "Mom! Mom, my *e-mail*! Hey Mom, get me my e-mail!"

A stew offered Eddy breakfast. He had a bowl of muesli and half a dozen boiled prunes. Then he broke out his travel card and ordered a mimosa. The booze didn't make him feel any more alert, though, so he ordered two more mimosas. Then he fell asleep.

Customs in Düsseldorf was awash. Summer tourists were pouring into the city like some vast migratory shoal of sardines. The people from outside Europe—from NAFTA, from the Sphere, from the South—were a tiny minority, though, compared to the vast intra-European traffic, who breezed through Customs completely unimpeded.

Uniformed inspectors were spexing the NAFTA and South baggage, presumably for guns or explosives, but their clunky government-issue spex looked a good five years out-of-date. Deep Eddy passed through the Customs chute without incident and had his passchip stamped. Passing out drunk on champagne and orange juice, then snoozing through the entire Atlantic crossing, had clearly been an excellent idea. It was 21:00 local time and Eddy felt quite alert and rested. Clearheaded. Ready for anything. Hungry.

Eddy wandered toward the icons signaling ground transport. A stocky woman in a bulky brown jacket stepped into his path. He stopped short. "Mr. Edward Dertouzas," she said.

"Right," Eddy said, dropping his bag. They stared at one another, spex to spex. "Actually, fraulein, as I'm sure you can see by my online bio, my friends call me Eddy. Deep Eddy, mostly."

"I'm not your friend, Mr. Dertouzas. I am your security escort. I'm called Sardelle today." Sardelle stooped and hefted his travel bag. Her head came about to his shoulder.

Deep Eddy's German translator, which he had restored to life, placed a yellow subtitle at the lower rim of his spex. "Sardelle," he noted. " *'Anchovy'?*"

"I don't pick the code names," Sardelle told him, irritated. "I have to use what the company gives me." She heaved her way through the crowd, jolting people aside with deft jabs of Eddy's travel bag. Sardelle wore a bulky air-conditioned brown trenchcoat, with multipocketed fawn-colored jeans and thicksoled black-and-white cop shoes. A crisp trio of small tattooed triangles outlined Sardelle's right cheek. Her hands, attractively small and dainty, were gloved in black-and-white pinstripe. She looked about thirty. No problem. He liked mature women. Maturity gave depth.

Eddy scanned her for bio data. "Sardelle," the spex read unhelpfully. Absolutely nothing else; no business, no employer, no address, no age, no interests, no hobbies, no personal ads. Europeans were rather weird about privacy. Then again, maybe Sardelle's lack of proper annotation had something to do with her business life.

Eddy looked down at his own hands, twitched bare fingers over a virtual menu in midair, and switched to some rude spexware he'd mail-ordered from Tijuana. Something of a legend in the spexing biz, X-Spex stripped people's clothing off and extrapolated the flesh beneath it in a full-color visual simulation. Sardelle, however, was so decked-out in waistbelts, holsters, and shoulderpads that the X-ware was baffled. The simulation looked alarmingly bogus, her breasts and shoulders waggling like drug-addled plasticine.

"Hurry out," she suggested sternly. "I mean hurry *up*."

"Where we going? To see the Critic?"

"In time," Sardelle said. Eddy followed her through the stomping, shuffling, heaving crowd to a set of travel lockers.

"Do you really need this bag, sir?"

"What?" Eddy said. "Sure I do! It's got all my stuff in it."

"If we take it, I will have to search it carefully," Sardelle informed him patiently. "Let's place your bag in this locker, and you can retrieve it when you leave Europe." She offered him a small gray handbag with the logo of a Berlin luxury hotel. "Here are some standard travel necessities."

"They scanned my bag in Customs," Eddy said. "I'm clean, really. Customs was a walk-through."

Sardelle laughed briefly and sarcastically. "One million people coming to Düsseldorf this weekend," she said. "There will be a Wende here. And you think the Customs searched you properly? Believe me, Edward. You have not been searched properly."

"That sounds a bit menacing," Eddy said.

"A proper search takes a lot of time. Some threats to safety are tiny—things woven into clothing, glued to the skin. . . ." Sardelle shrugged. "I like to have time. I'll *pay* you to have some time. Do you need money, Edward?"

"No," Eddy said, startled. "I mean, yeah. Sure I need money, who doesn't? But I have a travel card from my people. From CAPCLUG."

She glanced up sharply, aiming the spex at him. "Who is Kapklug?"

"Computer-Assisted Perception Civil Liberties Users Group," Eddy said. "Chattanooga Chapter."

"I see. The acronym in English." Sardelle frowned. "I hate all acronyms. . . . Edward, I will pay you forty ecu cash to put your bag into this locker and take this bag instead."

"Sold," Deep Eddy said. "Where's the money?"

Sardelle passed him four wellworn hologram bills. Eddy stuffed the cash in his pocket. Then he opened his own bag and retrieved an elderly hardbound book—*Crowds and Power,* by Elias Canetti. "A little light reading," he said unconvincingly.

"Let me see that book," Sardelle insisted. She leafed through the book rapidly, scanning pages with her pin-striped fingertips, flexing the covers and checking the book's binding, presumably for inserted razors, poisoned needles, or strips of plastic explosive. "You are smuggling data," she concluded sourly, handing it back.

"That's what we live for in CAPCLUG," Eddy told her, peeking at her over his spex and winking. He slipped the book into the gray hotel bag and zipped it. Then he heaved his own bag into the travel locker, slammed the door, and removed the numbered key.

"Give me that key," Sardelle said.

"Why?"

"You might return and open the locker. If I keep the key, that security risk is much reduced."

"No way," Eddy frowned. "Forget it."

"Ten ecu," she offered.

"Mmmmph."

"Fifteen."

"Okay, have it your way." Eddy gave her the key. "Don't lose it."

Sardelle, unsmiling, put the key into a zippered sleeve pocket. "I never lose things." She opened her wallet.

Eddy nodded, pocketing a hologram ten and five singles. Very attractive currency, the ecu. The ten had a hologram of René Descartes, a very deep zude who looked impressively French and rational.

Eddy felt he was doing pretty well by this, so far. In point of fact there wasn't anything in the bag he really needed: his underwear, spare jeans, tickets, business cards, dress shirts, tie, suspenders, spare shoes, toothbrush, aspirin, instant espresso, sewing kit, and earrings. So what? It wasn't as if she'd asked him to give up his spex.

He also had a complete crush on his escort. The name Anchovy suited her—she struck him as a small canned cold fish. Eddy found this perversely attractive. In fact he found her so attractive that he was having a hard time standing still and breathing normally. He really liked the way she carried her stripe-gloved hands, deft and feminine and mysteriously European, but mostly it was her hair. Long, light reddish-brown, and meticulously braided by machine. He loved women's hair when it was machine-braided. They couldn't seem to catch the fashion quite right in NAFTA. Sardelle's hair looked like a rusted mass of museum-quality chain-mail, or maybe some fantastically convoluted railway intersection. Hair that really *meant business*. Not only did Sardelle have not a hair out of place, but any unkemptness was *topologically impossible*. The vision rose unbidden of running his fingers through it in the dark.

"I'm starving," he announced.

"Then we will eat," she said. They headed for the exit.

Electric taxis were trying, without much success, to staunch the spreading hemorrhage of tourists. Sardelle clawed at the air with her pinstriped fingers. Adjusting invisible spex menus. She seemed to be casting the evil eye on a nearby family group of Italians, who reacted with scarcely concealed alarm. "We can walk to a city bus-stop," she told him. "It's quicker."

"Walking's quicker?"

Sardelle took off. He had to hurry to keep up. "Listen to me, Edward. If you follow my security suggestions, we will save time. If I save my time, then you will make money. If you make me work harder I will not be so generous."

"I'm easy," Eddy protested. Her cop shoes seemed to have some kind of computational cushion built into the soles; she walked as if mounted on springs. "I'm here to meet the Cultural Critic. An audience with him. I have a delivery for him. You know that, right?"

"It's the book?"

Eddy hefted the gray hotel bag. "Yeah. . . . I'm here in Düsseldorf to deliver an old book to some European intellectual. Actually, to give the book back to him. He, like, lent the book to the CAPCLUG Steering Committee, and it's time to give it back. How tough can that job be?"

"Probably not very tough," Sardelle said calmly. "But strange things happen during a Wende."

Eddy nodded soberly. "Wendes are very interesting

phenomena. CAPCLUG is studying Wendes. We might like to throw one someday."

"That's not how Wendes happen, Eddy. You don't 'throw' a Wende." Sardelle paused, considering. "A Wende throws *you*."

"So I gather," Eddy said. "I've been reading his work, you know. The Cultural Critic. It's deep work, I like it."

Sardelle was indifferent. "I'm not one of his partisans. I'm just employed to guard him." She conjured up another menu. "What kind of food do you like? Chinese? Thai? Eritrean?"

"How about German food?"

Sardelle laughed. "We Germans never eat German food. . . . There are very good Japanese cafes in Düsseldorf. Tokyo people fly here for the salmon. And the anchovies. . . ."

"You live here in Düsseldorf, Anchovy?"

"I live everywhere in Europe, Deep Eddy." Her voice fell. "Any city with a screen in front of it. . . . And they all have screens in Europe."

"Sounds fun. You want to trade some spexware?"

"No."

"You don't believe in *andwendungsoriente wissensverarbeitung*?"

She made a face. "How clever of you to learn an appropriate German phrase. Speak English, Eddy. Your accent is truly terrible."

"Thank you kindly," Eddy said.

"You can't trade wares with me, Eddy, don't be silly. I would not give my security spexware to civilian Yankee hacker-boys."

"Don't own the copyright, huh?"

"There's that, too." She shrugged, and smiled.

They were out of the airport now, walking south. Silent steady flow of electric traffic down Flughafenstrasse. The twilight air smelled of little white roses. They crossed at a traffic light. The German semiotics of ads and street signs began to press with gentle culture shock at the sur-

face of Deep Eddy's brain. Garagenhof. Spezialist fur
Mobil-Telefon. Burohausern. He put on some character-
recognition ware to do translation, but the instant dou-
bling of the words all around him only made him feel
schizophrenic.

They took shelter in a lit bus kiosk, along with a pair
of heavily tattooed gays toting grocery bags. A video-ad
built into the side of the kiosk advertised German-
language e-mail editors.

As Sardelle stood patiently, in silence, Eddy examined
her closely for the first time. There was something odd and
indefinitely European about the line of her nose. "Let's be
friends, Sardelle. I'll take off my spex if you take off your
spex."

"Maybe later," she said.

Eddy laughed. "You should get to know me. I'm a fun
guy."

"I already know you."

An overcrowded bus passed. Its riders had festooned
the robot bus with banners and mounted a klaxon on its
roof, which emitted a cacophony of rapidfire bongo music.

"The Wende people are already hitting the buses,"
Sardelle noted sourly, shifting on her feet as if trampling
grapes. "I hope we can get downtown."

"You've done some snooping on me, huh? Credit
records and such? Was it interesting?"

Sardelle frowned. "It's my business to research
records. I did nothing illegal. All by the book."

"No offense taken," Eddy said, spreading his hands.
"But you must have learned I'm harmless. Let's unwrap a
little."

Sardelle sighed. "I learned that you are an unmarried
male, age eighteen-to-thirty-five. No steady job. No steady
home. No wife, no children. Radical political leanings.
Travels often. Your demographics are very high-risk."

"I'm twenty-two, to be exact." Eddy noticed that
Sardelle showed no reaction to this announcement, but the
two eavesdropping gays seemed quite interested. He

smiled nonchalantly. "I'm here to network, that's all. Friend-of-a-friend situation. Actually, I'm pretty sure I share your client's politics. As far as I can figure his politics out."

"Politics don't matter," Sardelle said, bored and impatient. "I'm not concerned with politics. Men in your age group commit 80 percent of all violent crimes."

One of the gays spoke up suddenly, in heavily accented English. "Hey fraulein. We also have 80 percent of the charm!"

"And 90 percent of the fun," said his companion. "It's Wende time, Yankee boy. Come with us and we'll do some crimes." He laughed.

"Das ist sehr nett vohn Ihnen," Eddy said politely. "But I can't. I'm with nursie."

The first gay made a witty and highly idiomatic reply in German, to the effect, apparently, that he liked boys who wore sunglasses after dark, but Eddy needed more tattoos.

Eddy, having finished reading subtitles in midair, touched the single small black circle on his cheekbone. "Don't you like my solitaire? It's rather sinister in its reticence, don't you think?"

He'd lost them; they only looked puzzled.

A bus arrived.

"This will do," Sardelle announced. She fed the bus a ticket-chip and Eddy followed her on board. The bus was crowded, but the crowd seemed gentle; mostly Euro-Japanese out for a night on the town. They took a beanbag together in the back.

It had grown quite dark now. They floated down the street with machine-guided precision and a smooth dreamlike detachment. Eddy felt the spell of travel overcome him; the basic mammalian thrill of a live creature plucked up and dropped like a supersonic ghost on the far side of the planet. Another time, another place: whatever vast set of unlikelihoods had militated against his presence here had been defeated. A Friday night in Düsseldorf, July 13,

2035. The time was 22:10. The very specificity seemed magical.

He glanced at Sardelle again, grinning gleefully, and suddenly saw her for what she was. A burdened female functionary sitting stiffly in the back of a bus.

"Where are we now, exactly?" he said.

"We are on Danzigerstrasse heading south to the Alt-stadt," Sardelle said. "The old town center."

"Yeah? What's there?"

"Kartoffel. Beer. Schnitzel. Things for you to eat."

The bus stopped and a crowd of stomping, shoving rowdies got on. Across the street, a trio of police were struggling with a broken traffic securicam. The cops were wearing full-body pink riot-gear. He'd heard somewhere that all European cop riot-gear was pink. The color was supposed to be calming.

"This isn't much fun for you, Sardelle, is it?"

She shrugged. "We're not the same people, Eddy. I don't know what you are bringing to the Critic, and I don't want to know." She tapped her spex back into place with one gloved finger. "But if you fail in your job, at the very worst, it might mean some grave cultural loss. Am I right?"

"I suppose so. Sure."

"But if I fail in *my* job, Eddy, something *real* might *actually happen.*"

"Wow," Eddy said, stung.

The crush in the bus was getting oppressive. Eddy stood and offered his spot in the beanbag to a tottering old woman in spangled party gear.

Sardelle rose then, too, with bad grace, and fought her way up the aisle. Eddy followed, barking his shins on the thicksoled beastie-boots of a sprawling drunk.

Sardelle stopped short to trade elbow-jabs with a Nordic kamikaze in a horned baseball cap, and Eddy stumbled into her headlong. He realized then why people seemed so eager to get out of Sardelle's way: her trenchcoat was of woven ceramic and was as rough as sandpaper. He lurched one-handed for a strap. "Well," he puffed at Sardelle, swaying into her spex-to-spex, "if we can't enjoy each other's company, why not get this over with? Let me do my errand. Then I'll get right into your hair." He paused, shocked. "I mean, *out* of your hair. Sorry."

She hadn't noticed. "You'll do your errand," she said, clinging to her strap. They were so close that he could feel a chill air-conditioned breeze whiffling out of her trenchcoat's collar. "But on my terms. My time, my circumstances." She wouldn't meet his eyes; her head darted around as if from grave embarrassment. Eddy realized suddenly that she was methodically scanning the face of every stranger in the bus.

She spared him a quick, distracted smile. "Don't mind me, Eddy. Be a good boy and have fun in Düsseldorf. Just let me do my job, okay?"

"Okay then," Eddy muttered. "Really, I'm delighted to be in your hands." He couldn't seem to stop with the double entendres. They rose to his lips like drool from the id.

The glowing grids of Düsseldorf highrises shone outside the bus windows, patchy waffles of mystery. So many human lives behind those windows. People he would never meet, never see. Pity he still couldn't afford proper telephotos.

Eddy cleared his throat. "What's he doing out there right now? The Cultural Critic, I mean."

"Meeting contacts in a safehouse. He will meet a great many people during the Wende. That's his business, you know. You're only one of many that he bringed— brought—to this rendezvous." Sardelle paused. "Though in threat potential you do rank among the top five."

The bus made more stops. People piled in headlong, with a thrash and a heave and a jacking of kneecaps. Inside the bus they were all becoming anchovies. A smothered fistfight broke out in the back. A drunken woman tried, with mixed success, to vomit out the window.

Sardelle held her position grimly through several stops, then finally fought her way to the door.

The bus pulled to a stop and a sudden rush of massed bodies propelled them out.

They'd arrived by a long suspension bridge over a broad moonsilvered river. The bridge's soaring cables were lit end-to-end with winking party-bulbs. All along the bridge, flea-marketeers sitting cross-legged on glowing mats were doing a brisk trade in tourist junk. Out in the center, a busking juggler with smart-gloves flung lit torches in flaming arcs three stories high.

"Jesus, what a beautiful river," Eddy said.

"It's the Rhine. This is Oberkasseler Bridge."

"The Rhine. Of course, of course. I've never seen the Rhine before. Is it safe to drink?"

"Of course. Europe's very civilized."

"I thought so. It even smells good. Let's go drink some of it."

The banks were lined with municipal gardens: grape-musky vineyards, big pale meticulous flowerbeds. Tireless gardening robots had worked them over season by season with surgical trowels. Eddy stooped by the riverbank and scooped up a double-handful of backwash from a passing hydrofoil. He saw his own spex-clad face in the moony puddle of his hands. As Sardelle watched, he sipped a bit and flung the rest out as libation to the spirit of place.

"I'm happy now," he said. "Now I'm really here."

By midnight, he'd had four beers, two schnitzels, and a platter of kartoffels. Kartoffels were fried potato-batter waffles with a side of applesauce. Eddy's morale had soared from the moment he first bit into one.

They sat at a sidewalk cafe table in the midst of a centuries-old pedestrian street in the Altstadt. The entire street was a single block-long bar, all chairs, umbrellas, and cobbles, peaked-roof townhouses with ivy and windowboxes and ancient copper weathervanes. It had been invaded by an absolute throng of gawking, shuffling, hooting foreigners.

The gentle, kindly, rather bewildered Düsseldorfers were doing their level best to placate their guests and relieve them of any excess cash. A strong pink police presence was keeping good order. He'd seen two zudes in horned baseball-caps briskly hauled into a paddywagon—a "Pink Minna"—but the Vikings were pig-drunk and had it coming, and the crowd seemed very good-humored.

"I don't see what the big deal is with these Wendes," Deep Eddy said, polishing his spex on a square of oiled and lint-free polysilk. "This sucker's a walk-through. There's not gonna be any trouble here. Just look how calm and mellow these zudes are."

"There's trouble already," Sardelle said. "It's just not here in Altstadt in front of your nose."

"Yeah?"

"There are big gangs of arsonists across the river tonight. They're barricading streets in Neuss, toppling cars, and setting them on fire."

"How come?"

Sardelle shrugged. "They are anticar activists. They demand pedestrian rights and more mass transit. . . ." She paused a bit to read the inside of her spex. "Green radicals are storming the Lobbecke Museum. They want all extinct insect specimens surrendered for cloning. . . . Heinrich Heine University is on strike for academic freedom, and someone has glue-bombed the big traffic tunnel beneath the campus. . . . But this is nothing, not yet. Tomorrow England meets Ireland in the soccer finals at Rhein-Stadium. There will be hell to pay."

"Huh. That sounds pretty bad."

"Yes." She smiled. "So let's enjoy our time here, Eddy. Idleness is sweet. Even on the edge of dirty chaos."

"But none of those events by itself sounds all that threatening or serious."

"Not each thing by itself, Eddy, no. But it all happens all at once. That's what a Wende is like."

"I don't get it," Eddy said. He put his spex back on and lit the menu from within, with a fingersnap. He tapped the spex menu-bar with his right fingertip and light-amplifiers kicked in. The passing crowd, their outlines shimmering slightly from computational effects, seemed to be strolling through an overlit stage-set. "I guess there's trouble coming from all these outsiders," Eddy said, "but the Germans themselves seem so . . . well . . . so good-natured and tidy and civilized. Why do they even have Wendes?"

"It's not something we plan, Eddy. It's just something that happens to us." Sardelle sipped her coffee.

"How could this happen and not be planned?"

"Well, we knew it was coming, of course. Of course we knew *that*. Word gets around. That's how Wendes start." She straightened her napkin. "You can ask the Critic, when you meet him. He talks a lot about Wendes. He knows as much as anyone, I think."

"Yeah, I've read him," Eddy said. "He says that it's rumor, boosted by electronic and digital media, in a feedback-loop with crowd dynamics and modern mass transportation. A nonlinear networking phenomenon. That much I understand! But then he quotes some zude named Elias Canetti. . . ." Eddy patted the gray bag. "I tried to read Canetti, I really did, but he's twentieth-century, and as boring and stuffy as hell. . . . Anyway, we'd handle things differently in Chattanooga."

"People say that, until they have their first Wende," Sardelle said. "Then it's all different. Once you know a Wende can actually happen to you . . . well, it changes everything."

"We'd take steps to stop it, that's all. Take steps to control it. Can't you people take some steps?"

Sardelle tugged off her pinstriped gloves and set them on the tabletop. She worked her bare fingers gently, blew on her fingertips, and picked a big bready pretzel from the basket. Eddy noticed with surprise that her gloves had big rock-hard knuckles and twitched a little all by themselves.

"There are things you can do, of course," she told him. "Put police and firefighters on overtime. Hire more private security. Disaster control for lights, traffic, power, data. Open the shelters and stock first-aid medicine. And warn the whole population. But when a city tells its people that a Wende is coming, that *guarantees* the Wende will come. . . ." Sardelle sighed. "I've worked Wendes before. But this is a big one. A big, dark one. And it won't be over, it can't be over—not until everyone knows that it's gone, and feels that it's gone."

"That doesn't make much sense."

"Talking about it won't help, Eddy. You and I, talking about it—we become part of the Wende ourselves, you see? We're here because of the Wende. We met because of the Wende. And we can't leave each other, until the Wende goes away." She shrugged. "Can you go away, Eddy?"

"No . . . not right now. But I've got stuff to do here."

"So does everybody else."

Eddy grunted and killed another beer. The beer here was truly something special. "It's a Chinese finger-trap," he said, gesturing.

"Yes, I know those."

He grinned. "Suppose we both stop pulling? We could walk through it. Leave town. I'll throw the book in the river. Tonight you and I could fly back to Chattanooga. Together."

She laughed. "You wouldn't really do that, though."

"You don't know me after all."

"You spit in the face of your friends? And I lose my job? A high price to pay for one gesture. For a young man's pretense of free will."

"I'm not pretending, lady. Try me. I dare you."

"Then you're drunk."

"Well, there's that." He laughed. "But don't joke about liberty. Liberty's the realest thing there is." He stood up and hunted out the bathroom.

On his way back he stopped at a payphone. He gave it fifty centimes and dialed Tennessee. Djulia answered.

"What time is it?" he said.

"Nineteen. Where are you?"

"Düsseldorf."

"Oh." She rubbed her nose. "Sounds like you're in a bar."

"Bingo."

"So what's new, Eddy?"

"I know you put a lot of stock in honesty," Eddy said. "So I thought I'd tell you I'm planning an affair. I met this German girl here and frankly, she's irresistible."

Djulia frowned darkly. "You've got a lot of nerve telling me that kind of crap with your spex on."

"Oh yeah," he said. He took them off and stared into the monitor. "Sorry."

"You're drunk, Eddy," Djulia said. "I hate it when you're drunk! You'll say and do anything if you're drunk and on the far end of a phone line." She rubbed nervously at her newest cheek-tattoo. "Is this one of your weird jokes?"

"Yeah. It is, actually. The chances are eighty to one that she'll turn me down flat." Eddy laughed. "But I'm gonna try anyway. Because you're not letting me live and breathe."

Djulia's face went stiff. "When we're face to face, you always abuse my trust. That's why I don't like for us to go past virching."

"Come off it, Djulia."

She was defiant. "If you think you'll be happier with some weirdo virch-whore in Europe, go ahead! I don't know why you can't do that by wire from Chattanooga, anyway."

"This is Europe. We're talking actuality here."

Djulia was shocked. "If you actually touch another woman I never want to see you again." She bit her lip. "Or do wire with you, either. I mean that, Eddy. You know I do."

"Yeah," he said. "I know."

He hung up, got change from the phone, and dialed his parents' house. His father answered.

"Hi, Bob. Lisa around?"

"No," his father said, "it's her night for optic macrame. How's Europe?"

"Different."

"Nice to hear from you, Eddy. We're kind of short of money. I can spare you some sustained attention, though."

"I just dumped Djulia."

"Good move, son," his father said briskly. "Fine. Very serious girl, Djulia. Way too straitlaced for you. A kid your age should be dating girls who are absolutely jumping out of their skins."

Eddy nodded.

"You didn't lose your spex, did you?"

Eddy held them up on their neck chain. "Safe and sound."

"Hardly recognized you for a second," his father said. "Ed, you're such a serious-minded kid. Taking on all these responsibilities. On the road so much, spexware day in and day out. Lisa and I network about you all the time. Neither of us did a day's work before we were thirty, and we're all the better for it. You've got to live, son. Got to find yourself. Smell the roses. If you want to stay in Europe a couple of months, forget the algebra courses."

"It's calculus, Bob."

"Whatever."

"Thanks for the good advice, Bob. I know you mean it."

"It's good news about Djulia, son. You know we don't invalidate your feelings, so we never said a goddamn thing to you, but her glassware really sucked. Lisa says she's got no goddamn aesthetics at all. That's a hell of a thing, in a woman."

"That's my mom," Eddy said. "Give Lisa my best." He hung up.

He went back out to the sidewalk table. "Did you eat enough?" Sardelle asked.

"Yeah. It was good."

"Sleepy?"

"I dunno. Maybe."

"Do you have a place to stay, Eddy? Hotel reservations?"

Eddy shrugged. "No. I don't bother, usually. What's the use? It's more fun winging it."

"Good," Sardelle nodded. "It's better to wing. No one can trace us. It's safer."

She found them shelter in a park, where an activist group of artists from Munich had set up a squatter pavilion. As squatter pavilions went, it was quite a nice one, new and in good condition: a giant soap-bubble upholstered in cellophane and polysilk. It covered half an acre with crisp yellow bubblepack flooring. The shelter was illegal and therefore anonymous. Sardelle seemed quite pleased about this.

Once through the zippered airlock, Eddy and Sardelle were forced to examine the artists' multimedia artwork for an entire grueling hour. Worse yet, they were closely quizzed afterward by an expert-system, which bullied them relentlessly with arcane aesthetic dogma.

This ordeal was too high a price for most squatters. The pavilion, though attractive, was only half-full, and many people who had shown up bone-tired were fleeing the art headlong. Deep Eddy, however, almost always aced this sort of thing. Thanks to his slick responses to the computer's quizzing, he won himself quite a nice area, with a blanket, opaquable curtains, and its own light fixtures. Sardelle, by contrast, had been bored and minimal, and had won nothing more advanced than a pillow and a patch of bubblepack among the philistines.

Eddy made good use of a traveling pay-toilet stall, and bought some mints and chilled mineral water from a robot. He settled in cozily as police sirens, and some distant, rather choked-sounding explosions, made the night glamorous.

Sardelle didn't seem anxious to leave. "May I see your hotel bag," she said.

"Sure." He handed it over. Might as well. She'd given it to him in the first place.

He'd thought she was going to examine the book again, but instead she took a small plastic packet from within the bag, and pulled the packet's ripcord. A colorful jumpsuit jumped out, with a chemical hiss and a vague hot stink of catalysis and cheap cologne. The jumpsuit, a one-piece, had comically baggy legs, frilled sleeves, and was printed all over with a festive cut-up of twentieth-century naughty seaside postcards.

"Pajamas," Eddy said. "Gosh, how thoughtful."

"You can sleep in this if you want," Sardelle nodded, "but it's daywear. I want you to wear it tomorrow. And I want to buy the clothes you are wearing now, so that I can take them away for safety."

Deep Eddy was wearing a dress shirt, light jacket, American jeans, dappled stockings, and Nashville brogues of genuine blue suede. "I can't wear that crap," he protested. "Jesus, I'd look like a total loser."

"Yes," said Sardelle with an enthusiastic nod, "it's very cheap and common. It will make you invisible. Just one more party boy among thousands and thousands. This is very secure dress, for a courier during a Wende."

"You want me to meet the Critic in this get-up?"

Sardelle laughed. "The Cultural Critic is not impressed by taste, Eddy. The eye he uses when he looks at people . . . he sees things other people can't see." She paused, considering. "He *might* be impressed if you showed up dressed in *this*. Not because of what it is, of course. But because it would show that you can understand and manipulate popular taste to your own advantage . . . just as he does."

"You're really being paranoid," Eddy said, nettled.

"I'm not an assassin. I'm just some techie zude from Tennessee. You know that, don't you?"

"Yes, I believe you," she nodded. "You're very convincing. But that has nothing to do with proper security technique. If I take your clothes, there will be less operational risk."

"How much less risk? What do you expect to find in my clothes, anyway?"

"There are many, many things you *might* have done," she said patiently. "The human race is very ingenious. We have invented ways to kill, or hurt, or injure almost anyone, with almost nothing at all." She sighed. "If you don't know about such techniques already, it would only be stupid for me to tell you all about them. So let's be quick and simple, Eddy. It would make me happier to take your clothes away. A hundred ecu."

Eddy shook his head. "This time it's really going to cost you."

"Two hundred then," Sardelle said.

"Forget it."

"I can't go higher than two hundred. Unless you let me search your body cavities."

Eddy dropped his spex.

"Body cavities," Sardelle said impatiently. "You're a grown-up man, you must know about this. A great deal can be done with body cavities."

Eddy stared at her. "Can't I have some chocolate and roses first?"

"It's not chocolate and roses with us," Sardelle said sternly. "Don't talk to me about chocolate and roses. We're not lovers. We are client and bodyguard. It's an ugly business, I know. But it's only business."

"Yeah? Well, trading in body cavities is new to me." Deep Eddy rubbed his chin. "As a simple Yankee youngster I find this a little confusing. Maybe we could barter then? Tonight?"

She laughed harshly. "I won't sleep with you, Eddy. I won't sleep at all! You're only being foolish." Sardelle shook her head. Suddenly she lifted a densely braided mass of hair above her right ear. "Look here, Mr. Simple Yankee Youngster. I'll show you my favorite body cavity." There was a fleshcolored plastic duct in the side of her scalp. "It's illegal to have this done in Europe. I had it done in Turkey. This morning I took half a cc through there. I won't sleep until Monday."

"Jesus," Eddy said. He lifted his spex to stare at the small dimpled orifice. "Right through the blood-brain barrier? That must be a hell of an infection risk."

"I don't do it for fun. It's not like beer and pretzels. It's just that I won't sleep now. Not until the Wende is over." She put her hair back, and sat up with a look of composure. "Then I'll fly somewhere and lie in the sun and be very still. All by myself, Eddy."

"Okay," Eddy said, feeling a weird and muddy sort of pity for her. "You can borrow my clothes and search them."

"I have to burn the clothes. Two hundred ecu?"

"All right. But I keep these shoes."

"May I look at your teeth for free? It will only take five minutes."

"Okay," he muttered. She smiled at him, and touched her spex. A bright purple light emerged from the bridge of her nose.

At 08:00 a police drone attempted to clear the park. It flew overhead, barking robotic threats in five languages. Everyone simply ignored the machine.

Around 08:30 an actual line of human police showed up. In response, a group of the squatters brought out their own bullhorn, an enormous battery-powered sonic assault-unit.

The first earthshaking shriek hit Eddy like an electric prod. He'd been lying peacefully on his bubble-mattress, listening to the doltish yap of the robot chopper. Now he leapt quickly from his crash-padding and wormed his way

into the crispy bubblepack cloth of his ridiculous jumpsuit.

Sardelle showed up while he was still tacking the
jumpsuit's Velcro buttons. She led him outside the pavilion.

The squatter bullhorn was up on an iron tripod pedes-
tal, surrounded by a large group of grease-stained anarchists with helmets, earpads, and studded white batons.
Their bullhorn's enormous ululating bellow was reducing
everyone's nerves to jelly. It was like the shriek of Medusa.

The cops retreated, and the owners of the bullhorn
shut it off, waving their glittering batons in triumph. In the
deafened, jittery silence there were scattered shrieks, jeers,
and claps, but the ambience in the park had become very
bad: aggressive and surreal. Attracted by the apocalyptic
shriek, people were milling into the park at a trot, spoiling
for any kind of trouble.

They seemed to have little in common, these people:
not their dress, not language, certainly nothing like a coherent political cause. They were mostly young men, and
most of them looked as if they'd been up all night: red-
eyed and peevish. They taunted the retreating cops. A milling gang knifed one of the smaller pavilions, a scarlet one,
and it collapsed like a blood-blister under their trampling
feet.

Sardelle took Eddy to the edge of the park, where the
cops were herding up a crowd-control barricade-line of
ambulant robotic pink beanbags. "I want to see this," he
protested. His ears were ringing.

"They're going to fight," she told him.

"About what?"

"Anything. Everything," she shouted. "It doesn't matter. They'll knock our teeth out. Don't be stupid." She
took him by the elbow and they slipped through a gap in
the closing battle-line.

The police had brought up a tracked glue-cannon
truck. They now began to threaten the crowd with a past-
ing. Eddy had never seen a glue-cannon before—except on

television. It was quite astonishing how frightening the machine looked, even in pink. It was squat, blind, and nozzled, and sat there buzzing like some kind of wheeled warrior termite.

Suddenly several of the cops standing around the machine began to flinch and duck. Eddy saw a glittering object carom hard off the glue-truck's armored canopy. It flew twenty meters and landed in the grass at his feet. He picked it up. It was a stainless-steel ball-bearing the size of a cow's eyeball.

"Airguns?" he said.

"Slingshots. Don't let one hit you."

"Oh yeah. Great advice, I guess." To the far side of the cops a group of people—some kind of closely organized protestors—were advancing in measured step under a tall two-man banner. It read, in English: *The Only Thing Worse Than Dying Is Outliving Your Culture.* Every man jack of them, and there were at least sixty, carried a long plastic pike topped with an ominous-looking bulbous sponge. It was clear from the way they maneuvered that they understood military pike-tactics only too well; their phalanx bristled like a hedgehog, and some captain among them was barking distant orders. Worse yet, the pikemen had neatly outflanked the cops, who now began calling frantically for backup.

A police drone whizzed just above their heads, not the casual lumbering he had seen before, but direct and angry and inhumanly fast. "Run!" Sardelle shouted, taking his hands. "Peppergas . . ."

Eddy glanced behind him as he fled. The chopper, as if cropdusting, was farting a dense maroon fog. The crowd bellowed in shock and rage and, seconds later, that hellish bullhorn kicked in once more.

Sardelle ran with amazing ease and speed. She bounded along as if firecrackers were bursting under her feet. Eddy, years younger and considerably longer in leg, was very hard put to keep up.

In two minutes they were well out of the park, across

a broad street and into a pedestrian network of small shops and restaurants. There she stopped and let him catch his breath.

"Jesus," he puffed, "where can I buy shoes like that?"

"They're made-to-order," she told him calmly. "And you need special training. You can break your ankles, otherwise. . . ." She gazed at a nearby bakery. "You want some breakfast now?"

Eddy sampled a chocolate-filled pastry inside the shop, at a dainty, doily-covered table. Two ambulances rushed down the street, and a large group of drum-beating protesters swaggered by, shoving shoppers from the pavement; but otherwise things seemed peaceful. Sardelle sat with arms folded, staring into space. He guessed that she was reading security alerts from the insides of her spex.

"You're not tired, are you?" he said.

"I don't sleep on operations," she said, "but sometimes I like to sit very still." She smiled at him. "You wouldn't understand. . . ."

"Hell no I wouldn't," Eddy said, his mouth full. "All hell's breaking loose over there, and here you are sipping orange juice just as calm as a bump on a pickle. . . . Damn, these croissants, or whatever the hell they are, are really good. Hey! *Herr Ober!* Bring me another couple of those, *ja, danke*. . . ."

"The trouble could follow us anywhere. We're as safe here as any other place. Safer, because we're not in the open."

"Good," Eddy nodded, munching. "That park's a bad scene."

"It's not so bad in the park. It's very bad at the Rhein-Spire, though. The Mahogany Warbirds have seized the rotating restaurant. They're stealing skin."

"What are Warbirds?"

She seemed surprised. "You haven't heard of them? They're from NAFTA. A criminal syndicate. Insurance rackets, protection rackets, they run all the casinos in the Quebec Republic. . . ."

"Okay. So what's stealing skin?"

"It's a new kind of swindle; they take a bit of skin or blood, with your genetics, you see, and a year later they tell you they have a newborn son or daughter of yours held captive, held somewhere secret in the South. . . . Then they try to make you pay, and pay, and pay. . . ."

"You mean they're kidnapping genetics from the people in that restaurant?"

"Yes. Brunch in the Rhein-Spire is very prestigious. The victims are all rich or famous." Suddenly she laughed, rather bitter, rather cynical. "I'll be busy next year, Eddy, thanks to this. A new job—protecting my clients' skin."

Eddy thought about it. "It's kind of like the rent-a-womb business, huh? But really twisted."

She nodded. "The Warbirds are crazy, they're not even ethnic criminals, they are network interest-group creatures. . . . Crime is so damned ugly, Eddy. If you ever think of doing it, just stop."

Eddy grunted.

"Think of those children," she murmured. "Born from crime. Manufactured to order, for a criminal purpose. This is a strange world, isn't it? It frightens me sometimes."

"Yeah?" Eddy said cheerfully. "Illegitimate son of a millionaire, raised by a high-tech mafia? Sounds kind of weird and romantic to me. I mean, consider the possibilities."

She took off her spex for the first time, to look at him. Her eyes were blue. A very odd and romantic shade of blue. Probably tinted contacts.

"Rich people have been having illegitimate kids since the year zero," Eddy said. "The only difference is somebody's mechanized the process." He laughed.

"It's time you met the Cultural Critic," she said. She put the spex back on.

•   •   •

They had to walk a long way. The bus system was now defunct. Apparently the soccer fans made a sport of hitting public buses; they would rip all the beanbags out and kick them through the doors. On his way to meet the Critic, Eddy saw hundreds of soccer fans; the city was swarming with them. The English devotees were very bad news: savage, thick-booted, snarling, stamping, chanting, anonymous young men, in knee-length sandpaper coats, with their hair cropped short and their faces masked or war-painted in the Union Jack. The English soccer hooligans traveled in enormous packs of two and three hundred. They were armed with cheap cellular phones. They'd wrapped the aerials with friction tape to form truncheon handles, so that the high-impact ceramic phone-casing became a nasty club. It was impossible to deny a traveler the ownership of a telephone, so the police were impotent to stop this practice. Practically speaking, there was not much to be done in any case. The English hooligans dominated the streets through sheer force of numbers. Anyone seeing them simply fled headlong.

Except, of course, for the Irish soccer fans. The Irish wore thick elbow-length grappling gloves, some kind of workmen's gauntlets apparently, along with long green-and-white football-scarves. Their scarves had skull-denting weights sewn into pockets at their ends, and the tassels were fringed with little skin-ripping wire barbs. The weights were perfectly legitimate rolls of coins, and the wire—well, you could get wire anywhere. The Irish seemed to be outnumbered, but were, if anything, even drunker and more reckless than their rivals. Unlike the English, the Irish louts didn't even use the cellular phones to coordinate their brawling. They just plunged ahead at a dead run, whipping their scarves overhead and screaming about Oliver Cromwell.

The Irish were terrifying. They traveled down streets like a scourge. Anything in their way they knocked over and trampled: knickknack kiosks, propaganda videos, poster-booths, T-shirt tables, people selling canned jumpsuits. Even the postnatal abortion people, who were true fanatics, and the scary, eldritch, black-clad pro-euthanasia groups, would abandon their sidewalk podiums to flee from the Irish kids.

Eddy shuddered to think what the scene must be like at the Rhein-Stadium. "Those are some mean goddamn kids," he told Sardelle, as they emerged from hiding in an alley. "And it's all about *soccer*? Jesus, that seems so pointless."

"If they rioted in their *own* towns, *that* would be pointless," Sardelle said. "Here at the Wende, they can smash each other, and everything else, and tomorrow they will be perfectly safe at home in their own world."

"Oh, I get it," Eddy said. "That makes a lot of sense."

A passing blonde woman in a Muslim hijab slapped a button onto Eddy's sleeve. "Will your lawyer talk to God?" the button demanded aloud, repeatedly, in English. Eddy plucked the device off and stamped on it.

The Cultural Critic was holding court in a safehouse in Stadtmitte. The safehouse was an anonymous twentieth-century four-story dump, flanked by some nicely retrofitted nineteenth-century townhouses. A graffiti gang had hit the block during the night, repainting the street-surface with a sprawling polychrome mural, all big grinning green kitty-cats, fractal spirals, and leaping priapic pink pigs. "Hot Spurt!" one of the pigs suggested eagerly; Eddy skirted its word balloon as they approached the door.

The door bore a small brass plaque reading "E.I.S.—Elektronisches Invasionsabwehr-Systems GmbH." There was an inscribed corporate logo that appeared to be a melting ice-cube.

Sardelle spoke in German to the door video; it opened, and they entered a hall full of pale, drawn adults in suits, armed with fire-extinguishers. Despite their air of nervous resolution and apparent willingness to fight hand-to-hand, Eddy took them for career academics: modestly dressed, ties and scarves slightly askew, odd cheek-tattoos, dis-tracted gazes, too serious. The place smelled bad, like stale cottage-cheese and bookshelf dust. The dirt-smudged walls were festooned with schematics and wiring diagrams, amid a bursting mess of tower-stacked scrawl-labeled cartons—disk archives of some kind. The ceiling and floorboards were festooned with taped-down power-cables and fiber-optic network wiring.

"Hi, everybody!" Eddy said. "How's it going?" The building's defenders looked at him, noted his jumpsuit costume, and reacted with relieved indifference. They began talking in French, obviously resuming some briefly postponed and intensely important discussion.

"Hello," said a German in his thirties, rising to his feet. He had long, thinning, greasy hair and a hollow-cheeked, mushroom-pale face. He wore secretarial half-spex; and behind them he had the shiftiest eyes Eddy had ever seen, eyes that darted, and gloated, and slid around the room. He worked his way through the defenders, and smiled at Eddy, vaguely. "I am your host. Welcome, friend." He extended a hand.

Eddy shook it. He glanced sidelong at Sardelle. Sardelle had gone as stiff as a board and had jammed her gloved hands in her trenchcoat pockets.

"So," Eddy gabbled, snatching his hand back, "thanks a lot for having us over!"

"You'll be wanting to see my famous friend the Cultural Critic," said their host, with a cadaverous smile. "He is upstairs. This is my place. I own it." He gazed around himself, brimming with satisfaction. "It's my Library, you see. I have the honor of hosting the great man for the Wende. He appreciates my work. Unlike so many others." Their host dug into the pocket of his baggy slacks. Eddy, instinctively expecting a drawn knife, was vaguely surprised to see his host hand over an old-fashioned, dog-eared business card. Eddy glanced at it. "How are you, Herr Schreck?"

"Life is very exciting today," said Schreck with a smirk. He touched his spex and examined Eddy's online bio. "A young American visitor. How charming."

"I'm from NAFTA," Eddy corrected.

"And a civil libertarian. Liberty is the only word that still excites me," Schreck said, with itchy urgency. "I need many more American intimates. Do make use of me. And all my digital services. That card of mine—do call those network addresses and tell your friends. The more, the happier." He turned to Sardelle. *"Kaffee, fraulein? Zigaretten?"*

Sardelle shook her head minimally.

"It's good she's here," Schreck told Eddy. "She can help us to fight. You go upstairs. The great man is waiting for visitors."

"I'm going up with him," Sardelle said.

"Stay here," Schreck urged. "The security threat is to the Library, not to him."

"I'm a bodyguard," Sardelle said frostily. "I guard the body. I don't guard data-havens."

Schreck frowned. "Well, more fool you, then."

Sardelle followed Eddy up the dusty, flower-carpeted stairs. Upstairs to the right was an antique twentieth-century office-door in blond oak and frosted glass. Sardelle knocked; someone called out in French.

She opened the door. Inside the office were two long workbenches covered with elderly desktop computers. The windows were barred and curtained.

The Cultural Critic, wearing spex and a pair of datagloves, sat in a bright pool of sunlight-yellow glare from a trackmounted overhead light. He was pecking daintily with his gloved fingertips at a wafer-thin data-screen of woven cloth.

As Sardelle and Eddy stepped into the office, the Critic wrapped up his screen in a scroll, removed his spex, and unplugged his gloves. He had dark pepper-and-salt tousled hair, a dark wool tie, and a long maroon scarf draped over a beautifully cut ivory jacket.

"You would be Mr. Dertouzas from CAPCLUG," he said.

"Exactly. How are you, sir?"

"Very well." He examined Eddy briefly. "I assume his clothing was your idea, Frederika."

Sardelle nodded once, with a sour look. Eddy smiled at her, delighted to learn her real name.

"Have a seat," the Critic offered. He poured himself more coffee. "I'd offer you a cup of this, but it's been . . . adjusted."

"I brought you your book," Eddy said. He sat, and opened the bag, and offered the item in question.

"Splendid." The Critic reached into his pocket and, to Eddy's surprise, pulled a knife. The Critic opened its blade with one thumbnail. The shining blade was sawtoothed in a fractal fashion; even its serrations had tiny serrated serrations. It was a jack-knife the length of a finger, with a razor-sharp edge on it as long as a man's arm.

Under the knife's irresistible ripping caress, the tough cover of the book parted with a discreet shredding of cloth. The Critic reached into the slit and plucked out a thin, gleaming storage disk. He set the book down. "Did you read this?"

"That disk?" Eddy ad-libbed. "I assumed it was encrypted."

"You assumed correctly, but I meant the book."

"I think it lost something in translation," Eddy said.

The Critic raised his brows. He had dark, heavy brows with a pronounced frown-line between them, over sunken, gray-green eyes. "You have read Canetti in the original, Mr. Dertouzas?"

"I meant the translation between centuries," Eddy said, and laughed. "What I read left me with nothing but questions. . . . Can you answer them for me, sir?"

The Critic shrugged and turned to a nearby terminal. It was a scholar's workstation, the least dilapidated of the machines in the office. He touched four keys in order; a carousel whirled and spat out a disk. The Critic handed it to Eddy. "You'll find your answers here, to whatever extent I can give them," he said. "My Complete Works. Please take this disk. Reproduce it, give it to whomever you like, as long as you accredit it. The standard scholarly procedure. I'm sure you know the etiquette."

"Thank you very much," Eddy said with dignity, tucking the disk into his bag. "Of course I own your works already, but I'm glad of a fully up-to-date edition."

"I'm told that a copy of my Complete Works will get you a cup of coffee at any cafe in Europe," the Critic mused, slotting the encrypted disk and rapidly tapping keys. "Apparently digital commodification is not entirely a spent force, even in literature. . . ." He examined the screen. "Oh, this is lovely. I *knew* I would need this data again. And I certainly didn't want it in my house." He smiled.

"What are you going to do with that data?" Eddy said.

"Do you really not know?" the Critic said. "And you from CAPCLUG, a group of such carnivorous curiosity? Well, that's also a strategy, I suppose." He tapped more keys, then leaned back and opened a pack of zigarettes.

"What strategy?"

"New elements, new functions, new solutions—I don't know what 'culture' is, but I know exactly what I'm doing." The Critic drew slowly on a zigarette, his brows knotting.

"And what's that, exactly?"

"You mean, what is the underlying concept?" He waved the zigarette. "I have no 'concept.' The struggle here must not be reduced to a single simple idea. I am building a structure that must not, cannot, be reduced to a single simple idea. I am building a structure that perhaps *suggests* a concept. . . . If I did more, the system itself would become stronger than the surrounding culture. . . . Any system of rational analysis must live within the strong blind body of mass humanity, Mr. Dertouzas. If we learned anything from the twentieth century, we learned that much, at least." The Critic sighed, a fragrant medicinal mist. "I fight windmills, sir. It's a duty. . . . You often are hurt, but at the same time you

become unbelievably happy, because you see that you
have both friends and enemies, and that you are capable of
fertilizing society with contradictory attitudes."

"What enemies do you mean?" Eddy said.

"Here. Today. Another data-burning. It was necessary
to stage a formal resistance."

"This is an evil place," Sardelle—or rather Frederika—burst out. "I had no idea this was today's
safehouse. This is anything but safe. Jean-Arthur, you
must leave this place at once. You could be killed here!"

"An evil place? Certainly. But there is so much
megabytage devoted to works on goodness, and on doing
good—so very little coherent intellectual treatment of the
true nature of evil and being evil. . . . Of malice and stupidity and acts of cruelty and darkness. . . ." The Critic
sighed. "Actually, once you're allowed through the encryption that Herr Schreck so wisely imposes on his hold-
ings, you'll find the data here rather banal. The manuals
for committing crime are farfetched and badly written.
The schematics for bombs, listening devices, drug labs,
and so forth, are poorly designed and probably unwork-
able. The pornography is juvenile and overtly anti-erotic.
The invasions of privacy are of interest only to voyeurs.
Evil is banal—by no means so scarlet as one's instinctive
dread would paint it. It's like the sex-life of one's parents—a primal and forbidden topic, and yet, with objectiv-
ity, basically integral to their human nature—and of
course to your own."

"Who's planning to burn this place?" Eddy said.

"A rival of mine. He calls himself the Moral Referee."

"Oh yeah, I've heard of him!" Eddy said. "He's here
in Düsseldorf, too? Jesus."

"He is a charlatan," the Critic sniffed. "Something of
an ayatollah figure. A popular demagogue. . . ." He
glanced at Eddy. "Yes, yes—of course people do say much
the same of me, Mr. Dertouzas, and I'm perfectly aware of
that. But I have two doctorates, you know. The Referee is

a self-appointed digital Savonarola. Not a scholar at all.
An autodidactic philosopher. At best an artist."

"Aren't you an artist?"

"That's the danger. . . ." The Critic nodded. "Once I
was only a teacher, then suddenly I felt a sense of mission. . . . I began to understand which works are stron-
gest, which are only decorative. . . ." The Critic looked
suddenly restless, and puffed at his zigarette again. "In
Europe there is too much couture, too little culture. In
Europe everything is colored by discourse. There is too
much knowledge and too much fear to overthrow that
knowledge. . . . In NAFTA you are too naïvely
postmodern to suffer from this syndrome. . . . And the
Sphere, the Sphere, they are orthogonal to both our con-
cerns. . . . The South, of course, is the planet's last reser-
voir of authentic humanity, despite every ontological
atrocity committed there. . . ."

"I'm not following you," Eddy said.

"Take that disk with you. Don't lose it," the Critic
said somberly. "I have certain obligations, that's all. I
must know why I made certain choices, and be able to
defend them, and I *must* defend them, or risk losing everything. . . . Those choices are already made. I've drawn a
line here, established a position. It's my Wende today, you
know! My lovely Wende. . . . Through cusp-points like
this one, I can make things different for the whole of society." He smiled. "Not better, necessarily—but different,
certainly. . . ."

"People are coming," Frederika announced suddenly,
standing bolt upright and gesturing at the air. "A lot of
people marching in the streets outside . . . there's going
to be trouble."

"I knew he would react the moment that data left this
building," the Critic said, nodding. "Let trouble come! I
will not move!"

"God damn you, I'm being paid to see that you survive!" Frederika said. "The Referee's people burn data-

havens. They've done it before, and they'll do it again. Let's get out of here while there's still time!"

"We're all ugly and evil," the Critic announced calmly, settling deeply into his chair and steepling his fingers. "Bad knowledge is still legitimate self-knowledge. Don't pretend otherwise."

"That's no reason to fight them hand-to-hand here in Düsseldorf! We're not tactically prepared to defend this building! Let them burn it! What's one more stupid outlaw and his rat nest full of garbage?"

The Critic looked at her with pity. "It's not the access that matters. It's the principle."

"Bullseye!" Eddy shouted, recognizing a CAPCLUG slogan.

Frederika, biting her lip, leaned over a tabletop and began typing invisibly on a virtual keyboard. "If you call your professional backup," the Critic told her, "they'll only be hurt. This is not really your fight, my dear; you're not committed."

"Fuck you and your politics; if you burn up in here we don't get our bonuses," Frederika shouted.

"No reason *he* should stay, at least," the Critic said, gesturing to Eddy. "You've done well, Mr. Dertouzas. Thank you very much for your successful errand. It was most helpful." The Critic glanced at the workstation screen, where a program from the disk was still spooling busily, then back at Eddy again. "I suggest you leave this place while you can."

Eddy glanced at Frederika.

"Yes, go!" she said. "You're finished here, I'm not your escort anymore. Run, Eddy!"

"No way," Eddy said, folding his arms. "If you're not moving, I'm not moving."

Frederika looked furious. "But you're free to go. You heard him say so."

"So what? Since I'm at liberty, I'm also free to stay," Eddy retorted. "Besides, I'm from Tennessee, NAFTA's Volunteer State."

"There are hundreds of enemies coming," Frederika said, staring into space. "They will overwhelm us and burn this place to the ground. There will be nothing left of both of you and your rotten data but ashes."

"Have faith," the Critic said coolly. "Help will come, as well—from some unlikely quarters. Believe me, I'm doing my very best to maximize the implications of this event. So is my rival, if it comes to that. Thanks to that disk that just arrived, I am wirecasting events here to four hundred of the most volatile network sites in Europe. Yes, the Referee's people may destroy us, but their chances of escaping the consequences are very slim. And if we ourselves die here in flames, it will only lend deeper meaning to our sacrifice."

Eddy gazed at the Critic in honest admiration. "I don't understand a single goddamn word you're saying, but I guess I can recognize a fellow spirit when I meet one. I'm sure CAPCLUG would want me to stay."

"CAPCLUG would want no such thing," the Critic told him soberly. "They would want you to escape, so that they could examine and dissect your experiences in detail. Your American friends are sadly infatuated with the supposed potency of rational, panoptic, digital analysis. Believe me, please—the enormous turbulence in postmodern society is far larger than any single human mind can comprehend, with or without computer-aided perception or the finest computer-assisted frameworks of sociological analysis." The Critic gazed at his workstation, like a herpetologist studying a cobra. "Your CAPCLUG friends will go to their graves never realizing that every vital impulse in human life is entirely pre-rational."

"Well, I'm certainly not leaving here before I figure *that* out," Eddy said. "I plan to help you fight the good fight, sir."

The Critic shrugged, and smiled. "Thank you for just proving me right, young man. Of course a young American hero is welcome to die in Europe's political struggles. I'd hate to break an old tradition."

Glass shattered. A steaming lump of dry ice flew through the window, skittered across the office floor, and began gently dissolving. Acting entirely on instinct, Eddy dashed forward, grabbed it barehanded, and threw it back out the window.

"Are you okay?" Frederika said.

"Sure," Eddy said, surprised.

"That was a chemical gas bomb," Frederika said. She gazed at him as if expecting him to drop dead on the spot.

"Apparently the chemical frozen into the ice was not very toxic," the Critic surmised.

"I don't think it was a gas bomb at all," Eddy said, gazing out the window. "I think it was just a big chunk of dry ice. You Europeans are completely paranoid."

He saw with astonishment that there was a medieval pageant taking place in the street. The followers of the Moral Referee—there were some three or four hundred of them, well organized and marching forward in grimly disciplined silence—apparently had a weakness for medieval jerkins, fringed capes, and colored hose. And torches. They were very big on torches.

The entire building shuddered suddenly, and a burglar siren went off. Eddy craned to look. Half a dozen men were battering the door with a handheld hydraulic ram. They wore visored helmets and metal armor, which gleamed in the summer daylight. "We're being attacked by goddamn knights in shining armor," Eddy said. "I can't believe they're doing this in broad daylight!"

"The football game just started," Frederika said. "They have picked the perfect moment. Now they can get away with anything."

"Do these window-bars come out?" Eddy said, shaking them.

"No. Thank goodness."

"Then hand me some of those data-disks," he demanded. "No, not those shrimpy ones—give me the full thirty-centimeter jobs."

He threw the window up and began pelting the crowd

below with flung megabytage. The disks had vicious aero-
dynamics and were hefty and sharp-edged. He was re-
warded with a vicious barrage of bricks, which shattered
windows all along the second and third floors.

"They're very angry now," Frederika shouted over the
wailing alarm and roar of the crowd below. The three of
them crouched under a table.

"Yeah," Eddy said. His blood was boiling. He picked
up a long, narrow printer, dashed across the room, and
launched it between the bars. In reply, half a dozen long
metal darts—short javelins, really—flew up through the
window and embedded themselves in the office ceiling.

"How'd they get those through Customs?" Eddy
shouted. "Must've made them last night." He laughed.
"Should I throw 'em back? I can fetch them if I stand on a
chair."

"Don't, don't," Frederika shouted. "Control yourself!
Don't kill anyone, it's not professional."

"I'm not professional," Eddy said.

"Get down here," Frederika commanded. When he
refused, she scrambled from beneath the table and body-
slammed him against the wall. She pinned Eddy's arms,
flung herself across him with almost erotic intensity, and
hissed into his ear. "Save yourself while you can! This is
only a Wende."

"Stop that," Eddy shouted, trying to break her grip.
More bricks came through the window, tumbling past
their feet.

"If they kill these worthless intellectuals," she muttered hotly, "there will be a thousand more to take their
place. But if you don't leave this building right now, you'll
die here."

"Christ, I know that," Eddy shouted, finally flinging
her backward with a rasp at her sandpaper coat. "Quit
being such a loser."

"Eddy, listen!" Frederika yelled, knotting her gloved
fists. "Let me save your life! You'll owe me later! Go home
to your parents in America, and don't worry about the

Wende. This is all we ever do—it's all we are really good for."

"Hey, I'm good at this, too!" Eddy announced. A brick barked his ankle. In sudden convulsive fury, he up-ended a table and slammed it against a broken window, as a shield. As bricks thudded against the far side of the table, he shouted defiance. He felt superhuman. Her attempt to talk sense had irritated him enormously.

The door broke in downstairs, with a concussive blast. Screams echoed up the stairs. "That's torn it!" Eddy said.

He snatched up a multiplugged power outlet, dashed across the room, and kicked the office door open. With a shout, he jumped onto the landing, swinging the heavy power-strip over his head.

The Critic's academic cadre were no physical match for the Referee's knights-in-armor; but their fire extinguishers were surprisingly effective weapons. They coated everything in white caustic soda and filled the air with great blinding, billowing wads of flying, freezing droplets. It was clear that the defenders had been practicing.

The sight of the desperate struggle downstairs overwhelmed Eddy. He jumped down the stairs three at a time and flung himself into the midst of the battle. He conked a soda-covered helmet with a vicious overhead swing of his power-strip, then slipped and fell heavily on his back.

He began wrestling desperately across the soda-slick floor with a half-blinded knight. The knight clawed his visor up. Beneath the metal mask the knight was, if anything, younger than himself. He looked like a nice kid. He clearly meant well. Eddy hit the kid in the jaw as hard as he could, then began slamming his helmeted head into the floor.

Another knight kicked Eddy in the belly. Eddy fell off his victim, got up, and went for the new attacker. The two of them, wrestling clumsily, were knocked off balance by a sudden concerted rush through the doorway; a dozen Moral raiders slammed through, flinging torches and bottles of flaming gel. Eddy slapped his new opponent across the eyes with his soda-daubed hand, then lurched to his feet and jammed the loose spex back onto his face. He began coughing violently. The air was full of smoke; he was smothering.

He lurched for the door. With the panic strength of a drowning man, he clawed and jostled his way free.

Once outside the data-haven, Eddy realized that he was one of dozens of people daubed head to foot with white foam. Wheezing, coughing, collapsing against the side of the building, he and his fellow refugees resembled veterans of a monster cream-pie fight.

They didn't, and couldn't, recognize him as an enemy. The caustic soda was eating its way into Eddy's cheap jumpsuit, reducing the bubbled fabric to weeping red rags.

Wiping his lips, ribs heaving, Eddy looked around. The spex had guarded his eyes, but their filth subroutine had crashed badly. The internal screen was frozen. Eddy shook the spex with his foamy hands, fingersnapped at them, whistled aloud. Nothing.

He edged his way along the wall.

At the back of the crowd, a tall gentleman in a medieval episcopal mitre was shouting orders through a bullhorn. Eddy wandered through the crowd until he got closer to the man. He was a tall, lean man, in his late forties, in brocaded vestments, a golden cloak, and white gloves.

This was the Moral Referee. Eddy considered jumping this distinguished gentleman and pummeling him, perhaps wrestling his bullhorn away and shouting contradictory orders through it.

But even if he dared to try this, it wouldn't do Eddy much good. The Referee with the bullhorn was shouting in German. Eddy didn't speak German. Without his spex he couldn't read German. He didn't understand Germans or their issues or their history. In point of fact he had no real reason at all to be in Germany.

The Moral Referee noticed Eddy's fixed and calculating gaze. He lowered his bullhorn, leaned down a little from the top of his portable mahogany pulpit, and said something to Eddy in German.

"Sorry," Eddy said, lifting his spex on their neck chain. "Translation program crashed."

The Referee examined him thoughtfully. "Has the acid in that foam damaged your spectacles?" he said, in excellent English.

"Yes sir," Eddy said. "I think I'll have to strip 'em and blow-dry the chips."

The Referee reached within his robe and handed Eddy a monogrammed linen kerchief. "You might try this, young man."

"Thanks a lot," Eddy said. "I appreciate that, really."

"Are you wounded?" the Referee said, with apparently genuine concern.

"No, sir. I mean, not really."

"Then you'd better return to the fight," the Referee said, straightening. "I know we have them on the run. Be of good cheer. Our cause is just." He lifted his bullhorn again and resumed shouting.

The first floor of the building had caught fire. Groups of the Referee's people were hauling linked machines into the street and smashing them to fragments on the pavement. They hadn't managed to knock the bars from the windows, but they had battered some enormous holes through the walls. Eddy watched, polishing his spex.

Well above the street, the wall of the third floor began to disintegrate.

Moral Knights had broken into the office where Eddy had last seen the Cultural Critic. They had hauled their hydraulic ram up the stairs with them. Now its blunt nose was smashing through the brick wall as if it were stale cheese.

Fist-sized chunks of rubble and mortar cascaded to the street, causing the raiders below to billow away. In seconds, the raiders on the third floor had knocked a hole in the wall the size of a manhole cover. First, they flung down an emergency ladder. Then, office furniture began tumbling out to smash to the pavement below: voice mail-boxes, canisters of storage disks, red-spined European law-books, network routers, tape backup-units, color monitors. . . .

A trenchcoat flew out the hole and pinwheeled slowly to earth. Eddy recognized it at once. It was Frederika's sandpaper coat. Even in the midst of shouting chaos, with an evil billowing of combusting plastic now belching from the library's windows, the sight of that fluttering coat hooked Eddy's awareness. There was something in that coat. In its sleeve pocket. The key to his airport locker.

Eddy dashed forward, shoved three knights aside, and grabbed up the coat for himself. He winced and skipped aside as a plummeting office chair smashed to the street, narrowly missing him. He glanced up frantically.

He was just in time to see them throw out Frederika.

The tide was leaving Düsseldorf, and with it all the school-ing anchovies of Europe. Eddy sat in the departure lounge balancing eighteen separate pieces of his spex on a Velcro lap-table.

"Do you need this?" Frederika asked him.

"Oh yeah," Eddy said, accepting the slim chromed tool. "I dropped my dental pick. Thanks a lot." He placed it carefully into his black travel bag. He'd just spent all his European cash on a deluxe, duty-free German electronics repair kit.

"I'm not going to Chattanooga, now or ever," Frederika told him. "So you might as well forget that. That can't be part of the bargain."

"Change your mind," Eddy suggested. "Forget this Barcelona flight, and come transatlantic with me. We'll have a fine time in Chattanooga. There's some very deep people I want you to meet."

"I don't want anybody to meet," Frederika muttered darkly. "And I don't want you to show me off to your little hackerboy friends."

Frederika had taken a hard beating in the riot, while covering the Critic's successful retreat across the rooftop. Her hair had been scorched during the battle, and it had burst from its meticulous braiding like badly overused steel wool. She had a black eye, and her cheek and jaw were scorched and shiny with medicinal gel. Although Eddy had broken her fall, her three-story tumble to the street had sprained her ankle, wrenched her back, and barked both knees.

And she had lost her spex.

"You look just fine," Eddy told her. "You're very interesting, that's the point. You're deep! That's the appeal, you see? You're a spook, and a European, and a woman—those are all very deep entities, in my opinion." He smiled.

Eddy's left elbow felt hot and swollen inside his spare shirt; his chest, ribs, and left leg were mottled with enormous bruises. He had a bloodied lump on the back of his head where he'd smashed down into the rubble, catching her.

Altogether, they were not an entirely unusual couple among the departing Wende folk cramming the Düsseldorf airport. As a whole, the crowd seemed to be suffering a massive collective hangover—harsh enough to put many of them into slings and casts. And yet it was amazing how contented, almost smug, many of the vast crowd seemed as they departed their pocket catastrophe. They were wan and pale, yet cheerful, like people recovering from flu.

"I don't feel well enough to be deep," Frederika said, stirring in her beanbag. "But you did save my life, Eddy. I do owe you something." She paused. "It has to be something reasonable."

"Don't worry about it," Eddy told her nobly, rasping at the surface of a tiny circuit-board with a plastic spudger. "I mean, I didn't even break your fall, strictly speaking. Mostly I just kept you from landing on your head."

"You did save my life," she repeated quietly. "That crowd would have killed me in the street if not for you."

"You saved the Critic's life. I imagine that's a bigger deal."

"I was paid to save his life," Frederika said. "Anyway, I didn't save the bastard. I just did my job. He was saved by his own cleverness. He's been through a dozen of these damned things." She stretched cautiously, shifting in her beanbag. "So have I, for that matter. . . . I must be a real fool. I endure a lot to live my precious life. . . ." She took a deep breath. "Barcelona, *yo te quiero.*"

"I'm just glad we checked out of that clinic in time to catch our flights," Eddy told her, examining his work with a jeweler's loupe. "Could you believe all those soccer kids in there? They sure were having fun. . . . Why couldn't they be that good-tempered *before* they beat the hell out of each other? Some things are just a mystery, I guess."

"I hope you have learned a good lesson from this," Frederika said.

"Sure have," Eddy nodded. He blew dried crud from the point of his spudger, then picked up a chrome pinch-clamp and threaded a tiny screw through the earpiece of his spex. "I can see a lot of deep potential in the Wende. It's true that a few dozen people got killed here, but the city must have made an absolute fortune. That's got to look promising for the Chattanooga city council. And a Wende offers a lot of very useful exposure and influence for a cultural networking group like CAPCLUG."

"You've learned nothing at all," she groaned. "I don't know why I hoped it would be different."

"I admit it—in the heat of the action I got a little carried away," Eddy said. "But my only real regret is that you won't come with me to America. Or, if you'd really rather, take me to Barcelona. Either way, the way I see it you need someone to look after you for a while."

"You're going to rub my sore feet, yes?" Frederika said sourly. "How generous you are."

"I dumped my creep girlfriend. My dad will pick up my tab. I can help you manage better. I can improve your life. I can fix your broken appliances. I'm a nice guy."

"I don't want to be rude," she said, "but after this, the thought of being touched is repulsive." She shook her head, with finality. "I'm sorry, Eddy, but I can't give you what you want."

Eddy sighed, examined the crowd for a while, then repacked the segments of his spex and closed his tool kit. At last he spoke up again. "Do you virch?"

"What?"

"Do you do virtuality?"

She was silent for a long moment, then looked him in the eye. "You don't do anything really strange or sick on the wires, do you, Edward?"

"There's hardly any subjective time-lag if you use high-capacity transatlantic fiber," Eddy said.

"Oh. I see."

"What have you got to lose? If you don't like it, hang up."

Frederika tucked her hair back, examined the departure board for the flight to Barcelona, and looked at the toes of her shoes. "Would this make you happy?"

"No," Eddy said. "But it'd make me a whole lot more of what I already am."

BICYCLE REPAIRMAN

Repeated tinny banging woke Lyle in his hammock. Lyle groaned, sat up, and slid free into the tool-crowded aisle of his bike shop.

Lyle hitched up the black elastic of his skintight shorts and plucked yesterday's grease-stained sleeveless off the workbench. He glanced blearily at his chronometer as he picked his way toward the door. It was 10:04.38 in the morning, June 27, 2037.

Lyle hopped over a stray can of primer and the floor boomed gently beneath his feet. With all the press of work, he'd collapsed into sleep without properly cleaning the shop. Doing custom enameling paid okay, but it ate up time like crazy. Working and living alone was wearing him out.

Lyle opened the shop door, revealing a long sheer drop to dusty tiling far below. Pigeons darted beneath the hull of his shop through a soot-stained hole in the broken atrium glass, and wheeled off to their rookery somewhere in the darkened guts of the high-rise.

More banging. Far below, a uniformed delivery kid stood by his cargo tricycle, yanking rhythmically at the long dangling string of Lyle's spot-welded doorknocker.

Lyle waved, yawning. From his vantage point below the huge girders of the cavernous atrium, Lyle had a fine overview of three burnt-out interior levels of the old Tsatanuga Archiplat. Once-elegant handrails and battered pedestrian overlooks fronted on the great airy cavity of the atrium. Behind the handrails was a three-floor wilderness of jury-rigged lights, chicken coops, water tanks, and squatters' flags. The fire-damaged floors, walls, and ceilings were riddled with handmade descent-chutes, long coiling staircases, and rickety ladders.

Lyle took note of a crew of Chattanooga demolition workers in their yellow detox suits. The repair crew was deploying vacuum scrubbers and a high-pressure hose, off by the vandal-proofed western elevators of Floor Thirty-four. Two or three days a week, the city crew meandered into the damage zone to pretend to work, with a great hypocritical show of sawhorses and barrier tape. The lazy sons of bitches were all on the take.

Lyle thumbed the brake switches in their big metal box by the flywheel. The bike shop slithered, with a subtle hiss of cable-clamps, down three stories, to dock with a grating crunch onto four concrete-filled metal drums.

The delivery kid looked real familiar. He was in and out of the zone pretty often. Lyle had once done some custom work on the kid's cargo trike, new shocks and some granny-gearing as he recalled, but he couldn't remember the kid's name. Lyle was terrible with names. "What's up, zude?"

"Hard night, Lyle?"

"Just real busy."

The kid's nose wrinkled at the stench from the shop. "Doin' a lot of paint work, huh?" He glanced at his palmtop notepad. "You still taking deliveries for Edward Dertouzas?"

"Yeah. I guess so." Lyle rubbed the gear tattoo on one stubbled cheek. "If I have to."

The kid offered a stylus, reaching up. "Can you sign for him?"

Lyle folded his bare arms warily. "Naw, man, I can't sign for Deep Eddy. Eddy's in Europe somewhere. Eddy left months ago. Haven't seen Eddy in ages."

The delivery kid scratched his sweating head below his billed fabric cap. He turned to check for any possible sneak-ups by snatch-and-grab artists out of the squatter warrens. The government simply refused to do postal delivery on the Thirty-second, Thirty-third, and Thirty-fourth floors. You never saw many cops inside the zone, either. Except for the city demolition crew, about the only official functionaries who ever showed up in the zone were a few psychotically empathetic NAFTA social workers.

"I'll get a bonus if you sign for this thing." The kid gazed up in squint-eyed appeal. "It's gotta be worth something, Lyle. It's a really weird kind of routing; they paid a lot of money to send it just that way."

Lyle crouched down in the open doorway. "Let's have a look at it."

The package was a heavy shockproof rectangle in heat-sealed plastic shrinkwrap, with a plethora of intra-European routing stickers. To judge by all the overlays, the package had been passed from postal system to postal system at least eight times before officially arriving in the legal custody of any human being. The return address, if there had ever been one, was completely obscured. Someplace in France, maybe.

Lyle held the box up two-handed to his ear and shook it. Hardware.

"You gonna sign, or not?"

"Yeah." Lyle scratched illegibly at the little signature panel, then looked at the delivery trike. "You oughta get that front wheel trued."

The kid shrugged. "Got anything to send out today?"

"Naw," Lyle grumbled, "I'm not doing mail-order repair work anymore; it's too complicated and I get ripped off too much."

"Suit yourself." The kid clambered into the recumbent

seat of his trike and pedaled off across the heat-cracked ceramic tiles of the atrium plaza.

Lyle hung his hand-lettered OPEN FOR BUSINESS sign outside the door. He walked to his left, stamped up the pedaled lid of a jumbo garbage can, and dropped the package in with the rest of Dertouzas's stuff.

The can's lid wouldn't close. Deep Eddy's junk had finally reached critical mass. Deep Eddy never got much mail at the shop from other people, but he was always sending mail to himself. Big packets of encrypted diskettes were always arriving from Eddy's road jaunts in Toulouse, Marseilles, Valencia, and Nice. And especially Barcelona. Eddy had sent enough gigabyteage out of Barcelona to outfit a pirate data-haven.

Eddy used Lyle's bike shop as his safety-deposit box. This arrangement was okay by Lyle. He owed Eddy; Eddy had installed the phones and virching in the bike shop, and had also wangled the shop's electrical hookup. A thick elastic curly-cable snaked out the access crawlspace of Floor Thirty-five, right through the ceiling of Floor Thirty-four, and directly through a ragged punch-hole in the aluminum roof of Lyle's cable-mounted mobile home. Some unknown contact of Eddy's was paying the real bills on that electrical feed. Lyle cheerfully covered the expenses by paying cash into an anonymous post-office box. The setup was a rare and valuable contact with the world of organized authority.

During his stays in the shop, Eddy had spent much of his time buried in marathon long-distance virtuality sessions, swaddled head to foot in lumpy strap-on gear. Eddy had been painfully involved with some older woman in Germany. A virtual romance in its full-scale thumping, heaving, grappling progress, was an embarrassment to witness. Under the circumstances, Lyle wasn't too surprised that Eddy had left his parents' condo to set up in a squat.

Eddy had lived in the bicycle-repair shop, off and on, for almost a year. It had been a good deal for Lyle, because

Deep Eddy had enjoyed a certain clout and prestige with the local squatters. Eddy had been a major organizer of the legendary Chattanooga Wende of December '35, a monster street party that had climaxed in a spectacular looting-and-arson rampage that had torched the three floors of the Archiplat.

Lyle had gone to school with Eddy and had known him for years; they'd grown up together in the Archiplat. Eddy Dertouzas was a deep zude for a kid his age, with political contacts and heavy-duty network connections. The squat had been a good deal for both of them, until Eddy had finally coaxed the German woman into coming through for him in real life. Then Eddy had jumped the next plane to Europe.

Since they'd parted friends, Eddy was welcome to mail his European data-junk to the bike shop. After all, the disks were heavily encrypted, so it wasn't as if anybody in authority was ever gonna be able to read them. Storing a few thousand disks was a minor challenge, compared to Eddy's complex, machine-assisted love life.

After Eddy's sudden departure, Lyle had sold Eddy's possessions, and wired the money to Eddy in Spain. Lyle had kept the screen TV, Eddy's mediator, and the cheaper virching helmet. The way Lyle figured it—the way he remembered the deal—any stray hardware of Eddy's in the shop was rightfully his, for disposal at his own discretion. By now it was pretty clear that Deep Eddy Dertouzas was never coming back to Tennessee. And Lyle had certain debts.

Lyle snicked the blade from a roadkit multitool and cut open Eddy's package. It contained, of all things, a television cable set-top box. A laughable infobahn antique. You'd never see a cable box like that in NAFTA; this was the sort of primeval junk one might find in the home of a semiliterate Basque grandmother, or maybe in the armed bunker of some backward Albanian.

Lyle tossed the archaic cable box onto the beanbag in front of the wallscreen. No time now for irrelevant media

toys; he had to get on with real life. Lyle ducked into the
tiny curtained privy and urinated at length into a crockery
jar. He scraped his teeth with a flossing spudger and
misted some fresh water onto his face and hands. He
wiped clean with a towelette, then smeared his armpits,
crotch, and feet with deodorant.

Back when he'd lived with his mom up on Floor
Forty-one, Lyle had used old-fashioned antiseptic deodor-
ants. Lyle had wised up about a lot of things once he'd
escaped his mom's condo. Nowadays, Lyle used a gel roll-
on of skin-friendly bacteria that greedily devoured human
sweat and exuded as their metabolic by-product a pleas-
antly harmless reek rather like ripe bananas. Life was a lot
easier when you came to proper terms with your micro-
scopic flora.

Back at his workbench, Lyle plugged in the hot plate
and boiled some Thai noodles with flaked sardines. He
packed down breakfast with four hundred cc's of Dr.
Breasaire's Bioactive Bowel Putty. Then he checked last
night's enamel job on the clamped frame in the workstand.
The frame looked good. At three in the morning, Lyle was
able to get into painted detail work with just the right kind
of hallucinatory clarity.

Enameling paid well, and he needed the money bad.
But this wasn't real bike work. It lacked authenticity. Enameling was all about the owner's ego—that was what
really stank about enameling. There were a few rich kids
up in the penthouse levels who were way into "street aesthetic," and would pay good money to have some
treadhead decorate their machine. But flash art didn't help
the bike. What helped the bike was frame alignment and
sound cable-housings and proper tension in the derail-
leurs.

Lyle fitted the chain of his stationary bike to the shop's
flywheel, straddled up, strapped on his gloves and virching
helmet, and did half an hour on the 2033 Tour de France.
He stayed back in the pack for the uphill grind, and then,
for three glorious minutes, he broke free from the *domesti-*

ques in the *peloton* and came right up at the shoulder of
Aldo Cipollini. The champion was a monster, posthuman.
Calves like cinder blocks. Even in a cheap simulation with
no full-impact bodysuit, Lyle knew better than to try to
take Cipollini.

Lyle devirched, checked his heart-rate record on the
chronometer, then dismounted from his stationary trainer
and drained a half-liter squeeze bottle of antioxidant
carbo refresher. Life had been easier when he'd had a partner in crime. The shop's flywheel was slowly losing its
storage of inertia power these days, with just one zude
pumping it.

Lyle's disastrous second roommate had come from the
biking crowd. She was a criterium racer from Kentucky
named Brigitte Rohannon. Lyle himself had been a wan-
nabe criterium racer for a while, before he'd blown out a
kidney on steroids. He hadn't expected any trouble from
Brigitte, because Brigitte knew about bikes, and she
needed his technical help for her racer, and she wouldn't
mind pumping the flywheel, and besides, Brigitte was les-
bian. In the training gym and out at racing events, Brigitte
came across as a quiet and disciplined little politicized
tread-head person.

Life inside the zone, though, massively fertilized Brigitte's eccentricities. First, she started breaking training.
Then she stopped eating right. Pretty soon the shop was
creaking and rocking with all-night girl-on-girl hot-oil sessions, which degenerated into hooting pill-orgies with
heavily tattooed zone chyx who played klaxonized bongo
music, and beat each other up, and stole Lyle's tools. It
had been a big relief when Brigitte finally left the zone to
shack up with some well-to-do admirer on Floor Thirty-
seven. The debacle had left Lyle's tenuous finances in ruin.

Lyle laid down a new tracery of scarlet enamel on the
bike's chainstay, seat post, and stem. He had to wait for
the work to cure, so he left the workbench, picked up
Eddy's set-topper, and popped the shell with a hexkey.
Lyle was no electrician, but the insides looked harmless

enough: lots of bit-eating caterpillars and cheap Algerian silicon.

He flicked on Eddy's mediator, to boot the wallscreen. Before he could try anything with the cable box, his mother's mook pounced upon the screen. On Eddy's giant wallscreen, the mook's waxy, computer-generated face looked like a plump satin pillowcase. Its bow-tie was as big as a racing shoe.

"Please hold for an incoming vidcall from Andrea Schweik of Carnac Instruments," the mook uttered unctuously.

Lyle cordially despised all low-down, phone-tagging, artificially intelligent mooks. For a while, in his teenage years, Lyle himself had owned a mook, an off-the-shelf shareware job that he'd installed in the condo's phone. Like most mooks, Lyle's mook had one primary role: dealing with unsolicited phone calls from other people's mooks. In Lyle's case these were the creepy mooks of career counselors, school psychiatrists, truancy cops, and other official hindrances. When Lyle's mook launched and ran, it appeared online as a sly warty dwarf that drooled green ichor and talked in a basso grumble.

But Lyle hadn't given his mook the properly meticulous care and debugging that such fragile little constructs demanded, and eventually his cheap mook had collapsed into artificial insanity.

Once Lyle had escaped his mom's place to the squat, he had gone for the low-tech gambit and simply left his phone unplugged most of the time. But that was no real solution. He couldn't hide from his mother's capable and well-financed corporate mook, which watched with sleepless mechanical patience for the least flicker of video dial tone off Lyle's number.

Lyle sighed and wiped the dust from the video nozzle on Eddy's mediator.

"Your mother is coming online right away," the mook assured him.

"Yeah, sure," Lyle muttered, smearing his hair into some semblance of order.

"She specifically instructed me to page her remotely at any time for an immediate response. She really wants to chat with you, Lyle."

"That's just great." Lyle couldn't remember what his mother's mook called itself. "Mr. Billy," or "Mr. Ripley," or something else really stupid. . . .

"Did you know that Marco Cengialta has just won the Liege Summer Classic?"

Lyle blinked and sat up in the beanbag. "Yeah?"

"Mr. Cengialta used a three-spoked ceramic wheel with internal liquid weighting and buckyball hubshocks." The mook paused, politely awaiting a possible conversational response. "He wore breathe-thru Kevlar microlock cleatshoes," it added.

Lyle hated the way a mook cataloged your personal interests and then generated relevant conversation. The machine-made intercourse was completely unhuman and yet perversely interesting, like being grabbed and buttonholed by a glossy magazine ad. It had probably taken his mother's mook all of three seconds to snag and download every conceivable statistic about the summer race in Liege.

His mother came on. She'd caught him during lunch in her office. "Lyle?"

"Hi, Mom." Lyle sternly reminded himself that this was the one person in the world who might conceivably put up bail for him. "What's on your mind?"

"Oh, nothing much, just the usual." Lyle's mother shoved aside her platter of sprouts and tilapia. "I was idly wondering if you were still alive."

"Mom, it's a lot less dangerous in a squat than landlords and cops would have you believe. I'm perfectly fine. You can see that for yourself."

His mother lifted a pair of secretarial half-spex on a neckchain, and gave Lyle the computer-assisted once-over.

Lyle pointed the mediator's lens at the shop's aluminum door. "See over there, Mom? I got myself a shock-

baton in here. If I get any trouble from anybody, I'll just
yank that club off the door mount and give the guy fifteen
thousand volts!"

"Is that legal, Lyle?"

"Sure. The voltage won't kill you or anything, it just
knocks you out a good long time. I traded a good bike for
that shock-baton, it's got a lot of useful defensive features."

"That sounds really dreadful."

"The baton's harmless, Mom. You should see what
the cops carry nowadays."

"Are you still taking those injections, Lyle?"

"Which injections?"

She frowned. "You know which ones."

Lyle shrugged. "The treatments are perfectly safe.
They're a lot safer than a lifestyle of cruising for dates,
that's for sure."

"Especially dates with the kind of girls who live down
there in the riot zone, I suppose." His mother winced. "I
had some hopes when you took up with that nice bike-
racer girl. Brigitte, wasn't it? Whatever happened to her?"

Lyle shook his head. "Someone with your gender and
background oughta understand how important the treatments are, Mom. It's a basic reproductive-freedom issue.
Antilibidinals give you real freedom, freedom from the
urge to reproduce. You should be glad I'm not sexually
involved."

"I don't mind that you're not involved, Lyle, it's just
that it seems like a real cheat that you're not even *interested*."

"But, Mom, nobody's interested in me, either. Nobody. No woman is banging at my door to have sex with a
self-employed fanatical dropout bike mechanic who lives
in a slum. If that ever happens, you'll be the first to
know."

Lyle grinned cheerfully into the lens. "I had girlfriends
back when I was in racing. I've been there, Mom. I've
done that. Unless you're coked to the gills with hormones,

sex is a major waste of your time and attention. Sexual Deliberation is the greatest civil-liberties movement of modern times."

"That's really weird, Lyle. It's just not natural."

"Mom, forgive me, but you're not the one to talk about natural, okay? You grew me from a zygote when you were fifty-five." He shrugged. "I'm too busy for romance now. I just want to learn about bikes."

"You were working with bikes when you lived here with me. You had a real job and a safe home where you could take regular showers."

"Sure, I was working, but I never said I wanted a *job*, Mom. I said I wanted to *learn about bikes*. There's a big difference! I can't be a loser wage-slave for some lousy bike franchise."

His mother said nothing.

"Mom, I'm not asking you for any favors. I don't need any bosses, or any teachers, or any landlords, or any cops. It's just me and my bike work down here. I know that people in authority can't stand it that a twenty-four-year-old man lives an independent life and does exactly what he wants, but I'm being very quiet and discreet about it, so nobody needs to bother about me."

His mother sighed, defeated. "Are you eating properly, Lyle? You look peaked."

Lyle lifted his calf muscle into camera range. "Look at this leg! Does that look like the gastrocnemius of a weak and sickly person?"

"Could you come up to the condo and have a decent meal with me sometime?"

Lyle blinked. "When?"

"Wednesday, maybe? We could have pork chops."

"Maybe, Mom. Probably. I'll have to check. I'll get back to you, okay? Bye." Lyle hung up.

Hooking the mediator's cable to the primitive set-top box was a problem, but Lyle was not one to be stymied by a merely mechanical challenge. The enamel job had to wait as he resorted to miniclamps and a cable cutter. It was a handy thing that working with modern brake cabling had taught him how to splice fiber optics.

When the set-top box finally came online, its array of services was a joke. Any decent modern mediator could navigate through vast information spaces, but the set-top box offered nothing but "channels." Lyle had forgotten that you could even obtain old-fashioned "channels" from the city fiber-feed in Chattanooga. But these channels were government-sponsored media, and the government was always quite a ways behind the curve in network development. Chattanooga's huge fiber-bandwidth still carried the ancient government-mandated "public-access channels," spooling away in their technically fossilized obscurity, far below the usual gaudy carnival of popular virching, infobahnage, demo-splintered comboards, public-service rants, mudtrufflage, remsnorkeling, and commercials.

The little set-top box accessed nothing but political channels. Three of them: Legislative, Judicial, and Executive. And that was the sum total, apparently. A set-top box that offered nothing but NAFTA political coverage. On the Legislative Channel there was some kind of parliamentary debate on proper land use in Manitoba. On the Judicial Channel, a lawyer was haranguing judges about the stock market for air-pollution rights. On the Executive Channel, a big crowd of hicks was idly standing around on windblown tarmac somewhere in Louisiana waiting for something to happen.

The box didn't offer any glimpse of politics in Europe or the Sphere or the South. There were no hotspots or pips or index tagging. You couldn't look stuff up or annotate it—you just had to passively watch whatever the channel's masters chose to show you, whenever they chose to show it. This media setup was so insultingly lame and halt and primitive that it was almost perversely interesting. Kind of like peering through keyholes.

Lyle left the box on the Executive Channel, because it looked conceivable that something might actually happen there. It had swiftly become clear to him that the intolerably monotonous fodder on the other two channels was about as exciting as those channels ever got. Lyle retreated to his workbench and got back to enamel work.

At length, the president of NAFTA arrived and decamped from his helicopter on the tarmac in Louisiana. A swarm of presidential bodyguards materialized out of the expectant crowd, looking simultaneously extremely busy and icily unperturbable.

Suddenly a line of text flickered up at the bottom of the screen. The text was set in a very old-fashioned computer font, chalk-white letters with little visible jagged pixel-edges. *"Look at him hunting for that camera mark,"* the subtitle read as it scrolled across the screen. *"Why wasn't he briefed properly? He looks like a stray dog!"*

The president meandered amiably across the sun-blistered tarmac, gazing from side to side, and then stopped briefly to shake the eager outstretched hand of a local politician. *"That must have hurt,"* commented the text. *"That Cajun dolt is poison in the polls."* The president chatted amiably with the local politician and an elderly harridan in a purple dress who seemed to be the man's wife. *"Get him away from those losers!"* raged the subtitle. *"Get the Man up to the podium, for the love of Mike! Where's the chief of staff? Doped up on so-called smart drugs as usual? Get with your jobs, people!"*

The president looked well. Lyle had noticed that the president of NAFTA always looked well; it seemed to be a professional requirement. The big political cheeses in Europe always looked somber and intellectual, and the Sphere people always looked humble and dedicated, and the South people always looked angry and fanatical, but the NAFTA prez always looked like he'd just done a few laps in a pool and had a brisk rubdown. His large, glossy, bluffly cheerful face was discreetly stenciled with tattoos: both cheeks, a chorus line of tatts on his forehead above both eyebrows, plus a few extra logos on his rocklike chin. A president's face was the ultimate billboard for major backers and interest groups.

"Does he think we have all day?" the text demanded. *"What's with this dead air time? Can't anyone properly arrange a media event these days? You call this public access? You call this informing the electorate? If we'd known the infobahn would come to this, we'd have never built the thing!"*

The president meandered amiably to a podium covered with ceremonial microphones. Lyle had noticed that politicians always used a big healthy cluster of traditional big fat microphones, even though nowadays you could build working microphones the size of a grain of rice.

"Hey, how y'all?" asked the president, grinning.

The crowd chorused back at him, with ragged enthusiasm.

"Let these fine folks up a bit closer," the president ordered suddenly, waving airily at his phalanx of bodyguards. "Y'all come on up closer, everybody! Sit right on the ground, we're all just folks here today." The president smiled benignly as the sweating, straw-hatted summer crowd hustled up to join him, scarcely believing their luck.

"Marietta and I just had a heck of a fine lunch down in Opelousas," commented the president, patting his flat, muscular belly. He deserted the fiction of his official podium to energetically press the Louisianan flesh. As he moved from hand to grasping hand, his every word was picked up infallibly by an invisible mike, probably implanted in one of his molars. "We had dirty rice, red beans—were they hot!—and crawdads big enough to body-slam a Maine lobster!" He chuckled. "What a sight them mudbugs were! Can y'all believe that?"

The president's guards were unobtrusively but methodically working the crowd with portable detectors and sophisticated spex equipment. They didn't look very concerned by the president's supposed change in routine.

"I see he's gonna run with the usual genetics malarkey," commented the subtitle.

"Y'all have got a perfect right to be mighty proud of the agriculture in this state," intoned the president.

"Y'all's agroscience know-how is second to none! Sure, I know there's a few pointy-headed Luddites up in the snowbelt, who say they prefer their crawdads dinky."

Everyone laughed.

"Folks, I got nothin' against that attitude. If some jasper wants to spend his hard-earned money buyin' and peelin' and shuckin' those little dinky ones, that's all right by me and Marietta. Ain't that right, honey?"

The first lady smiled and waved one power-gloved hand.

"But folks, you and I both know that those whiners who waste our time complaining about 'natural food' have never sucked a mudbug head in their lives! 'Natural,' my left elbow! Who are they tryin' to kid? Just 'cause you're country, don't mean you can't hack DNA!"

"He's been working really hard on the regional accents," commented the text. *"Not bad for a guy from Minnesota. But look at that sloppy, incompetent camera work! Doesn't anybody care anymore? What on earth is happening to our standards?"*

By lunchtime, Lyle had the final coat down on the enameling job. He ate a bowl of triticale mush and chewed up a mineral-rich handful of iodized sponge.

Then he settled down in front of the wallscreen to work on the inertia brake. Lyle knew there was big money in the inertia brake—for somebody, somewhere, sometime. The device smelled like the future.

Lyle tucked a jeweler's loupe in one eye and toyed methodically with the brake. He loved the way the piezoplastic clamp and rim transmuted braking energy into electrical-battery storage. At last, a way to capture the energy you lost in braking and put it to solid use. It was almost, but not quite, magical.

The way Lyle figured it, there was gonna be a big market someday for an inertia brake that captured energy and then fed it back through the chaindrive in a way that just felt like human pedaling energy, in a direct and intuitive and muscular way, not chunky and buzzy like some loser battery-powered moped. If the system worked out right, it would make the rider feel completely natural and yet subtly superhuman at the same time. And it had to be simple, the kind of system a shop guy could fix with hand tools. It wouldn't work if it was too brittle and fancy, it just wouldn't feel like an authentic bike.

Lyle had a lot of ideas about the design. He was pretty sure he could get a real grip on the problem, if only he weren't being worked to death just keeping the shop going. If he could get enough capital together to assemble the prototypes and do some serious field tests.

It would have to be chip-driven, of course, but true to the biking spirit at the same time. A lot of bikes had chips in them nowadays, in the shocks or the braking or in reactive hubs, but bicycles simply weren't like computers. Computers were black boxes inside, no big visible working parts. People, by contrast, got sentimental about their bike gear. People were strangely reticent and traditional about bikes. That's why the bike market had never really gone for recumbents, even though the recumbent design had a big mechanical advantage. People didn't like their bikes too complicated. They didn't want bicycles to bitch and complain and whine for attention and constant upgrading the way that computers did. Bikes were too personal. People wanted their bikes to wear.

Someone banged at the shop door.

Lyle opened it. Down on the tiling by the barrels stood a tall brunette woman in stretch shorts, with a short-sleeve blue pullover and a ponytail. She had a bike under one arm, an old lacquer-and-paper-framed Taiwanese job. "Are you Edward Dertouzas?" she said, gazing up at him.

"No," Lyle said patiently. "Eddy's in Europe."

She thought this over. "I'm new in the zone," she confessed. "Can you fix this bike for me? I just bought it secondhand and I think it kinda needs some work."

"Sure," Lyle said. "You came to the right guy for that job, ma'am, because Eddy Dertouzas couldn't fix a bike

for hell. Eddy just used to live here. I'm the guy who actually owns this shop. Hand the bike up."

Lyle crouched down, got a grip on the handlebar stem,
and hauled the bike into the shop. The woman gazed up at
him respectfully. "What's your name?"

"Lyle Schweik."

"I'm Kitty Casaday." She hesitated. "Could I come up
inside there?"

Lyle reached down, gripped her muscular wrist, and
hauled her up into the shop. She wasn't all that
good-looking, but she was in really good shape—like a
mountain biker or triathlon runner. She looked about
thirty-five. It was hard to tell, exactly. Once people got
into cosmetic surgery and serious biomaintenance, it got
pretty hard to judge their age. Unless you got a good, close
medical exam of their eyelids and cuticles and internal
membranes and such.

She looked around the shop with great interest, brown
ponytail twitching. "Where you hail from?" Lyle asked
her. He had already forgotten her name.

"Well, I'm originally from Juneau, Alaska."

"Canadian, huh? Great. Welcome to Tennessee."

"Actually, Alaska used to be part of the United
States."

"You're kidding," Lyle said. "Hey, I'm no historian,
but I've seen Alaska on a map before."

"You've got a whole working shop and everything
built inside this old place! That's really something, Mr.
Schweik. What's behind that curtain?"

"The spare room," Lyle said. "That's where my roommate used to stay."

She glanced up. "Dertouzas?"

"Yeah, him."

"Who's in there now?"

"Nobody," Lyle said sadly. "I got some storage stuff
in there."

She nodded slowly, and kept looking around, apparently galvanized with curiosity. "What are you running on that screen?"

"Hard to say, really," Lyle said. He crossed the room, bent down, and switched off the set-top box. "Some kind of weird political crap."

He began examining her bike. All its serial numbers had been removed. Typical zone bike.

"The first thing we got to do," he said briskly, "is fit it to you properly: set the saddle height, pedal stroke, and handlebars. Then I'll adjust the tension, true the wheels, check the brake pads and suspension valves, tune the shifting, and lubricate the drivetrain. The usual. You're gonna need a better saddle than this—this saddle's for a male pelvis." He looked up. "You got a charge card?"

She nodded, then frowned. "But I don't have much credit left."

"No problem." He flipped open a dog-eared catalog. "This is what you need. Any halfway decent gel-saddle. Pick one you like, and we can have it shipped in by tomorrow morning. And then"—he flipped pages—"order me one of these."

She stepped closer and examined the page. "The 'cotterless crank-bolt ceramic wrench set,' is that it?"

"That's right. I fix your bike, you give me those tools, and we're even."

"Okay. Sure. That's cheap!" She smiled at him. "I like the way you do business, Lyle."

"You'll get used to barter, if you stay in the zone long enough."

"I've never lived in a squat before," she said thoughtfully. "I like the attitude here, but people say that squats are pretty dangerous."

"I dunno about the squats in other towns, but Chattanooga squats aren't dangerous, unless you think anarchists are dangerous, and anarchists aren't dangerous unless they're really drunk." Lyle shrugged. "People will steal your stuff all the time, that's about the worst part. There's a couple of tough guys around here who claim they have handguns. I never saw anybody actually use a handgun. Old guns aren't hard to find, but it takes a real chemist to make working ammo nowadays." He smiled back at her. "Anyway, you look to me like you can take care of yourself."

"I take dance classes."

Lyle nodded. He opened a drawer and pulled a tape measure.

"I saw all those cables and pulleys you have on top of this place. You can pull the whole building right up off the ground, huh? Kind of hang it right off the ceiling up there."

"That's right, it saves a lot of trouble with people breaking and entering." Lyle glanced at his shock-baton, in its mounting at the door. She followed his gaze to the weapon and then looked at him, impressed.

Lyle measured her arms, torso length, then knelt and measured her inseam from crotch to floor. He took notes. "Okay," he said. "Come by tomorrow afternoon."

"Lyle?"

"Yeah?" He stood up.

"Do you rent this place out? I really need a safe place to stay in the zone."

"I'm sorry," Lyle said politely, "but I hate landlords and I'd never be one. What I need is a roommate who can really get behind the whole concept of my shop. Someone who's qualified, you know, to develop my infrastructure or do bicycle work. Anyway, if I took your cash or charged you for rent, then the tax people would just have another excuse to harass me."

"Sure, okay, but . . ." She paused, then looked at him under lowered eyelids. "I've gotta be a lot better than having this place go empty."

Lyle stared at her, astonished.

"I'm a pretty useful woman to have around, Lyle. Nobody's ever complained before."

"Really?"

"That's right." She stared at him boldly.

"I'll think about your offer," Lyle said. "What did you say your name was?"

"I'm Kitty. Kitty Casaday."

"Kitty, I got a whole lot of work to do today, but I'll see you tomorrow, okay?"

"Okay, Lyle." She smiled. "You think about me, all right?"

Lyle helped her down out of the shop. He watched her stride away across the atrium until she vanished through the crowded doorway of the Crowbar, a squat coffee shop. Then he called his mother.

"Did you forget something?" his mother said, looking up from her workscreen.

"Mom, I know this is really hard to believe, but a strange woman just banged on my door and offered to have sex with me."

"You're kidding, right?"

"In exchange for room and board, I think. Anyway, I said you'd be the first to know if it happened."

"Lyle—" His mother hesitated. "Lyle, I think you better come right home. Let's make that dinner date for tonight, okay? We'll have a little talk about this situation."

"Yeah, okay. I got an enameling job I gotta deliver to Floor Forty-one, anyway."

"I don't have a positive feeling about this development, Lyle."

"That's okay, Mom. I'll see you tonight."

Lyle reassembled the newly enameled bike. Then he set the flywheel onto remote, and stepped outside the shop. He mounted the bike, and touched a password into the remote control. The shop faithfully reeled itself far out of reach and hung there in space below the fire-blackened ceiling, swaying gently.

Lyle pedaled away, back toward the elevators, back toward the neighborhood where he'd grown up.

He delivered the bike to the delighted young idiot who'd commissioned it, stuffed the cash in his shoes, and then went down to his mother's. He took a shower, shaved, and shampooed thoroughly. They had pork chops and grits and got drunk together. His mother complained about the breakup with her third husband and wept bitterly, but not as much as usual when this topic came up. Lyle got the strong impression she was thoroughly on the mend and would be angling for number four in pretty short order.

Around midnight, Lyle refused his mother's ritual offers of new clothes and fresh leftovers, and headed back down to the zone. He was still a little clubfooted from his mother's sherry, and he stood breathing beside the broken glass of the atrium wall, gazing out at the city-smeared summer stars. The cavernous darkness inside the zone at night was one of his favorite things about the place. The queasy twenty-four-hour security lighting in the rest of the Archiplat had never been rebuilt inside the zone.

The zone always got livelier at night when all the normal people started sneaking in to cruise the zone's unlicensed dives and nightspots, but all that activity took place behind discreetly closed doors. Enticing squiggles of red and blue chemglow here and there only enhanced the blessed unnatural gloom.

Lyle pulled his remote control and ordered the shop back down.

The door of the shop had been broken open.

Lyle's latest bike-repair client lay sprawled on the floor of the shop, unconscious. She was wearing black military fatigues, a knit cap, and rappelling gear.

She had begun her break-in at Lyle's establishment by pulling his shock-baton out of its glowing security socket beside the doorframe. The booby-trapped baton had immediately put fifteen thousand volts through her, and sprayed her face with a potent mix of dye and street-legal incapacitants.

Lyle turned the baton off with the remote control, and then placed it carefully back in its socket. His surprise guest was still breathing, but was clearly in real metabolic distress. He tried clearing her nose and mouth with a tissue. The guys who'd sold him the baton hadn't been kidding about the "indelible" part. Her face and throat were drenched with green and her chest looked like a spin-painting.

Her elaborate combat spex had partially shielded her eyes. With the spex off she looked like a viridian-green raccoon.

Lyle tried stripping her gear off in conventional fashion, realized this wasn't going to work, and got a pair of metal-shears from the shop. He snipped his way through the eerily writhing power-gloves and the Kevlar laces of the pneumoreactive combat boots. Her black turtleneck had an abrasive surface and a cuirass over chest and back that looked like it could stop small-arms fire.

The trousers had nineteen separate pockets and they were loaded with all kinds of eerie little items: a matte-black electrode stun-weapon, flash capsules, fingerprint dust, a utility pocketknife, drug adhesives, plastic handcuffs, some pocket change, worry beads, a comb, and a makeup case.

Close inspection revealed a pair of tiny microphone amplifiers inserted in her ear canals. Lyle fetched the tiny devices out with needlenose pliers. Lyle was getting pretty seriously concerned by this point. He shackled her arms and legs with bike-security cable, in case she regained consciousness and attempted something superhuman.

Around four in the morning she had a coughing fit and began shivering violently. Summer nights could get pretty cold in the shop. Lyle thought over the design problem for some time, and then fetched a big heat-reflective blanket out of the empty room. He cut a neat poncho-hole in the center of it, and slipped her head through it. He got the bike cables off her—she could probably slip the cables anyway—and sewed all four edges of the blanket shut from the outside, with sturdy monofilament thread from his saddle-stitcher. He sewed the poncho edges to a tough fabric belt, cinched the belt snugly around her neck, and padlocked it. When he was done, he'd made a snug bag that contained her entire body, except for her head, which had begun to drool and snore.

A fat blob of superglue on the bottom of the bag kept her anchored to the shop's floor. The blanket was cheap but tough upholstery fabric. If she could rip her way through blanket fabric with her fingernails alone, then he was probably a goner anyway. By now, Lyle was tired and stone sober. He had a squeeze bottle of glucose rehydrator, three aspirins, and a canned chocolate pudding. Then he climbed in his hammock and went to sleep.

Lyle woke up around ten. His captive was sitting up inside the bag, her green face stony, eyes red-rimmed, and brown hair caked with dye. Lyle got up, dressed, ate breakfast, and fixed the broken door-lock. He said nothing, partly because he thought that silence would shake her up, but mostly because he couldn't remember her name. He was almost sure it wasn't her real name anyway.

When he'd finished fixing the door, he reeled up the string of the doorknocker so that it was far out of reach. He figured the two of them needed the privacy.

Then Lyle deliberately fired up the wallscreen and turned on the set-top box. As soon as the peculiar subtitles started showing up again, she grew agitated.

"Who are you really?" she demanded at last.

"Ma'am, I'm a bicycle repairman."

She snorted.

"I guess I don't need to know your name," he said, "but I need to know who your people are, and why they sent you here, and what I've got to do to get out of this situation."

"You're not off to a good start, mister."

"No," he said, "maybe not, but you're the one who's blown it. I'm just a twenty-four-year-old bicycle repairman from Tennessee. But you, you've got enough specialized gear on you to buy my whole place five times over."

He flipped open the little mirror in her makeup case and showed her her own face. Her scowl grew a little stiffer below the spattering of green.

"I want you to tell me what's going on here," he said.

"Forget it."

"If you're waiting for your backup to come rescue you, I don't think they're coming," Lyle said. "I searched you very thoroughly and I've opened up every single little gadget you had, and I took all the batteries out. I'm not even sure what some of those things are or how they work, but hey, I know what a battery is. It's been hours now. So I don't think your backup people even know where you are."

She said nothing.

"See," he said, "you've really blown it bad. You got caught by a total amateur, and now you're in a hostage situation that could go on indefinitely. I got enough water and noodles and sardines to live up here for days. I dunno, maybe you can make a cellular phone call to God off some gizmo implanted in your thighbone, but it looks to me like you've got serious problems."

She shuffled around a bit inside the bag and looked away.

"It's got something to do with the cable box over there, right?"

She said nothing.

"For what it's worth, I don't think that box has anything to do with me or Eddy Dertouzas," Lyle said. "I think it was probably meant for Eddy, but I don't think he asked anybody for it. Somebody just wanted him to have it, probably one of his weird European contacts. Eddy used to be in this political group called CAPCLUG, ever heard of them?"

It looked pretty obvious that she'd heard of them.

"I never liked 'em much, either," Lyle told her. "They kind of snagged me at first with their big talk about freedom and civil liberties, but then you'd go to a CAPCLUG meeting up in the penthouse levels, and there were all these potbellied zudes in spex yapping off stuff like, 'We must follow the technological imperatives or be jettisoned into the history dump-file.' They're a bunch of useless blowhards who can't tie their own shoes."

"They're dangerous radicals subverting national sovereignty."

Lyle blinked cautiously. "Whose national sovereignty would that be?"

"Yours, mine, Mr. Schweik. I'm from NAFTA, I'm a federal agent."

"You're a fed? How come you're breaking into people's houses, then? Isn't that against the Fourth Amendment or something?"

"If you mean the Fourth Amendment to the Constitution of the United States, that document was superseded years ago."

"Yeah . . . okay, I guess you're right." Lyle shrugged. "I missed a lot of civics classes. . . . No skin off my back anyway. I'm sorry, but what did you say your name was?"

"I said my name was Kitty Casaday."

"Right. Kitty. Okay, Kitty, just you and me, person to person. We obviously have a mutual problem here. What do you think I ought to do in this situation? I mean, speaking practically."

Kitty thought it over, surprised. "Mr. Schweik, you should release me immediately, get me my gear, and give me the box and any related data, recordings, or diskettes. Then you should escort me from the Archiplat in some confidential fashion so I won't be stopped by police and questioned about the dye stains. A new set of clothes would be very useful."

"Like that, huh?"

"That's your wisest course of action." Her eyes narrowed. "I can't make any promises, but it might affect your future treatment very favorably."

"You're not gonna tell me who you are, or where you came from, or who sent you, or what this is all about?"

"No. Under no circumstances. I'm not allowed to reveal that. You don't need to know. You're not supposed to know. And anyway, if you're really what you say you are, what should you care?"

"Plenty. I care plenty. I can't wander around the rest of my life wondering when you're going to jump me out of a dark corner."

"If I'd wanted to hurt you, I'd have hurt you when we first met, Mr. Schweik. There was no one here but you and me, and I could have easily incapacitated you and taken anything I wanted. Just give me the box and the data and stop trying to interrogate me."

"Suppose you found me breaking into your house, Kitty? What would you do to me?"

She said nothing.

"What you're telling me isn't gonna work. If you don't tell me what's really going on here," Lyle said heavily, "I'm gonna have to get tough."

Her lips thinned in contempt.

"Okay, you asked for this." Lyle opened the mediator and made a quick voice call. "Pete?"

"Nah, this is Pete's mook," the phone replied. "Can I do something for you?"

"Could you tell Pete that Lyle Schweik has some big trouble, and I need him to come over to my bike shop immediately? And bring some heavy muscle from the Spiders."

"What kind of big trouble, Lyle?"

"Authority trouble. A lot of it. I can't say any more. I think this line may be tapped."

"Right-o. I'll make that happen. Hoo-ah, zude." The mook hung up.

Lyle left the beanbag and went back to the workbench. He took Kitty's cheap bike out of the repair stand and angrily threw it aside. "You know what really bugs me?" he said at last. "You couldn't even bother to charm your way in here, set yourself up as my roommate, and then steal the damn box. You didn't even respect me that much. Heck, you didn't even have to steal anything, Kitty. You could have just smiled and asked nicely and I'd have given you the box to play with. I don't watch media, I hate all that crap."

"It was an emergency. There was no time for more extensive investigation or reconnaissance. I think you should call your gangster friends immediately and tell them you've made a mistake. Tell them not to come here."

"You're ready to talk seriously?"

"No, I won't be talking."

"Okay, we'll see."

After twenty minutes, Lyle's phone rang. He answered it cautiously, keeping the video off. It was Pete from the City Spiders. "Zude, where is your doorknocker?"

"Oh, sorry, I pulled it up, didn't want to be disturbed. I'll bring the shop right down." Lyle thumbed the brake switches.

Lyle opened the door and Pete broad-jumped into the shop. Pete was a big man but he had the skeletal, wiry build of a climber, bare dark arms and shins and big sticky-toed jumping shoes. He had a sleeveless leather bodysuit full of clips and snaps, and he carried a big fabric shoulder bag. There were six vivid tattoos on the dark skin of his left cheek, under the black stubble.

Pete looked at Kitty, lifted his spex with wiry callused fingers, looked at her again bare-eyed, and put the spex back in place. "Wow, Lyle."

"Yeah."

"I never thought you were into anything this sick and twisted."

"It's a serious matter, Pete."

Pete turned to the door, crouched down, and hauled a second person into the shop. She wore a beat-up air-conditioned jacket and long slacks and zipsided boots and wire-rimmed spex. She had short ratty hair under a green cloche hat. "Hi," she said, sticking out a hand. "I'm Mabel. We haven't met."

"I'm Lyle." Lyle gestured. "This is Kitty here in the bag."

"You said you needed somebody heavy, so I brought Mabel along," said Pete. "Mabel's a social worker."

"Looks like you pretty much got things under control here," said Mabel liltingly, scratching her neck and looking about the place. "What happened? She break into your shop?"

"Yeah."

"And," Pete said, "she grabbed the shock-baton first thing and blasted herself but good?"

"Exactly."

"I told you that thieves always go for the weaponry first," Pete said, grinning and scratching his armpit. "Didn't I tell you that? Leave a weapon in plain sight, man, a thief can't stand it, it's the very first thing they gotta grab." He laughed. "Works every time."

"Pete's from the City Spiders," Lyle told Kitty. "His people built this shop for me. One dark night, they hauled this mobile home right up thirty-four stories in total darkness, straight up the side of the Archiplat without anybody seeing, and they cut a big hole through the side of the building without making any noise, and they hauled the whole shop through it. Then they sank explosive bolts through the girders and hung it up here for me in midair. The City Spiders are into sport-climbing the way I'm into bicycles, only, like, they are very *seriously* into climbing and there are *lots* of them. They were some of the very first people to squat the zone, and they've lived here ever since, and they are pretty good friends of mine."

Pete sank to one knee and looked Kitty in the eye. "I love breaking into places, don't you? There's no thrill like some quick and perfectly executed break-in." He reached casually into his shoulder bag. "The thing is"—he pulled out a camera—"to be sporting, you can't steal anything. You just take trophy pictures to prove you were there." He snapped her picture several times, grinning as she flinched.

"Lady," he breathed at her, "once you've turned into a little wicked greedhead, and mixed all that evil cupidity and possessiveness into the beauty of the direct action, then you've prostituted our way of life. You've gone and spoiled our sport." Pete stood up. "We City Spiders don't like common thieves. And we especially don't like thieves who break into the places of clients of ours, like Lyle here. And we thoroughly, especially, don't like thieves who are so brickhead dumb that they get caught red-handed on the premises of friends of ours."

Pete's hairy brows knotted in thought. "What I'd like to do here, Lyle ol' buddy," he announced, "is wrap up your little friend head to foot in nice tight cabling, smuggle her out of here down to Golden Gate Archiplat—you know, the big one downtown over by MLK and Highway Twenty-seven?—and hang her head-down in the center of the cupola."

"That's not very nice," Mabel told him seriously.

Pete looked wounded. "I'm not gonna charge him for it or anything! Just imagine her, spinning up there beautifully with all those chandeliers and those hundreds of mirrors."

Mabel knelt and looked into Kitty's face. "Has she had any water since she was knocked unconscious?"

"No."

"Well, for heaven's sake, give the poor woman something to drink, Lyle."

Lyle handed Mabel a bike-tote squeeze bottle of electrolyte refresher. "You zudes don't grasp the situation yet," he said. "Look at all this stuff I took off her." He showed them the spex, and the boots, and the stun-gun, and the gloves, and the carbon-nitride climbing plectra, and the rappelling gear.

"Wow," Pete said at last, dabbing at buttons on his spex to study the finer detail, "this is no ordinary burglar! She's gotta be, like, a street samurai from the Mahogany Warbirds or something!"

"She says she's a federal agent."

Mabel stood up suddenly, angrily yanking the squeeze bottle from Kitty's lips. "You're kidding, right?"

"Ask her."

"I'm a grade-five social counselor with the Department of Urban Redevelopment," Mabel said. She presented Kitty with an official ID. "And who are you with?"

"I'm not prepared to divulge that information at this time."

"I can't believe this," Mabel marveled, tucking her dog-eared hologram ID back in her hat. "You've caught somebody from one of those nutty reactionary secret black-bag units. I mean, that's gotta be what's just happened here." She shook her head slowly. "Y'know, if you work in government, you always hear horror stories about these right-wing paramilitary wackos, but I've never actually seen one before."

"It's a very dangerous world out there, Miss Social Counselor."

"Oh, tell me about it," Mabel scoffed. "I've worked suicide hot lines! I've been a hostage negotiator! I'm a career social worker, girlfriend! I've seen more horror and suffering than you *ever* will. While you were doing push-ups in some comfy cracker training camp, I've been out here in the real world!" Mabel absently unscrewed the top from the bike bottle and had a long glug. "What on earth are you doing trying to raid the squat of a bicycle repairman?"

Kitty's stony silence lengthened. "It's got something to do with that set-top box," Lyle offered. "It showed up here in delivery yesterday, and then she showed up just a few hours later. Started flirting with me, and said she wanted to live in here. Of course I got suspicious right away."

"Naturally," Pete said. "Real bad move, Kitty. Lyle's on antilibidinals."

Kitty stared at Lyle bitterly. "I see," she said at last. "So that's what you get, when you drain all the sex out of one of them. . . . You get a strange malodorous creature that spends all its time working in the garage."

Mabel flushed. "Did you hear that?" She gave Kitty's bag a sharp angry yank. "What conceivable right do you have to question this citizen's sexual orientation? Especially after cruelly trying to sexually manipulate him to abet your illegal purposes? Have you lost all sense of decency? You . . . you should be sued."

"Do your worst," Kitty muttered.

"Maybe I will," Mabel said grimly. "Sunlight is the best disinfectant."

"Yeah, let's string her up somewhere real sunny and public and call a bunch of news crews," Pete said. "I'm way hot for this deep ninja gear! Me and the Spiders got real mojo uses for these telescopic ears, and the tracer dust, and the epoxy bugging devices. And the press-on climbing-claws. And the carbon-fiber rope. Everything, really! Everything except these big-ass military shoes of hers, which really suck."

"Hey, all that stuff's mine," Lyle said sternly. "I saw it first."

"Yeah, I guess so, but . . . okay, Lyle, you make us a deal on the gear, we'll forget everything you still owe us for doing the shop."

"Come on, those combat spex are worth more than this place all by themselves."

"I'm real interested in that set-top box," Mabel said cruelly. "It doesn't look too fancy or complicated. Let's take it over to those dirty circuit zudes who hang out at the Blue Parrot, and see if they can't reverse-engineer it. We'll post all the schematics up on twenty or thirty progressive activist networks, and see what falls out of cyberspace."

Kitty glared at her. "The terrible consequences from that stupid and irresponsible action would be entirely on your head."

"I'll risk it," Mabel said airily, patting her cloche hat. "It might bump my soft little liberal head a bit, but I'm pretty sure it would crack your nasty little fascist head like a coconut."

Suddenly Kitty began thrashing and kicking her way furiously inside the bag. They watched with interest as she ripped, tore, and lashed out with powerful side and front kicks. Nothing much happened.

"All right," she said at last, panting in exhaustion. "I've come from Senator Creighton's office."

"Who?" Lyle said.

"Creighton! Senator James P. Creighton, the man who's been your senator from Tennessee for the past thirty years!"

"Oh," Lyle said. "I hadn't noticed."

"We're anarchists," Pete told her.

"I've sure heard of the nasty old geezer," Mabel said, "but I'm from British Columbia, where we change senators the way you'd change a pair of socks. If you ever changed your socks, that is. What about him?"

"Well, Senator Creighton has deep clout and seniority! He was a United States Senator even before the first NAFTA Senate was convened! He has a very large, and powerful, and very well seasoned personal staff of twenty thousand hard-working people, with a lot of pull in the Agriculture, Banking, and Telecommunications Committees!"

"Yeah? So?"

"So," Kitty said miserably, "there are twenty thousand of us on his staff. We've been in place for decades now, and naturally we've accumulated lots of power and importance. Senator Creighton's staff is basically running some quite large sections of the NAFTA government, and if the senator loses his office, there will be a great deal of . . . of unnecessary political turbulence." She looked up. "You might not think that a senator's staff is all that important politically. But if people like you bothered to learn anything about the real-life way that your government functions, then you'd know that Senate staffers can be really crucial."

Mabel scratched her head. "You're telling me that even a lousy senator has his own private black-bag unit?"

Kitty looked insulted. "He's an excellent senator! You can't have a working organization of twenty thousand staffers without taking security very seriously! Anyway, the Executive wing has had black-bag units for years! It's only right that there should be a balance of powers."

"Wow," Mabel said. "The old guy's a hundred and twelve or something, isn't he?"

"A hundred and seventeen."

"Even with government health care, there can't be a lot left of him."

"He's already gone," Kitty muttered. "His frontal lobes are burned out. . . . He can still sit up, and if he's stoked on stimulants he can repeat whatever's whispered to him. So he's got two permanent implanted hearing aids, and basically . . . well . . . he's being run by remote control by his mook."

"His mook, huh?" Pete repeated thoughtfully.

"It's a very good mook," Kitty said. "The coding's old, but it's been very well looked after. It has firm moral values and excellent policies. The mook is really very much like the senator was. It's just that . . . well, it's old. It still prefers a really old-fashioned media environment. It spends almost all its time watching old-fashioned public political coverage, and lately it's gotten cranky and started broadcasting commentary."

"Man, never trust a mook," Lyle said. "I hate those things."

"So do I," Pete offered, "but even a mook comes off pretty good compared to a politician."

"I don't really see the problem," Mabel said, puzzled. "Senator Hirschheimer from Arizona has had a direct neural link to his mook for years, and he has an excellent progressive voting record. Same goes for Senator Marmalejo from Tamaulipas; she's kind of absentminded, and everybody knows she's on life support, but she's a real scrapper on women's issues."

Kitty looked up. "You don't think it's terrible?"

Mabel shook her head. "I'm not one to be judgmental about the intimacy of one's relationship to one's own digital alter ego. As far as I can see it, that's a basic privacy issue."

"They told me in briefing that it was a very terrible business, and that everyone would panic if they learned that a high government official was basically a front for a rogue artificial intelligence."

Mabel, Pete, and Lyle exchanged glances. "Are you guys surprised by that news?" Mabel said.

"Heck no," said Pete.

"Big deal," Lyle added.

Something seemed to snap inside Kitty then. Her head sank. "Disaffected émigrés in Europe have been spreading boxes that can decipher the senator's commentary. I mean, the senator's mook's commentary. . . . The mook speaks just like the senator did, or the way the senator used to speak, when he was in private and off the record. The way he spoke in his diaries. As far as we can tell, the mook *was* his diary. . . . It used to be his personal laptop computer. But he just kept transferring the files, and upgrading the software, and teaching it new tricks like voice recognition and speechwriting, and giving it power of attorney and such. . . . And then, one day the mook made a break for it. We think that the mook sincerely believes that it's the senator."

"Just tell the stupid thing to shut up for a while, then."

"We can't do that. We're not even sure where the mook is, physically. Or how it's been encoding those sarcastic comments into the video-feed. The senator had a lot of friends in the telecom industry back in the old days. There are a lot of ways and places to hide a piece of distributed software."

"So that's all?" Lyle said. "That's it, that's your big secret? Why didn't you just come to me and ask me for the box? You didn't have to dress up in combat gear and kick my door in. That's a pretty good story, I'd have probably just given you the thing."

"I couldn't do that, Mr. Schweik."

"Why not?"

"Because," Pete said, "her people are important government functionaries, and you're a loser techie wacko who lives in a slum."

"I was told this is a very dangerous area," Kitty muttered.

"It's not dangerous," Mabel told her.

"No?"

"No. They're all too broke to be dangerous. This is just a kind of social breathing space. The whole urban infrastructure's dreadfully overplanned here in Chattanooga. There's been too much money here too long. There's been no room for spontaneity. It was choking the life out of the city. That's why everyone was secretly overjoyed when the rioters set fire to these three floors."

Mabel shrugged. "The insurance took care of the damage. First the looters came in. Then there were a few hideouts for kids and crooks and illegal aliens. Then the permanent squats got set up. Then the artist's studios, and the semilegal workshops and red-light places. Then the quaint little coffeehouses, then the bakeries. Pretty soon the offices of professionals will be filtering in, and they'll restore the water and the wiring. Once that happens, the real-estate prices will kick in big-time, and the whole zone will transmute right back into gentryville. It happens all the time."

Mabel waved her arm at the door. "If you knew anything about modern urban geography, you'd see this kind of, uh, spontaneous urban renewal happening all over the place. As long as you've got naive young people with plenty of energy who can be suckered into living inside rotten, hazardous dumps for nothing, in exchange for imagining that they're free from oversight, then it all works out just great in the long run."

"Oh."

"Yeah, zones like this turn out to be extremely handy for all concerned. For some brief span of time, a few people can think mildly unusual thoughts and behave in mildly unusual ways. All kinds of weird little vermin show up, and if they make any money then they go legal, and if they don't then they drop dead in a place really quiet where it's all their own fault. Nothing dangerous about it." Mabel laughed, then sobered. "Lyle, let this poor dumb cracker out of the bag."

"She's naked under there."

"Okay," she said impatiently, "cut a slit in the bag and throw some clothes in it. Get going, Lyle."

Lyle threw in some biking pants and a sweatshirt.

"What about my gear?" Kitty demanded, wriggling her way into the clothes by feel.

"I tell you what," said Mabel thoughtfully. "Pete here will give your gear back to you in a week or so, after his friends have photographed all the circuitry. You'll just have to let him keep all those knickknacks for a while, as his reward for our not immediately telling everybody who you are and what you're doing here."

"Great idea," Pete announced, "terrific, pragmatic solution!" He began feverishly snatching up gadgets and stuffing them into his shoulder bag. "See, Lyle? One phone call to good ol' Spider Pete, and your problem is history, zude! Me and Mabel-the-Fed have crisis negotiation skills that are second to none! Another potentially lethal confrontation resolved without any bloodshed or loss of life." Pete zipped the bag shut. "That's about it, right, everybody? Problem over! Write if you get work, Lyle buddy. Hang by your thumbs." Pete leapt out the door and bounded off at top speed on the springy soles of his reactive boots.

"Thanks a lot for placing my equipment into the hands of sociopathic criminals," Kitty said. She reached out of the slit in the bag, grabbed a multitool off the corner of the workbench, and began swiftly slashing her way free.

"This will help the sluggish, corrupt, and underpaid Chattanooga police to take life a little more seriously," Mabel said, her pale eyes gleaming. "Besides, it's profoundly undemocratic to restrict specialized technical knowledge to the coercive hands of secret military elites."

Kitty thoughtfully thumbed the edge of the multitool's ceramic blade and stood up to her full height, her eyes slitted. "I'm ashamed to work for the same government as you."

Mabel smiled serenely. "Darling, your tradition of deep dark government paranoia is far behind the times! This is the postmodern era! We're now in the grip of a government with severe schizoid multiple-personality disorder."

"You're truly vile. I despise you more than I can say." Kitty jerked her thumb at Lyle. "Even this nutcase eunuch anarchist kid looks pretty good, compared to you. At least he's self-sufficient and market-driven."

"I thought he looked good the moment I met him," Mabel replied sunnily. "He's cute, he's got great muscle tone, and he doesn't make passes. Plus he can fix small appliances and he's got a spare apartment. I think you ought to move in with him, sweetheart."

"What's that supposed to mean? You don't think I could manage life here in the zone like you do, is that it? You think you have some kind of copyright on living outside the law?"

"No, I just mean you'd better stay indoors with your boyfriend here until that paint falls off your face. You look like a poisoned raccoon." Mabel turned on her heel. "Try to get a life, and stay out of my way." She leapt outside, unlocked her bicycle, and methodically pedaled off.

Kitty wiped her lips and spat out the door. "Christ, that baton packs a wallop." She snorted. "Don't you ever ventilate this place, kid? Those paint fumes are gonna kill you before you're thirty."

"I don't have time to clean or ventilate it. I'm real busy."

"Okay, then I'll clean it. I'll ventilate it. I gotta stay here a while, understand? Maybe quite a while."

Lyle blinked. "How long, exactly?"

Kitty stared at him. "You're not taking me seriously, are you? I don't much like it when people don't take me seriously."

"No, no," Lyle assured her hastily. "You're very serious."

"You ever heard of a small-business grant, kid? How about venture capital, did you ever hear of that? Ever heard of federal research-and-development subsidies, Mr. Schweik?" Kitty looked at him sharply, weighing her words. "Yeah, I thought maybe you'd heard of that one, Mr. Techie Wacko. Federal R-and-D backing is the kind of thing that only happens to other people, right? But Lyle, when you make good friends with a senator, you *become* 'other people.' Get my drift, pal?"

"I guess I do," Lyle said slowly.

"We'll have ourselves some nice talks about that subject, Lyle. You wouldn't mind that, would you?"

"No. I don't mind it now that you're talking."

"There's some stuff going on down here in the zone that I didn't understand at first, but it's important." Kitty paused, then rubbed dried dye from her hair in a cascade of green dandruff. "How much did you pay those Spider gangsters to string up this place for you?"

"It was kind of a barter situation," Lyle told her.

"Think they'd do it again if I paid 'em real cash? Yeah? I thought so." She nodded thoughtfully. "They look like a heavy outfit, the City Spiders. I gotta pry 'em loose from that leftist gorgon before she finishes indoctrinating them in socialist revolution." Kitty wiped her mouth on her sleeve. "This is the senator's own constituency! It was stupid of us to duck an ideological battle, just because this is a worthless area inhabited by reckless sociopaths who don't vote. Hell, that's exactly why it's important. This could be a vital territory in the culture war. I'm gonna call the office right away, start making arrangements. There's no way we're gonna leave this place in the hands of the self-styled Queen of Peace and Justice over there."

She snorted, then stretched a kink out of her back.

"With a little self-control and discipline, I can save those Spiders from themselves and turn them into an asset to law and order! I'll get 'em to string up a couple of trailers here in the zone. We could start a dojo."

Eddy called, two weeks later. He was in a beachside cabana somewhere in Catalunya, wearing a silk floral-print shirt and a new and very pricey looking set of spex. "How's life, Lyle?"

"It's okay, Eddy."

"Making out all right?" Eddy had two new tattoos on his cheekbone.

"Yeah. I got a new paying roommate. She's a martial artist."

"Girl roommate working out okay this time?"

"Yeah, she's good at pumping the flywheel and she lets me get on with my bike work. Bike business has been picking up a lot lately. Looks like I might get a legal electrical feed and some more floorspace, maybe even some genuine mail delivery. My new roomie's got a lot of useful contacts."

"Boy, the ladies sure love you, Lyle! Can't beat 'em off with a stick, can you, poor guy? That's a heck of a note."

Eddy leaned forward a little, shoving aside a silver tray full of dead gold-tipped zigarettes. "You been getting the packages?"

"Yeah. Pretty regular."

"Good deal," he said briskly, "but you can wipe 'em all now. I don't need those backups anymore. Just wipe the data and trash the disks, or sell 'em. I'm into some, well, pretty hairy opportunities right now, and I don't need all that old clutter. It's kid stuff anyway."

"Okay, man. If that's the way you want it."

Eddy leaned forward. "D'you happen to get a package lately? Some hardware? Kind of a set-top box?"

"Yeah, I got the thing."

"That's great, Lyle. I want you to open the box up, and break all the chips with pliers."

"Yeah?"

"Then throw all the pieces away. Separately. It's trouble, Lyle, okay? The kind of trouble I don't need right now."

"Consider it done, man."

"Thanks! Anyway, you won't be bothered by mailouts from now on." He paused. "Not that I don't appreciate your former effort and goodwill, and all."

Lyle blinked. "How's your love life, Eddy?"

Eddy sighed. "Frederika! What a handful! I dunno, Lyle, it was okay for a while, but we couldn't stick it together. I don't know why I ever thought that private cops were sexy. I musta been totally out of my mind. . . . Anyway, I got a new girlfriend now."

"Yeah?"

"She's a politician, Lyle. She's a radical member of the Spanish Parliament. Can you believe that? I'm sleeping with an elected official of a European local government." He laughed. "Politicians are *sexy,* Lyle. Politicians are *hot*! They have charisma. They're glamorous. They're powerful. They can really make things happen! Politicians get around. They know things on the inside track. I'm having more fun with Violeta than I knew there was in the world."

"That's pleasant to hear, zude."

"More pleasant than you know, my man."

"Not a problem," Lyle said indulgently. "We all gotta make our own lives, Eddy."

"Ain't it the truth."

Lyle nodded. "I'm in business, zude!"

"You gonna perfect that inertial whatsit?" Eddy said.

"Maybe. It could happen. I get to work on it a lot now. I'm getting closer, really getting a grip on the concept. It feels really good. It's a good hack, man. It makes up for all the rest of it. It really does."

Eddy sipped his mimosa. "Lyle."

"What?"

"You didn't hook up that set-top box and look at it, did you?"

"You know me, Eddy," Lyle said. "Just another kid with a wrench."

TAKLAMAKAN

A bone-dry frozen wind tore at the earth outside, its lethal howling cut to a muffled moan. Katrinko and Spider Pete were camped deep in a crevice in the rock, wrapped in furry darkness. Pete could hear Katrinko breathing, with a light rattle of chattering teeth. The neuter's yeasty armpits smelled like nutmeg.

Spider Pete strapped his shaven head into his spex.

Outside their puffy nest, the sticky eyes of a dozen gelcams splayed across the rock, a sky-eating web of perception. Pete touched a stud on his spex, pulled down a glowing menu, and adjusted his visual take on the outside world.

Flying powder tumbled through the yardangs like an evil fog. The crescent moon and a billion desert stars, glowing like pixelated bruises, wheeled above the eerie wind-sculpted landscape of the Taklamakan. With the exceptions of Antarctica, or maybe the deep Sahara—locales Pete had never been paid to visit—this central Asian desert was the loneliest, most desolate place on Earth.

Pete adjusted parameters, etching the landscape with a busy array of false colors. He recorded an artful series of panorama shots, and tagged a global positioning fix onto the captured stack. Then he signed the footage with a cryptographic time-stamp from a passing NAFTA spy-sat.

Pete saved the stack onto a gelbrain. This gelbrain was a walnut-sized lump of neural biotech, carefully grown to mimic the razor-sharp visual cortex of an American bald eagle. It was the best, most expensive piece of photographic hardware that Pete had ever owned. Pete kept the thing tucked in his crotch.

Pete took a deep and intimate pleasure in working with the latest federally subsidized spy gear. It was quite the privilege for Spider Pete, the kind of privilege that he might well die for. There was no tactical use in yet another spy-shot of the chill and empty Taklamakan. But the tagged picture would prove that Katrinko and Pete had been here at the appointed rendezvous. Right here, right now. Waiting for the man.

And the man was overdue.

During their brief professional acquaintance, Spider Pete had met the Lieutenant Colonel in a number of deeply unlikely locales. A parking garage in Pentagon City. An outdoor seafood restaurant in Cabo San Lucas. On the ferry to Staten Island. Pete had never known his patron to miss a rendezvous by so much as a microsecond.

The sky went dirty white. A sizzle, a sparkle, a zenith full of stink. A screaming-streaking-tumbling. A nasty thunderclap. The ground shook hard.

"Dang," Pete said.

They found the Lieutenant Colonel just before eight in the morning. Pieces of his landing pod were violently scattered across half a kilometer.

Katrinko and Pete skulked expertly through a dirty yellow jumble of wind-grooved boulders. Their camou gear switched coloration moment by moment, to match the landscape and the incidental light.

Pete pried the mask from his face, inhaled the thin,

pitiless, metallic air, and spoke aloud. "That's our boy all right. Never missed a date."

The neuter removed her mask and fastidiously smeared her lips and gums with silicone anti-evaporant. Her voice fluted eerily over the insistent wind. "Space-defense must have tracked him on radar."

"Nope. If they'd hit him from orbit, he'd really be spread all over. . . . No, something happened to him really close to the ground." Pete pointed at a violent scattering of cracked ochre rock. "See, check out how that stealth-pod hit and tumbled. It didn't catch fire till after the impact."

With the absent ease of a gecko, the neuter swarmed up a three-story-high boulder. She examined the surrounding forensic evidence at length, dabbing carefully at her spex controls. She then slithered deftly back to earth. "There was no anti-aircraft fire, right? No interceptors flyin' 'round last night."

"Nope. Heck, there's no people around here in a space bigger than Delaware."

The neuter looked up. "So what do you figure, Pete?"

"I figure an accident," said Pete.

"A what?"

"An accident. A lot can go wrong with a covert HALO insertion."

"Like what, for instance?"

"Well, G-loads and stuff. System malfunctions. Maybe he just blacked out."

"He was a federal military spook, and you're telling me he *passed out*?" Katrinko daintily adjusted her goggled spex with gloved and bulbous fingertips. "Why would that matter anyway? He wouldn't fly a spacecraft with his own hands, would he?"

Pete rubbed at the gummy line of his mask, easing the prickly indentation across one dark, tattooed cheek. "I kinda figure he would, actually. The man was a pilot. Big military prestige thing. Flyin' in by hand, deep in Sphere territory, covert insertion, way behind enemy lines. . . .

That'd really be something to brag about, back on the
Potomac."

The neuter considered this sour news without apparent resentment. As one of the world's top technical climbers, Katrinko was a great connoisseur of pointless displays
of dangerous physical skill. "I can get behind that." She
paused. "Serious bad break, though."

They resealed their masks. Water was their greatest
lack, and vapor exhalation was a problem. They were re-
cycling body-water inside their suits, topped off with a few
extra cc's they'd obtained from occasional patches of
frost. They'd consumed the last of the trail-goop and
candy from their glider shipment three long days ago.
They hadn't eaten since. Still, Pete and Katrinko were getting along pretty well, living off big subcutaneous lumps of
injected body fat.

More through habit than apparent need, Pete and Katrinko segued into evidence-removal mode. It wasn't hard
to conceal a HALO stealth pod. The spycraft was radar-
transparent and totally biodegradable. In the bitter wind
and cold of the Taklamakan, the bigger chunks of wreck-
age had already gone all brown and crispy, like the shed
husks of locusts. They couldn't scrape up every physical
trace, but they'd surely get enough to fool aerial surveillance.

The Lieutenant Colonel was extremely dead. He'd
come down from the heavens in his full NAFTA military
power-armor, a leaping, brick-busting, lightning-spewing
exoskeleton, all acronyms and input jacks. It was powerful, elaborate gear, of an entirely different order than the
gooey and fibrous street tech of the two urban intrusion
freaks.

But the high-impact crash had not been kind to the
armored suit. It had been crueler still to the bone, blood,
and tendon housed inside.

Pete bagged the larger pieces with a heavy heart. He
knew that the Lieutenant Colonel was basically no good:
deceitful, ruthlessly ambitious, probably crazy. Still, Pete

sincerely regretted his employer's demise. After all, it was precisely those qualities that had led the Lieutenant Colonel to recruit Spider Pete in the first place.

Pete also felt sincere regret for the gung-ho, clear-eyed young military widow, and the two little redheaded kids in Augusta, Georgia. He'd never actually met the widow or the little kids, but the Lieutenant Colonel was always fussing about them and showing off their photos. The Lieutenant Colonel had been a full fifteen years younger than Spider Pete, a rosy-cheeked cracker kid really, never happier than when handing over wads of money, nutty orders, and expensive covert equipment to people whom no sane man would trust with a burnt-out match. And now here he was in the cold and empty heart of Asia, turned to jam within his shards of junk.

Katrinko did the last of the search-and-retrieval while Pete dug beneath a ledge with his diamond hand-pick, the razored edges slashing out clods of shale.

After she'd fetched the last blackened chunk of their employer, Katrinko perched birdlike on a nearby rock. She thoughtfully nibbled a piece of the pod's navigation console. "This gelbrain is good when it dries out, man. Like trail mix, or a fortune cookie."

Pete grunted. "You might be eating part of *him*, y'know."

"Lotta good carbs and protein there, too."

They stuffed a final shattered power-jackboot inside the Colonel's makeshift cairn. The piled rock was there for the ages. A few jets of webbing and thumbnail dabs of epoxy made it harder than a brick wall.

It was noon now, still well below freezing, but as warm as the Taklamakan was likely to get in January. Pete sighed, dusted sand from his knees and elbows, stretched. It was hard work, cleaning up; the hardest part of intrusion work, because it was the stuff you had to do after the thrill was gone. He offered Katrinko the end of a fiber-optic cable, so that they could speak together without using radio or removing their masks.

Pete waited until she had linked in, then spoke into his mike. "So we head on back to the glider now, right."

The neuter looked up, surprised. "How come?"

"Look, Trink, this guy that we just buried was the actual spy in this assignment. You and me, we were just his gophers and backup support. The mission's an abort."

"But we're searching for a giant, secret rocket base."

"Yeah, sure we are."

"We're supposed to find this monster high-tech complex, break in, and record all kinds of crazy top secrets that nobody but the mandarins have ever seen. That's a totally hot assignment, man."

Pete sighed. "I admit it's very high-concept, but I'm an old guy now, Trink. I need the kind of payoff that involves some actual money."

Katrinko laughed. "But Pete! It's a *starship*! A whole fleet of 'em, maybe! Secretly built in the desert, by Chinese spooks and Japanese engineers!"

Pete shook his head. "That was all paranoid bullshit that the flyboy made up, to get himself a grant and a field assignment. He was tired of sitting behind a desk in the basement, that's all."

Katrinko folded her lithe and wiry arms. "Look Pete, you saw those briefings just like me. You saw all those satellite shots. The traffic analysis, too. The Sphere people are up to something way big out here."

Pete gazed around him. He found it painfully surreal to endure this discussion amid a vast and threatening tableau of dust-hazed sky and sand-etched mudstone gullies. "They built something big here once, I grant you that. But I never figured the Colonel's story for being very likely."

"What's so unlikely about it? The Russians had a secret rocket base in the desert a hundred years ago. American deserts are full of secret mil-spec stuff and space-launch bases. So now the Asian Sphere people are up to the same old game. It all makes sense."

"No, it makes no sense at all. Nobody's space-racing to build any starships. Starships aren't a space race. It takes four hundred years to fly to the stars. Nobody's gonna finance a major military project that'll take four hundred years to pay off. Least of all a bunch of smart and thrifty Asian economic-warfare people."

"Well, they're sure building *something*. Look, all we have to do is find the complex, break in, and document some stuff. We can do that! People like us, we never needed any federal bossman to help us break into buildings and take photos. That's what we always do, that's what we live for."

Pete was touched by the kid's game spirit. She really had the City Spider way of mind. Nevertheless, Pete was fifty-two years old, so he found it necessary to at least try to be reasonable. "We should haul our sorry spook asses back to that glider right now. Let's skip on back over the Himalayas. We can fly on back to Washington, tourist class out of Delhi. They'll debrief us at the puzzle-palace. We'll give 'em the bad news about the bossman. We got plenty of evidence to prove *that*, anyhow. . . . The spooks will give us some walkin' money for a busted job, and tell us to keep our noses clean. Then we can go out for some pork chops."

Katrinko's thin shoulders hunched mulishly within the bubblepak warts of her insulated camou. She was not taking this at all well. "Peter, I ain't looking for pork chops. I'm looking for some professional validation, okay? I'm sick of that lowlife kid stuff, knocking around raiding network sites and mayors' offices. . . . This is my chance at the big-time!"

Pete stroked the muzzle of his mask with two gloved fingers.

"Pete, I know that you ain't happy. I know that already, okay? But you've *already made it* in the big-time, Mr. City Spider, Mr. Legend, Mr. Champion. Now here's my big chance come along, and you want us to hang up our cleats."

Pete raised his other hand. "Wait a minute, I never said that."

"Well, you're tellin' me you're walking. You're turning your back. You don't even want to check it out first."

"No," Pete said weightily, "I reckon you know me too well for that, Trink. I'm still a Spider. I'm still game. I'll always at least check it out."

Katrinko set their pace after that. Pete was content to let her lead. It was a very stupid idea to continue the mission without the overlordship of the Lieutenant Colonel. But it was stupid in a different and more refreshing way than the stupid idea of returning home to Chattanooga.

People in Pete's line of work weren't allowed to go home. He'd tried that once, really tried it, eight years ago, just after that badly busted caper in Brussels. He'd gotten a straight job at Lyle Schweik's pedal-powered aircraft factory. The millionaire sports tycoon had owed him a favor. Schweik had been pretty good about it, considering.

But word had swiftly gotten around that Pete had once been a champion City Spider. Dumb-ass co-workers would make significant remarks. Sometimes they asked him for so-called "favors," or tried to act street-wise. When you came down to it, straight people were a major pain in the ass.

Pete preferred the company of seriously twisted people. People who really cared about something, cared enough about it to really warp themselves for it. People who looked for more out of life than mommy, daddy, money, and the grave.

Below the edge of a ridgeline they paused for a recce. Pete whirled a tethered eye on the end of its reel and flung it. At the peak of its arc, six stories up, it recorded their surroundings in a panoramic view.

Pete and Katrinko studied the image together through their linked spex. Katrinko highlit an area downhill with a fingertip gesture. "Now there's a tipoff."

"That gully, you mean?"

"You need to get outdoors more, Pete. That's what we rockjocks technically call a road."

Pete and Katrinko approached the road with professional caution. It was a paved ribbon of macerated cinderblock, overrun with drifting sand. The road was made of the coked-out clinker left behind by big urban incinerators, a substance that Asians used for their road surfaces because all the value had been cooked out of it.

The cinder road had once seen a great deal of traffic. There were tire-shreds here and there, deep ruts in the shoulder, and post-holes that had once been traffic signs, or maybe surveillance boxes.

They followed the road from a respectful distance, cautious of monitors, tripwires, landmines, and many other possible unpleasantries. They stopped for a rest in a savage arroyo where a road bridge had been carefully removed, leaving only neat sockets in the roadbed and a kind of conceptual arc in midair.

"What creeps me out is how clean this all is," Pete said over cable. "It's a road, right? Somebody's gotta throw out a beer can, a lost shoe, something."

Katrinko nodded. "I figure construction robots."

"Really."

Katrinko spread her swollen-fingered gloves. "It's a Sphere operation, so it's bound to have lots of robots, right? I figure robots built this road. Robots used this road. Robots carried in tons and tons of whatever they were carrying. Then when they were done with the big project, the robots carried off everything that was worth any money. Gathered up the guideposts, bridges, everything. Very neat, no loose ends, very Sphere-type way to work." Katrinko set her masked chin on her bent knees, gone into reverie. "Some very weird and intense stuff can happen, when you got a lot of space in the desert, and robot labor that's too cheap to meter."

Katrinko hadn't been wasting her time in those intelligence briefings. Pete had seen a lot of City Spider wannabes, even trained quite a few of them. But Katrinko had what it took to be a genuine Spider champion: the desire, the physical talent, the ruthless dedication, and even the smarts. It was staying out of jails and morgues that was gonna be the tough part for Katrinko. "You're a big fan of the Sphere, aren't you, kid? You really like the way they operate."

"Sure, I always liked Asians. Their food's a lot better than Europe's."

Pete took this in stride. NAFTA, Sphere, and Europe: the trilateral superpowers jostled about with the uneasy regularity of sunspots, periodically brewing storms in the proxy regimes of the South. During his fifty-plus years, Pete had seen the Asian Cooperation Sphere change its public image repeatedly, in a weird political rhythm. Exotic vacation spot on Tuesdays and Thursdays. Baffling alien threat on Mondays and Wednesdays. Major trading partner each day and every day, including weekends and holidays.

At the current political moment, the Asian Cooperation Sphere was deep into its Inscrutable Menace mode, logging lots of grim media coverage as NAFTA's chief economic adversary. As far as Pete could figure it, this basically meant that a big crowd of goofy North American economists were trying to act really macho. Their major complaint was that the Sphere was selling NAFTA too many neat, cheap, well-made consumer goods. That was an extremely silly thing to get killed about. But people perished horribly for much stranger reasons than that.

At sunset, Pete and Katrinko discovered the giant warning signs. They were titanic vertical plinths, all epoxy and clinker, much harder than granite. They were four stories tall, carefully rooted in bedrock, and painstakingly chiseled with menacing horned symbols and elaborate textual warnings in at least fifty different languages. English was language number three.

"Radiation waste," Pete concluded, deftly reading the

text through his spex, from two kilometers away. "This is
a radiation waste dump. Plus, a nuclear test site. Old Red
Chinese hydrogen bombs, way out in the Taklamakan desert." He paused thoughtfully. "You gotta hand it to 'em.
They sure picked the right spot for the job."

"No way!" Katrinko protested. "Giant stone warning
signs, telling people not to trespass in this area? That's got
to be a con job."

"Well, it would sure account for them using robots,
and then destroying all the roads."

"No, man. It's like—you wanna hide something big
nowadays. You don't put a safe inside the wall anymore,
because hey, everybody's got magnetometers and sonic
imaging and heat detection. So you hide your best stuff in
the garbage."

Pete scanned their surroundings on spex telephoto.
They were lurking on a hillside above a playa, where the
occasional gullywasher had spewed out a big alluvial fan
of desert-varnished grit and cobbles. Stuff was actually
growing down there—squat leathery grasses with fat waxy
blades like dead men's fingers. The evil vegetation didn't
look like any kind of grass that Pete had ever seen. It
struck him as the kind of grass that would blithely gobble
up stray plutonium. "Trink, I like my explanations simple.
I figure that so-called giant starship base for a giant
radwaste dump."

"Well, maybe," the neuter admitted. "But even if
that's the truth, that's still news worth paying for. We
might find some busted-up barrels, or some badly managed fuel rods out there. That would be a big political
embarrassment, right? Proof of that would be worth
something."

"Huh," said Pete, surprised. But it was true. Long experience had taught Pete that there were always useful
secrets in other people's trash. "Is it worth glowin' in the
dark for?"

"So what's the problem?" Katrinko said. "I ain't having kids. I fixed that a long time ago. And you've got enough kids already."

"Maybe," Pete grumbled. Four kids by three different women. It had taken him a long sad time to learn that women who fell head-over-heels for footloose, sexy tough guys would fall repeatedly for pretty much any footloose, sexy tough guy.

Katrinko was warming to the task at hand. "We can do this, man. We got our suits and our breathing masks, and we're not eating or drinking anything out here, so we're practically radiation-tight. So we camp way outside the dump tonight. Then before dawn we slip in, we check it out real quick, we take our pictures, we leave. Clean, classic intrusion job. Nobody living around here to stop us, no problem there. And then, we got something to show the spooks when we get home. Maybe something we can sell."

Pete mulled this over. The prospect didn't sound all that bad. It was dirty work, but it would complete the mission. Also—this was the part he liked best—it would keep the Lieutenant Colonel's people from sending in some other poor guy. "Then, back to the glider?"

"Then, back to the glider."

"Okay, good deal."

Before dawn the next morning, they stoked themselves with athletic performance enhancers, brewed in the guts of certain gene-spliced ticks that they had kept hibernating in their armpits. Then they concealed their travel gear, and swarmed like ghosts up and over the great wall.

They pierced a tiny hole through the roof of one of the dun-colored, half-buried containment hangars, and oozed a spy-eye through.

Bomb-proofed ranks of barrel-shaped sarcophagi, solid and glossy as polished granite. The big fused radwaste containers were each the size of a tanker truck. They sat there neatly ranked in hermetic darkness, mute as sphinxes. They looked to be good for the next twenty thousand years.

Pete liquefied and retrieved the gelcam, then resealed the tiny hole with rock putty. They skipped down the slope of the dusty roof. There were lots of lizard tracks in the sand drifts, piled at the rim of the dome. These healthy traces of lizard cheered Pete up considerably.

They swarmed silently up and over the wall. Back uphill to the grotto where they'd stashed their gear. Then they removed their masks to talk again.

Pete sat behind a boulder, enjoying the intrusion afterglow. "A cakewalk," he pronounced it. "A pleasure hike." His pulse was already normal again, and, to his joy, there were no suspicious aches under his caraco-acromial arch.

"You gotta give them credit, those robots sure work neat."

Pete nodded. "Killer application for robots, your basic lethal waste gig."

"I telephotoed that whole cantonment," said Katrinko, "and there's no water there. No towers, no plumbing, no wells. People can get along without a lot of stuff in the desert, but nobody lives without water. That place is stone dead. It was always dead." She paused. "It was all automated robot work from start to finish. You know what that means, Pete? It means no human being has ever seen that place before. Except for you and me."

"Hey, then it's a first! We scored a first intrusion! That's just dandy," said Pete, pleased at the professional coup. He gazed across the cobbled plain at the walled cantonment, and pressed a last set of spex shots into his gelbrain archive. Two dozen enormous domes, built block by block by giant robots, acting with the dumb persistence of termites. The sprawling domes looked as if they'd congealed on the spot, their rims settling like molten taffy into the desert's little convexities and concavities. From a satellite view, the domes probably passed for natural features. "Let's not tarry, okay? I can kinda feel those X-ray fingers kinking my DNA."

"Aw, you're not all worried about that, are you, Pete?"

Pete laughed and shrugged. "Who cares? Job's over, kid. Back to the glider."

"They do great stuff with gene damage nowadays, y'know. Kinda re-weave you, down at the spook lab."

"What, those military doctors? I don't wanna give them the excuse."

The wind picked up. A series of abrupt and brutal gusts. Dry, and freezing, and peppered with stinging sand.

Suddenly, a faint moan emanated from the cantonment. Distant lungs blowing the neck of a winebottle.

"What's that big weird noise?" demanded Katrinko, all alert interest.

"Aw no," said Pete. "Dang."

Steam was venting from a hole in the bottom of the thirteenth dome. They'd missed the hole earlier, because the rim of that dome was overgrown with big thriving thornbushes. The bushes would have been a tip-off in themselves, if the two of them had been feeling properly suspicious.

In the immediate area, Pete and Katrinko swiftly discovered three dead men. The three men had hacked and chiseled their way through the containment dome—from the inside. They had wriggled through the long, narrow crevice they had cut, leaving much blood and skin.

The first man had died just outside the dome, apparently from sheer exhaustion. After their Olympian effort, the two survivors had emerged to confront the sheer four-story walls.

The remaining men had tried to climb the mighty wall with their handaxes, crude woven ropes, and pig-iron pitons. It was a nothing wall for a pair of City Spiders with modern handwebs and pinpression cleats. Pete and Katrinko could have camped and eaten a watermelon on that

wall. But it was a very serious wall for a pair of very weary
men dressed in wool, leather, and homemade shoes.

One of them had fallen from the wall, and had broken
his back and leg. The last one had decided to stay to com-
fort his dying comrade, and it seemed he had frozen to
death.

The three men had been dead for many months,
maybe over a year. Ants had been at work on them, and
the fine salty dust of the Taklamakan, and the freeze-
drying. Three desiccated Asian mummies, black hair and
crooked teeth and wrinkled dusky skin, in their funny
bloodstained clothes.

Katrinko offered the cable lead, chattering through
her mask. "Man, look at these *shoes*! Look at this shirt
this guy's got—would you call this thing a *shirt*?"

"What I would call this is three very brave climbers,"
Pete said. He tossed a tethered eye into the crevice that the
men had cut.

The inside of the thirteenth dome was a giant forest of
monitors. Microwave antennas, mostly. The top of the
dome wasn't sturdy sintered concrete like the others, it
was some kind of radar-transparent plastic. Dark inside,
like the other domes, and hermetically sealed—at least before the dead men had chewed and chopped their hole
through the wall. No sign of any radwaste around here.

They discovered the little camp where the men had
lived. Their bivouac. Three men, patiently chipping and
chopping their way to freedom. Burning their last wicks
and oil lamps, eating their last rations bite by bite, emptying their leather canteens and scraping for frost to drink.
Surrounded all the time by a towering jungle of satellite
relays and wavepipes. Pete found that scene very ugly.
That was a very bad scene. That was the worst of it yet.

Pete and Katrinko retrieved their full set of intrusion gear.
They then broke in through the top of the dome, where the
cutting was easiest. Once through, they sealed the hole

behind themselves, but only lightly, in case they should need a rapid retreat. They lowered their haulbags to the stone floor, then rappelled down on their smart-ropes. Once on ground level, they closed the escape tunnel with web and rubble, to stop the howling wind, and to keep contaminants at bay.

With the hole sealed, it grew warmer in the dome. Warm, and moist. Dew was collecting on walls and floor. A very strange smell, too. A smell like smoke and old socks. Mice and spice. Soup and sewage. A cozy human reek from the depths of the earth.

"The Lieutenant Colonel sure woulda loved this," whispered Katrinko over cable, spexing out the towering machinery with her infrareds. "You put a clip of explosive ammo through here, and it sure would put a major crimp in somebody's automated gizmos."

Pete figured their present situation for an excellent chance to get killed. Automated alarm systems were the deadliest aspect of his professional existence, somewhat tempered by the fact that smart and aggressive alarm systems frequently killed their owners. There was a basic engineering principle involved. Fancy, paranoid alarm systems went false-positive all the time: squirrels, dogs, wind, hail, earth tremors, horny boyfriends who forgot the password. . . . They were smart, and they had their own agenda, and it made them troublesome.

But if these machines were alarms, then they hadn't noticed a rather large hole painstakingly chopped in the side of their dome. The spars and transmitters looked bad, all patchy with long-accumulated rime and ice. A junkyard look, the definite smell of dead tech. So somebody had given up on these smart, expensive, paranoid alarms. Someone had gotten sick and tired of them, and shut them off.

At the foot of a microwave tower they found a rat-sized manhole chipped out, covered with a laced-down lid of sheep's hide. Pete dropped a spy-eye down, scoping out a machine-drilled shaft. The tunnel was wide enough to swallow a car, and it dropped down as straight as a plumb bob for farther than his eye's wiring could reach.

Pete silently yanked a rusting pig-iron piton from the edge of the hole, and replaced it with a modern glue anchor. Then he whipped a smart-rope through and carefully tightened his harness.

Katrinko began shaking with eagerness. "Pete, I am way hot for this. Lemme lead point."

Pete clipped a crab into Katrinko's harness, and linked their spex through the fiber-optic embedded in the rope. Then he slapped the neuter's shoulder. "Get bold, kid."

Katrinko flared out the webbing on her gripgloves, and dropped in feetfirst.

The would-be escapees had made a lot of use of cabling already present in the tunnel. There were ceramic staples embedded periodically, to hold the cabling snug against the stone. The climbers had scrabbled their way up from staple to staple, using ladder-runged bamboo poles and iron hooks.

Katrinko stopped her descent and tied off. Pete sent their haulbags down. Then he dropped and slithered after her. He stopped at the lead chock, tied off, and let Katrinko take lead again, following her progress with the spex.

An eerie glow shone at the bottom of the tunnel. Pay day. Pete felt a familiar transcendental tension overcome him. It surged through him with mad intensity. Fear, curiosity, and desire: the raw, hot, thieving thrill of a major-league intrusion. A feeling like being insane, but so much better than craziness, because now he felt so awake. Pete was awash in primal spiderness, cravings too deep and slippery to speak about.

The light grew hotter in Pete's infrareds. Below them was a slotted expanse of metal, gleaming like a kitchen sink, louvers with hot slots of light. Katrinko planted a foamchock in the tunnel wall, tied off, leaned back, and dropped a spy-eye through the slot.

Pete's hands were too busy to reach his spex. "What do you see?" he hissed over cable.

Katrinko craned her head back, gloved palms pressing the goggles against her face. "I can see *everything,* man! Gardens of Eden, and cities of gold!"

The cave had been ancient solid rock once, a continental bulk. The rock had been pierced by a Russian-made drilling rig. A dry well, in a very dry country. And then some very weary, and very sunburned, and very determined Chinese Communist weapons engineers had installed a one-hundred megaton hydrogen bomb at the bottom of their dry hole. When their beast in its nest of layered casings achieved fusion, seismographs jumped like startled fawns in distant California.

The thermonuclear explosion had left a giant gasbubble at the heart of a crazy webwork of faults and cracks. The deep and empty bubble had lurked beneath the desert in utter and terrible silence, for ninety years.

Then Asia's new masters had sent in new and more sophisticated agencies.

Pete saw that the distant sloping walls of the cavern were daubed with starlight. White constellations, whole and entire. And amid the space—that giant and sweetly damp airspace—were three great glowing lozenges, three vertical cylinders the size of urban highrises. They seemed to be suspended in midair.

"Starships," Pete muttered.

"Starships," Katrinko agreed. Menus appeared in the shared visual space of their linked spex. Katrinko's fingertip sketched out a set of tiny moving sparks against the walls. "But check that out."

"What are those?"

"Heat signatures. Little engines." The envisioned world wheeled silently. "And check out over here, too—

and crawlin' around deep in there, dozens of the things. And Pete, see these? Those big ones? Kinda on patrol."

"Robots."

"Yep."

"What the hell are they up to, down here?"

"Well, I figure it this way, man. If you're inside one of those fake starships, and you look out through those windows—those *portholes*, I guess we call 'em—you can't see anything but shiny stars. Deep space. But with spex, we can see right through all that business. And Pete, that whole stone sky down there is crawling with machinery."

"Man-oh-man."

"And nobody inside those starships can see *down*, man. There is a whole lot of very major weirdness going on down at the bottom of that cave. There's a lot of hot steamy water down there, deep in those rocks and those cracks."

"Water, or a big smelly soup maybe," Pete said. "A chemical soup."

"Biochemical soup."

"Autonomous self-assembly proteinaceous biotech. Strictly forbidden by the Nonproliferation Protocols of the Manila Accords of 2037," said Pete. Pete rattled off this phrase with practiced ease, having rehearsed it any number of times during various background briefings.

"A whole big lake of way-hot, way-illegal, self-assembling goo down there."

"Yep. The very stuff that our covert-tech boys have been messing with under the Rockies for the past ten years."

"Aw Pete, everybody cheats a little bit on the accords. The way we do it in NAFTA, it's no worse than bathtub gin. But this is *huge*! And Lord only knows what's inside those starships."

"Gotta be people, kid."

"Yep."

Pete drew a slow moist breath. "This is a big one, Trink. This is truly major league. You and me, we got ourselves an intelligence coup here of historic proportions."

"If you're trying to say that we should go back to the glider now," Katrinko said, "don't even start with me."

"We need to go back to the glider," Pete insisted, "with the photographic proof that we got right now. That was our mission objective. It's what they pay us for."

"Whoop-de-doo."

"Besides, it's the patriotic thing. Right?"

"Maybe I'd play the patriot game, if I was in uniform," said Katrinko. "But the army don't allow neuters. I'm a total freak and I'm a free agent, and I didn't come here to see Shangri-la and then turn around first thing."

"Yeah," Pete admitted. "I really know that feeling."

"I'm going down in there right now," Katrinko said. "You belay for me?"

"No way, kid. This time, I'm leading point."

Pete eased himself through a crudely broken louver and out onto the vast rocky ceiling. Pete had never much liked climbing rock. Nasty stuff, rock—all natural, no guaranteed engineering specifications. Still, Pete had spent a great deal of his life on ceilings. Ceilings he understood.

He worked his way out on a series of congealed lava knobs till he hit a nice solid crack. He did a rapid set of fist-jams, then set a pair of foam-clamps, and tied himself off on anchor.

Pete panned slowly in place, upside down on the ceiling, muffled in his camou gear, scanning methodically for the sake of Katrinko back on the fiber-optic spex link. Large sections of the ceiling looked weirdly worm-eaten, as if drills or acids had etched the rock away. Pete could discern in the eerie glow of infrared that the three fake starships were actually supported on columns. Huge hollow tubes, lacelike and almost entirely invisible, made of something black and impossibly strong, maybe carbon-fiber. There were water pipes inside the columns, and electrical power.

Those columns were the quickest and easiest ways to climb down or up to the starships. Those columns were also very exposed. They looked like excellent places to get killed.

Pete knew that he was safely invisible to any naked human eye, but there wasn't much he could do about his heat signature. For all he knew, at this moment he was glowing like a Christmas tree on the sensors of a thousand heavily armed robots. But you couldn't leave a thousand machines armed to a hair-trigger for years on end. And who would program them to spend their time watching ceilings?

The muscular burn had faded from his back and shoulders. Pete shook a little extra blood through his wrists, unhooked, and took off on cleats and gripwebs. He veered around one of the fake stars, a great glowing glassine bulb the size of a laundry basket. The fake star was cemented into a big rocky wart, and it radiated a cold, enchanting, and gooey firefly light. Pete was so intrigued by this bold deception that his cleat missed a smear. His left foot swung loose. His left shoulder emitted a nasty-feeling, expensive-sounding pop. Pete grunted, planted both cleats, and slapped up a glue patch, with tendons smarting and the old forearm clock ticking fast. He whipped a crab through the patchloop and sagged within his harness, breathing hard.

On the surface of his spex, Katrinko's glowing fingertip whipped across the field of Pete's vision, and pointed. Something moving out there. Pete had company.

Pete eased a string of flashbangs from his sleeve. Then he hunkered down in place, trusting to his camouflage, and watching.

A robot was moving toward him among the dark pits of the fake stars. Wobbling and jittering.

Pete had never seen any device remotely akin to this robot. It had a porous, foamy hide, like cork and plastic. It had a blind compartmented knob for a head, and fourteen long fibrous legs like a frayed mess of used rope, terminating in absurdly complicated feet, like a boxful of grip pliers. Hanging upside down from bits of rocky irregularity too small to see, it would open its big warty head and flick out a forked sensor like a snake's tongue. Sometimes it would dip itself close to the ceiling, for a lingering chemical smooch on the surface of the rock.

Pete watched with murderous patience as the device backed away, drew nearer, spun around a bit, meandered a little closer, sucked some more ceiling rock, made up its mind about something, replanted its big grippy feet, hoofed along closer yet, lost its train of thought, retreated a bit, sniffed the air at length, sucked meditatively on the end of one of its ropy tentacles.

It finally reached him, walked deftly over his legs, and dipped up to lick enthusiastically at the chemical traces left by his gripweb. The robot seemed enchanted by the taste of the glove's elastomer against the rock. It hung there on its fourteen-plier feet, loudly licking and rasping.

Pete lashed out with his pick. The razored point slid with a sullen crunch right through the thing's corky head.

It went limp instantly, pinned there against the ceiling. Then with a nasty rustling it deployed a whole unsuspected set of waxy and filmy appurtenances. Complex bug-tongue things, mandible scrapers, delicate little spatulas, all reeling and trembling out of its slotted underside.

It was not going to die. It couldn't die, because it had never been alive. It was a piece of biotechnical machinery. Dying was simply not on its agenda anywhere. Pete photographed the device carefully as it struggled with obscene mechanical stupidity to come to workable terms with its new environmental parameters. Then Pete levered the pick loose from the ceiling, shook it loose, and dropped the pierced robot straight down to hell.

Pete climbed more quickly now, favoring the strained shoulder. He worked his way methodically out to the relative ease of the vertical wall, where he discovered a large

mined-out vein in the constellation Sagittarius. The vein
was big snaky recess where some kind of ore had been
nibbled and strained from the rock. By the look of it, the
rock had been chewed away by a termite host of tiny robots with mouths like toenail clippers.

He signaled on the spex for Katrinko. The neuter followed along the clipped and anchored line, climbing like a
fiend while lugging one of the haulbags. As Katrinko settled in to their new base camp, Pete returned to the louvers
to fetch the second bag. When he'd finally heaved and
grappled his way back, his shoulder was aching bitterly
and his nerves were shot. They were done for the day.

Katrinko had put up the emission-free encystment
web at the mouth of their crevice. With Pete returned to
relative safety, she reeled in their smart-ropes and fed them
a handful of sugar.

Pete cracked open two capsules of instant fluff, then
sank back gratefully into the wool.

Katrinko took off her mask. She was vibrating with
alert enthusiasm. Youth, thought Pete, youth, and the
eight percent metabolic advantage that came from lacking
sex organs. "We're in so much trouble now," Katrinko
whispered, with a feverish grin in the faint red glow of
single indicator light. She no longer resembled a boy or
young woman. Katrinko looked completely diabolical.
This was a nonsexed creature. Pete liked to think of her as
a "she," because this was somehow easier on his mind, but
Katrinko was an "it." Now it was filled with glee, because
finally it had placed itself in a proper and pleasing situation. Stark and feral confrontation with its own stark and
feral little being.

"Yeah, this is trouble," Pete said. He placed a fat med-
icated tick onto the vein inside of his elbow. "And you're
taking first watch."

Pete woke four hours later, with a heart-fluttering rise
from the stunned depths of chemically assisted delta-sleep.

He felt numb, and lightly dusted with a brain-clouding amnesia, as if he'd slept for four straight days. He had been profoundly helpless in the grip of the drug, but the risk had been worth it, because now he was thoroughly rested. Pete sat up, and tried the left shoulder experimentally. It was much improved.

Pete rubbed feeling back into his stubbled face and scalp, then strapped his spex on. He discovered Katrinko squatting on her haunches, in the radiant glow of her own body heat, pondering over an ugly mess of spines, flakes, and goo.

Pete touched spex knobs and leaned forward. "What you got there?"

"Dead robots. They ate our foamchocks, right out of the ceiling. They eat anything. I killed the ones that tried to break into camp." Katrinko stroked at a midair menu, then handed Pete a fiber lead for his spex. "Check this footage I took."

Katrinko had been keeping watch with the gelcams, picking out passing robots in the glow of their engine heat. She'd documented them on infrared, saving and editing the clearest live-action footage. "These little ones with the ball-shaped feet, I call them 'keets,'" she narrated, as the captured frames cascaded across Pete's spex-clad gaze. "They're small, but they're really fast, and all over the place—I had to kill three of them. This one with the sharp spiral nose is a 'drillet.' Those are a pair of 'dubits.' The dubits always travel in pairs. This big thing here, that looks like a spilled dessert with big eyes and a ball on a chain, I call that one a 'lurchen.' Because of the way it moves, see? It's sure a lot faster than it looks."

Katrinko stopped the spex replay, switched back to live perception, and poked carefully at the broken litter before her booted feet. The biggest device in the heap resembled a dissected cat's head stuffed with cables and bristles. "I also killed this 'piteen.' Piteens don't die easy, man."

"There's lots of these things?"

"I figure hundreds, maybe thousands. All different kinds. And every one of 'em as stupid as dirt. Or else we'd be dead and disassembled a hundred times already."

Pete stared at the dissected robots, a cooling mass of nerve-netting, batteries, veiny armor plates, and gelatin. "Why do they look so crazy?"

" 'Cause they grew all by themselves. Nobody ever designed them." Katrinko glanced up. "You remember those big virtual spaces for weapons design that they run out in Alamogordo?"

"Yeah, sure, Alamogordo. Physics simulations on those super-size quantum gelbrains. Huge virtualities, with ultra-fast, ultra-fine detail. You bet I remember New Mexico! I love to raid a great computer lab. There's something so traditional about the hack."

"Yeah. See, for us NAFTA types, physics virtualities are a military app. We always give our tech to the military whenever it looks really dangerous. But let's say you don't share our NAFTA values. You don't wanna test new weapons systems inside giant virtualities. Let's say you want to make a can opener, instead."

During her sleepless hours huddling on watch, Katrinko had clearly been giving this matter a lot of thought. "Well, you could study other people's can openers and try to improve the design. Or else you could just set up a giant high-powered virtuality with a bunch of virtual cans inside it. Then you make some can-opener simulations, that are basically blobs of goo. They're simulated goo, but they're also programs, and those programs trade data and evolve. Whenever they pierce a can, you reward them by making more copies of them. You're running, like, a million generations of a million different possible can openers, all day every day, in a simulated space."

The concept was not entirely alien to Spider Pete. "Yeah, I've heard the rumors. It was one of those stunts like Artificial Intelligence. It might look really good on paper, but you can't ever get it to work in real life."

"Yeah, and now it's illegal, too. Kinda hard to police,

though. But let's imagine you're into economic warfare and you figure out how to do this. Finally, you evolve this super weird, super can opener that no human being could ever have invented. Something that no human being could even *imagine*. Because it grew like a mushroom in an entire alternate physics. But you have all the specs for its shape and proportions, right there in the supercomputer. So to make one inside the real world, you just print it out like a photograph. And it works! It runs! See? Instant cheap consumer goods."

Pete thought it over. "So you're saying the Sphere people got that idea to work, and these robots here were built that way?"

"Pete, I just can't figure any other way this could have happened. These machines are just too alien. They had to come from some totally nonhuman, autonomous process. Even the best Japanese engineers can't design a jelly robot made out of fuzz and rope that can move like a caterpillar. There's not enough money in the world to pay human brains to think that out."

Pete prodded at the gooey ruins with his pick. "Well, you got that right."

"Whoever built this place, they broke a lot of rules and treaties. But they did it all *really cheap*. They did it in a way that is so cheap that it is *beyond economics*." Katrinko thought this over. "It's *way* beyond economics, and that's exactly *why* it's against all those rules and the treaties in the first place."

"Fast, cheap, and out of control."

"Exactly, man. If this stuff ever got loose in the real world, it would mean the end of everything we know."

Pete liked this last statement not at all. He had always disliked apocalyptic hype. He liked it even less now because under these extreme circumstances it sounded very plausible. The Sphere had the youngest and the biggest population of the three major trading blocs, and the youngest and the biggest ideas. People in Asia knew how to get things done. "Y'know, Lyle Schweik once told me that the weirdest bicycles in the world come out of China these days."

"Well, he's right. They do. And what about those Chinese circuitry chips they've been dumping in the NAFTA markets lately? Those chips are dirt cheap and work fine, but they're full of all this crazy leftover wiring that doubles back and gets all snarled up. . . . I always thought that was just shoddy workmanship. Man, 'workmanship' had nothing to do with those chips."

Pete nodded soberly. "Okay. Chips and bicycles, that much I can understand. There's a lot of money in that. But who the heck would take the trouble to create a giant hole in the ground that's full of robots and fake stars? I mean, *why?*"

Katrinko shrugged. "I guess it's just the Sphere, man. They still do stuff just because it's wonderful."

The bottom of the world was boiling over. During the passing century, the nuclear test cavity had accumulated its own little desert aquifer, a pitch-black subterranean oasis. The bottom of the bubble was an unearthly drowned maze of shattered cracks and chemical deposition, all turned to simmering tidepools of mechanical self-assemblage. Oxygen-fizzing geysers of black fungus tea.

Steam rose steadily in the darkness amid the crags, rising to condense and run in chilly rivulets down the spherical star-spangled walls. Down at the bottom, all the water was eagerly collected by aberrant devices of animated sponge and string. Katrinko instantly tagged these as "smits" and "fuzzens."

The smits and fuzzens were nightmare dishrags and piston-powered spaghetti, leaping and slopping wetly from crag to crag. Katrinko took an unexpected ease and pleasure in naming and photographing the machines. Speculation boiled with sinister ease from the sexless youngster's vulpine head, a swift off-the-cuff adjustment to this alien toy world. It would seem that the kid lived rather closer to the future than Pete did.

They cranked their way from boulder to boulder, crack to liquid crack. They documented fresh robot larvae, chewing their way to the freedom of darkness through plugs of goo and muslin. It was a whole miniature creation, designed in the senseless gooey cores of a Chinese supercomputing gelbrain, and transmuted into reality in a hot broth of undead mechanized protein. This was by far the most amazing phenomenon that Pete had ever witnessed. Pete was accordingly plunged into gloom. Knowledge was power in his world. He knew with leaden certainty that he was taking on far too much voltage for his own good.

Pete was a professional. He could imagine stealing classified military secrets from a superpower, and surviving that experience. It would be very risky, but in the final analysis it was just the military. A rocket base, for instance—a secret Asian rocket base might have been a lot of fun.

But this was not military. This was an entire new means of industrial production. Pete knew with instinctive street-level certainty that tech of this level of revolutionary weirdness was not a spy thing, a sports thing, or a soldier thing. This was a big, big money thing. He might survive discovering it. He'd never get away with revealing it.

The thrilling wonder of it all really bugged him. Thrilling wonder was at best a passing thing. The sober implications for the longer term weighed on Pete's soul like a damp towel. He could imagine escaping this place in one piece, but he couldn't imagine any plausible aftermath for handing over nifty photographs of thrilling wonder to military spooks on the Potomac. He couldn't imagine what the powers-that-were would do with that knowledge. He rather dreaded what they would do to him for giving it to them.

Pete wiped a sauna cascade of sweat from his neck.

"So I figure it's either geothermal power, or a fusion generator down there," said Katrinko.

"I'd be betting thermonuclear, given the circumstances." The rocks below their busy cleats were a-skitter with bugs: gippers and ghents and kebbits, dismantlers and glue-spreaders and brain-eating carrion disassemblers. They were profoundly dumb little devices, as specialized as centipedes. They didn't seem very aggressive, but it surely would be a lethal mistake to sit down among them.

A barnacle thing with an iris mouth and long whipping eyes took a careful taste of Katrinko's boot. She retreated to a crag with a yelp.

"Wear your mask," Pete chided. The damp heat was bliss after the skin-eating chill of the Taklamakan, but most of the vents and cracks were spewing thick smells of hot beef stew and burnt rubber, all varieties of eldritch mechano-metabolic by-product. His lungs felt sore at the very thought of it.

Pete cast his foggy spex upward the nearest of the carbon-fiber columns, and the golden, glowing, impossibly tempting lights of those starship portholes up above.

Katrinko led point. She was pitilessly exposed against the lacelike girders. They didn't want to risk exposure during two trips, so they each carried a haulbag.

The climb went well at first. Then a machine rose up from wet darkness like a six-winged dragonfly. Its stinging tail lashed through the thready column like the kick of a mule. It connected brutally. Katrinko shot backward from the impact, tumbled ten meters, and dangled like a ragdoll from her last backup chock.

The flying creature circled in a figure eight, attempting to make up its nonexistent mind. Then a slower but much larger creature writhed and fluttered out of the starry sky, and attacked Katrinko's dangling haulbag. The bag burst like a Christmas pinata in a churning array of taloned wings. A fabulous cascade of expensive spy gear splashed down to the hot pools below.

Katrinko twitched feebly at the end of her rope. The dragonfly, cruelly alerted, went for her movement. Pete launched a string of flashbangs.

The world erupted in flash, heat, concussion, and flying chaff. Impossibly hot and loud, a thunderstorm in a closet. The best kind of disappearance magic: total overwhelming distraction, the only real magic in the world.

Pete soared up to Katrinko like a balloon on a bungee cord. When he reached the bottom of the starship, twenty-seven heart-pounding seconds later, he had burned out both the smart-ropes.

The silvery rain of chaff was driving the bugs to mania. The bottom of the cavern was suddenly a-crawl with leaping mechanical heat-ghosts, an instant menagerie of skippers and humpers and floppers. At the rim of perception there were new things rising from the depths of the pools, vast and scaly, like golden carp to a rain of fish chow.

Pete's own haulbag had been abandoned at the base of the column. That bag was clearly not long for this world.

Katrinko came to with a sudden winded gasp. They began free-climbing the outside of the starship. Its surface was stony, rough and uneven, something like pumice, or wasp spit.

They found the underside of a monster porthole and pressed themselves flat against the surface.

There they waited, inert and unmoving, for an hour. Katrinko caught her breath. Her ribs stopped bleeding. The two of them waited for another hour, while crawling and flying heat-ghosts nosed furiously around their little world, following the tatters of their programming. They waited a third hour.

Finally they were joined in their haven by an oblivious gang of machines with suckery skirts and wheelbarrows for heads. The robots chose a declivity and began filling it with big mandible trowels of stony mortar, slopping it on and jaw-chiselling it into place, smoothing everything over, tireless and pitiless.

Pete seized this opportunity to attempt to salvage their lost equipment. There had been such fabulous federal bounty in there: smart audio bugs, heavy-duty gelcams, sensors and detectors, pulleys, crampons, and latches, priceless vials of programmed neural goo. . . . Pete crept back to the bottom of the spacecraft.

Everything was long gone. Even the depleted smart-ropes had been eaten, by a long trail of foraging keets. The little machines were still squirreling about in the black lace of the column, sniffing and scraping at the last molecular traces, with every appearance of satisfaction.

Pete rejoined Katrinko, and woke her where she clung rigid and stupefied to her hiding spot. They inched their way around the curved rim of the starship hull, hunting for a possible weakness. They were in very deep trouble now, for their best equipment was gone. It didn't matter. Their course was very obvious now, and the loss of alternatives had clarified Pete's mind. He was consumed with a burning desire to break in.

Pete slithered into the faint shelter of a large, deeply pitted hump. There he discovered a mess of braided rope. The rope was woven of dead and mashed organic fibers, something like the hair at the bottom of a sink. The rope had gone all petrified under a stony lacquer of robot spit.

These were climber's ropes. Someone had broken out here—smashed through the hull of the ship, from the inside. The robots had come to repair the damage, carefully resealing the exit hole, and leaving this ugly hump of stony scar tissue.

Pete pulled his gelcam drill. He had lost the sugar reserves along with the haulbags. Without sugar to metabolize, the little enzyme-driven rotor would starve and be useless soon. That fact could not be helped. Pete pressed the device against the hull, waited as it punched its way through, and squirted in a gelcam to follow.

He saw a farm. Pete could scarcely have been less astonished. It was certainly farmland, though. Cute, toy farmland, all under a stony blue ceiling, crisscrossed with hot grids of radiant light, embraced in the stony arch of the enclosing hull. There were fishponds with reeds. Ditches, and a wooden irrigation wheel. A little bridge of bamboo. There were hairy melon vines in rich black soil and neat, entirely weedless fields of dwarfed red grain. Not a soul in sight.

Katrinko crept up and linked in on cable. "So where is everybody?" Pete said.

"They're all at the portholes," said Katrinko, coughing.

"What?" said Pete, surprised. "Why?"

"Because of those flashbangs," Katrinko wheezed. Her battered ribs were still paining her. "They're all at the portholes, looking out into the darkness. Waiting for something else to happen."

"But we did that stuff hours ago."

"It was very big news, man. Nothing ever happens in there."

Pete nodded, fired with resolve. "Well then. We're breakin' in."

Katrinko was way game. "Gonna use caps?"

"Too obvious."

"Acids and fibrillators?"

"Lost 'em in the haulbags."

"Well, that leaves cheesewires," Katrinko concluded. "I got two."

"I got six."

Katrinko nodded in delight. "Six cheesewires! You're loaded for bear, man!"

"I love cheesewires," Pete grunted. He had helped to invent them.

Eight minutes and twelve seconds later they were inside the starship. They reset the cored-out plug behind them, delicately gluing it in place and carefully obscuring the hair-thin cuts.

Katrinko sidestepped into a grove of bamboo. Her

camou bloomed in green and tan and yellow, with such
instant and treacherous ease that Pete lost her entirely.
Then she waved, and the spex edge detectors kicked in on
her silhouette.

Pete lifted his spex for a human naked-eye take on the
situation. There was simply nothing there at all. Katrinko
was gone, less than a ghost, like pitchforking mercury with
your eyelashes.

So they were safe now. They could glide through this
bottled farm like a pair of bad dreams.

They scanned the spacecraft from top to bottom, looking
for dangerous and interesting phenomena. Control rooms
manned by Asian space technicians maybe, or big lethal
robots, or video monitors—something that might cramp
their style or kill them. In the thirty-seven floors of the
spacecraft, they found no such thing.

The five thousand inhabitants spent their waking
hours farming. The crew of the starship were preindus-
trial, tribal, Asian peasants. Men, women, old folks, little
kids.

The local peasants rose every single morning, as their
hot networks of wiring came alive in the ceiling. They
would milk their goats. They would feed their sheep, and
some very odd, knee-high, dwarf Bactrian camels. They
cut bamboo and netted their fishponds. They cut down
tamarisks and poplar trees for firewood. They tended
melon vines and grew plums and hemp. They brewed alcohol, and ground grain, and boiled millet, and squeezed
cooking oil out of rapeseed. They made clothes out of
hemp and raw wool and leather, and baskets out of reeds
and straw. They ate a lot of carp.

And they raised a whole mess of chickens. Somebody
not from around here had been fooling with the chickens.
Apparently these were super space-chickens of some kind,
leftover lab products from some serious long-term attempt
to screw around with chicken DNA. The hens produced

five or six lumpy eggs every day. The roosters were enormous, and all different colors, and very smelly, and distinctly reptilian.

It was very quiet and peaceful inside the starship. The animals made their lowing and clucking noises, and the farm workers sang to themselves in the tiny round-edged fields, and the incessant foot-driven water pumps would clack rhythmically, but there were no city noises. No engines anywhere. No screens. No media.

There was no money. There were a bunch of tribal elders who sat under the blossoming plum trees outside the big stone granaries. They messed with beads on wires, and wrote notes on slips of wood. Then the soldiers, or the cops—they were a bunch of kids in crude leather armor, with spears—would tramp in groups, up and down the dozens of stairs, on the dozens of floors. Marching like crazy, and requisitioning stuff, and carrying stuff on their backs, and handing things out to people. Basically spreading the wealth around.

Most of the weird bearded old guys were palace accountants, but there were some others, too. They sat cross-legged on mats in their homemade robes, and straw sandals, and their little spangly hats, discussing important matters at slow and extreme length. Sometimes they wrote stuff down on palm leaves.

Pete and Katrinko spent a special effort to spy on these old men in the spangled hats, because after close study, they had concluded that this was the local government. They pretty much had to be the government. These old men with the starry hats were the only part of the population who weren't being worked to a frazzle.

Pete and Katrinko found themselves a cozy spot on the roof of the granary, one of the few permanent structures inside the spacecraft. It never rained inside the starship, so there wasn't much call for roofs. Nobody ever trespassed up on the roof of the granary. It was clear that the very idea of doing this was beyond local imagination. So Pete and Katrinko stole some bamboo water jugs, and some lovely handmade carpets, and a lean-to tent, and set up camp there.

Katrinko studied an especially elaborate palm-leaf book that she had filched from the local temple. There were pages and pages of dense alien script. "Man, what do you suppose these yokels have to write about?"

"The way I figure it," said Pete, "they're writing down everything they can remember from the world outside."

"Yeah?"

"Yeah. Kinda building up an intelligence dossier for their little starship regime, see? Because that's all they'll ever know, because the people who put them inside here aren't giving 'em any news. And they're sure as hell never gonna let 'em out."

Katrinko leafed carefully through the stiff and brittle pages of the handmade book. The people here spoke only one language. It was no language Pete or Katrinko could even begin to recognize. "Then this is their history. Right?"

"It's their lives, kid. Their past lives, back when they were still real people, in the big real world outside. Transistor radios, and shoulder-launched rockets. Barbed wire, pacification campaigns, ID cards. Camel caravans coming in over the border, with mortars and explosives. And very advanced Sphere mandarin bosses, who just don't have the time to put up with armed, Asian, tribal fanatics."

Katrinko looked up. "That kinda sounds like *your* version of the outside world, Pete."

Pete shrugged. "Hey, it's what happens."

"You suppose these guys really believe they're inside a real starship?"

"I guess that depends on how much they learned from the guys who broke out of here with the picks and the ropes."

Katrinko thought about it. "You know what's truly pathetic? The shabby illusion of all this. Some spook mandarin's crazy notion that ethnic separatists could be squeezed down tight, and spat out like watermelon seeds into interstellar space. . . . Man, what a *come-on,* what an enticement, what an empty promise."

"I could sell that idea," Pete said thoughtfully. "You know how *far away* the stars really are, kid? About *four hundred years* away, that's how far. You seriously want to get human beings to travel to another star, you gotta put human beings inside of a sealed can for four hundred solid years. But what are people supposed to do in there, all that time? The only thing they *can* do is quietly run a farm. Because that's what a starship is. It's a desert oasis."

"So you want to try a dry-run starship experiment," said Katrinko. "And in the meantime, you happen to have some handy religious fanatics in the backwoods of Asia, who are shooting your ass off. Guys who refuse to change their age-old lives, even though you are very, very high-tech."

"Yep. That's about the size of it. Means, motive, and opportunity."

"I get it. But I can't believe that somebody went through with that scheme in real life. I mean, rounding up an ethnic minority, and sticking them down in some godforsaken hole, just so you'll never have to think about them again. That's just impossible!"

"Did I ever tell you that my grandfather was a Seminole?" Pete said.

Katrinko shook her head. "What's that mean?"

"They were American tribal guys who ended up stuck in a swamp. The Florida Seminoles, they called 'em. Y'know, maybe they just *called* my grandfather a Seminole. He dressed really funny. . . . Maybe it just *sounded good* to call him a Seminole. Otherwise, he just would have been some strange, illiterate geezer."

Katrinko's brow wrinkled. "Does it *matter* that your grandfather was a Seminole?"

"I used to think it did. That's where I got my skin color—as if that matters, nowadays. I reckon it mattered plenty to my grandfather, though. . . . He was always stompin' and carryin' on about a lot of weird stuff we couldn't understand. His English was pretty bad. He was never around much when we needed him."

"Pete. . . ." Katrinko sighed. "I think it's time we got out of this place."

"How come?" Pete said, surprised. "We're safe up here. The locals are not gonna hurt us. They can't even *see* us. They can't touch us. Hell, they can't even *imagine* us. With our fantastic tactical advantages, we're just like gods to these people."

"I know all that, man. They're like the ultimate dumb straight people. I don't like them very much. They're not much of a challenge to us. In fact, they kind of creep me out."

"No way! They're fascinating. Those baggy clothes, the acoustic songs, all that menial labor. . . . These people got something that we modern people just don't have anymore."

"Huh?" Katrinko said. "Like *what*, exactly?"

"I dunno," Pete admitted.

"Well, whatever it is, it can't be very important." Katrinko sighed. "We got some serious challenges on the agenda, man. We gotta sidestep our way past all those angry robots outside, then head up that shaft, then hoof it back, four days through a freezing desert, with no haulbags. All the way back to the glider."

"But Trink, there are two other starships in here that we didn't break into yet. Don't you want to see those guys?"

"What I'd like to see right now is a hot bath in a four-star hotel," said Katrinko. "And some very big international headlines, maybe. All about *me*. That would be lovely." She grinned.

"But what about the people?"

"Look, I'm not 'people,'" Katrinko said calmly. "Maybe it's because I'm a neuter, Pete, but I can tell you're way off the subject. These people are none of our business. Our business now is to return to our glider in an

operational condition so that we can complete our as-
signed mission, and return to base with our data. Okay?"

"Well, let's break into just one more starship first."

"We gotta move, Pete. We've lost our best equipment,
and we're running low on body fat. This isn't something
that we can kid about and live."

"But we'll never come back here again. Somebody
will, but it sure as heck won't be us. See, it's a Spider
thing."

Katrinko was weakening. "One more starship? Not
both of 'em?"

"Just one more."

"Okay, good deal."

The hole they had cut through the starship's hull had been
rapidly cemented by robots. It cost them two more
cheesewires to cut themselves a new exit. Then Katrinko
led point, up across the stony ceiling, and down the carbon column to the second ship. To avoid annoying the
lurking robot guards, they moved with hypnotic slowness
and excessive stealth. This made it a grueling trip.

This second ship had seen hard use. The hull was ex-
tensively scarred with great wads of cement, entombing
many lengths of dried and knotted rope. Pete and Katrinko found a weak spot and cut their way in.

This starship was crowded. It was loud inside, and it
smelled. The floors were crammed with hot and sticky little bazaars, where people sold handicrafts and liquor and
food. Criminals were being punished by being publicly
chained to posts and pelted with offal by passersby. Big
crowds of ragged men and tattooed women gathered
around brutal cockfights, featuring spurred mutant chickens half the size of dogs. All the men carried knives.

The architecture here was more elaborate, all kinds of
warrens, and courtyards, and damp, sticky alleys. After
exploring four floors, Katrinko suddenly declared that she
recognized their surroundings. According to Katrinko,

they were a physical replica of sets from a popular Japanese interactive samurai epic. Apparently the starship's designers had needed some pre-industrial Asian village settings, and they hadn't wanted to take the expense and trouble to design them from scratch. So they had programmed their construction robots with pirated game designs.

This starship had once been lavishly equipped with at least three hundred armed video camera installations. Apparently, the mandarins had come to the stunning realization that the mere fact that they were recording crime didn't mean that they could control it. Their spy cameras were all dead now. Most had been vandalized. Some had gone down fighting. They were all inert and abandoned.

The rebellious locals had been very busy. After defeating the spy cameras, they had created a set of giant hullbreakers. These were siege engines, big crossbow torsion machines, made of hemp and wood and bamboo. The hullbreakers were starship community efforts, elaborately painted and ribboned, and presided over by tough, aggressive gang bosses with batons and big leather belts.

Pete and Katrinko watched a labor gang, hard at work on one of the hullbreakers. Women braided rope ladders from hair and vegetable fiber, while smiths forged pitons over choking, hazy charcoal fires. It was clear from the evidence that these restive locals had broken out of their starship jail at least twenty times. Every time they had been corralled back in by the relentless efforts of mindless machines. Now they were busily preparing yet another breakout.

"These guys sure have got initiative," said Pete admiringly. "Let's do 'em a little favor, okay?"

"Yeah?"

"Here they are, taking all this trouble to hammer their way out. But we still have a bunch of caps. We got no more use for 'em, after we leave this place. So the way I figure it, we blow their wall out big-time, and let a whole

bunch of 'em loose at once. Then you and I can escape real
easy in the confusion."

Katrinko loved this idea, but had to play devil's advo-
cate. "You really think we ought to interfere like that?
That kind of shows our hand, doesn't it?"

"Nobody's watching anymore," said Pete. "Some
technocrat figured this for a big lab experiment. But they
wrote these people off, or maybe they lost their anthropol-
ogy grant. These people are totally forgotten. Let's give the
poor bastards a show."

Pete and Katrinko planted their explosives, took cover
on the ceiling, and cheerfully watched the wall blow out.

A violent gust of air came through as pressures equal-
ized, carrying a hemorrhage of dust and leaves into interstellar space. The locals were totally astounded by the
explosion, but when the repair robots showed up, they
soon recovered their morale. A terrific battle broke out, a
general vengeful frenzy of crab-bashing and sponge-
skewering. Women and children tussled with the keets and
bibbets. Soldiers in leather cuirasses fought with the bigger
machines, deploying pikes, crossbow quarrels, and big
robot-mashing mauls.

The robots were profoundly stupid, but they were indifferent to their casualties, and entirely relentless.

The locals made the most of their window of opportunity. They loaded a massive harpoon into a torsion cata-
pult, and fired it into space. Their target was the
neighboring starship, the third and last of them.

The barbed spear bounded off the hull. So they reeled
it back in on a monster bamboo hand-reel, cursing and
shouting like maniacs.

The starship's entire population poured into the fight.
The walls and bulkheads shook with the tramp of their
angry feet. The outnumbered robots fell back. Pete and
Katrinko seized this golden opportunity to slip out the
hole. They climbed swiftly up the hull, and out of reach of
the combat.

The locals fired their big harpoon again. This time the
barbed tip struck true, and it stuck there quivering.

Then a little kid was heaved into place, half-naked,
with a hammer and screws, and a rope threaded through
his belt. He had a crown of dripping candles set upon his
head.

Katrinko glanced back, and stopped dead.

Pete urged her on, then stopped as well.

The child began reeling himself industriously along
the trembling harpoon line, trailing a bigger rope. An airborne machine came to menace him. It fell back twitching,
pestered by a nasty scattering of crossbow bolts.

Pete found himself mesmerized. He hadn't felt the des-
peration of the circumstances, until he saw this brave little
boy ready to fall to his death. Pete had seen many climbers
who took risks because they were crazy. He'd seen professional climbers, such as himself, who played games with
risk as masters of applied technique. He'd never witnessed
climbing as an act of raw, desperate sacrifice.

The heroic child arrived on the grainy hull of the alien
ship, and began banging his pitons in a hammer-swinging
frenzy. His crown of candles shook and flickered with his
efforts. The boy could barely see. He had slung himself out
into stygian darkness to fall to his doom.

Pete climbed up to Katrinko and quickly linked in on
cable. "We gotta leave now, kid. It's now or never."

"Not yet," Katrinko said. "I'm taping all this."

"It's our big chance."

"We'll go later." Katrinko watched a flying vacuum
cleaner batting by, to swat cruelly at the kid's legs. She
turned her masked head to Pete and her whole body stiff-
ened with rage. "You got a cheesewire left?"

"I got three."

"Gimme. I gotta go help him."

Katrinko unplugged, slicked down the starship's wall in a
daring controlled slide, and hit the stretched rope. To

Pete's complete astonishment, Katrinko lit there in a crouch, caught herself atop the vibrating line, and simply ran for it. She ran along the humming tightrope in a thrumming blur, stunning the locals so thoroughly that they were barely able to fire their crossbows.

Flying quarrels whizzed past and around her, nearly skewering the terrified child at the far end of the rope. Then Katrinko leapt and bounded into space, her gloves and cleats outspread. She simply vanished.

It was a champion's gambit if Pete had ever seen one. It was a legendary move.

Pete could manage well enough on a tightrope. He had experience, excellent balance, and physical acumen. He was, after all, a professional. He could walk a rope if he was put to the job.

But not in full climbing gear, with cleats. And not on a slack, handbraided, homemade rope. Not when the rope was very poorly anchored by a homemade pig-iron harpoon. Not when he outweighed Katrinko by twenty kilos. Not in the middle of a flying circus of airborne robots. And not in a cloud of arrows.

Pete was simply not that crazy anymore. Instead, he would have to follow Katrinko the sensible way. He would have to climb the starship, transverse the ceiling, and climb down to the third starship onto the far side. A hard three hours' work at the very best—four hours, with any modicum of safety.

Pete weighed the odds, made up his mind, and went after the job.

Pete turned in time to see Katrinko busily cheesewiring her way through the hull of Starship Three. A gout of white light poured out as the cored plug slid aside. For a deadly moment, Katrinko was a silhouetted goblin, her camou useless as the starship's radiance framed her. Her clothing fluttered in a violent gust of escaping air.

Below her, the climbing child had anchored himself to the wall and tied off his second rope. He looked up at the sudden gout of light, and he screamed so loudly that the whole universe rang.

The child's many relatives reacted by instinct, with a ragged volley of crossbow shots. The arrows veered and scattered in the gusting wind, but there were a lot of them. Katrinko ducked, and flinched, and rolled headlong into the starship. She vanished again.

Had she been hit? Pete set an anchor, tied off, and tried the radio. But without the relays in the haulbag, the weak signal could not get through.

Pete climbed on doggedly. It was the only option left.

After half an hour, Pete began coughing. The starry cosmic cavity had filled with a terrible smell. The stench was coming from the invaded starship, pouring slowly from the cored-out hole. A long-bottled, deadly stink of burning rot.

Climbing solo, Pete gave it his best. His shoulder was bad and, worse yet, his spex began to misbehave. He finally reached the cored-out entrance that Katrinko had cut. The locals were already there in force, stringing themselves a sturdy rope bridge, and attaching it to massive screws. The locals brandished torches, spears, and crossbows. They were fighting off the incessant attacks of the robots. It was clear from their wild expressions of savage glee that they had been longing for this moment for years.

Pete slipped past them unnoticed, into Starship Three. He breathed the soured air for a moment, and quickly retreated again. He inserted a new set of mask filters, and returned.

He found Katrinko's cooling body, wedged against the ceiling. An unlucky crossbow shot had slashed through her suit and punctured Katrinko's left arm. So, with her usual presence of mind, she had deftly leapt up a nearby wall, tied off on a chock, and hidden herself well out of harm's way. She'd quickly stopped the bleeding. Despite its awkward location, she'd even managed to get her wound bandaged.

Then the foul air had silently and stealthily overcome her.

With her battered ribs and a major wound, Katrinko hadn't been able to tell her dizziness from shock. Feeling sick, she had relaxed, and tried to catch her breath. A fatal gambit. She was still hanging there, unseen and invisible, dead.

Pete discovered that Katrinko was far from alone. The crew here had all died. Died months ago, maybe years ago. Some kind of huge fire inside the spacecraft. The electric lights were still on, the internal machinery worked, but there was no one left here but mummies.

These dead tribal people had the nicest clothes Pete had yet seen. Clearly they'd spent a lot of time knitting and embroidering, during the many weary years of their imprisonment. The corpses had all kinds of layered sleeves, and tatted aprons, and braided belt-ties, and lacquered hairclips, and excessively nifty little sandals. They'd all smothered horribly during the sullen inferno, along with their cats and dogs and enormous chickens, in a sudden wave of smoke and combustion that had filled their spacecraft in minutes.

This was far too complicated to be anything as simple as mere genocide. Pete figured the mandarins for gentlemen technocrats, experts with the best of intentions. The lively possibility remained that it was mass suicide. But on mature consideration, Pete had to figure this for a very bad, and very embarrassing, social-engineering accident.

Though that certainly wasn't what they would say about this mess, in Washington. There was no political mess nastier than a nasty ethnic mess. Pete couldn't help but notice that these well-behaved locals hadn't bothered to do any harm to their spacecraft's lavish surveillance equipment. But their cameras were off and their starship was stone dead anyway.

The air began to clear inside the spacecraft. A pair of soldiers from Starship Number Two came stamping down the hall, industriously looting the local corpses. They couldn't have been happier about their opportunity. They were grinning with awestruck delight.

Pete returned to his comrade's stricken body. He stripped the camou suit—he needed the batteries. The neuter's lean and sexless corpse was puffy with subcutaneous storage pockets, big encystments of skin where Katrinko stored her last-ditch escape tools. The battered ribs were puffy and blue. Pete could not go on.

Pete returned to the break-in hole, where he found an eager crowd. The invaders had run along the rope-bridge and gathered there in force, wrinkling their noses and cheering in wild exaltation. They had beaten the robots; there simply weren't enough of the machines on duty to resist a whole enraged population. The robots just weren't clever enough to out-think armed, coordinated human resistance—not without killing people wholesale, and they hadn't been designed for that. They had suffered a flat-out defeat.

Pete frightened the cheering victors away with a string of flashbangs.

Then he took careful aim at the lip of the drop, and hoisted Katrinko's body, and flung her far, far, tumbling down, into the boiling pools.

Pete retreated to the first spacecraft. It was a very dispiriting climb, and when he had completed it, his shoulder had the serious, familiar ache of chronic injury. He hid among the unknowing population while he contemplated his options.

He could hide here indefinitely. His camou suit was slowly losing its charge, but he felt confident that he could manage very well without the suit. The starship seemed to feature most any number of taboo areas. Blocked-off no-go spots, where there might have been a scandal once, or bloodshed, or a funny noise, or a strange, bad, panicky smell.

Unlike the violent, reckless crowd in Starship Two,

these locals had fallen for the cover story. They truly believed they were in the depths of space, bound for some better, brighter pie in their starry stone sky. Their little stellar ghetto was full of superstitious kinks. Steeped in profound ignorance, the locals imagined that their every sin caused the universe to tremble.

Pete knew that he should try to take his data back to the glider. This was what Katrinko would have wanted. To die, but leave a legend—a very City Spider thing.

But it was hard to imagine battling his way past resurgent robots, climbing the walls with an injured shoulder, then making a four-day bitter trek through a freezing desert, all completely alone. Gliders didn't last forever, either. Spy gliders weren't built to last. If Pete found the glider with its batteries flat, or its cute little brain gone sour, Pete would be all over. Even if he'd enjoyed a full set of equipment, with perfect health, Pete had few illusions about a solo spring outing, alone and on foot, over the Himalayas.

Why risk all that? After all, it wasn't like this subterranean scene was breaking news. It was already many years old. Someone had conceived, planned, and executed this business a long time ago. Important people with brains and big resources had known all about this for years. Somebody knew. Maybe not the Lieutenant Colonel, on the lunatic fringe of NAFTA military intelligence. But . . .

When Pete really thought about the basic implications. . . . This was a great deal of effort, and for not that big a payoff. Because there just weren't that many people cooped up down here. Maybe fifteen thousand of them, tops. The Asian Sphere must have had tens of thousands of unassimilated tribal people, maybe hundreds of thousands. Possibly millions. And why stop at that point? This wasn't just an Asian problem. It was a very general problem. Ethnic, breakaway people, who just plain couldn't, or wouldn't, play the twenty-first century's games.

How many Red Chinese atom-bomb tests had taken place deep in the Taklamakan? They'd never bothered to brief him on ancient history. But Pete had to wonder if, by

now, maybe they hadn't gotten this stellar concept down
to a fine art. Maybe the Sphere had franchised their plan
to Europe and NAFTA. How many forgotten holes were
there, relic pockets punched below the hide of the twenty-
first century, in the South Pacific, and Australia, and Ne-
vada? The deadly trash of a long-derailed armageddon.
The sullen trash-heaps where no one would ever want to
look.

Sure, he could bend every nerve and muscle to force
the world to face all this. But why? Wouldn't it make better sense to try to think it through first?

Pete never got around to admitting to himself that he
had lost the will to leave.

As despair slowly loosened its grip on him, Pete grew genuinely interested in the locals. He was intrigued by the
stark limits of their lives and their universe, and in what he
could do with their narrow little heads. They'd never had
a supernatural being in their midst before; they just imagined them all the time. Pete started with a few poltergeist
stunts, just to amuse himself. Stealing the spangled hats of
the local graybeards. Shuffling the palm-leaf volumes in
their sacred libraries. Hijacking an abacus or two.

But that was childish.

The locals had a little temple, their special holy of
holies. Naturally Pete made it his business to invade the
place.

The locals kept a girl locked up in there. She was very
pretty, and slightly insane, so this made her the perfect
candidate to become their Sacred Temple Girl. She was the
Official Temple Priestess of Starship Number One. Apparently, their modest community could only afford one, single, awe-inspiring Virgin High Priestess. But they were
practical folks, so they did the best with what they had
available.

The High Priestess was a pretty young woman with a
stiflingly pretty life. She had her own maidservants, a

wardrobe of ritual clothing, and a very time-consuming hairdo. The High Priestess spent her entire life carrying out highly complex, totally useless ritual actions. Incense burnings, idol dustings, washings and purifications, forehead knockings, endless chanting, daubing special marks on her hands and feet. She was sacred and clearly demented, so they watched her with enormous interest, all the time. She meant everything to them. She was doing all these crazy, painful things so the rest of them wouldn't have to. Everything about her was completely and utterly foreclosed.

Pete quite admired the Sacred Temple Girl. She was very much his type, and he felt a genuine kinship with her. She was the only local who Pete could bear to spend any personal time with.

So after prolonged study of the girl and her actions, one day Pete manifested himself to her. First, she panicked. Then she tried to kill him. Naturally that effort failed. When she grasped the fact that he was hugely powerful, totally magical, and utterly beyond her ken, she slithered around the polished temple floor, rending her garments and keening aloud, clearly in the combined hope/fear of being horribly and indescribably defiled.

Pete understood the appeal of her concept. A younger Pete would have gone for the demonic subjugation option. But Pete was all grown up now. He hardly saw how that could help matters any, or, in fact, make any tangible difference in their circumstances.

They never learned each other's languages. They never connected in any physical, mental, or emotional way. But they finally achieved a kind of status quo, where they could sit together in the same room, and quietly study one another, and fruitlessly speculate on the alien contents of one another's heads. Sometimes, they would even get together and eat something tasty.

That was every bit as good as his connection with these impossibly distant people was ever going to get.

•   •   •

It had never occurred to Pete that the stars might go out.

He'd cut himself a sacred, demonic bolt-hole, in a taboo area of the starship. Every once in a while, he would saw his way through the robot's repair efforts and nick out for a good long look at the artificial cosmos. This reassured him, somehow. And he had other motives as well. He had a very well-founded concern that the inhabitants of Starship Two might somehow forge their way over, for a violent racist orgy of looting, slaughter, and rapine.

But Starship Two had their hands full with the robots. Any defeat of the bubbling gelbrain and its hallucinatory tools could only be temporary. Like an onrushing mudslide, the gizmos would route around obstructions, infiltrate every evolutionary possibility, and always, always keep the pressure on.

After the crushing defeat, the bubbling production vats went into biomechanical overdrive. The old regime had been overthrown. All equilibrium was gone. The machines had gone back to their cybernetic dreamtime. Anything was possible now.

The starry walls grew thick as fleas with a seething mass of new-model jailers. Starship Two was beaten back once again, in another bitter, uncounted, historical humiliation. Their persecuted homeland became a mass of grotesque cement. Even the portholes were gone now, cruelly sealed in technological spit and ooze. A living grave.

Pete had assumed that this would pretty much finish the job. After all, this clearly fit the parameters of the system's original designers.

But the system could no longer bother with the limits of human intent.

When Pete gazed through a porthole and saw that the stars were fading, he knew that all bets were off. The stars were being robbed. Something was embezzling their energy.

He left the starship. Outside, all heaven had broken loose. An unspeakable host of creatures were migrating up the rocky walls, bounding, creeping, lurching, rappelling on a web of gooey ropes. Heading for the stellar zenith.

Bound for transcendence. Bound for escape.

Pete checked his aging cleats and gloves, and joined the exodus at once.

None of the creatures bothered him. He had become one of them now. His equipment had fallen among them, been absorbed, and kicked open new doors of evolution. Anything that could breed a can opener could breed a rock chock and a piton, a crampon, and a pulley, and a carabiner. His haulbags, Katrinko's bags, had been stuffed with generations of focused human genius, and it was all about one concept: UP. Going up. Up and out.

The unearthly landscape of the Taklamakan was hosting a robot war. A spreading mechanical prairie of inching, crawling, biting, wrenching, hopping mutations. And pillars of fire: Sphere satellite warfare. Beams pouring down from the authentic heavens, invisible torrents of energy that threw up geysers of searing dust. A bio-engineer's final nightmare. Smart, autonomous hell. They couldn't kill a thing this big and keep it secret. They couldn't burn it up fast enough. No, not without breaking the containment domes, and spilling their own ancient trash across the face of the earth.

A beam crossed the horizon like the finger of God, smiting everything in its path. The sky and earth were thick with flying creatures, buzzing, tumbling, sculling. The beam caught a big machine, and it fell spinning like a multi-ton maple seed. It bounded from the side of a containment dome, caromed like a dying gymnast, and landed below Spider Pete. He crouched there in his camou, recording it all.

It looked back at him. This was no mere robot. It was a mechanical civilian journalist. A brightly painted, ultramodern, European network drone, with as many cameras on board as a top-flight media mogul had martinis. The machine had smashed violently against the secret wall, but it was not dead. Death was not on its agenda. It was way game. It had spotted him with no trouble at all. He was a human interest story. It was looking at him.

Glancing into the cold spring sky, Pete could see that the journalist had brought a lot of its friends.

The robot rallied its fried circuits, and centered him within a spiraling focus. Then it lifted a multipronged limb, and ceremonially spat out every marvel it had witnessed, up into the sky and out into the seething depths of the global web.

Pete adjusted his mask and his camou suit. He wouldn't look right, otherwise.

"Dang," he said.

About the
Author

BRUCE STERLING IS THE AUTHOR OF THE NONFICTION BOOK *The Hacker Crackdown*, as well as the novels *Holy Fire, Heavy Weather, Schismatrix,* and *Islands in the Net*. With William Gibson he co-authored the acclaimed novel *The Difference Engine*. He also writes popular science and travel journalism. He lives with his wife and two daughters in Austin, Texas.